THE CHRISTIAN PROBLEM

THE CHRISTIAN PROBLEM
A Jewish View

Stuart E. Rosenberg

HIPPOCRENE BOOKS
New York

IN MEMORY OF MY GRANDFATHER
YEHOSHUA ZEV ROSENBERG
WHO PERISHED WITH
THE SIX MILLION

Except where otherwise noted, the author's source for biblical quotations is the *Revised Standard Version:* New Testament (New York: Thomas Nelson and Sons, 1946); Old Testament (New York: Thomas Nelson and Sons, 1952).

Acknowledgment is made to the following for their kind permission to reprint material from copyright sources:

The Christian Century Foundation: "Again, Silence in the Churches" by Alice and A. Roy Eckardt. Copyright 1967 Christian Century Foundation. Reprinted by permission from the August 2, 1967 issue of *The Christian Century.*

Columbia University Press: *A Social and Religious History of the Jews* by Salo W. Baron; and *Jewish Influence on Christian Reform Movements* by Louis I. Newman.

Commentary: "What the Fundamentalists Want" (May 1985) by Richard J. Neuhaus.

Harvard University Press: *Judaism in the First Centuries of the Christian Era* by George Foot Moore.

Holmes & Meier Publishers, Inc.: Reprinted from Raul Hilberg's *Destruction of the European Jews* (Chicago: Quadrangle Press, 1961).

The Jewish Publication Society: *Students, Scholars and Saints* by Louis Ginzberg.

New American Library: *The Meaning of the Dead Sea Scrolls* by A. Powell Davies. Copyright © 1956 by A. Powell Davies. Copyright © 1984 by Muriel A. Davies. Reprinted by arrangement with New American Library, New York, New York.

Paulist Press: *Is the New Testament Anti-Semitic?* by Gregory Baum.

Schocken Books, Inc.: *Economic History of the Jews* by Baron, Kahn, *et al.*

The Winston Seabury Press: *Faith and Fratricide* by Rosemary Ruether. © 1974 The Seabury Press, Minneapolis, Minnesota. All rights reserved. Used with permission.

For information, address: Hippocrene Books, Inc.
171 Madison Avenue, New York, NY 10016.

Published in the United States of America by
Hippocrene Books, Inc.

Library of Congress Cataloging-in-Publication Data

Rosenberg, Stuart E.
  The Christian problem.

  Bibliography: p. 225.
  Includes index.
  1. Christianity—Controversial literature.
2. Judaism—Apologetic works. 3. Judaism—Relations—
Christianity. 4. Christianity and other religions—
Judaism. I. Title.
BM590.R57 1986   296.3   86-19528

ISBN 0-87052-284-1

Printed in the United States of America.

Contents

Foreword

A. ROY ECKARDT

WE ARE THE BENEFICIARIES OF A SCORE OF BOOKS UPON JEWISH LIFE AND thought from the pen of Dr. Stuart E. Rosenberg, distinguished scholar, rabbi, and community leader.

The Christian Problem is to date and in a most vital respect Rabbi Rosenberg's foremost contribution to the Jewish-Christian dialogue and to Jewish-Christian understanding. This new work constitutes a logical next stage after two other studies of his published in 1985. *Christians and Jews* celebrates the eternal bond between the Jewish and Christian communities, while *The New Jewish Identity in America* chronicles the socially and religiously revitalized station of today's Jewish community, its burgeoning human victory over an old *apologia pro sua vita*. Yet precisely because the Jewish-Christian bond remains real and unbroken, our author can in his latest study speak straightforwardly and openly to his Christian sisters and brothers. Dr. Rosenberg has now turned his attention, not without sympathy yet with noteworthy prophetic-critical fervor, to the basically "adversarial character of Christianity," its sectarian condition of triumphalism and antipathy toward Judaism and the Jewish people. However, we are given anything but one more lamentation upon Christian antisemitism. *The Christian Problem* is a serious, scholarly appraisal of the continuing Christian plight written in lively fashion and bringing to bear a wealth of historical and theological learning. Within the majority world of Christendom, the so-called Jewish problem is not that at all. There is only a Christian problem.

A fresh era in the Jewish-Christian encounter began in 1967, following upon the failure of the Second Vatican Council to renounce traditionalist Christian supersessionism, and in conjunction with the Six Day War and the woeful silence of Christian church bodies amidst still further menaces to Jewish survival. In this new period the Jewish people are increasingly standing up for themselves and their rights. And they are more and more calling Christians to task for persisting Christian arrogance, exclusivism, and antisemitism. Rabbi Rosenberg is a leading member in this blessed Jewish company, a group that includes such other contemporary figures as Eliezer Berkovits, Emil L. Fackenheim, and Hyam Maccoby.

In *The Christian Problem* Rosenberg never waffles or falls into being "nice." He tells things as they are: Jesus was *not* the Jewish Messiah; the Jewish community did *not* band together to "reject" Jesus; the Hebrew Bible is *not* the Old Testament; the Christian church is *not* the "new Israel"; the Jewish covenant remains *unbroken;* the people Israel *lives*—full stop (as our British friends like to say). The moral and religious errors and evils of Christianity are neither to be qualified nor passed over. They are to be laid out for all to see, and then red tagged with a steady moral demand that the Christian community shape up. (It is as a Christian that I heartily accept and applaud Stuart Rosenberg's findings.)

The Jewish community can and does exist completely independent of the Christian church. But the converse does not apply: the church's very foundation is Jewish. Here, as Rosenberg shows, is where the Christian problem begins. While the church's originative identity was wholly Jewish, "by creating myths that have closed Jews out of history" the church afflicted itself with a most grievous condition. The professedly "new Israel" fabricated a quite new and different religion, all the while pretending to itself and to the world that it was not doing this.

As Dr. Rosenberg reminds us, the primordial culprit here was the apostle Paul and his Christianizing theology. It is through Paul, I should argue, that the line must be traced from the first century of the Christian era to the death camps of Europe's Jews. For Paul was the paganizing founder of Christian anti-Jewish supersessionism. He radically betrayed Judaism and his own people. (Any rapprochement of Judaism and Nazism is a contradiction in terms, whereas the consanguinity of historic Christianity and Nazism is a categorical truth of history; cf., e.g., the Concordat between Germany and the Holy See in July 1933.) A final irony of Christianity is that its ostensible "Lord," Jesus of Nazareth, would never have dreamed of founding a new religion outside the people Israel. He was wholly devoted to prophetic-Torah Judaism. The Christian church stays impaled upon the dilemma of worshipping a figure whose whole life and entire conviction rule out his ever being worshipped. As a faithful Jew, Jesus of Nazareth is the unrelenting foe of the church's Christological idolatries.

It is the case, as Rabbi Rosenberg points out, that Jews are able to discern a blessing of God in the church's perpetuation. For they do not equate human unity with human uniformity. Our author would never sanction an attack upon the Christian community or the Christian faith as such. Nevertheless, he is loyal to the great, unfulfilled Jewish mission: to rid the world of its paganism and idolatries. The church is called to join in that same mission. Yet many discrete aspects of the Christian problem stand in the way of Jewish-Christian conciliation. These include a shameful ideology according to which Jewish legitimacy and vitality ceased with the advent of the church; Christian falsification of the Hebrew Bible whereby the national and religious literature of the Jewish people was turned into a propaedeutic of the New Testament; the perpetuating of an outmoded sacrificial-priestly cult; the defaming of the Pharisees; the myth of the "wandering Jew" spurned by God; the truncating of Jewish universalism (there are many pathways to God) into a Christian narrowness that admits of salvation only in Christ; and a failure or refusal to grapple with the critical meaning and lessons of the Holocaust and the State of Israel for the Jewish people but also for Christian teaching and morality. Rabbi Rosenberg provides an especially profound interpretation of the linkage among Christian silence, the Holocaust, the State of Israel, and the new Jewish self-affirmation.

Along the way, our author effectively reenforces a number of salient facts, convictions, and teachings from within the Jewish tradition. To exemplify: The biblical prophets are not foretellers but forthtellers—of the moral truths of God. The Messiah is a purely human, not divine, being who will act to deliver Israel from her oppressors, a figure through whom, with his people, the sovereignty of God will be established in the world. The Pharisees were humanist, liberal, never literalist, interpreters of the Torah-law—leaders who, through the instituting of the synagogue, paved the way for the survival of Jewry everywhere in the world. Pharisee-rabbinic Judaism was and remains—in contrast to sectarian Catholic and Protestant Christianity—the savior of biblical religion.

Through my study of *The Christian Problem*, I am encouraged to envision the kind of Christian church that could one day incarnate the moral and spiritual inspiration and power represented by Stuart Rosenberg and the Jewish people. That Christian community will venerate the Hebrew Bible on its own terms. That community will do its utmost to restore a non-exclusionary Jesus to the circle of his followers (cf. Paul F. Knitter, *No Other Name? A Critical Survey of Christian Attitudes Toward the World Religions*, 1985). That community will have been delivered from pagan-Gentile distortions and returned to a life-giving Jewishness. That community will represent and implement the moral and spiritual universalism for which the synagogue stands. That community will have abandoned its fatal proclivity to absolutize things that are relative. That community will be victorious over a missionizing policy and attitude that betrays Jewish integrity and truth. That community will have redeemed itself from the anti-Israelism that is a cover for antisemitism. That community will fully recognize and proclaim to the world the massive Jewish contribution to our conceptions and applications of social justice, to the modern welfare state, to international cooperation, to human freedom, to the solidarity and pricelessness of the family, to education, and to new ways of thought and life for Christendom and within modern nationhood. Above all, that community will offer continuing thanksgiving for the ongoing presence of God's people Israel.

 Our author would not say it but as a Christian I can: Whatever is truthful and good in Christianity is Jewish.

In closing, I may be permitted a personal note. The friendship between the author and me extends back more than forty years, beginning at Brooklyn College where as undergraduates we were enrolled in a small seminar studying the works of George Santayana. Whenever I read Rabbi Rosenberg's books, the happy memories of those good, young days are rekindled for me. My admiration for him and his distinctive contribution continues unabated. We who are Christians sorely need his kind of Jewish witness. We need it for the sake of our souls. Dr. Stuart E. Rosenberg has rendered signal service to the Christian community. I thank him and I say to him, my old friend: May you go from strength to strength.

Introduction

THIS IS NOT STILL ANOTHER ANGRY BOOK INVEIGHING AGAINST THE EVILS of antisemitism. It is a book about religious dialogue, or, more correctly, one intended as a serious preface to dialogue. My purpose is to help Christians and Jews meet in a more balanced spiritual equilibrium, so that if they choose to encounter one another, they may do so as religious equals. Without such parity, we may have conversation, but we do not truly meet.

I take for granted that many Christians and Jews know very little about why one group is now in the majority and the other in the minority. Fewer still understand what happened in the past to create what has been, until now, their imbalanced, and often adversarial, relationship. Here I have turned to *speak to the majority*, although I speak *for* the minority. I hope that in the process, both will also learn more about themselves, and not only of the other.

"The subject of antisemitism," I recently wrote, "treated historically, or as a topical reality based upon some recent issue or event, creeps into a clear majority of the sermons given by [North] American rabbis. It is the Jewish counterpart to Christian ministers haranguing their parishioners about the Devil, or its latest incarnation. These talks are sure winners; but they merely reflect the vainglorious and pointless victory that comes from preaching to the converted."[1]

What follows here are words addressed to the "unconverted," to open-minded Jews and Christians alike. In this context, by "unconverted," I simply mean those who lack any previous religious tradition or personal experience of learning how to deal humanely and democratically with the religious problems they share, yet who are open to such opportunities, and willing to learn. I have singled out here my Jewish view of "the Christian problem" because I profoundly

3

believe that Christians can meet Jews with a balanced spiritual attitude only by first recognizing and analyzing how their majority faith should deal with so intimately-related a minority faith and culture as Judaism. I am also convinced that unless open-minded Christians initiate these self-reviews as a courageous first step, it may well be impossible for them to proceed with Christian-Jewish encounters that will have any lasting worth. Only a frank recognition of the problem can spur the necessary solutions. I also see this work as a logical and, for me, necessary sequel to two of my recent books, both of which appeared in 1985. The first was *The New Jewish Identity in America*, which was followed, a few months later, by *Christians and Jews: The Eternal Bond*. The latter was an attempt to show how Christianity was, in its origin, and remains, profoundly related to Jewish ideas and religious celebrations. It serves principally as an introduction to the Jewishness of Christianity.

The former book is a historical and sociological analysis of the ways Jews have thought of themselves—their changing social and religious identity as it developed among American Jews out of the heritage they or their ancestors had brought to the new world from Europe.

What is "new" about that identity is principally the result of their changed world-views during the last two decades. It was then that a new self-awareness and group-consciousness began to make themselves manifest in ways which pointed toward more robust private or public espousals of their own ethnic and religious culture than those of the generations which had preceded them. The "old" Jewish identity was content to practice a Judaism which could be regarded as an alternate version of "American religion," by the side of Catholicism and Protestantism. What mattered most was that Jewish practices should appear to be "American." Differences between Jews and the others should not loom large in the public view, while similarities between the three branches of the so-called "Judeo-Christian tradition" were to be widely trumpeted. All of this went over very well in an age dominated by the idea of the "melting pot."

But Jews now bear a "new" identity and they are less awed by issues related to the need to look, think, and behave like all the others. For them, as for North America itself, pluralism—religious as well as cultural—has displaced the older and now surpassed idea that one's citizenship is enhanced when religious or cultural differences are downplayed, or even obliterated. The spirit of this "new pluralism" has settled in on America itself, so that the "new Jew" of our time fits the landscape well. Then, of course, a new ecumenical spirit began to pervade major Christian groups, after Vatican II was convened in 1962.

Catholic-Protestant ecumenism was designed to help Christian partners to the dialogue to live in charity until the day that all Christians regard as their ultimate fulfillment—when "all may be one," and the scandal of Christian disunity is eradicated. But how should the Jew react to Christian ecumenism and its possible consequences? Does "Christian unity" resolve old questions or does it, rather, pose new problems for him? What religious responses can he possibly make to those ecumenists whose search for Christian unity is now extended to him and to his brethren?

While proselytizing between Protestants and Catholics has now been set aside by the spirit of Christian ecumenism, can the same be said of the continuing Christian need for Jews to "enter into the fullness"? Dr. Gregory Baum, a leading Catholic ecumenist in Canada, has been quick to admit that "Jews have suffered so much from an aggressive Christian missionary approach." This, he goes on to explain, is why "they are extremely sensitive and easily suspect the Christian partner in conversation of being inspired by a will to convert. Jews are afraid that the friendliness of the Christian and his eagerness to engage in dialogue are simply the ways of a new missionary technique: while the old missionary came with threats, the new one comes with a smile."[2]

Indeed, there is still another problem: neither Jews nor Christians have been fully prepared for such dialogues. Secular democracy may have made them into citizens equal before the law. But neither the synagogues nor the churches have had any prior experience in training their adherents to meet others as religious equals.

Jews were always reticent on this subject. They knew themselves to be and were regarded by others as a small religious minority in a vast Christian community. Close religious encounters, however, encourage—indeed, they require—continuous challenges and confrontations from all sides. Jews had been prepared to leave well enough alone, so that they could continue to live undisturbed within the shelter of secular, democratic safeguards.

But within a single generation, the contemporary Jewish community experienced two alpine events—death and resurrection. The "new Jew" arose in response to both of these traumas.

The first of these, the slaughter of six million, destroyed fully one-third of their number. The Holocaust brought them to the brink of oblivion—closer to the doom and prophecies of perdition than could have been wildly preached across the centuries by even the most mean-spirited of their many antagonists within Christendom. But it happened, inside Christian Europe, while the Church and the western world slept. Jews in the free world—especially in America—were traumatized, and they, too, were enfeebled.

At war's end, that same Christian world maintained its unruffled calm and complacency while a relative handful of Jewish survivors of the death camps roamed the seas and the forests in search of warm haven and permanent shelter. The doors of western countries remained bolted; only a trickle squeezed through, here and there. Then came the new hour. Phoenix-like, rising from the flames and ashes of destroyed homes, synagogues, schools and families, they mustered the spiritual strength to become themselves again. When they established the third Jewish commonwealth, the State of Israel, the Jews meant to begin again. They intended to wipe clean the slate of older hostile memories. Or, better still, they would re-enter world history on their own, as equals, unfettered by the distortions and obsessions of their religious or secular antagonists whose fabricated Jewish myths had made them into the outcasts of society, a pariah people unfit to live. This time, marching in step with the new spirit of hope, Jews everywhere were quickened and reawakened. They saw themselves in the front lines of a braver, newer Jewish world.

Yet as recently as 1984, even Jews in democratic, pluralist America, when polled by social scientists studying their political and social outlooks, responded in a manner that indicated that "roughly half or more still expressed in various ways their concern with contemporary anti-Semitism." A two-to-one majority agreed that "when it comes to the crunch, few non-Jews will come to Israel's side in its struggle to survive." Over three-quarters of the respondents agreed that "anti-Semitism in America, may, in the future, become a serious problem for American Jews." And more to the point: almost half of America's Jews still believe that Protestants—both the Fundamentalist and "mainstream" varieties—and to a slightly lesser extent, Catholics, too, are antisemitic.[3] If these are the views of Jews who reside in what is regarded as the freest diaspora-community of all, what, indeed, shall we say, for example, of those Jews who live today in some Latin American or European countries? Surely, past conditioning helps to account for the lingering sense of insecurity that abides deep inside the Jewish psyche.

Before dialogue with Jews can truly begin, Christians facing them cannot overlook either history or memory.

Within Christendom, for almost two millennia, Jews had been well schooled in the business of "death and resurrection." They were repeatedly expelled from one exile to another. They became perennial and blameless victims of the Church. Yet, over and again, they began again. They never gave up the ghost, though theirs was a holy spirit fashioned very differently from that of their trinitarian neighbors.

Indeed, in the name of the Trinity, Christians have had a continuing problem with "rejectionist" Jews—those who persisted in surviving. They have generally refused to reconcile themselves to the autonomy and selfhood of the Jewish faith and people. Instead, they created for themselves—and for the world as well—a uniquely Christian problem. Let it be perfectly clear from the outset, however, that while I speak here of "the Christian problem" no blame is to be attached to individual Christians. In the words of Dr. Eugene Fisher, a leading American Catholic ecumenist, "the issue is not Christians, but Christianity, not personal guilt but the objective impact of Christian teaching on the minds and hearts of Jesus' followers in their relations with their Jewish neighbors through the centuries."[4]

The central, continuing Christian problem, it will be seen, is Judaism, and the people who practice it, the Jews. From this crucial issue many other difficulties also flow, all relating in one form or another to the need to rule the world in God's name. As if the one God required one Church, and none other, to worship in one way, and none other. This is the Christian "scandal"; brooking no "disunity," the Church would label every deviation from its own doctrine as heresy; for Jewish "outsiders," their fate was even worse—perdition. Uniformity, not unity, would be a better word to describe its dominant desire and ruling style.

What went wrong? *Chesterton*

Should we perhaps take seriously what George Bernard Shaw said ironically: "There's really nothing wrong with Christianity; its only problem is that it has never been tried"? No. Christianity's problem is real, and it is further compounded because it has behaved as if it did not have a problem. Christianity's "Jewish problem," however, is not a Jewish problem—though Jews have been hurt and tormented because of it. The question I am concerned with here is integral to the very nature of the Christian religion. It arises, I am confident, not because Christianity "was never tried," but because before it can be tried, that problem must be confronted courageously.

The first twenty centuries of Christianity coincided with various ages of authoritarian rule, and the temper of those times suited an imperial Christendom very well. When that religion was riding high in the saddle; when Throne and Altar were wedded in what was often unholy matrimony; when autocracy and uniformity were the rule of the day, *the Christian problem* could easily be covered over, and would never even surface to trouble conscience. But as the next century looms on the near horizon, we seem headed for what can be a post-Christian, democratic age, wherein human and group rights—and especially the rights of dissident minorities—will dominate political imagination.

Is it not a time for sensitive Christians to turn their attention to the very nature of Christian thought, to examine how its autocratic "political" theology came into being with the founding of their religion? This is the time to come forward at last, not merely with a fleeting Church resolution here, or a liberal Vatican document there, which "proclaim" anti-Jewishness as "un-Christian," but with a thorough investigation and review of the basic adversarial character of Christianity versus the Jews and their religion.

I suggest that the continuing need to reduce Judaism to a dispossessed and outdated religious system actually began with the strange and unusual way the Church regarded itself at the first hours of its birth. Ancient cultures and religions habitually draw on the sources of neighboring civilizations, or build into their own way of life, styles and ideas borrowed—usually unwittingly—from the peoples of their region. This is the way of history: hardly anything is ever new; cultures continually beg, borrow, or steal from one another. Indeed, all of us—even our ancestors—are cross-fertilized descendants of a variety of intermixed streams of thought, habit, and ideas that have flowed into our lives from outside sources. Sociologists give these flows and processes technical names: cultural accommodation, or assimilation, or acculturation, as in the case of a minority group which accepts elements of a majority's lifestyle.

From the start, however, Christian teachers did none of these things. They proclaimed a *new* faith, called it Christianity, and they did so in a startling fashion—by wholly ingesting the Jewish religion. The painful irony—as we shall note later in greater detail—is that they spoke as Jews but behaved as Christians. But they were zealous, arbitrary, and very often vindictive about Jewish neighbors who refused to accept their leader, Jesus, as the only true leader (not merely a leader, but god, as well) for all Jews. This, of course, is the way of religious bigots and zealots: either you believe in my way, or be forever doomed. It had happened before in Jewish history—as in the case of the Samaritans—and it repeats itself throughout the world, through the ages. It is the intolerant philosophy of "either-or." But what makes the claim of these first Christians fairly bizarre—and unique—is their ironical and adamant insistence that in calling themselves Christians they were not actually creating a new or revolutionary religion. They were the "real" Jews, and Judaism, to be true to itself, had to become Christianity. When their leader-god, Jesus, was not accepted as such by the majority of the members of the Jewish community, they proceeded to do something that had not been done before. They endowed their own minority status with a divine mandate—they, the minority, had been transformed by the Lord himself into the true Israel. They did not borrow, absorb, or receive Judaism from the outside. They wholly appropriated the entire Jewish tradition, and made it theirs alone.

What then would be the status of those Jews who protested, or who refused to accept a Christianized Judaism as appropriate for themselves? The answers which the infant Church proposed to questions such as these reveal how it was that the Christian problem first arose, and why, to this day, it has not yet been fully resolved. Christianity, in reply to these questions, created for itself the *myth of successionism*. Had the first Christians remained only what they really were—a small Jewish sect—we might scarcely have heard from them again. But they maintained that they had, in fact, wholly succeeded the older Judaism. To justify this claim, they were forced to build what, in fact, amounted to a new and distinctive religion. All of it was based on a Jewish foundation, supported by Jewish structures, and filled with Jewish ideas. Christianity bonded itself to Judaism from the very outset, and established an ongoing, symbiotic relationship with it, for one principal reason: to "prove" its passionate insistence that Christianity was nothing more and nothing less than Judaism fulfilled.

From *successionism*, Christians went a step beyond, to *supersessionism*: for Christians, the "old" Jewish community was no longer Israel at all. Because Jews had missed the spiritual opportunity God himself had offered them, the new Christian Church had justly replaced them altogether. This triumphant Christian answer to the question of Jewish survival was really not a helpful response, but still another self-defeating Christian problem. Of course, as Christians read history, their answer did not appear problematical: they simply transformed Jewish persons into objects, regarded Judaism as an obsolete, fossil religion, and blithely—and blindly—used their worldly power to fuel their arrogance toward a defeated target. Over and over again they kept burying a dead religion that would not die: because the Jews would not play the game by Christian rules. Jews survived inside Church-sponsored ghettos, or under stringent social and economic dictates which virtually turned them into untouchable outcasts.

This is the Christian problem, too: the persistent, creative survival of autonomous Jews. It is similarly linked to the Church's own "bondage" to Jews—its Christian need which, in diverse ways, forced Christians to link themselves to the Jewish fate. In a word, the proof of Christian truths was made to depend on Jewish failings; Christian victory seemed always to require Jewish defeat. Such triumphalist views, even if sanctified in the name of theology, were somehow related to a sense of historical insecurity. The younger brother wanted to be the older brother.

Can it not be that questions related to spiritual genealogy—we might say "sibling rivalry"—are deeply at the heart of this ongoing, unresolved "Christian problem"? That Jesus was a Jew should have prevented all other Jews from serving as the basis of this Christian problem. In point of fact, as we shall see, for even those who did remember this (some Christians still think Jesus was a Christian) his Jewishness often compounded this problem, instead of helping to solve it.

The religion of Jesus was Judaism, while the religion about Jesus developed into Christianity. The Christian problem begins at this very point: without Jews and Judaism there can be no Church, yet the teachings of Christianity are not integral to the ongoing life of the Jews or to the faith of Judaism. The Jews have become the Christian problem because Christianity has mishandled many questions related to its own Jewish identity by creating myths that have closed Jews out of history. And because the Church appropriated for itself both the purpose and role of Judaism.

Before they can free themselves from their dilemma, Christians must first undo the myths they created about Jews in order to bolster their image as the younger brother who has bested the older brother. To do this, in this day of pluralism, they must accommodate to the fact that the Jews have their own history, one that not only predates, but also postdates the rise of Christianity.

But Jews, too, especially those of us who have lived through the Holocaust, must also know how to address Christians. As one of these, I have written this book for Jews, too. Without a proper perspective of their own history, Jews cannot offer Christians the Jewish challenge they require: ill-informed Jews can only encourage the continuation of the Christian problem, and can do nothing to help Christians remove their self-induced blind-spots. Yet, before Jews can speak to Christians of these delicate matters, they themselves must first be taught to redeem Judaism from the oblivion assigned to it by Christian historians.

Indeed, Jews have very special messages to bring to their Christian partners-in-dialogue. Those messages, to be sure, emerge from our uniqueness, as creative survivors within the context of the traditional Christian world. But we also have biblical and rabbinic messages which transcend that history's place. The latter may serve as a long-stifled Jewish contribution to the enlargement of universal religious life and thought, from antiquity until the present.

Our first set of messages, however, must serve as a preamble to any serious conversation, and these form the ground rules for Jewish dialogue with Christians. Indeed, without prior acceptance of these as fundamental postulates, there can be no true dialogue:

(1) Judaism is a living religion; it never died; it does not exist as a propaedeutic to Christianity. The Jewish people is a living people with its own religious, cultural, and historical destiny. We cannot begin to speak as Jews facing Christians unless the spiritual integrity of a living Judaism and of a vital people of Israel is accepted as fact.

(2) Antisemitism and anti-Judaism, history teaches, feed upon each other; they are twin phenomena. We cannot begin dialogue with Christians whose insensitivity to these facts prevents them from recognizing the past role of the church in preserving Christian hostility to Judaism, and, therefore, to Jews.

(3) We cannot speak as Jews facing Christians unless they can say to us what we can say to them: We do not seek to convert you; we are willing to leave to God's doing what is surely God's planning.

There are other personal messages I would send my Christian colleagues and neighbors. At times, what will be said here may be painful to you. Yet as one who has helped to pioneer and foster serious Jewish-Christian exchanges, let it be perfectly clear that what follows in these pages is not an attack upon your faith, but rather an attempt to make possible serious and meaningful discussion between our two faith groups. If Jews are no longer willing to listen to you until you first listen to us, it is because, at last, we have regained our voice and one might say, our mission. Six million unfulfilled Jewish lives remind us of our old, unfulfilled mission: to rid the world of its paganism and its assorted idolatries. And we think that you have a special role to play in these matters. It is, however, a part you can not seriously undertake without first expunging the lingering pagan heritage still stowed away deep in the heart of the Christian tradition.

What I have undertaken here is not a pleasant task; neither for me nor for you. After all, you do not like to be told that Christianity is linked inexorably to the historical antipathy of its teachings to Judaism, any more than I want to be blamed for what some Jews are purported to have done to Jesus. Yet unless Jews like me, who respect and honor you because of your faithfulness to your own tradition, help you to come to grips with many of the root-issues that have come between us in the name of that tradition, there will never be honest dialogue—or trust and deep understanding—between our groups. Unless, at long last, in the spirit of openness and love, and without fear of angry retaliation, we Jews can faithfully speak these truths to you, as preamble to our dialogue, all talk and conversation between us will end up as word games—perhaps as good "public relations," but never as profound and deeply-motivated private relations. Vast progress has indeed been made in the last two decades which has advanced the cause of mutual understanding between Christians and Jews. Yet we are really only at the beginning. There are still large preserves and pockets of confusion and misunderstanding which we must jointly address and enlighten.

*   *   *

Truth to tell, this book has actually been inspired by what many Christian ecumenists have told me concerning their own need to relearn Christian history in a new light, from the Jewish perspective. I take heart from, and am inspired by, their views, which can best be summarized in the words of a cherished Catholic colleague, Father John Sheerin, General Consultant to the American Bishops' Secretariat for Catholic-Jewish Relations. He has pithily written: "The fact is the Christian story is a reinterpretation of Israel as the early Christians learned it as Jews. Therefore . . . the dialogue has to be structured by the Jewish frame of reference rather than the Christian."[5] I do not, of course, expect my Christian readers to accept my Jewish views of Paul, for example, as wholly appropriate for them. But I would hope that by explaining to them why many Jews think of Paul—or Jesus, or other matters—as they do, Christians may begin to consider the need to reinterpret their own tradition more sensitively, and from a new perspective. I am convinced that whenever they seek to take the Jewish tradition into account, they will also succeed in clarifying and ennobling their own traditions more authentically and creatively than they have in the past. Happily, this is slowly coming to pass. One Christian authority, speaking for many others, has reported that "in dialogue with the Jewish faith, and in acknowledging the abiding validity of the Jewish religion, one describes his/her faith in Jesus differently . . . A factor which emerges after one surveys the recent history of the Jewish-Christian encounter is the profound way that the posture of dialogue has affected the content of what Christians are saying about their belief in Christ . . . we have noticed how their language about Jesus is less absolutist, their claim about messianic fulfillment less univocal."[6]

Here, then, I have tried to help both groups understand who they really are and what has happened to them as a result of the encrustations of two millennia of anti-Jewish traditions, and that this new understanding will point to a day not yet known, when each may go its own separate way, secure and firm in the knowledge that neither threatens the other.

In the face of our true and common adversary—old paganisms dressed in new raiment—this book is placed before Christians and Jews, so that all will learn to become true brothers who love each other because they need each other.

Indeed, I offer this up in the spirit of Pope John XXIII. Shortly before his death in 1963 he composed this little-known beautiful prayer of penitence: "We now acknowledge that for many, many centuries blindness has covered our eyes, so that we no longer see the beauty of Thy chosen people and no longer recognize in its face the features of our first-born brother. We acknowledge that the mark of Cain is upon our brow. For centuries Abel lay low in blood and tears, because we forgot Thy love. Forgive us the curse that we wrongfully pronounced upon the name of the Jews. Forgive us that we crucified Thee in the flesh for the second time. For we knew not what we did . . ."[7]

NOTES

1. Stuart E. Rosenberg, *The Real Jewish World* (New York: Philosophical Library, 1984) and (Toronto: Clarke Irwin, 1984), pp. 121–22.

2. Gregory Baum, "What the Vatican Council Can Do for the Jews," in *Ecumenical Theology Today,* edited by Gregory Baum (New York: Paulist Press, 1964), p. 229.

3. See Steven M. Cohen, *The 1984 National Survey of American Jews: Political and Social Outlooks* (New York: American Jewish Committee, 1984), pp. 28–30.

4. Eugene J. Fisher, "The Holocaust and Christian Responsibility," in *America* (Vol. 144, No. 6; February 14, 1981), p. 10.

5. John B. Sheerin, "Has Interfaith a Future?" *Judaism*, Summer, 1978, p. 312.

6. Michael B. McGarry, *Christology After Auschwitz* (New York: Paulist Press, 1977), pp. 91; 103.

7. See Werner Keller, *Diaspora: The Post-Biblical History of the Jews* (New York: Harcourt, Brace and World, 1966), flyleaf.

PART ONE

Christian Myths About Jews and Judaism

In the light of the real issues, the Jewish-Christian dialogue has been a singular failure. It has failed because the Jews as well as the Christians who are engaged in it do not have the moral courage to face the truth about Jewish-Christian relationships. The matter at hand is not one of differences in creed and dogma; the task is not to further mutual theological understanding of religious differences. The fundamental issue is the meaning of the Jewish experience in the midst of Christendom all through history. The first truth to note is the realization that, in its effect upon the life of the Jew and the Jewish people, Christianity's New Testament has been the most dangerous anti-Semitic tract in history . . .

. . . To face this truth is the first condition of a meaningful Jewish-Christian dialogue. Is Christianity morally capable of doing it? And what is it able to do about it?[1]

Eliezer Berkovits

15

We project upon the Jews our own hatred of Christ. Yet to utilize "the Jewish crucifixion" of Christ both as a means of ridding ourselves of Christ and of exonerating any trespass of ours is to aggravate our plight, for in continuing to punish the Jews we merely sharpen the apprehension of guilt over having rejected Christ in them . . .

[Speaking as a Christian] suppose that one day we must face the agony of choice between the "true faith" and reconciliation with our elder brother. I speak for no one save myself here, but I believe that I shall pray for the courage to choose reconciliation, in the name of Jesus Christ himself. For we cannot work around our disavowal of Christ; we can only pierce through it to something else. And the only provision we may ourselves bring for the journey is a handclasp with the brother we have wronged.[2]

A. Roy Eckardt

To be effective, an act of contrition must include a firm purpose of amendment, and our amendment could begin with a resolve to do what we can to dissipate the multitudinous misconceptions and the lying fables that Christians have often used in the past to justify their harsh treatment of the Jews.[3]

Rev. John B. Sheerin, C.S.P.

NOTES

1. Eliezer Berkovits, "Facing the Truth," *Judaism*, Summer, 1978, pp. 323, 325.

2. A. Roy Eckardt, "Anti-Semitism," in *Jews and Christians*, edited by George A. F. Knight (Philadelphia: The Westminster Press, 1965), pp. 161 ff.

3. John B. Sheerin, "Evaluating the Past in Catholic-Jewish Relations: Lessons for Today from the Pain of the Past," in *Torah and Gospel*, edited by Philip Scharper (New York: Sheed and Ward, 1966), p. 24.

CHAPTER I

Jesus Was Not a Christian

Jesus as the Christ: The Heart of the Christian Problem

IF JESUS WERE SOMEHOW TO ARISE, WALK THIS EARTH, AND WISH TO commune with "his father in heaven," where might he choose to pray? I have often asked this of Christian audiences. The question is not flippant, nor is it intended as an irreverent, clever ploy. Because the question is indeed very serious, although clearly hypothetical, history's answers are profoundly disturbing and unsettling. The straight-forward, unavoidable evidence—if the historical Jesus is at all to be believed—throws clear light on the fundamental, still unresolved ambivalence which Christians continue to demonstrate about their own inherited Jewish identity. They must deal with his life, not only with his death and resurrection. As the disciples of Jesus on earth—the man, the teacher, and the Jewish herald of their salvation—they must somehow acknowledge and appreciate his own Jewish ways. Yet they are to be found in their churches, which they call his, while he, as even their own sacred texts attest, never left his synagogue.

It is precisely here that the unacknowledged but persistent Christian problem begins. It is rooted in the Jewishness of the Lord whom Christians claim as their own: the crucified Jesus. But what of the living Jesus? Ironically, had Jesus been born, or had he lived, as a Christian, there would be no "Christian problem." Had he emerged from the stock of any of the other ancient but now defunct civiliza-

17

tions of his day (say the Roman or the Greek) to found a new religion completely unconnected with Judaism, Christians would never have had to cope or even deal with the issue of Jewish survival. They would have been indifferent to Jews, and undisturbed by their continuing presence in history—if they even bothered to take notice at all.

Indeed, they might have become as neutral towards the Jews as they later were towards the Romans, even though the latter had ruled over them meanly and despotically, while the former had actually paid them little attention. (There are, for example, no references to Jesus in the Jewish literature of his time; and only a few stray comments about Christianity in the Talmud, which was edited five centuries after the time of Jesus.) Christians surely had more reason to remain hostile to the Romans, who had, after all, crucified Jesus, and whom Tertullian, a famous second-and-third-century Christian writer, had regarded as bigoted, heathen tyrants madly bent on Christianity's total annihilation. "If the Tiber rose to the walls of the city," he once lamented, "if the inundations of the Nile failed to give the fields enough water, if the heavens did not send rain, if an earthquake occurred, if famine threatened, if pestilence raged, the cry resounded: 'Throw the Christians to the lions!' " (If Tertullian had lived during the Christian middle ages, he would surely have noted that in their attitudes towards Jews, his own co-religionists had adopted the very bigotry he himself had ascribed to the Romans.)[1]

But Rome, after all, perished, and what had remained of the Empire after the fifth century, was wholly ingested by the Roman Catholic Church. The Church had defeated all the Caesars, converting almost all of their pagan subjects. Why, then, not forgive and forget what had happened centuries earlier, at the hands of anti-Christian pagan rulers? The Altar was now mightier than the imperial Throne and Rome was no longer a threat. Christians could relax in what was now their Holy Roman Empire. So they did forget and did forgive.

Christianity, however, has remained to this day neither neutral towards the Jews nor relaxed in their historical presence. Politically, the Jews, too, had been vanquished—long years before, by Rome itself. But spiritually and psychologically the Jews became, and still remain, the quintessential Christian problem: rival claimants who would not go away. They were an enduring puzzlement: if the mighty Roman Empire could convert to become the Holy Roman Empire, why should not the synagogue also join the Church? Because Jews held firmly to their own ground, their universal survival became an affront to a powerful and expanding Church. Christian leaders never forgave or forgot that.

That the people of Jesus could survive after he came to them and they refused to follow him, has confused benign Christians and provoked the less gentle among them. That Jews should possess a divine right to follow leaders of their own choosing never seemed to impress the Christian mind. And that Jews should have been as critical of Jesus as of *all* of their would-be messiahs—both before and after him—still remains unacceptable, or at best, inexplicable, to many Christians.

I think there is profound irony here, one that continues to trigger the ongoing Christian problem. Jews think of Jesus as a living person, a maverick, apocalyptic Jew to be sure, but they do not deny Christians the right to worship and adore him as they please. To Christians, however, Jesus is the crucified Messiah, a veritable Christian god, who was brazenly rejected by his own people. To put the matter bluntly: to Jews, Jesus was a human "Jewish option" they did not follow; to Christians he is the singular, divine, "Christian option."

To many Christians, in their deepest psyches, Jesus the Jew has become Jesus the Christian. And Jews are guilty of offending his— and now, their—Christianity. As a consequence, what many Christians widely trumpeted and labelled as the "Jewish problem" is really their own. *The Christian problem* starts with Jesus, the living Jew, before his death and resurrection and continues with the whole Jewish people who survived him and who still see him as a Jew, in human, not Christian terms.

It is important to realize how this Christian problem serves not only as a continuing impasse in general Christian-Jewish relations, but even as a block to enlightened dialogue. If I, the Jew, were to ask my Christian friend to see Jesus *only* as a Jew, I would, in effect, be asking him to give up Christianity, and our dialogue would end abruptly there. On the other hand, if my Christian friend were to ask me to see Jesus as he sees him—as much more than a Jew, to be sure—he would really be inviting me to convert to Christianity, and that would also end the dialogue. But what would happen if I asked my Christian neighbor or colleague to see Jesus not only as a Jew, but also as a Jew? Need the dialogue falter at that point? On the contrary: I would say that this must be the starting point of all Jewish discussion with Christians:—to begin to understand the human, Jewish Jesus.

Indeed, the Christian-Jewish dialogue depends for its integrity upon the ability of the Christian to detach himself from all attempts to make Judaism the object of the Christian mission. These hangovers from the past often block Christians from permitting Judaism to serve as its own subject. By learning to understand the Jewish Jesus before he became a "Christian" Jesus there is a chance that my Christian neighbors and colleagues may also understand me as a Jew, and the Judaism I practice. Indeed, such awareness is acutely necessary to help my neighbors understand why Jews wish to remain faithful to Judaism to the end of their days, even as Jesus had done.

At the same time, as Christians review the life of Jesus from an internal Jewish standpoint, they must also confront still another problem of their own making. This question arises from their view of the meaning of his death. If the death of Jesus resulted in the universal and glorious benefit they believe it to have done—the atonement for all human sin—then why do they continue to impose unforgiving blame, whether on the Romans, or more often, on the Jewish people as a whole, for causing the benefit? "If," as one writer put it, "as the Gospels, especially John, suppose, Jesus knew and predicted long in advance that the particular events would happen, and the events were neither a surprise nor a defeat, then were not the events merely a working out of some antecedently arrived-at divine schedule? If it was part of a divine schedule, then why blame mere men for acting out the preordained human role?"[2] Christians cannot begin the dialogue with Jews without first disposing of their own long-standing, self-imposed Christian problem: they must purge themselves of any identification with that part of their Christian heritage which vilified Jews and Judaism in the name of the crucified Jesus.

When they can come to understand both of these issues—first, about his life; then, about his death—they may also come to see how their ancestors (and perhaps even their own priests or preachers) have been involved in a centuries-old psychological game—sometimes also known as "theology"—to help Christians relieve themselves of their own problems by loading them onto the backs of Jews.

They may also begin to realize that historical Christianity had for so long succeeded in evading its own problem by concentrating principally upon the death, and not the life, of Jesus. For example, for three centuries after the founding of their religion, Christians did not celebrate Christmas, which related to the birth and life of Jesus. Their principal feast was Easter, which concentrated only on the death and resurrection. The Cross, or crucifix, not the star of Bethlehem, became the essential symbol of Christianity; Calvary, not Nazareth, was the chief sacred locus. These served as holy reminders of the "saving" mystery of his atoning death. Indeed, to identify with Jesus as a living Jew is difficult: it requires Christians to study the Torah of Moses, and all the Hebrew prophets and writings that form the basis of the demanding system of Jewish ethics. These were the core of Jesus' public teaching—in the market places, the public squares, the hill-tops, and the synagogues of ancient Israel.

Moreover, one need not be a Freudian to recognize that intense preoccupation with the death of Jesus not only has led many Christians to regard Jews as "Christ-killers," but may also have covered over a deeper, unconscious desire on the part of some who became profoundly hostile to Jews. Did they wish to obliterate the Jews as "Christ-killers" because they really longed to obliterate them as the "Christ-givers"? Indeed, I have the feeling that by obsessively focussing upon the so-called Jewish "rejection" of Jesus, they are demonstrating, perhaps unconsciously, their own revolt against the full acceptance of his stringent Jewish demands. For although Christianity is a belief in a man-god who died as a Christian deity, in virtually all respects, Jesus himself had lived as a self-regarding and faithful *Jew*. In sum, before dialogue can truly commence, Christians must carefully examine their own ambivalences and hangups. It will not do for them to use the Jew or his religion as the handy objects of their own unresolved anxieties.

In medieval times, the urge to deny was much stronger than the will to understand. This explains why the Church frequently arranged public disputations between priests and rabbis, all of which had predictably unhappy endings: victory for the Church, defeat for the Jews—and often the burning of Jewish religious books in the town square. There followed inevitably the expulsion of the entire Jewish community from the area: their patent "error" could not be tolerated by an autocratic Church. *Shape up or ship out!*

But in our new age of openness and dialogue, there are at last some Christians who are willing to listen to Jewish interpretations of their own faith and history. For those who are prepared for this, there can be hopeful solutions to the Christian problem. To begin with I propose that those who are willing, try to fathom how Jews understand the answers to two fundamental questions: Who was Jesus—in Jewish history? What was Jesus—in Christian theology?

Who Was Jesus?

"Jesus was the son of the covenant and behaved as an ardently religious, practicing Jew."

Henry Daniel-Rops, the distinguished French Catholic scholar who was responsible for this particular quotation, also made it clear why no Christian can truly understand his own religion unless he also understands the Judaism which Jesus practiced. He wrote:

> When he began his ministry, in what context did he do so, and who were his helpers, his collaborators? The physical context was that of the Jewish land, that Palestine which he practically never left in all his many journeys. His disciples, the twelve apostles, were all Jews, most of them peasants and fishermen from Galilee: their names alone show this— Simon, John, Jude and Judas, Levi, who was to be Matthew, and the others. When he spoke, his style was so impregnated with the Jewish manner of expression that the rhythms, the balanced repetitions and alliterations of Hebrew poetry are to be felt even in the Greek of the gospels, just as in his parables we are aware of the same manner of thought as that which produced the *midrash* [the Rabbinic literature] of Israel. . . .
>
> . . . But it was not only by birth, breeding, manner of life, friendship and means of expression that Jesus, as a man, was a Jew and so wholly a Jew. . . . He was also a Jew in that he recognized that his people had a particular mission and a destiny entirely of their own. He, like all his countrymen, was a son of the covenant.[3]

If a modern Christian scholar can say these things about Jesus— words which some of his Jewish counterparts can also endorse—why has it been so difficult, and often almost impossible, for other Christians to see things this way, too? This question leads us back again to a cluster of Christian problems.

Many Christians suffer from what I call "double vision" when they behold their Savior. When he is referred to as "Jesus," they can vaguely envision him as a Jew. But to avoid any confusion, they almost never call him simply Jesus, or "Jesus of Nazareth," or "the Nazarene," the way Jews do. They almost always refer to him as "our Lord Jesus," or as Jesus Christ. Jesus the man may have been Jewish, but by deifying him Christians have in essence read him out of his strictly Jewish context.[4]

A related Christian problem is the inability to see Jesus the Jew without also seeing him as the divine Christ the Jews had "rejected." This begins with the earliest documents of the Church: its sacred scripture, the New Testament. To compound the issue, none of these scriptural writers were contemporaries of Jesus. They neither witnessed the events they described nor did they personally hear Jesus say the words they quoted. The Four Gospels—Matthew, Mark, Luke

the very oldest
1 by scholars to
several genera-
as if they are
ıl were actually
And even they
ıatic, as Oxford
fact that in his
ˈhenever asked
ʹ after his death
ıspels, publicly
their budding
ɛsus.[5]

f these records
ɡious history as
ɛre based upon
ıe truth of past
y were actually
Epistles or the
with Jesus, the
so he is hardly
From Paul we
lieved, he was
and that Jesus
der of the new
—Paul was not
ʋas: the divine,
ɪly incidental to
ɛr of Jesus was
ine being.
difficult it is to
studying these
ɔunts of his life.
ɛscribe his birth
Jesus. Despite
ır Gospels con-
one overriding
ı earth, which
ɛe events, there

is some confusion: the trial and crucifixion, in John, take place on the day before Passover; in the other three Gospels, these events occur on the first day of Passover. The resurrected Jesus, in Matthew, appears in Galilee; Luke identifies the location somewhere else altogether—in Emmaus, near Jerusalem. Mark does not contain an account of the reappearance of the resurrected Jesus at all.

But these, as I see it, are mere quibbles. Infinitely more significant is the fact that not only later generations of Christian theologians but the New Testament writers themselves seem much less interested in the Jewish traditions of Jesus than they are in explaining why they regard him as their supernatural Messiah. There is good historical reason for this. At first, they were addressing only their own fellow Jews, urging them to accept Jesus as the foretold Jewish Messiah. In putting Jesus forth in this manner to their own co-religionists, it was of little import to convince them that he was actually one of them; that was taken for granted. It was extremely vital, however, to persuade their fellow Jews that Jesus was indeed a supernatural Messiah, and this explains why it is this aspect of Jesus, his divinity rather than his humanity, which became the central concern of the New Testament authors.[6] Later, when it appeared that the Jewish community would not accept the "divine" Jesus as its Messiah, the Christian message was presented principally to the Gentiles, to whom Jewish life and traditions were alien, and in many ways too rigorous. To stress the Jewishness of Jesus to a Jewish audience was clearly unnecessary. But to do so to a Gentile audience was totally irrelevant, perhaps even counterproductive—considering the difficulties pagans had in accepting monotheism, let alone the ethical and ritual "burdens" of Jewish religious teaching.

So it was that New Testament authors subordinated the religion *of* Jesus to their new religion-in-the-making: the religion *about* Jesus, which was centered not so much on his life and teachings as upon his mystical death and resurrection. This is christology, wherein all of life and creation are centered in the belief in the crucified and risen Christ. Christology, and those who preached or accepted it, transformed the religion *of* Jesus into the religion *about* Jesus—no longer the man, but the eternal Christ who died to bring salvation to the whole world through his church.

From that time forward, the Jewish ethical and religious teachings, as embodied in the Torah-law and the Hebrew prophets, were viewed as transcended, even overturned, by the atoning death of Christ. As Paul himself had put it, "if justification were through the law [Torah] then Christ died to no purpose" (Galatians 2:21). What Jesus had become in Christian thought, not who he was, became paramount. In such a situation the Jewishness of Jesus was expressly rendered insignificant, as if it had never been. All of which helps to explain why Jesus, in Anglo-Saxon countries, has been portrayed by artists and sculptors as if he were an Anglo-Saxon; and in other regions of the world, too, visualized by different cultures—from the Orient to the Occident—as if he had lived and grown up in their own world. In bringing Jesus to the world by all manner of missionary means, the churches have all but denied his Jewish heritage. To make Christ accessible to everyone, he could no longer belong to one in particular. His Jewishness would serve as an impediment. For if his own people did not accept him as Messiah, why should any other people see him as their savior? In practice, then, while the churches borrowed the idea of messiah from Judaism, the pagans, whom they especially sought to convert to Christianity, were not taught about Jesus the Jew. To do so would probably have been too great a source of confusion. Many scholars believe that large numbers of converts to Christianity were drawn from those pagans who had first been attracted to Judaism. To preach the Jewishness of Jesus to these recent converts would have been counterproductive: it could have perhaps led some of them back to Judaism, not forward to Christianity.

But the problem did not end there. In the years before Constantine the Great converted to Christianity (and with his conversion made the entire Roman Empire Christian in the fourth century, c.e.), pagans in the Empire saw active and spiritually vibrant synagogue communities all around them. To complicate things further, many of them, especially the more learned, were also attending Jewish services, either as converts, or as interested candidates for admission to the Jewish faith. Indeed, there were even many recent Christians who still admired Judaism and continued to engage in Jewish practices. You might say that they wished to live the Jewish religious life of their Christian Savior. Understandably, these "Judaizers," as the Church contemptuously called them, were not to be tolerated by the official Christian community.

It is at this point that the Christian problem becomes exacerbated. Most pagan converts to Christianity had joined a universal religion of salvation, one that offered each of them—as private persons—life everlasting. For these, even if Judaism had never existed, this new and glittering faith was powerful enough on its own. Its promises of eternal bliss for those who believed in its Savior were sufficient rewards in themselves. It was only because Jews still continued to survive, whether in the earlier days of Paul and the writers of the Gospels, or during the pre-Christian centuries of the Roman Empire, that church leaders could not fully avoid dealing with the Jewishness of Jesus. In their minds, however, Jesus the Jew could be viewed in only one way: as an eternal reminder of the error of Jews who refused to recognize him as the long-awaited Messiah, prophesied by their own Hebrew prophets.

So we are forced back to our starting point: the only purpose Judaism served to Christians called upon to take the Jewishness of

Jesus into serious account was to proclaim the good tidings that the "Christian Messiah" had lived among them. But instead of seeing this positively, they used this inescapable fact as a theological weapon. Jewish rejection of him would always remain a stain; the "mark of Cain," the Bible's first murderer, would forever accompany them. They deserved their punishment: destruction of their Temple; exile and banishment from their own land; and wandering throughout the world forever. This argument would clearly help the rapidly expanding Church to dissuade would-be converts from joining this wretched people. Judaism was no longer even a rival claimant of the truth, but an accursed religion. The only way to come to God the Father was through his divine son, the Christ. And he was not to be found in the surpassed Synagogue, but only in the Church, his divine body. For as the Fathers of the Church taught, "outside the Church there is no salvation." In one fell swoop, they had done away with the need to deal with, or to appreciate, the Jewishness of Jesus.

Leading Protestant ecumenists, like Bishop Stephen Neill, while devoutly hoping for Jewish-Christian dialogue often fail to take the autonomy and self-sufficiency of Judaism into account. "The Christian faith may learn much from other faiths," he writes, reaching out his hands in brotherly love. Half a sentence later, however, he takes it all back, without being aware of the full impact of his religious imperialism on his Jewish "brothers-in-dialogue." His complete sentence reads as follows: "The Christian faith may learn much from other faiths; but it is universal in its claims; *in the end Christ must be acknowledged as Lord of all.*"[7] (Italics added.)

The Christian Temptation

There are other well-intentioned Christian scholars who wish to achieve reconciliation between Christians and Jews despite the hostility of ages past. Far from seeing Jesus as the stumbling block that has set the two groups apart, they affirm the Christian need to understand his Jewishness, and they also go to great lengths to "prove" that nothing in the New Testament can be said to be *explicitly* anti-Jewish. One of these, the liberal Catholic scholar Gregory Baum, provides us with an interesting example of this "Christian problem."

In 1965, Baum wrote a lengthy book whose title asked the tell-tale question: *"Is the New Testament Anti-Semitic?"* He wrote then that "the Christian Church of today facing Judaism cannot regard itself, as it [did] 1900 years ago, as the fulfillment and replacement of Jewish religion contemporary to it." To prove this, he earnestly set out to show that only a misreading of the New Testament would permit the conclusion that its writers were antagonistic to the Jewish people and religion. "The hard words," he then thought, "that biblical writers addressed to impenitent Jews [*sic!*] of their day are God's message to the Christian Church, for the resistance to the Gospel of Jesus' contemporaries and Paul's audiences is today the temptation of the Christian believer. The temptation of the Synagogue then was to resist the Christ who made demands in the context of its traditional faith. This temptation today exists only in the Church."[8] Whatever else Baum was saying about Christians today, he had still regarded the Jews of the time of Jesus as sinful and "impenitent" simply because they did not accept him as Christ. In 1965, Baum was still very far from offering Jews the hand of reconciliation because he, like others, still refused to understand that Jesus *the Jew* does not, and did not, stand between Jews and Christians as a great divide. It is Christ Jesus, and the claims made in his name, which do.

Toward the end of that earlier work, Baum had fallen right back into the old Christian theological straitjacket, despite the preceding three hundred and more pages of closely reasoned hermeneutics which sought to deny any explicit anti-Jewishness in the New Testament. "Since the Christian creed," he wrote, "is opposed to Jewish doctrine, since Christian faith is the antithesis of the religion of Law, since the Church of Christ regards herself as superseding the Synagogue, *there is contained in Christianity a perpetual possibility that its radical opposition to Judaism may deteriorate into animosity and hate against the Jews. The intrinsic opposition to Judaism of the Christian faith can, of course, never be removed or mitigated, for we believe, what the Jews deny, that with Christ the messianic king has come and humanity has entered the last days initiating the kingdom of glory.*"[9] (Italics added.)

In fairness to Baum, it should be noted that even then he firmly believed that with "Christian love" the implicit "temptation" to anti-Jewishness contained in classical Christianity can, and should, be overcome. Yet he did not deny, for the reasons he had himself enumerated earlier, that there is a built-in "Christian temptation" to be hostile to Jews.

But Baum had a profound change of heart a few years later. He had obviously been grappling with *his* "Christian problem" ever since he had tried, with great effort, to prove that the New Testament was not responsible for anti-Jewish teachings. Finally, in 1974, he recanted and publicly confessed his radical change of mind. In his introduction to a noteworthy work by a fellow Catholic theologian, Rosemary Ruether, he explained why he was ready to deal with this serious question in a radically different fashion than before. He wrote there:

> While I was bound to acknowledge that already the New Testament proclaimed the Christian message with a polemical edge against the religion of Israel, I refused to draw the consequences from this. I was still convinced that the anti-Jewish trends in Christianity were peripheral and accidental, not grounded in the New Testament itself but due to later development, and that it would consequently be fairly easy to purify the preachings of the Church from anti-Jewish bias. Since then, especially under the influence of Rosemary Ruether's writings, I have had to change my mind . . .
>
> All attempts of Christian theologians to derive a more positive conclusion from Paul's teaching in *Romans* 9–11 (and I have done this as much as others) are grounded in wishful thinking. *What Paul and the entire Christian tradition taught is unmistakeably negative: the religion of Israel is now superseded, the Torah abrogated, the promises fulfilled in the Christian Church, the Jews struck with blindness, and whatever remains of the election to Israel rests as a burden upon them in the present age. If the Church wants to clear itself of the anti-Jewish trends built into its teaching, a few marginal correctives (as in the Vatican Declaration on the Jews of 1965) will not do. It must examine the very center of its proclamation and reinterpret the meaning of the gospel for our times . . . It was not until the Holocaust of six million Jewish victims that some Christian theologians have been willing to face this question in a radical way.*[10] (Italics added.)

Here we have a supreme example of the way one leading Catholic thinker was moved to realize that key Church documents, in this case, its very own Scriptures, had served to impede the practice of Christian love and charity, at least as they had applied to Jews and Judaism. Indeed, we find here echoes of the hallowed prayer of Pope John XXIII: "Forgive us the curse which we unjustly laid upon the name of the Jews. Forgive us that, with our curse, we crucified Thee a second time." Baum and others like him have performed a major ecumenical service and advanced Christian self-understanding by their bold, giant steps.

Yet for all this new-found awareness on the part of a select few the larger problems unhappily still remain. Despite all the Christian "love" and "charity" Jews might some day receive, I would contend that Christianity is structured on a foundation that makes it "tempting" to nullify and even to try to abolish Judaism. The still-unresolved, twenty centuries long, Christian problem remains.

As a Jew, I ask my colleagues what seems to me an obvious question: Why do you not amend your Christian doctrine and teachings to reflect your "Christian love"? Why permit your mortal, sin-prone communicants to remain eternally vulnerable to their historically conditioned, anti-Jewish "temptations"? Why not, as Roy Eckardt put it, choose between reconciliation and winning battles for the "true faith" of Christianity? And I would add: you cannot have both.

How, indeed, did it come about that Christians were put into so awkward a position in the first place? Put another way: what happened in the past to make it possible for Christians to take an original Jewish idea of Messiah, and so radically alter it, that it was transformed into God incarnate in the divine person of Jesus the Christ?

It is time to let the simple facts of Jewish history speak for themselves.

NOTES

1. Tertullian himself went on to become an important Church Father and anti-Jewish polemicist who equated the Jewish faith with the work of the devil. His diatribe *In Answer to the Jews*, written about the year 200 c.e. became an early and popular Church source of antisemitic attitudes. See A. Lukyn Williams, *Adversus Judaeos* (Cambridge University Press, 1935), pp. 43–52. A contemporary Christian theologian, Michael Ryan, suggests that Tertullian "argued vehemently for the theological supersession of Judaism by Christianity, viewing Jews as an inferior and condemned people, a negative witness to the Christian faith, with circumcision as the sign of God's disfavor." See Seymour Cain, "The Holocaust and Christian Responsibility," *Midstream*, April, 1982, p. 25.

2. See Samuel Sandmel, *We Jews and Jesus* (New York: Oxford University Press, 1965), p. 140.

3. Henry Daniel-Rops, *Daily Life in Palestine in the Time of Christ* (London: Weidenfeld, 1962), pp. 481–3.

4. Michael Wyschogrod, a contemporary Jewish theologian, has noted the following: "[Among] those difficult issues which most distinctly separate Judaism from Christianity . . . none is more significant than the problem of Christology, the evaluation of the person of Jesus as an equal person of the triune God. For the Jew, this raises the ultimate danger of idolatry, of the deification of a human being. It must be clearly understood that this is a far more serious issue than the question of whether Jesus was the messiah." See Michael Wyschogrod, "A New Stage in Jewish-Christian Dialogue," *Judaism*, Summer, 1982, pp. 361–62.

5. Geza Vermes, *Jesus the Jew* (London: Collins, 1973); see especially pp. 58–69.

6. Martin Buber pointed out that this "process of deification" began with Paul, and continued with the Gospels, including John. He indicated that "the fundamental and persistent character of the Messiah, as of one rising from humanity and clothed with power [the original Jewish view], was displaced by one substantially different: a heavenly being, who came down to the world, sojourned in it, left it, ascended to heaven and now enters upon the dominion of the world which originally belonged to him." See his *Two Types of Faith* (London: Routledge & Kegan Paul, 1951), p. 113.

7. Stephen Neill, *Christian Faith and Other Faiths* (London: Oxford University Press, 1962), p. 229f.

8. Gregory Baum, *Is the New Testament Anti-Semitic?* (New York: Paulist Press: 1965), p. 9.

9. *Ibid.*, pp. 329–30.

10. See his "Introduction" to Rosemary Ruether, *Faith and Fratricide* (New York: The Seabury Press, 1974), pp. 3–4; 6–7. See also my later chapter on the "Holocaust" (Chapter 11).

CHAPTER II

The Jewish Messiah Was Not Jesus

The Jewish Idea of Messiah in Biblical Times

IT IS CRUCIALLY IMPORTANT TO MAKE SOMETHING VERY CLEAR: THE great Hebrew prophets were not seers, crystal-ball gazers, or magical diviners. "To prophesy," as the Hebrew language itself indicates, is "to give utterance" to great moral truths, not to deal in end-of-the-world scenarios. These towering Jewish teachers spoke to their own generations, to men of high or low station without the least regard for power or rank—to all who flouted or perverted the moral law of God. They frequently risked their lives, and often suffered rebuke and privation.

As one writer tells it:

> Nathan did not hesitate to denounce David the mighty king for his murderous action against Uriah the Hittite (II Samuel 12). Elijah had to flee for his life because of his vehement denunciations of Ahab and Jezebel. Micaiah was hit on the cheek and thrown into prison (I Kings 22:24–27). Amos the Judean risked limb and life when he audaciously invaded the royal sanctary at Bethel, and he minced no words in telling the royal house and its supporters what lay in store for them as retribution for their rebellion against the Lord. Because he bitterly denounced the foreign policy of his government, Jeremiah's life was threatened, he was beaten, he was put in stocks, and he was thrown into a dungeon, so that he was constrained to cry out, "And I was like a docile lamb that is

31

led to the slaughter" (11:9). The Second Isaiah echoed these words when he described himself as "a lamb that is led to the slaughter, and as a sheep that is dumb before her shearers" (53:7). Ezekiel was told by God, "And you, son of man, be not afraid of them, neither be afraid of their words, though briers and thorns be with you and you dwell among scorpions" (Ezekiel 2:6). Uriah the prophet was killed by King Jehoiakim (Jeremiah 26:20–23), and the prophet Zechariah was stoned to death (II Chronicles 24:20–21).[1]   *John Baptist.*

But a strange fate was to overtake the words and pronouncements which these and other Hebrew prophets brought to bear on the events of their own time. Later generations, living under changed and dramatically different circumstances, turned back to these "prophecies" meant for their own time and endowed them with the magical powers of foretelling and prediction. To later generations, these prophecies were quoted as intended not only to foretell distant, unknown future events, but to be "signs" of the wonders God would perform against all manner of evil at the very end of time itself!

A few examples from Isaiah can help us understand how prophets came to be seen as "foretellers" of the distant future, rather than serving as moral prods to the corrupt rulers of their own day. In the eighth pre-Christian century, a prophet known as Isaiah, a native of Jerusalem, was pondering the question of how to save his beloved city, and with her, the entire kingdom of Judah. Isaiah had analyzed the efforts of King Pekah of Israel (in the north) and King Rezin of Aram to force his own kingdom of Judah into a coalition against the expanding Assyrian empire (Isaiah 7–8). He urged his own government not to enter any such alliance, warning that neither Israel nor its Aramean ally would succeed, and both would surely be defeated. "Behold," he said, "a young woman shall conceive and bear a son, and shall call his name Immanuel . . . For before the child knows how to refuse the evil and choose the good, the land before whose two kings you are in dread will be deserted" (7:14ff.).

Jewish scholars are of one mind concerning what it was that Isaiah was trying to achieve. The historical context makes it abundantly clear that he was essentially analyzing the moral and political forces of the world in which he lived, hoping to convince his compatriots to accept his own analysis of the situation, as he understood it. Of course, the prophets used parables, similes, and metaphors; these helped to endow their eloquent public orations with drama and clarity.

Orlinsky describes the moment in this fashion:

Read in this light [Isaiah's parable] the reference to the young woman and her child becomes nothing more than a dramatic measure of time, a warning that before the unborn child will be old enough to know the difference between good and evil, the Lord will bring devastation on Judah's enemies. [Later Christian generations introduced an additional error, namely, that the pregnant young woman in question was a virgin. The Hebrew word in Isaiah 7:14, *almah,* means "young woman"—even one recently married—not "virgin."] A similar statement was made by Isaiah in this very connection about his own wife and child, whom he called symbolically *Maher-shalal-hash-baz,* literally, "the spoil speeds, the prey hastes," the double name referring to the two kingdoms of Aram and Israel (Isaiah 8:1–4). Yet when passages of this sort were read in a later and wholly different set of conditions they laid the basis for the common belief that the prophets were foretellers and that their gift was based not merely on their power of analysis of an immediate situation, but that it derived from divine inspiration and implied distant and mystical promises.[2]

Sometime close to the destruction of the Jewish state, (in 70 C.E.) the post-biblical Jews were coming to believe that the power of prediction was, in fact, the most significant aspect of prophetic literature. The scrupulous analysis of long-past political and military situations no longer concerned them, and they began to read their own present back into the past. The literary powers of the prophets were so great that their works were read and searched increasingly to find meanings relevant to the new age and the new situation. Those older prophetic warnings of defeat and destruction were no longer meaningful after the Dispersion—and yet, the temptation to find hidden promises of an ultimate restoration and a final triumph was to become overpowering.

The Anointed One

The biblical idea of the messiah is, nevertheless, rooted in the primary meaning given to it in the message and teachings of several Hebrew prophets. In the Bible, a "messiah," literally "the anointed one," was the product of the prophetic belief that after the destruction of the Temple of Solomon (586 B.C.E.), God would restore his people to the land, under the rule of a descendant of the house of David. But the word "messiah" must be understood from its original biblical context. Anyone who was selected by God through his prophets to be the ruler of his people was regarded as "his messiah"—the anointed one. In this way, Saul, Israel's first king, was called "the Lord's anointed," and so were other kings like David and Zedekiah. Even King Cyrus of Persia, whom the Second Isaiah regarded as God's agent for destroying Babylonia and restoring Israel to its land, is called "God's anointed one" (45:1). Always, and in every biblical case, the "anointed one" is a human, not a divine being. And as for the connection to King David, Bible readers will remember that when the first Babylonian exile was indeed terminated and the people restored to their land, it was Zerubbabel, of the house of David, who led the restoration.

Clearly, from the Hebrew Bible itself, there is no warrant whatever to consider the Jewish idea of a messiah in superhuman terms, or to endow "the anointed one"—*mashiach*—with any of the miracle-making attributes which his first Jewish disciples had ascribed to Jesus of Nazareth. Not a single word in the Hebrew Bible, Jewish scholars aver, can be brought forward as proof that Jesus Christ was already pointed to, in Hebrew Scripture, long before his own arrival in time. To arrive at that kind of messiah—a messiah with a capital "M"—who would become the Christian Christ, we have to look elsewhere.

Where, then, shall we look?

How the Idea Changed in Rabbinic Times

The idea of a superhuman, anointed leader is the product of a much later time, and the result of changed circumstances. The view that God would send a Messiah (with a capital "M") at some early or distant future time to intervene directly in defending Israel against its oppressors—or for that matter, to protect all of the righteous against the wicked—is a development that occurs only in later rabbinic times, many centuries after the older Hebrew prophets. The trigger for these new views was, in fact, the oppressive, imperial rule of Rome. Seeking desperately to find some comfort and national hope in this difficult time, Jews began to look for new answers that might mitigate their dark feelings of entrapment in the meshes of an all-powerful, arrogant, and pagan empire.

In these circumstances, which occurred only a few decades before the beginning of the Christian Era, a number of sects began to sprout within the Jewish community, each with a "formula" intended to serve as a way out of national despair. Until recently, what we knew about the nature of some of these Jewish sects derived principally from the pen of the leading Jewish reporter of his times, the historian Josephus. From him we learn of the existence of at least four such groups: Pharisees, Sadducees, Essenes, and "the Fourth Philosophy." This last sect got its unusual name because Josephus described the first three sects as "philosophies," and lacking a name for the last, he merely gave it a number. It should be noted that since Josephus, although a Jew, was writing for Greek readers—and often indulged in propaganda rather than straightforward reportage—we should read him with many grains of salt. For example, we must be very skeptical of his description of the Pharisees as Stoics and the Essenes as Pythagoreans. Moreover, it will soon become clear why we must not—indeed we can not—assume that these four groups of Josephus accounted for all the sects that may have existed. Of them, only two, the Pharisees and Sadducees, are mentioned in the New Testament, or in the Talmud of the rabbis.

Briefly, we can say that the Pharisees comprised the main rabbinical party. They asserted that henceforward, lay teachers—not only the priests—by reason of their learning and piety, could interpret Scripture. The second of these parties was the Sadducees, a priestly sect whose literal interpretation of the Torah-law the Pharisee-rabbis regarded as much too rigid. The latter were liberal, broad-constructionists, when it came to applying the traditional laws to their own times.[3] From them, we have inherited no literature at all, while the Talmud, that vast repository of law and learning which was accumulated from the first century B.C.E. to the sixth century C.E., is the product of the ruling Pharisee-party. As for Josephus' "Fourth Philosophy," we should understand it not as a "philosophy" at all, but as a band of activist "guerrillas," sporadic and loosely organized, whose answer to the oppressiveness of the Romans was more militaristic than spiritual.

But it is the Pharisees who set the stage for two separate, conflicting, and amazing phenomena. They first ensured Jewish survival after the fall of Jerusalem in 70 C.E. by expanding Judaism into a world religion, capable of and interested in receiving new converts into the fold. At the same time the "oral law," their Talmudic reinterpretations of biblical laws, created the conditions necessary for a national religion like Judaism to live on, even when its people were dispersed throughout the world, exiled from their beloved Jerusalem and its central sanctuary, the Temple.

As for a demonstration of the novel humanistic and unauthoritarian approach—as Erich Fromm has noted—of the Pharisees, compared to the legal, biblical tradition espoused by their rivals, the Sadducees, a single trenchant story from the Talmud tellingly makes the point.

Several distinguished scholars had disagreed with Rabbi Eliezer's view on a point of ritual law. Then, as the story is detailed, on that day Rabbi Eliezer brought forward every imaginable argument. Said he to them:

"If the law is as I think it is then this tree shall let us know." Whereupon the tree jumped from its place a hundred yards (others say four hundred yards). His colleagues said to him, "One does not prove anything from a tree." He said, "If I am right then this brook shall let us know." Whereupon the brook ran upstream. His colleagues said to him, "One does not prove anything from a brook." He continued and said, "If the law is as I think then the walls of this house will tell." Whereupon the walls began to fall. But Rabbi Joshua shouted at the walls and said, "If scholars argue a point of law, what business have you to fall?" So the walls fell no further out of respect for Rabbi Joshua but out of respect for Rabbi Eliezer did not straighten up. And that is the way they still are. Rabbi Eliezer took up the argument again and said, "If the law is as I think, they shall tell us from heaven." Whereupon a voice from heaven said, "What have you against Rabbi Eliezer, because the law is as he says." Whereupon Rabbi Joshua got up and said, "It is written in the Bible: The law is not in heaven. What does this mean? According to Rabbi Yirmiyahu it means since the Torah has been given on Mount Sinai we no longer pay attention to voices from heaven because it is written: You make your decision according to the majority opinion." It then happened that Rabbi Nathan [one of the participants in the discussion] met the Prophet Elijah [who had taken a stroll on earth] and he asked the Prophet, "What did God himself say when we had this discussion?" The Prophet answered, "God smiled and said, My children have won, my children have won."[4]

Commenting on this poignant tale, Fromm adds: "This story is hardly in need of comment. It emphasizes the autonomy of man's reason with which even the supernatural voices from heaven cannot interfere. God smiles, man has done what God wanted him to do, he has become his own master, capable and resolved to make his decisions by himself according to rational, democratic methods."[5]

Beyond their insistence upon rationality as a basis for their new religious jurisprudence, there was another important side to the Pharisees. The age in which they lived, one of national decline under the heel of the Roman oppressor, moved them to graft onto the biblical Judaism they inherited a new interpretation of God's justice. A deep mystical strain was thus introduced into the Pharisaic worldview. In older Israel, as depicted in the Bible, death was the end of life and the dead went to a common abode of all who once lived: to the depths of the earth, called *Sheol*, or the netherworld. The prophets had delivered their message to the nation: their teaching about retribution, repentance, and restoration, because it was *national*, was of *this world*, and not addressed to a hereafter. The Pharisees, however, came to believe in their own novel doctrine of *individual retribution after death*, perhaps because they were anticipating a great crisis in the history of the Jewish people, and of the world. In short, God's justice would now be extended to the world to come; in anticipating the "end of time," each *individual's merit or demerit* would determine whether he would be re-created, to emerge revivified after his time on earth.

It is within the matrix of these Pharisaic teachings that the rabbinic idea of the Messiah emerges, connected in spirit to the older expectations of the prophets, yet altered to a great extent to suit their view of the national crisis facing Israel under Rome. While the biblical prophets stressed the nature of the age called "the End of Days," the Pharisees focussed, as well, on the person of their Messiah, who gives "the Messianic age" its very name. In their view, although the Messiah may be endowed with special powers, as the future King of Israel, he is a human being; only an *agent of God*, and never an atoning Savior as Christians later believed. He is expected to attain for Israel the idyllic blessings of the prophets. He is a *comforter* of his suffering people, Israel. Never is he seen as a *suffering, or atoning* Messiah. He was to defeat the enemies of Israel, restore his people to the land, reconcile them with God, and introduce a period of universal, spiritual, and physical bliss. He was, indeed, to be many things in one: prophet, comforter, warrior, judge, king, and teacher of Torah! He would appear as the scion of the house of David, to rule his people "at the end of days." Then, at the climax of human history, the Messiah together with his people was to serve as the instrument by which the sovereignty of God was established on earth.

It would be a serious mistake and a grievous misreading of the Pharisees to conclude that they were seized by mystical leaps of faith, or that they had concentrated their spiritual energies on "forcing God's hand" to send a Messiah forthwith, quickly, to put an end to their earthly miseries under Rome. They were much more preoccupied with life on this earth, and in the process, centered their attention on performing *mitzvot*, divine commandments, here on earth, as prescribed in the Torah-law of Moses. It was in this essential way that they transformed Judaism into a system of monotheistic ethics. The Talmud, the recorded result of their efforts in this direction, is ample testimony of their dedication to the perfection of man and the building of a just society *in this world*.

To uncover the essential Jewish "messianists" of those times, we have to look beyond the Pharisees to the various apocalyptic sects, religious enthusiasts of a very different kind. The former were indeed innovators, but still in the center of community life. The latter were on the fringe.

Apocalyptics: The Essenes and the "Dead Sea Sect"

The greatest archaeological excitement of the century, sometimes bordering on commotion, has been about the Essenes, who for so long had been regarded as a quaint and unique Jewish sect, but about whom very little was known. Like the Sadducees, the Essenes, it appeared until a few decades ago, had left the world without a trace; they had no known literature or written record. All of this changed with the discovery in the late 1940s of the now famous "Dead Sea Scrolls."

The Essenes, like other Jewish apocalyptic sects of the time, rooted their basic doctrine in their fervent expectation of the imminence of "the end of days." With its advent, evil was to be destroyed and Israel would finally be freed from the "yoke of the nations"—freed from its political subjugation. In varying degrees of intensity, all of these sects shared a common belief: either preceding the great event, or during the "final era," God would raise up (some even believed had *already* raised up) for himself a community of "elect" who were destined to be saved, as a nucleus of the future Israel. For two hundred years, beginning with the first century B.C.E. until the fall of the Temple in 70 C.E., this relatively small but deeply pious sect had split off into a variety of highly organized communities—not unlike monastic orders—who had dedicated themselves to living in a state of religious purity to await the great day coming.

For decades now, some scholars have been suggesting that since the dominant theme of early Christianity is the "renunciation of life," as part of its messianic expectancy, its connecting link to Judaism, if not its very origin, was to be found in the Essene sect or some variant of it. Indeed, some like Heinrich Graetz, the great nineteenth century Jewish historian, believed that John the Baptist was himself an Essene—or at least deeply influenced by this unusual Jewish sect. He and other similarly minded scholars felt that if we could somehow know more about their beliefs and practices than Josephus had sketchily detailed, we might also find the "missing link" between Pharisaic Judaism and early Christianity. Then, in 1947, ancient Hebrew scrolls, dating to a time very close to the era of John the

Baptist and Jesus, were discovered near the Dead Sea. It was later determined that they were the work of a Jewish sect that dwelled nearby along the shore of the sea at a place called Qumran. Ever since, the sect of the scrolls was called the "Qumran or Dead Sea Sect," and to this quaint group the attention of a host of Jewish and Christian scholars around the world now turned. In their initial excitement, some were even sure that this was the very apocalyptic sect to which John the Baptist belonged, and from whose sectarian teachings he had drawn his repetitive refrain: "Repent now, for the Kingdom of heaven is at hand!"

This is not the place to delve deeply into the vast new scholarly literature that has been developing around these important archaeological finds. I believe, however, that it will simply no longer do for anyone seriously interested in understanding the origins of the Jewish-Christian schism to mouth old saws about "the blindness of the Jews" in "rejecting" Jesus. We now discover that the models for the first Christians had pre-dated John the Baptist and Jesus by over a century. These were Jews who lived as a small sectarian community at Qumran, presided over by their chief ruler and priest, their Teacher of Righteousness (or "Righteous Teacher"). They practised a religious way of life that was already, one hundred and more years before the time of Jesus, at the farthest fringes of the organized community. It was the sectarian Jews who had "rejected" Judaism by fleeing to the desert. It was *they* who established a "substitute" Judaism, not the organized community.

What kind of Judaism were they advocating?

They lived an ascetic life, set apart from other Jews in their Judean desert habitat near the Dead Sea. According to one of their scrolls, "The Manual of Discipline," as scholars now call it, they were apocalyptics who had left the evil priests in Jerusalem, to dwell together in ritual and ethical purity in the desert, there to await the coming of the Jewish messiah. (Indeed, many investigators believe that they anticipated the arrival of *three* separate and distinctive messiahs: a priest-messiah, a king-messiah, and a prophet-messiah.) They ardently believed in the Torah-law of Moses, regarding themselves as its most pious and pure fulfillers, in contrast to the "wicked priests"—the Sadducees—who administered the cultic ritual in the Jerusalem Temple. As a community, they regarded themselves as constituting "God's elect" who had entered into a "new covenant" to help all of Israel return in purity to the first covenant, the law God gave them at the hand of Moses at Sinai. (Shades of Christianity!) The key personality of the sect was their Teacher-Priest. It was he who had led his followers into this new Mosaic covenant, formed them into this religious order, and instructed them in the meaning of the scriptures, adding his own teachings and prophecies. He remained the martyred leader of the order, adored, venerated, and expected to play a part in the messianic age of the future.

Some of the commotion created by the discovery of the sect's scrolls was centered in the mistaken conclusion some scholars had jumped to: they were sure that, at long last, direct evidence had been unearthed of Jesus, and they loudly trumpeted their belief that Qumran's Teacher of Righteousness was none other than Jesus himself! When all the clamoring had died down, and especially after dating tests of the documents were made, it became clear that Qumran's Teacher of Righteousness had lived almost a century before the time of Jesus.

By now, many believe that this teacher may have been Onias the Righteous, who, according to Josephus, was stoned to death in 65 B.C.E. The scrolls refer to the "Wicked Priest" and to the "Man of the Lie," and it is suggested that the former referred to the leader of the Sadducees, and the latter to the head of the Pharisees. Both of these larger parties were opposed to Onias, and both seem to have blamed his death on the other. In any event, while other apocalyptic sects had stressed either the kingly or the prophetic attributes of the messiah they anticipated, the Qumranites were essentially geared to the ideal type of the messiah-priest, their Teacher of Righteousness, and believed that either he or one of his progeny would soon lead Israel in the imminent "end of days."

What actually emerges from a careful study of this Dead Sea sect is a clear refutation of the claims of Christianity concerning Israel's "rejection" of Jesus—not to speak of the recurrent physical and mortal terror which have been inflicted on generations of Jews in the name of those claims. It is wrong to use loaded words like "rejection" when describing the relationship of a far-out messianic sect like the Qumranites to the central Jewish community led by the Pharisees. Neither totally rejected the other or read them out of Jewish life. Theirs were simply different religious approaches to the overwhelming Jewish problem of their time: how to survive the Roman oppressor. The Sadducees had remained static, drawing their religious program and inspiration principally from the Temple, which they controlled. The Essene groups, of which the Qumranites, we now know, were an integral part, turned their minds away from this world, and sought to override and transcend the Roman problem, by relying on messianic intervention: peace and well-being for Israel would be achieved with the imminent "end of days." The Pharisees, or scribes, comprised the only party with an essentially pragmatic, this-world view, with a program that was compatible with the looming possibility of a broad and protracted dispersion of the Jews.

It was the Pharisees, as we shall see, who gave meaning to the synagogue, as a "small sanctuary"—one that could survive anywhere in the world, even should the Temple fall or Jerusalem be destroyed. In their academies of Torah-learning, where they assiduously searched and re-searched the enduring and universal applications of Scripture, they set the stage for Judaism as a world religion. There, scholars, later to be known as "rabbis," sought to enlarge the meaning of the older biblical religion of cult and sacrificial altar, and to apply with new and creative spiritual energies the teachings of Moses and of the other Hebrew prophets. Although these Pharisees, like all other religious people, could not live *only* as rational men—they too, were deeply pious, and sometimes mystical—they did not eschew the rational. Theirs, however, was a patient messianism: they were unwilling to force God's hand, then and there, to bring an immediate end to human history. This, perhaps, is why they regarded fellow Jews—the mystical Essenes and their like—as persons unwilling or incapable of submitting to the day-to-day *rational*, human quest to overthrow evil and to build by just and ethical means the better world God had commanded as their Jewish duty. For the Pharisees, total and other-worldly absorption into the mystical realms of messianic speculation seemed to be an evasion of religious responsibility. Man needs God, they believed; but God, those Pharisees were bold to proclaim, needed man, as co-creator of the present and future human community.

So now we have it, the "hard" archaeological evidence of the Qumran literature, and are thus able to open up the long-shut book of Essene history and religious thought. As a result, we also have a better fix on the question of the Jewish "rejection" of Jesus and his Jewish followers, the sect of the "Nazarenes," who may be regarded as proto-Christians. And we also have the so-called "missing link" between Judaism and Christianity, inscribed in the scrolls of that Essene-like sect, the Qumranites.

Upon analysis, however, the long-sought missing link turns out to be much more than a link; it is also our earliest source of radical Christian departure. Which is to say that several generations before the birth of Jesus the very Jewish movement which had served as his model and spiritual paradigm was already far out of the mainstream of Pharisaic Jewish life. Had there been no Pharisees, Judaism would probably have died with the death of the Temple and the loss of Jerusalem. Pharisaic, or more properly, rabbinic Judaism, saved biblical religion for all men, and for all time. It saved the Jews from despair in exile, and from spiritual dehydration in their wide and vast dispersions. If it were not for rabbinic Judaism, the biblical books, prophets, teachings, laws—indeed, the monotheistic inspiration itself—would probably have become as strange, remote, and unknown to us as all the forgotten religions of the ancient world.

The scroll-discovery is also important as a reminder that the Jews of Qumran, like their fellow Essenes, had opted for a Judaism of another style, one that was not destined to survive within the Jewish world, but which, in effect, did become the cornerstone of the future Christian church. To the majority of Jews in their day, the Essenes and their various off-shoots seemed to have strayed very far from the biblically correct Judaism they were taught by their Pharisee teachers. It turns out, then, that the earliest forerunners of Jesus and the Nazarenes were themselves fringe sectarian Jews whose philosophy and practice of religion was already regarded as unacceptable by the principal Jewish community, long before Jesus even arrived on the scene.

With this new knowledge now at hand, it strikes me as wilful and prejudiced for many Christians to continue to maintain even today, as they have steadfastly done for almost twenty centuries, that the Jews rejected Jesus. It was not Jesus, as such, they refused to follow, but also virtually thousands of their fellow Jews, members of one or another Essene-type sect whose apocalyptic fixations seemed to them excessive, non-rational, and thus unattractive. Yet were it not for Paul, it is possible that the Nazarenes would have remained within the Jewish fold, despite their minority status and their radical messianic claims. After all, there were other small Jewish splinter sects who had also made claims in behalf of a messiah of their own.

But with the coming of Paul, a generation after the time of Jesus, the Nazarenes would wholly adopt his views—a theology so far removed from the strict monotheism Jews had nurtured that it would be obvious that Paul was, in fact, founding a new religion. (Indeed, he himself understood this, for he had successfully held out against James, the brother of Jesus, who had urged a "mission" only to their fellow Jews, while Paul turned his attention to the pagan, gentile world as the major target for his Christianizing.) His religion used

Judaism as its base, but it was equally indebted to the pagan and Greek mystery cults he had known in his native town of Tarsus, in Asia Minor, while still known by his Hebrew name of Saul. Pauline religion was thus no longer only a variant form of Judaism and to expect Jews to accept his paganized reinterpretation of their own ancestral heritage as the "real Judaism" is not merely wrong; it is nothing less than far-fetched, wishful thinking.

In what way did Paul's new religion (which constitutes the basic Christian theology that has endured through the centuries) differ from, and even appear to subvert, the meaning of Judaism itself?

Paul and the Pagan Cults

The New Testament, as a result of Paul's radical revamping of Jewish doctrines and his borrowings from pagan cults, differs fundamentally in major respects from all Jewish literature, including the apocalyptic, messianic writings of some small sects; or the Dead Sea scrolls; or any rabbinic works. "The New Testament," writes one Jewish scholar, "tells us about the death of a god who was resurrected on the third day. Unless the death of a divine figure marks the end of an outworn religious cult, like the death of Pan, it can be given meaning only in terms of a scheme of salvation: and this is how the New Testament interprets it. The death of Jesus atones for the sins of mankind, who can escape damnation only by sharing in his death and resurrection. Where in Jewish literature is the concept of the death of God to be found? The answer is simple: nowhere. Such a concept, associated everywhere in the ancient world with the renewal of nature in the spring, was banished forever from Judaism by its theology of a God superior to nature."[6]

But if this is the Jewish view, are there no Christians who see these matters in a similar vein? Unfortunately, the answer is mostly negative. What of Christian scholars? Are they not also committed to "objective research," and do they not also seek to reconstruct the past with cool dispassion, as would behoove true scholarship? Again, the reply is hardly positive. Very few of them are willing to open up a wide and ranging discussion of these topics with laymen; and even within their own circles, a certain conservative reticence reigns—this because many academic Christians are also ordained clergymen, whose intention is to preserve the older tradition, not amend it. They continue to hold to the "consensus" of church tradition, for the most part. Few indeed have written for general consumption and discussion what A. Powell Davies has done so compellingly in his popular book on the scrolls:

> The traditional view of the founding of Christianity taken by the typical layman is that Jesus preached its gospel, died as Messiah and Redeemer, arose from the dead and founded the Christian church, which spread out through the world, beginning with the work of the apostles. Or, if he does not believe in the Resurrection, he supposes that the apostles, moved by the spirit of Jesus, founded the church upon his gospel . . .
>
> . . . In any case, he assumes the originality of Christian doctrine, and it does not occur to him that much of it existed previously (except perhaps as it was foreshadowed by Moses and the prophets), or that a great deal of it is indebted to sources that do not appear in the Bible.
>
> What the layman does not know, and the scholar does, is that there were many Pagan dieties for whom quite similar claims were made and in whose names were preached quite similar doctrines. Mithras was a Redeemer of mankind; so were Tammuz, Adonis, and Osiris. The view eventually taken of Jesus as a Redeemer was not a Judaic concept; nor was it held by the first Christians in Palestine. The Messiah the Jews and the Judaic Christians expected was not the Son of God but a messenger from God, not one who saved by blood-atonement but one whose salvation came from his rule of the earth in a Messianic kingdom. . . .
>
> . . . It was when Christianity spread out into the Pagan world that the idea of Jesus as a Savior God emerged. This idea was patterned on those already existing, especially upon Mithras. It was the birthday of Mithras, the 25th of December (the winter solstice) that was taken over by the Pagan Christians to be the birthday of Jesus. Even Sabbath, the Jewish seventh day appointed by God in the Mosaic Law and hallowed by his own resting on this day after the work of Creation, had to be abandoned in favor of the Mithraic first day, the Day of the Conquering Sun . . .
>
> . . . In the Mediterranean area during the time of Christian expansion, nowhere was there absent the image of the Virgin Mother and her Dying Son. Originally, it was the earth itself that was the goddess, virginal again with every spring. Her son was the fruit of the earth, born only to die, and in dying, to be implanted once more in the earth, as the seed that would renew the cycle. This was the "vegetation myth" from which the drama of the "Savior-God" and the *Mater Dolorosa* was drawn, soon to be elaborated . . .
>
> . . . These examples are but the barest indications of what must be

encountered in the quest for historicity in the New Testament scriptures . . .

. . . This obviously does mean . . . that when there are new suggestions, such as those arising from the discovery of the (Dead Sea) Scrolls, it is entirely appropriate to give them full consideration. *If they are disturbing to the consensus, or quasi-historical field of reference, formerly arrived at by scholars, it may be because we need a new consensus.*[7] (Emphasis added.)

Toward a New Beginning

Several truths now emerge. In the first instance, there can be no doubt that in its origins what we now call Christianity was a Jewish sect. The first followers of Jesus, we have seen, were sectarian Jews—not yet full-blown Christians—who differed from other Jews principally in believing that their messiah-claimant had not died but would soon return to resume his interrupted mission of *liberating his people from Roman rule.* It was Paul, as we have seen, tilting toward the pagans after the days of Jesus, whose missionary zeal latched onto ideas anchored in the Greek and pagan mystery cults. In so doing, he de-nationalized Judaism, divided faith from folk, and transformed the meaning of the death of Jesus into a world-wide invitation to share in the salvation offered by his atoning sacrifice. One would hardly expect the mass of Palestinian Jews, with their undiluted loyalties to their own people, to accept his bidding. But as the eminent classicist Michael Grant has shown, even "the Jews of Asia Minor [who were acculturated to Greek ideas] mostly rejected Paul because they regarded his doctrine of the divinity of Jesus Christ as a blasphemous betrayal of their tradition of monotheism. So he turned to the Gentiles instead, infusing his reinterpretation of Jesus' message, at times, with some degree of Hellenism in order to make it more palatable."[8] In the process of becoming the Apostle to the Gentiles, Paul also became the "arch-apostate" of the Jews.

Indeed, Grant suggests that Paul not only *changed* but also *subverted* the teachings of Jesus. "Comparisons," he notes, "between the instruction ascribed to Jesus and to Paul scarcely even touch on the most vital difference between them. The faith which Paul himself came to hold, and desired others to hold with him, was faith in the Crucifixion and Resurrection of Jesus Christ and in the consequences of those events for mankind. This was by far the most important part of his

beliefs and his preachings and teachings, and it means that they can
scarcely be compared at all with those of Jesus. For, even if Jesus in his
last days came to foresee his own violent death as in some way
redemptive, this idea had manifestly *not* stood in the forefront of his
ministry which, throughout his career, had centered instead upon the
dawning and shortly to be consummated Kingdom of God. It was
scarcely surprising, then, that Paul showed so little interest in Jesus'
life. What the two men preached was quite different, and the Christianity that we have today is largely Paul's creation."[9]

How Paul won the day in his desire to attract new converts has been
pithily described by one acute observer:

> The infant Church was split in twain on the issue of the validity of
> Mosaic precepts for Gentile proselytes. The Gentile converts brought
> with them into Christianity their own legalist and cultural system; they
> viewed with abhorrence the civilization and law of Jewry, both on
> theological and national grounds. Peter and the so-called "Judaizing"
> group championed the opinion that no Gentile could enter Christianity
> except through the gate of Judaism; Paul on the other hand urged the
> admittance of Gentiles without circumcision and observance of Jewish
> food-laws. The Council of Jerusalem discussed these problems and
> attempted to fix rules for future action. The Gentile group in the
> Christian communion triumphed; Paul, though at moments he relapsed
> into adherence to the Old Law, rejected its authority and literal validity
> for Christian believers.[10]

Paul, however, could never fully resolve the internal Jewish contra-
dictions of his Christianizing theology, which, as we have been seeking to demonstrate, has remained at the heart of the continuing
Christian problem. He needed to retain his ties to his Jewish heritage
in order to validate Jesus as the true Messiah. This is why some regard
him as a Jewish "loyalist" who was still able to think of himself as a
committed Pharisee even *after* his conversion. "Brethren," he said, I
am a Pharisee, a son of Pharisees." (See Acts 23:6.) Yet Paul also
needed to discard the Jewish nation—his very own—as a living or-
ganism, since it was the essential vehicle of the ongoing expression of
the fullness of the Jewish faith he was rejecting, as surpassed by
Christ. It thus turns out that Paul needed the Jews *for their past*—but
as for their *future*, as a "real-life" people, I believe that he needed them
not at all. He was preoccupied as the Apostle to the Gentiles. The
future he foresaw for Jews was only as a christianized "Israel"—either
converted in this life, or restored to Christ in the world to come.

Even when Paul referred to "Israel" as the "old stock whom God *will not forever reject and which could flower again,"* which Israel did he really mean? "Paul takes Israel seriously," a Jewish writer correctly observed, "but it is an Israel in which no Jew believed. The Israel of Paul is a theological construction and a theological necessity; it is an intermediate device which must be employed [by him] that the pagan world be redeemed in Christ—at which point, hopefully in the spirit of Romans (11:13–24), God might return to graft on once more the broken shoots of the old stock of Israel. Israel is for Paul and for the Christian the first thought and the last [in the end of days] but the middle is all of Christ. Such a use of the presence of Israel cannot be less than a falsehood in our [Jewish] sight."[11]

In my view, I also see him as guilt-ridden, ambivalent, and, at times even a self-hating Jew, whose relationship to his Pharisaic roots after his "conversion to Jesus" on the road to Damascus bears all the marks of the love-hate mechanism of many another apostate. To prove the zeal of their new love, they often go to odd lengths to reject their old one. Following what sociologist Lewis Coser has said about the nature of social conflict—"the closer the relationship, the more intense the conflict"—Paul's volatile and often contradictory views about the destiny of a Christless Jewry may perhaps be traced to his obsessive remorse and his wrenching, inner conflicts as an apostate Jew.

Finally, to conclude this discussion of what the generations after Paul had made of Jesus as the Christ, I rely on the historical record to substantiate my claim that Christians have a moral, psychological, and spiritual problem, not only with Jews and Judaism, but also with themselves. To that record I would also add this personal, admittedly, subjective, intuition: I continue to ask myself whether Christians— unwittingly, and even unconsciously—have perhaps often understood (as did Paul, on many introspective, mystical occasions) that it was *they* who were the renegades—*from Judaism.* It has been said that the renegade is one whose "attack on the values of his previous group does not cease with his departure, but continues long after the rupture has been completed."[12] It strikes me that this psychological side of "the Christian problem"—its "protesting too much" against Judaism for long centuries after the initial rupture took place—has not been sufficiently probed or discussed.

The position which sees Christianity as the religious heir of Judaism is a rather extravagant view, as we have seen. It should be clear that Jesus himself could never repudiate, deny, revile, or wish to expunge his own people from the annals of history and of human hope. Even if, in the confusion or insecurity of their own hearts, some Christians still feel that they "owe" Jews nothing, they surely *owe Jesus* this much: to resolve this Pauline-Christian problem they have made of the Jews, in his name.

This alone can constitute the new ecumenical beginning so ardently desired, especially by those who truly prize peace on earth and good will among men.

NOTES

1. See Harry Orlinsky, *Ancient Israel* (Ithaca, New York: Cornell University Press, 1954), p. 157.

2. *Ibid.*, p. 159.

3. The Sadducees, according to Talmudic sources, were a conservative, upper-class party of priestly aristocrats who, it is believed, derived their name from that of Zadok, the High Priest, in the days of King David.

Pharisees—*perushim*, in Hebrew—or "people who set themselves apart from the rest of the community," and therefore are out of the mainstream, is the name given to these forerunners of rabbinic Judaism by the Sadducees.

This epithet was intended derisively to suggest that the Pharisees were "schismatic," "deviationist," and "separatist." The Pharisees themselves usually referred to their own group as *haverim*, "members of the fellowship"; as *hahamim*, the sages or teachers of Israel; or, as scribes, *soferim*.

4. Based on the Babylonian Talmud: *Baba Mezia*, 59b.

5. Erich Fromm, *Psychoanalysis and Religion* (New Haven: Yale University Press, 1950), pp. 46–7.

6. Hyam Maccoby, "Christianity's Break with Judaism," *Commentary*, August, 1984, p. 39. Maccoby, correctly in my view, links Paul with the pagan Gnostic sects. Earlier, he wrote: "It used to be thought that the Gnostic sects, of which there were many, were all heresies derived from Christianity, but it seems probable that Gnostic sects existed before Christianity began, and it may be closer to the facts to explain [Pauline] Christianity in terms of Gnosticism rather than the reverse . . . In Gnosticism there was a Savior (in Greek, 'Soter') who was one of a Trinity of divine beings . . . He redeemed mankind by his suffering and then ascended to Heaven to sit by the side of the Father in glory. An interesting and significant fact is that the Gnostic writings, even before the birth of Christianity, were bitterly anti-Jewish." Accordingly, Maccoby pointedly concludes: "The bulk of Paul's adherents certainly had a pagan Hellenistic background which enabled them to respond to the Gnostic aspects of his teaching." See his *Revolution in Judaea* (New York: Taplinger, 1981), p. 88. My own views of Paul are further elaborated in Chapter 5.

7. A. Powell Davies, *The Meaning of the Dead Sea Scrolls* (New York: New American Library, 1961), pp. 89–92. For a good overview of the scrolls, see Geza Vermes, *The Dead Sea Scrolls: Qumran in Perspective* (London: Collins, 1977). A controversial but interesting work is the book by John M. Allegro, *The Dead Sea Scrolls and the Christian Myth* (London: Westbridge Books, 1979).

8. Michael Grant, *From Alexander to Cleopatra: The Hellenist World* (New York: Charles Scribner's Sons, 1982), p. 79. Concerning his views of Paul as the "arch-apostate," see my Chapter 5, footnote 5.

9. Michael Grant, *Saint Paul* (New York: Charles Scribner's Sons, 1976), p. 194.

10. Louis I. Newman, *Jewish Influence on Christian Reform Movements* (New York: Columbia University Press, 1925), p. 9.

11. Arthur A. Cohen, *The Myth of the Judeo-Christian Tradition* (New York: Harper and Row, 1970), p. 47.

Indeed, Chapters 9–11 of *Romans* are often cited by Christians as "proof" of Paul's continuing "love of Israel." Here again readers are reminded that Paul is discussing an allegorical, ethereal "Israel" of his own invention, made to suit his theological designs, or his christology, and not the living Jewish community. What he says in these chapters is primarily addressed to pagan Gentiles, and not spoken directly, or even lovingly, to Jews themselves.

12. Lewis Coser, *The Functions of Social Conflict* (Glencoe: The Free Press, 1965). See also Michael Grant, "Paul the Discontented Jew," *Midstream,* Aug./Sept. 1976, pp. 32–40.

CHAPTER III

The Synagogue Is Neither Temple Nor Church

IF THE RABBI IS NOT A CLERGYMAN, AND THE SYNAGOGUE IS NOT A church, what, then is a Jew?

Christianity has been wrestling with this question for centuries. Its difficulty in coming to grips with this matter is the result of an unwillingness to recognize that unlike itself, Judaism is not constituted as a church and was not, like itself, organized by a founder and established as an ecclesiastical community. To make matters more confusing, Judaism also refuses to pattern its faith solely along creedal lines, unlike the Christian churches.

Christianity, on the other hand, is a religion, not a culture. It is a faith-community one joins and is not born into, or to which one is converted, both by means of baptism. Even those born to Christian parents are not considered fully Christian until they are "converted" to it by the rite or sacrament of baptism, born again, as it were, in Christ.

Accordingly, doctrines and creeds play a crucial and major role in Christianity. Presbyterians are not Baptists, Methodists, or Lutherans—though all call themselves Protestants—because their separate church creeds and doctrines differ. Sometimes even ritual differences, or mere nuances or shades of liturgical meanings, can define and divide one Christian group from another. This is so because from the very beginning, Christianity was formed and founded on a theological base, and distinctive articles of faith became the essential vehicle of the group's purpose and goal. Competing theologies led to competing ministries and missions, and one or another heresy, schism, or reform has given birth to a vast proliferation of Christian sects and churches.

Despite the lip-service now being paid to it, Christian ecumenism has still not fully produced Christian unity—not even between disparate elements in the Protestant sector itself, not to speak of the older and continuous antagonism that still abides between Roman Catholics, Greek Orthodox, Eastern Churches, and Protestants of all varieties. The crucial need to convert all believers to its "singular truth" has been so strong and compelling that for centuries it has created inter-church rivalries as Catholics seek to convert Protestants, and one denomination tries to lure other Protestants into its own fold!

Imagine, then, the serious problem Christians have in confronting Jews, whose religion is neither comprehended nor carried by confessional institutions, but rather by a folk and a community who bear their own culture. Judaism, it has been properly claimed, is best defined not as "the Jewish church," but as the evolving religious civilization of the Jewish people. It is the people that carries the culture, and the culture that bears the special imprint and insights of the religious tradition. It is called "Judaism," not "Mosaism," because it is not the product of any single founder—not even Moses. The culture of this people created and later shaped its changing spiritual views. As the Jewish civilization faced new and changing ideas and values, its communal will responded in an organic way, not only religiously, but socially and politically as well. To be Jewish was a total experience, incorporating both the sacred *and* the secular, not seeing either as locked in eternal combat with the other. To be Jewish has also meant to regard oneself as a member of a world-wide family group, always as persons in community, never as a single, isolated, lonely heart in search of private salvation. Had Jews lost their collective sense of peoplehood and become like Christianity only a church-type religion—purely a confessional faith-group—they would surely have gone over to Christianity or Islam long ago. History is witness that a minority faith not linked to its own universal folk and civilization, with its own distinctive cultural and social expressions, tends to be gobbled up by the majority religion.

At one crucial juncture of its history Judaism seemed destined to become a large and expansive world religion. This became possible when the Pharisees, and their heirs, the rabbis, introduced a revolutionary and daring concept to the world—a missionary, proselytizing community with doors opened to the stranger. Their new form of

Judaism went far beyond anything the Hebrew prophets had taught, for in that older world a people's religion and national culture were one and the same, and outsiders could not enter the closed society created by "ethnic religion." It was the post-biblical Jewish community under the impact of its new teachers, the Pharisee rabbis who created the Talmud, which was the first in history to reject the idea of a biologically determined, nationally autonomous society. It welcomed into the life of the nation as Jews all who voluntarily accepted the Jewish religious tradition and granted them full equality with those native born. But since Judaism was not just a "religion," by accepting its teachings one also became a member of the Jewish people. Indeed, even before the Temple fell in 70 c.e., one out of every twenty persons living in the city of Rome was Jewish—some 40,000 of the total population of 800,000. Clearly, a goodly portion of Rome's Jews had converted, left their pagan ties, and joined as faithful members of the Jewish community.

If we required proof that the Pharisees were diligent, even zealous, in their efforts to recruit converts into Judaism, we need only turn to the Gospel According to Matthew, wherein the apostle testifies that the Pharisees "traverse sea and land to make a single proselyte."[1] We can see from estimates of Jewish population at the time that the number of Jews was increased by these converts. In the first century c.e., they were already as many as seven million Jews. Accordingly, even after the infant Church was launched and still struggling to survive, a relatively high percentage of persons then living in the Roman Empire was Jewish—most were native born, but many were surely converts.

Paradoxically, the universalist religion of Judaism, with its message of international peace and harmony, did not win over the nations to monotheism, in its own name. Judaism, instead, remained the national faith of the Jewish people. Despite the fact that so many Romans had converted to Judaism, it became clear that to be a Jew in the Roman Empire was a severe liability. After all, Rome had brought Judea to its knees, destroyed its vaunted Temple in Jerusalem, and reduced Jews to the status of an enslaved nation. Could Romans be expected to accept as their own, the religion of a subject people—one, indeed, they themselves had defeated?

Nevertheless, despite this difficult psychological and political impasse, the rabbis did not narrow their world view or reduce their concern for universal man. In the realm of religious and ethical ideology they continued their daring and their creativity. In practical terms, however, they withdrew from the "missionary race" with Christianity and set about building a new religious and social structure for the Jewish people. They made possible the survival of Jews as a minority beyond the fall of the Temple, the loss of Zion, and through every other exile and disperson as "God's witnesses" to the end of time.

They could not, however, have achieved their blueprint for creative exile if they had not radically altered the religious lifestyle and culture inherited from earlier generations—those who had neither lost their Temple nor been exiled from their native habitat. Everywhere one turns in contemporary Jewish life and thought, the genius of Pharisaic or rabbinic Judaism is still to be found. It assured the Jewish future by means of two novel religious developments, the synagogue-school and the rabbinate, neither of which were known in earlier, biblical religion.

When the Torah and Prophets became a Book, the day of the prophets was over, but it was far from the end of Judaism. Now that God's word was committed to writing, a new type of communal and religious leader came to the force—neither a prophet, nor a priest. First known as scribe, and only after the fall of the Temple called rabbi (Hebrew for "scholar-teacher"), he was seriously challenged and rebuffed by the priests, despite the fact that he never laid claim to their biblical prerogatives as leaders of the cultic-worship practiced in the Jerusalem Temple.

When Jerusalem fell to the Romans, the day of the Temple and the priests was over too; but this was not the end of Judaism. Now the rabbi became the authoritative and unchallenged heir of both prophet and priest. Now, too, the synagogue emerged as a new and uniquely rabbinic center, a school and a sanctuary. The rabbis did not create the synagogue. It grew, as we shall see, from the grass-roots, from the inner soul of the people themselves. But it was the rabbis who shaped and adapted it as a major vehicle for their ethical universalism and their faith in Israel's future, even in far-flung exiles and diasporas.

The Temple Is Not the Synagogue

When contemporary Jews or Christians refer to synagogues as temples they are in error. There was only one Temple, with a capital "T": the Jerusalem Temple on Mount Zion. That Temple was first built by Solomon but destroyed by the Babylonian Nebuchadnezzar in 586 B.C.E. Then it was rebuilt as the Second Temple, only to be destroyed by the Romans in the year 70 of the Christian era. That temple had a biblical mandate. How it came to be built, maintained, and operated was fully described in the Bible. A full set of laws and practices was minutely formulated to govern the institution of the Temple, the plan and purpose of which were believed to be divinely inspired. Each day, morning and afternoon, there were sacrifices on the altar. Pilgrims from all over the land thronged to it, particularly during the three harvest festivals of spring, summer, and fall. The building itself was elaborately and splendidly built, and its physical majesty was matched by the rich aura of the religious service conducted by the priests, and the levitical choirs and orchestra whose tones overflowed into the chambers and the outer courts.

The Temple was regarded as the place where God himself, his spirit, lived. It was also a meeting place for pilgrims, but above all, the Temple was essentially the *domus dei*, the house of God, his very dwelling-place. Virtually all ancient temples, as for example, those of the Greeks, were viewed as a kind of "heavenly precinct." Indeed, the very word "temple" (from the Greek *temenos*) refers to the marking out of a special area of the heavens where divine signs might be seen. Thus, the temple, or *temenos*, becomes the corresponding place on earth where divine actions occur, omens are given, and sacrifices are offered in its sacred precincts. But alone among ancient civilizations which stressed sacrifices, in addition to its sacrificial cults, the Jerusalem Temple also encouraged prayer. It was not *merely* a house for the deity, guarded from attacks of evil powers, where man performed the necessary cultic rites to protect or strengthen the deity. It was not only a "house of God," but also a place where the God of Israel heard prayer and answered, judged and pardoned, showed compassion, and delivered man from sin. Since only one Temple was sanctioned— the central sanctuary in Jerusalem atop Mount Zion—local deities and semi-pagan rites often associated with scattered regional altars and holy places were effectively rooted out, and the worship of the singular God by all of Israel in its lone Temple was assured.[3]

Priests and Prophets

Priests are almost always conservative. They wish to protect their own institutional powers, and so, priestly religions invariably reflect a rigid and authoritarian lifestyle. Priests promote theocracies, because in this social and political climate their oligarchical position remains in place, protected from the vagaries of changing public demands. Israel's priests were no exception. The prophets of Israel and their stinging perorations are eloquent testimonies of the longing for a larger view of the universe—more humane, more moral, and more socially conscious than the ritualistic rigidities offered by the priests.

The prophetic tradition, with its emphasis on man's ethical responsibilities to his fellow men, was coupled to the religious obligation to build a better society. These views were regarded as their own special legacy by the Pharisees and later by their heirs, the rabbis. Caste and class—the social armor which had protected and preserved priestly oligarchies—were replaced by a grass-roots spiritual movement which stressed novel, non-cultic ideals, and which were anchored in a new system of moral education. The rabbis made learning and the study of Scripture into a religious exercise. In this process, the synagogue, which was regarded, at first, as only a poor and temporary substitute for the Temple—to be restored only when the Messiah came—became the new community center, the rational academy for higher religious learning and insight, and the house of community prayer. It revolutionized biblical Judaism, by replacing its priestly caste with men of learning as the new religious leaders, and by spiritualizing the manner in which God's nearness, love, and compassion were to be sought. The synagogue, not the Temple, would be the religous answer to exile. Holiness would no longer be the exclusive, tribal possession of the priests and their Temple: the synagogue would be the house of all the people. Instead of becoming a holy place, it became the house of a people in search of holiness.

The Synagogue: More Than a House of Worship

The ancient Jewish Temple had an altar; and virtually every Christian church has an altar. Logic therefore suggests that churches are related to an archaic, Temple-like Judaism, and not to synagogue-Judaism, which from its inception was careful not to try to emulate or substitute for the lone and irreplaceable Jerusalem temple.

Why have churches retained an "outmoded" altar? What, indeed, is still being "sacrificed" at church services to require altars that hark back to the days when Jewish priests still presided over the Temple's sacrificial cult?

Of course, there are no animal sacrifices in either contemporary or ancient churches. Altars in Christian churches are, however, reminders of a "sacrifice" of another kind. On these, Jesus as the "lamb of God" has become the human-divine sacrifice that is repeatedly offered in Catholic churches at every mass, and in many Protestant churches at communion or eucharist time.

All of this is another way of suggesting that early Christianity based itself on the Temple-religion of biblical Judaism with its priests, altars, and sacrifices, and not upon post-Christian Judaism, which in the hands of the rabbis and the synagogues they fostered had transcended the sacrificial cult of an earlier time. Despite a good deal of current confusion, Christians and Jews should realize that churchly religion is "Temple religion," while the synagogue is neither church nor Temple. It is rather a religious institution of a new order. And it reflects the fact that Jews, after the Temple had fallen and the dispersion had set in, retained their uniqueness as a people and a culture even in exile. They were not merely a local church or sect on the run, flitting from one diaspora to another, but a universal family—a worldwide people sharing the same religious culture wherever they lived. So it was that their synagogue—their "national center" in microcosm—became a portable sanctuary which no longer served only as a "house of God," as had the Temple: it became the "house of the people." Every church is always *domus dei;* every synagogue is first a *domus ecclesiae*—the house of the congregation. It is as much people-centered as it is God-oriented.

How did it happen that the synagogue became what it was, *sui generis,* unique unto itself, neither a substitute for the biblical Temple, nor a parallel to the Christian church, itself patterned along Temple lines? The answer to these questions sheds light on the serious stumbling block Christians often put in their own way, when they view Judaism only as the "religion of the Jews." The synagogue—unlike the Temple—is not primarily a religious institution, the place where the cult is performed authentically. And it is also unlike the church, whose principal quest is theological, offering personal salvation to a collection of individual believers called Christians, and insuring their private hopes for immortality in a future life to come. The church altar is the stage whereon this divine Christian mystery is played out, and the priest or minister is God's agent in this drama, not the emissary of the community or congregation.

The synagogue, it must be noted, represents a changed form: it is an examplar of the fact that after the fall of Jerusalem, Judaism was reconstituted as the global culture of the Jewish people. It was not established by a founder as a conversionary church, whose doctrines assured the individual convert or communicant life everlasting by accepting its creeds and doctrines. It is both the sacred *and* secular center of the Jewish communal experience. Above the synagogue is the community and the traditions it carries. As for Christians, without a church there can be no altar, and without both, there would be no Christianity.

The exact origins of the synagogue are still not clear or precise. It is believed, however, to have come upon the scene as a human accommodation to the changed circumstances of Jewish history, sometime after the first Temple had been destroyed. Ironically, a negative factor, the exile of the Jews to Babylonia, was probably responsible for establishing the need for some "portable" Jewish institution: ultimately, this became the synagogue. We can picture them gathering in their homes on the sacred day of the week, the Sabbath, to read to one another from those sacred writings that may already have been committed to parchment. After reading these texts someone might lead in prayer, perhaps using the very psalms that had been earlier incorporated into the Temple service. Still others might interpret portions of these sacred texts, relying upon the oral traditions that customarily were handed down from father to son and from teacher to pupil.

It is out of these new needs and conditions that the synagogue arose. From the start, it centered in the congregation rather than in a sacred shrine, a magnificent building, or a putative holy place. Even when the exiles returned to their land to build the Second Temple they carried attachments to this new and popular form of community expression. From that time forward, despite the existence of the Temple, emphasis began to shift, at first almost imperceptibly, from the sanctity of the priests to the people themselves as a community; from the place of worship to the gathering of worshippers, the people as a holy congregation. This is the *edah*—the congregation, or "flock"—which the rabbis came to sanction as a formal religious community of ten or more males. Wherever they would assemble—in private homes, at the gates of the city, or in the open fields—it was their religious motivations as a congregation, not the sacramental leadership of the priests, the sacred ritual of the Temple, its sacrificial altar, or sanctified vessels, which came to dominate Jewish thought. This new spirit was catching, and synagogues sprouted all over the land without plan or design, and without an established hereditary or hierarchical clergy.

Under the influence of the "rabbis" the synagogue was made into a higher academy for adult learning, a "House of Study," or in Hebrew, *Beth Hamidrash*. The reading and teaching of Scripture became a central characteristic feature of Jewish public worship, and a lecture or a homily given by recognized scholars was a regular instructional device which was built into the service. (It was because of this feature that Jesus could preach in Galilean synagogues, and later still, that Paul could proselytize Jews in the Roman diaspora from the pulpits of their own synagogues.) Learning God's will by studying and applying the teachings of the Torah and Prophets (and now, their novel rabbinical interpretations, too) was made into a veritable act of worship. To this day, synagogues continue to emulate their earliest counterparts: even the smallest congregation will rarely fail to have a study hall, known as the "house of study," with a formidable library of books dealing with the ethics, theology, jurisprudence, and philosophy of Judaism. Three-dimensional pictorial art was precluded from both Temple and synagogue by the commandment prohibiting graven images. So as not to rival or replace the Temple, neither grand architecture nor furnishings were ever lavished upon any synagogue: its old and rare books became the "art" of the synagogue, the library its treasure house. Indeed, so central to the life of the synagogue is the idea of study and learning that in Yiddish it is still called *shul*, from the German *schule*, which of course means "school."

In addition to the two functions of prayer and study, the synagogue was regarded as a community center, and also called *Beth Knesset*, a "House of Assembly." The synagogue building served as a public center where matters of interest and concern could be aired. Courts of Jewish law met in its rooms, heard testimony, administered oaths, and proclaimed judgments. Strangers to the community were welcomed into its hostel, the poor were invited there to receive alms, and community philanthropies were administered by its councils. Asylums for the homeless and the aged were often connected with the synagogue, too. (Such a hospice is recorded in the ancient synagogue of Theodotus in Jerusalem. A stone inscribed "the guest house" was found even in the small community of Ramah, between Safed and Acre). In time, these communal functions of the synagogue became so integrated with its religious and educational purposes that by the Middle Ages the practice had developed whereby one could even interrupt public worship in order to inform the entire community of wrongs and injustices not yet redressed.

As a result of these paramount socio-ethical and educational concerns, the synagogue's role as a house of worship had become secondary. This bred a certain indifference to synagogue architecture; in fact, some Talmudic rabbis resented the diversion of substantial building funds from educational and social welfare budgets. When Rabbi Hama ben Hanina pointed out to Rabbi Hoshiah a beautiful synagogue in Lydda in which his ancestors had "sunk [invested] a lot of money," the latter exclaimed: *"And how many souls did they sink here? Were there no men willing to study the Torah?"* The strong emphasis the synagogue placed on the human needs of the community rather than its physical setting led to a more universal social outreach than had ever been possible in the days of the Temple.

As a building, the synagogue was almost always nondescript, hardly apparent as a religious landmark, and from country to country, an uninspiring structure reflecting the style of its time and place. Yet it was necessary to distinguish the synagogue from the Temple and from a church. Every synagogue had to have windows to allow light to illumine the interior and permit those within its halls to see the world outside. That illumination spoke volumes. It said: this is a rational center, rooted in the here-and-now human experience. This was surely in great contrast to the stained glass windows of churches and cathedrals, intended to give their interiors the mysterious light that made the telling Christian point: those who entered the church could experience a foretaste of the world to come. The light of this world was artfully transformed into the light of the resurrection.

In sum, the synagogue was neither church nor Temple; it became a unique place, without sacrifice or altar. More than a prayer house, it served as a community and teaching center for Jews who had lost their patrimony.

Many Christians when thinking of Judaism think only of those Jewish religious habits and styles which are biblical. As will later be noted in detail, they choose to disregard and discount the value of all forms of Judaism that grew up after the death of Jesus. But there is great irony here: while classical Christianity positioned itself on the Temple base and carried on as a priestly religion after the fall of the Temple, the rabbis caused Judaism to change course, and to chart these new directions described above, thus moving Judaism farther and farther away from both Temple and church.

Every synagogue was a virtual community in itself, serving a wide range of human and social needs. It was also a small piece of the Holy Land taken into exile, where Jews could remain unestranged and retain their spiritual autonomy, even in foreign lands. It represented the dynamic response of the resilient Jewish spirit to a changing and challenging environment, a unique institution molded and directed, to this day, by the religious teachings of rabbinic Judaism.

The Rabbi

Without the emergence of the rabbinate as an institution parallel to the synagogue, and the ultimate establishment of the rabbi as the authoritative heir of prophet and priest, the synagogue would have been bereft of the rationale and ideology necessary for its universalism. Today, synagogue and rabbis are institutionally united: rabbis usually function as the spiritual leaders of specific congregations. But when rabbis first appeared on the scene as scribes, their ideas were not altogether popular. True, the prophets were laymen, and they often opposed the priestly ways, but they were chosen by God himself, and in any case, prophecy was said to have come to an end. Who, then, could serve as the legitimate successors to the prophets? Who would be the new teachers of Israel and the world?

As long as the Sadducees were "enthroned," the Pharisee party had no official influence over the affairs of the community. Even after the Romans came to power, the Sadducees were regarded by the Emperor and his pro-consul as the "Establishment"—the recognized representatives of the Jews. Nevertheless, almost two centuries before the rise of Christianity, the scribes were already beginning to gain the confidence of the rank and file of the people. Soon they came to be regarded as the backbone of the Pharisee party.

With the destruction of the Temple and the consequent waning of the priesthood, leadership was gradually transferred to those who could serve as judges. By reason of his knowledge of the law and his technical abilities as a student of Scripture, the scribe slowly assumed some of the powers once held by the priest. After the destruction— but not before—the scribe was called "Rabbi," a title for what we might call the "diplomate doctor of the law." (All attempts by Christians or Jews to regard Jesus as a rabbi are not grounded in historical reality, since the title "Rabbi" did not come into use until several generations after Jesus' death.)[4] The main question that had plagued the community since the close of prophecy had now been answered. Who, indeed, were the authentic successors of the prophets, the teachers and the conscience of the Jewish community? The rabbis, of course! And who could be a rabbi? Those who attended the academies and were authorized by their scholar-teachers to be one of them. The master laid his hands upon his student, ordaining him as a rabbi, and the official transference of authority from master to pupil was made known to all in a public ceremony.

Even today, when rabbis have become the interpreters of Judaism through their personal leadership of specific congregations rather than through their attachment to the academies alone, they still retain many of the characteristics of their ancient colleagues. Like his first precursors, the contemporary rabbi is not a priest, because he performs no ritual for his group—only with it. But neither is the rabbi a minister, because he never acts as God's authorized agent in offering access to personal salvation. This is why I have referred to him as a layman—he is a "teaching elder." And this is why, both in theory and fact, his ritual functions at Jewish services have never been of any greater significance than those of the humblest members of the congregation. Since he does not administer sacraments, as do Catholic priests, or perform sacred rituals, as do Protestant ministers, he is only one of the members of the community, not a representative of divinity. His principal functions are as teacher, judge, and expounder of the laws of the tradition. The authority of the rabbi is primarily an "authority of influence" rather than an "authority of jurisdiction." He exercises leadership by virtue of his scholarship, learning and moral virtue, rather than by any legal or "divine right."

This is the revolution wrought by the first rabbis who had shaped the school and the synagogue in this new religious spirit. They were devoted to making the life of each individual Jew a reflection of his own personal "priesthood," as a member of the holy people who were to fulfill the prophetic role as the "light to the nations." Moreover, they also taught their people to regard other "righteous men"—particularly those who shared their monotheism—as partners, not as rivals or outcasts. Among the many traditionally Jewish ideas which Paul, and those who followed him through the centuries, dismissed as useless—or what is worse, as both obsolete and misleading—were these rabbinic views about the oneness of a diverse mankind under one God.

* * *

All signs point to a human, if not a christological, truth which needs constant reiteration: this Christian problem harkens back to the reluctance of the church then—and often even now—to regard Jews as equals in the sight of God, neither as rivals nor outcasts, but as partners.

Contemporary Christians are still caught up in the problem of learning how to confront the reality of a living and vital synagogue-community, a problem that concerns the Jewish present and future. Furthermore, they have not as yet rid themselves of their fixation regarding the Jewish past. This confusion is especially manifested in the way in which the churches still read Hebrew Scriptures. That they labelled the biblical books sacred to Jews as the "Old Testament" also speaks volumes for their attitude: what is "old" may be venerable, but it also denotes something surpassed and transcended by the "new."

As a Jew, I pose the obvious question: How can one truly venerate what he has already rendered spiritually obsolete? This is still a nagging and persistent Christian problem. Let us examine it more closely.

NOTES

1. Matthew: 23:15. Of course, the latent rivalry to Judaism, and therefore the hostility of the New Testament writer, is more fully comprehended when we read the entire verse. "Woe to you, scribes and Pharisees, hypocrites! For you traverse sea and land to make a single proselyte, and when he becomes a proselyte, you make him twice as much a child of hell as yourselves."

2. A census of the Jewish population taken by Emperor Claudius in 48 c.e. discovered no less than 6,944,000 Jews within the confines of the Empire. According to Salo W. Baron, "it stands to reason that shortly before the fall of Jerusalem the world Jewish population exceeded 8,000,000 of whom probably not more than 2,350,000—2,500,000 lived in Palestine." Other Jewish settlements were found in Egypt, Syria, Asia Minor and Babylonia, each probably embracing more than 1,000,000 Jews. "Even Rome, the capital of the Empire, seems to have included a Jewish community of about 40,000 in a total population of some 800,000 . . ."

When these numbers are compared with the estimates of Jewish population in Palestine—not to speak of the Diaspora—before the Pharisees began their active proselytizing, it appears likely that *a very large number of converts must have entered the Jewish community in Roman times.*

See Salo W. Baron, "Population," in *Encyclopedia Judaica* (Jerusalem, 1970), Vol. 13, pp. 870–1.

3. For a comprehensive and original view of the ways in which ancient "temples" differed from synagogues see Harold Turner, *From Temple to Meeting House: The Phenomenology and Theology of Places of Worship* (The Hague: Mouton Publishers, 1979). See especially Chapter 14: "The Experiences of Other Traditions: Judaism."

4. It is discouraging to note that even usually reliable contemporary Christian scholars and theologians, perhaps out of their zeal to see the human Jesus from within his Jewish context, go to the untenable extreme of labeling him "rabbi." See, for example, the opening chapter "Jesus as Rabbi" in Jaroslav Pelikan, *Jesus Through the Centuries: His Place in the History of Culture* (New Haven: Yale University Press, 1985).

CHAPTER IV

The Hebrew Bible Is Not the "Old Testament"

SOMETIMES JUDAISM HAS TO BE PROTECTED EVEN FROM ITS CHRISTIAN friends.

One of these, a highly regarded scholar who thinks of himself as a philo-semite, while damning Judaism with faint praise, proclaims loudly his friendly intentions. He proudly claims that he is "not of those who depreciate the Judaism of the post-exilic period, or of subsequent ages," and he recognizes "with gratitude the rich heritage the Christian Church received from Judaism, and all that our Lord and the early Christians owed to the mother faith from whose womb the Church was born." In the next breath, however, he reveals an attitude to Judaism which clearly belies his protestations. Despite his scholarly credentials, he emerges with a view of the Hebrew Bible (or Old Testament) that is a "virtuous" model of Christian prejudice. He goes on to write: "Not in any spirit of hostility or controversy, but as a simple statement of fact [sic!] it must be observed that with all its cherishing of the high ethical values of the Old Testament, post-Biblical Judaism is an interlude that neither continues to obey the law of Moses, nor yet offers in itself the fulfillment of the hopes which the Old Testament holds before men. It is an interlude that is worthy of high respect, and marked by a noble spirit which calls for deep admiration. Nevertheless, it is an interlude. . . The promise set forth in the Old Testament is not fulfilled in Judaism."[1]

The language may sound friendly, but the words alert us that we are dealing once again with a Christian, no matter how seemingly

65

respectful, and *his* Jewish problem. He wants us to believe that the essential value of the Hebrew Bible is appreciated only if we accept his tortured logic: the "Old" Testament can be understood only as a bridge to the "New" Testament—its hopes and dreams are fulfilled only in Christianity, not in Judaism. For Jews, however, the Old Testament is neither "old," nor is it only a testament, or a theological document.

No matter what else such "friends" of Judaism may think of the Hebrew Bible, they are really saying that it has merit only if it is read as a Christian Bible.

Are Jews really expected to see these views as the highest compliment an informed Christian can pay Judaism? Yet, the author quoted above and many others like him continue to boast of their "understanding" and "appreciation" of the Jewish spiritual contribution. The preceding should give us a good idea of how much more difficult matters can be when dealing with laypersons whose limited Sunday school education makes them vulnerable to more fundamentalist pulpit preachers, whose "appreciation" of the Jews or their religion is rarely, if ever, proclaimed.

Proof-Texts

What are some of the sources of this Christian problem?

The first of these can be traced to the early Christian habit of proof-texting—reading into the Old Testament text a special Christian meaning, which often was not actually there or is clearly far-fetched. To be sure, the first Christians borrowed this method from the Pharisees, and later from the rabbis. At first it involved the search for specific texts in order to establish earlier "scriptural proof" which would authenticate their own later ideas. But in the hands of the Gospel writers, especially Matthew, and in the Epistles of Paul, this rabbinic method was put to christological use in ways that strained the facts of history and the context or intention of texts spoken centuries before by Jewish scriptural authors to a different audience and under different conditions altogether. Often, in order to prove that Jesus was indeed the Messiah already foretold in the Hebrew Bible, Gospel writers felt the need to demonstrate that even the most trivial details of his life and career were either foretold by the Hebrew prophets or were alluded to in other parts of Jewish Scripture.

A few examples of this use of "Old Testament" texts to justify the new religion will show how the Hebrew Bible was made to serve the pressing Christian need for authenticity.

(1) Micah had prophesied that Bethlehem, the birthplace of King David, would once again be the cradle of a ruler of Israel: "But you, O Bethlehem . . . from you shall come forth for me one who is to be a ruler in Israel" (Micah 5:2). In the New Testament (Matthew 2:3–6) we come upon the following verses, written more than seven centuries later: "He [King Herod] was troubled . . . and assembling all the chief priests and scribes of the people he inquired of them where the Christ was to be born. They told him, 'In Bethlehem of Judea: for so it is written by the prophet: And thou Bethlehem in the land of Judah art by no means least among the rulers of Judah; for from thee shall come a ruler who will govern my people Israel.' "

(2) Similarly, Zechariah's vision is taken literally to prove that Jesus was the intended Messiah. The Hebrew prophet had written: "Rejoice greatly, O daughter of Zion! Shout aloud, O daughter of Jerusalem! Lo, your king comes to you: triumphant and victorious is he, humble and riding on an ass, on a colt the foal of an ass" (Zechariah 9:9). Both Matthew and John use the prophet's text as proof of Jesus' authenticity as the Jewish Messiah, making certain to portray him even regarding the most minute details of his entry into Jerusalem: ". . . Jesus sent two disciples saying to them, 'Go into the village opposite you, and immediately you will find an ass tied, and a colt with her; untie them and bring them to me. If any one says anything to you, you shall say, 'The Lord has need of them,' and he will send them immediately.' This took place to fulfill what was spoken by the prophet. . ." (Matthew 21:2–5; see also John 12:14–15). Again, although the Gospels were written many centuries after the time of Zechariah, their writers combed all those prophetic texts they believed had some relationship to the Messiah figure. Then they made certain to replicate as many details as possible, so that it would appear clear to all that Jesus was the only Messiah that Zechariah, Isaiah—or other venerable Jewish figures—had in mind.

(3) From the Psalms, too, New Testament writers brought texts which related wholly to Jewish life and history; they simply appropriated them without regard to original context or meaning, exploiting them as pre-texts for their pro-Christian, often anti-Jewish message. Thus the Psalmist's bitter complaint about the rebelliousness of the nations against God and his anointed: "Why do the nations conspire and the people plot in vain? The kings of the earth set themselves,

and the rulers take counsel together, against the Lord and his anointed . . ." (Psalms 2:1–2). The New Testament writer of the Book of Acts quotes these passages as if they referred specifically to the plot against Jesus (Acts 4:25 ff). With the same ease, the Gospels appropriate other Psalms as if they too were clear prophecies of the rejection of Jesus by the Jews: "The very stone which the builders rejected has become the head of the corner; this was the Lord's doing, and it is marvelous in our eyes." (See Matthew 21:42; Mark 12:10–11.)

It was especially important for the Gospel writers to come up with "proofs" from the Hebrew Bible for both the Davidic descent of Jesus and for their (mistaken) belief that the Jewish Messiah foretold by Isaiah would be born to a virgin woman. That the evidence for Jesus' relationship to the family of David was considered flimsy even by his contemporaries is easily seen in a passage from the *Gospel According to John*. It records the perplexity of the people in trying the reconcile the tradition of his Galilean origin, for which many other proof-texts were also adduced, with the messianic promises. And so they asked: "Is the Christ to come from Galilee? Has not the scripture said that the Christ is descended from David and comes from Bethlehem, the village where David was [born]?" (John 7:41–2). Indeed, many objective scholars—Christians among them—now believe that Jesus was not born in Bethlehem, as depicted by the New Testament, but in Nazareth.

(4) Probably the most widely discussed New Testament reinterpretation of a Hebrew text given christological twists of meaning is a verse in Isaiah which, correctly translated, reads as follows: "Behold, a young woman shall conceive and bear a son, and shall call his name Immanuel" (Isaiah 7:14). I have already pointed out how the plain meaning of verses like this would be torn out of context by later generations of Christian apocalyptics and messianists. The remarkable Christian dogma of the "Virgin Birth" is based four-square on a faulty translation of a Hebrew word. *Alma*, meaning "young woman," is incorrectly rendered in the Greek Bible version by the word *partenos*—a virgin. Today, serious Christian Bible scholars readily admit that this passage in Isaiah does not speak of a "virgin" but of a "young woman." Untouched by all this, many still hold fast to their dogma.[2]

One Christian scholar puts the matter clearly:

> But when the New Testament finally emerged in its official form, it included a great deal of material whose purpose was to find in Hebrew history a series of mechanically "inspired" predictions pointing to

Jesus. This feature of the New Testament originated in the struggle which had been going on to explain the relation between Israel and the Christian Churches . . . New Testament pragmatism, accordingly, is responsible for dislocating the Hebrew prophets from their actual character as champions of justice and metamorphosing them into mechanically inspired foretellers, thus giving prophecy the character of mere unintelligent prediction . . .

. . . An instructive example of such manipulation is found in the treatment of Isaiah (7:14) by the book of Matthew. The Isaiah passage, written more than seven hundred years before Christ, relates to the fast-approaching invasion of Israel by the Assyrians and predicts that before the event a young woman *(alma)* shall bear a son. . . .

. . . The Isaiah passage is used in the book of Matthew in the interests of Christian dogma, as a prediction of the birth of Jesus.[3]

(5) As might be expected, the crucifixion story, which serves as the central theme of Christianity, and often even minor incidents and episodes relating to it were subjected to intense proof-texting in the New Testament. To list but a few of these, I begin with the reference to the betrayal of Jesus by Judas Iscariot: his remorse, his turning over the thirty silver pieces to the Temple, and the priests' purchase with this money of the potter's field as a burial ground. These events were incorrectly regarded as a fulfillment of some verses in Zechariah (11:12 ff.) The New Testament writers, however, probably because of his association with the purchase of a field (see Matthew 27:3–10), mistakenly ascribe this to a different prophet, Jeremiah.

According to the New Testament, when his body was taken off the cross, Jesus' legs were not broken as was the Roman custom. This, too, in the view of the writer, was regarded as a direct fulfillment of the Old Testament, namely, the prohibition of the breaking of the bones of the paschal lamb (Exodus 12:46; Numbers 9:12). It was, moreover, also regarded as a christological fulfillment of what Jews had always understood as the Psalmist's solace to the righteous: "Many are the afflictions of the righteous; but the Lord delivers him out of them all. He keeps all his bones; not one of them is broken" (Psalms 34:19–20). In the New Testament these passages from Psalms are regarded as referring directly to Jesus, and they are specifically applied to his crucifixion. Thus, John writes: "But when they came to Jesus and saw that he was already dead, they did not break his legs . . . For these things took place that the scripture might be fulfilled. 'Not a bone of him shall be broken' " (John 19:33–36). Later generations of Christians used these very references to the Hebrew paschal lamb, which was originally sacrificed on the Passover, as the basis of their new theology.

The "sacrifice" of Jesus as the "lamb of God," it is said, fulfilled and transcended the Old Testament practices of the Passover, and moved Christianity onto a higher plane. The Old Testament, it was then said, was concerned with animal sacrifices, while the death of Jesus was seen as the sacrifice *par excellence* of the new Christian covenant. Christians return repeatedly to their own reworked theme of "sacrifice," the means whereby Jesus, as the lamb of God, took upon himself the sins of the world. (See John 18:28 ff.) The church altar is a perennial reminder of his ultimate sacrifice.

Old Testament, New Testament

To Christians, the Hebrew Bible is to be studied and sometimes admired—but inevitably, they find "the promise set forth in the Old Testament is not fulfilled in Judaism," only in Christianity. Its chief, and sometimes only, value consists, therefore, in being the preparation, or "schoolmaster," that leads inexorably to the New Testament. Only therein, they believe, are all of its promises fulfilled—in the life and death of Jesus Christ.

To Jews, the Hebrew Bible is conceived altogether differently. It spans a national library of thirty-nine books, from Genesis to Chronicles, and covers a period of almost two thousand years, from the time of Abraham forward. There are sagas of families, biographies of heroes, proverbs, chronicles, poems, philosophical tracts, a novelette, love songs, and a verse-play in this Bible—all of which comprise the national literature of the Jewish people. The Hebrew religion it depicts is not static. It changes over the course of the centuries, as well it should, considering that the biblical record describes the birth, growth, and evolution of the Jewish people across many centuries.

The Hebrew Bible would ultimately be divided into three parts: the Torah, or Pentateuch (sometimes also called "The Law"); the Prophets, former and latter, major and minor; and the general miscellany, called the Writings, or Hagiographa. Yet, the road that led to the final canonization of the entire Bible with all of its thirty-nine books, was long and arduous. First there had been only a series of oral traditions which circulated among the people for centuries. Some of these were later discarded, while others were committed to writing. Still later, these earliest manuscripts were changed and edited; and again, some were sifted out and discarded altogether. At some point in time, various unknown compilers or redactors brought together all of those books which were deemed authentic and acceptable.

It is probable that the idea of forming an official canon came from Greek culture and the growth of Greek literature, while the more immediate cause and outcome of this was the popularity of various apocalyptic books written by and circulating among the Jews. Because the religious leaders regarded this as erroneous or even pernicious literature, it became necessary to decide which of the mass of books then current were to be regarded as containing the truth. As a result, what we now call the Hebrew Bible was finally canonized, probably by the end of the first Christian century.

The principle behind canonization was "divine inspiration": whether or not the books contained God's own word and were therefore regarded as sacred. If a book was written before "divine inspiration" had ceased to be revealed unto men, the rabbis judged it to be sacred; if later, it was deemed unacceptable. Accordingly, many of those books which had not made their way into Hebrew Scripture were labeled "Apocrypha" ("hidden" from the ordinary reader) by the Church, which also did not regard them as being part of the Old Testament. This literature is often called the intertestamentary writing because it bridges the gap between the Hebrew Bible and the New Testament.

There are differences of opinion about these books, however. Martin Luther, for example, in the preface to his Bible translation, rejected the Apocrypha as non-canonical, referring to its books as "books that are not equally esteemed with the Holy Scripture, but nevertheless are profitable and good to read." In this matter, he adopted the Jewish view. At the Council of Trent in 1546, however, the Roman Catholic Church clearly defined its position in opposition to Luther, accepting the Apocrypha as sacred writing, even if not as part of the Old Testament. It held: "If any man does not accept as sacred and canonical these books, entire, with all their parts, as they have customarily been read in the Catholic church and are contained in the ancient common Latin edition . . . let him be anathema!" (Fourth session of the Council of Trent, April 8, 1546). In effect, then, Protestants as well as Jews regard as sacred only those books which were officially part of the Hebrew Bible, while Roman Catholics accept the apocryphal (and some apocalyptical) writings as canonical.

Once the Hebrew Bible was canonized it would be important to insure that all the standardized, authoritative texts were preserved intact, free from errors, omissions, or unwarranted additions. The creation of an official "received Text," called in Hebrew the *Masorah*, was the result. It was the careful, reverent and loving work of humble scholars who devoted themselves to the preservation of the text and its protection from the intrusion of later mistakes or innovations. After the Hebrew, this is called the "Masoretic Text."

As we have seen, the Dead Sea scrolls were of enormous help in providing some of the important links between sectarian Judaism and the beginnings of Christianity. They have been of great importance concerning the text of the Hebrew Bible, as well, helping to support the fidelity of the Masoretic tradition. Now, for the first time, we have the actual manuscripts of various books of the Hebrew Bible (and still others, contemporary with but not included in, the canon) which go back almost a thousand years before those previously in the possession of scholars.

The Masoretic text in our hands goes back only to the ninth and tenth Christian centuries, and there are always scholarly doubts about material that is so far removed from the period of its production. "Considering how widely the earliest manuscripts of the New Testament vary," wrote Millar Burrows, a leading Christian scholar, "how radically the ancient Greek versions differ from the traditional Hebrew text, and what a long time intervened between the Dead Sea Scrolls and the oldest of medieval manuscripts, one might have expected a much larger number of variant readings and a much wider degree of divergence. It is a matter for wonder that through something like a thousand years, the [ancient Hebrew] text underwent so little revision."[4]

The Masoretic text now emerges as a highly reliable version of the original. The Dead Sea scrolls lend scientific evidence to the spiritual fidelity and painstaking concern of those to whom the copying of Scripture was a religious act, not a secretarial or professional chore. The remarkable thing about the Hebrew Bible is that alone among the literature of ancient cultures, it survived the silt of time's deluge. It was not buried in the ruins of the ages, nor covered by the sands of history. It emerged from antiquity as the lone, protected record of the earlier epochs. That this occurred in the face of man's normal forgetfulness of the past is no mean feat.

The Book and the "People of the Book"

Despite the frequently negative attitude to the Hebrew Bible by an ambivalent Christian church, the Jewish people has remarkably maintained its own spiritual integrity. It did this by protecting its own national literature, its Scriptures. No amount of rationalizing after the fact can alter, amend, or eradicate this truth: for Jews, the Hebrew Bible was never in need of fulfillment by other religions nor does it now need to be propped up by the support of those who see in it a secondary, not a principal role. The Hebrew Bible lives today because the Jewish people protected and cared for it. Not without reason did the frustrated Muhammed call them "The People of the Book." He was acknowledging the principal reason they would not convert to Islam: their loyalty and love for their own sacred writings as God's word. In their view, their own covenant with God did not need to be "embroidered," "improved," or redefined by others whose connection to their own Jewish Scripture was exploitative, self-vindicating, and self-fulfilling as prophecy.

We have seen how the first Christians, in order to compete with Judaism, felt the need to furnish evidence that they, too, had received a revelation that was authentic. They pointed to Jesus as the symbol and focal point of this revelation, and they identified his "new covenant" with their supreme and pressing mission to proselytize at first only their fellow Jews, but later, following Paul's insistence, among the pagan Gentiles of the area. In the tradition-minded Orient, claims to authority had to be authenticated by means of ancestor proof. Early Christianity acquired such justification by the bold claim that all the messianic predictions of the Hebrew Bible were based and focused on none other than Jesus. So it was that the Bible of the Jewish people became for them the "Old Testament"—important only because of its predictions of the messiahship of Jesus. It was, in short, the deed and title of the Christian claim. A Christian scholar summed this up very neatly: "The life of Christ, the doctrines of the new dispensation, the fortunes of the Church would stand out clearly to the Christian eye on the pages of Scripture; the old congregation of Israel was felt to be a preparation for and a prediction of the new congregation of Christ; the chief interest for the Christian lay in the discovery of references to the gospel times, and in a thousand Old Testament passages he might find prophecies and illustrations of what was going on around him."[5]

* * *

For all their pious study or reverent use of the Hebrew Bible, to Christians it is still an Old Testament—profoundly in need of a New Testament. To Jews, however, their Bible constitutes the core of their past and present uniqueness, the source of their ongoing spirituality, and the promise of their future. It is, consciously or not, the very matrix of their Jewish identity.

As long as even wise and scholarly Christian advocates keep missing these Jewish messages of the "Old Testament," they will remain enmeshed in this and other Christian problems of their own making. It is time for a change. We live in an age of democratic pluralism, where appeals to ancient authority are no longer necessary or even relevant. Christian statesmanship, I contend, must seek to produce self-confidence in the churches based on a new mood of openness toward the non-Christian world. It must be willing to reconsider those older and surpassed ecclesiastical notions, based principally on Paul's view, which held that for Christianity to missionize and rule the world it had to absorb, and thus dethrone, both the covenant and the people of Israel.

And there is no better way to start democratizing the Christian world-view than by learning to give back the Book to the People of the Book.

NOTES

1. H. H. Rowley, *The Unity of the Bible* (New York: Meridian Books, 1957), pp. 91–2. Yet, for Rowley even the Old Testament itself is deficient from a Christian point of view. He writes: "Not a little in the Old Testament is superseded in the New, and even where there is no explicit supersession Christians recognize that whatever is alien to the spirit of Christ and His revelation of God has no validity for them. In other words, Christ is for them the standard whereby the Old Testament must be judged as a revelation of the character and will of God." See *supra*, p. 25.

2. It is instructive to note that while the prestigious Protestant translation, the *Revised Standard Version* (1952), does use "young woman" in the text, it still finds it necessary to offer the alternative reading—"or virgin"—as a footnote to the text.

3. Louis D. Wallis, *The Bible Is Human* (New York: Columbia University Press, 1943), pp. 11ff.

4. Millar Burrows, *The Dead Sea Scrolls* (New York: Viking Press, 1955), p. 394. The oldest dated Masoretic text of the Hebrew Bible is the so-called "Ben Asher Codex" of the Prophets (895 C.E.) The oldest dated scroll of the entire Hebrew Bible was preserved in the synagogue of Aleppo, Syria, and it has been dated to about 929 C.E. "What is astonishing," wrote Professor Yigael

Yadin, "is that despite their antiquity . . . the [Dead Sea] scrolls . . . are on the whole almost identical with the Masoretic text known to us." See his *The Message of the Scrolls* (New York: Simon and Schuster, 1969), p. 83.

5. Crawford H. Toy, *Judaism and Christianity* (Boston: Little, Brown, 1892), p. 137.

CHAPTER V

The Church Is Not the "New Israel"

"Among Christian scholars seeking to undermine the theological and scriptural bases of Christian anti-Judaism," writes one of their number, "no figure has been discussed more frequently, or proven more controversial than Paul."[1] For Jews, however, it would be difficult to alter their view that his life and teachings still constitute an important part of the Christian problem.

The final separation of Christianity from the Jewish people is the work of the real founder of the Church, Saul, later called Paul, of Tarsus. He broke the ties that bound the early Judeo-Christians to their ancestral heritage by announcing in effect: "The Old Israel is dead! Long live the Christians, the New Israel!"

In many ways, he was an eclectic, ambivalent Jew. Like other zealous reformers, he was often impatient to see his hopes realized, and eager to overwhelm those who stood in his way. Consider this description of Paul by the eminent Jewish historian Salo W. Baron:

> In contrast to Jesus, the Galilean, he [Paul] may be classified as the intellectual spokesman of Hellenistic Jewry, particularly of the type prevalent in Asia Minor . . . As a rule, he thought in terms of world Jewry, rather than in those of Palestine. From this standpoint he was easily induced to abandon many revolutionary and communistic elements of the earlier movement. Largely accepting the existing social order, he visualized the victory of Christianity as a prolongation and coronation of the expansion of Judaism . . . Very soon, however, Paul discovered the chief obstacle to the expansion of Judaism. Even full-fledged Jews in his country must have felt the yoke of the law much more heavily than the Jews in Palestine. Those among them who were

recent proselytes suffered from it in a still higher degree. It may be taken for granted that many of these Diaspora Jews, like the Galilean Am Ha-Ares [the uneducated], could not adhere strictly to the rigid law. Perhaps the poor among them, including slaves and hired workers, had often to disregard dietary laws, the laws of the Sabbath, etc. Such religious transgressors were deeply troubled; their conscience told them that they were sinners. Others belonging to the large class of sebomenoi [semi-converts to Judaism] wanted to become [full] Jews, but did not see their way to accepting the burden of the law. *For all these, probably constituting a majority of the Jewish people in Asia Minor and neighboring countries, Paul found a formula. All of you are Jews, he told them, as long as you believe in the spiritual tenets of Judaism.* For a time the ritual law in all its ramifications had been necessary. But with the advent of the Messiah, "who had already come," it was nullified. Faith had now taken the place of the law . . . Using the terminology of Jeremiah and of Philo, he substituted the circumcision of the heart for the circumcision of the flesh. Here was the symbol of the new covenant between man and God. *In one word, the Law had been abolished, and with it its bearer, the Jewish national group. Israel in the flesh had been replaced by a more universal body of men, Israel in the spirit* (italics added).[2]

Paul's attacks on his own people were the result of their unwillingness to join his own group. This led him to turn to the Gentiles more and more. He let out his wrath on his own people and contemptuously explained why he turned away from them: "It was necessary that the word of God should be spoken first to you. Since you thrust it from you, and judge yourselves unworthy of eternal life, behold, we turn to the Gentiles" (Acts 13:46). As part of his religious propaganda, he freely offered the pagan communities of Asia Minor, Greece and Rome to which he travelled the place once occupied by Israel, as God's elect. If they would join him and his fellow Christians, *they* would be the true and new Israel, the "Israel of God" (Galatians 6:16).

It was no coincidence that Paul's missionary journeys never led him either to Egypt or Babylonia, Jewish communities whose spirit of national sentiment was exceedingly strong. Alexandria, in particular, was then the intellectual and economic center of the Western world, and Paul's omission of this metropolis from his itinerary, and his concentration, instead, on remoter outposts, where Jews had weaker national ties, gives us an insight into his shrewd and calculating program. He must have known that neither in the Egyptian or Babylonian diaspora communities would his denunciations of the Jewish people and its external symbol, the Torah-law, have much effect in luring Jews to accept his new doctrines.[3] Indeed, his anti-Jewish diatribes in communities such as these would have been profoundly counter-productive.

We can see his mind at work as he turned from the Jews toward the Gentiles. The more he succeeded with these new converts, those "outsiders-turned-insiders" to whom the promise of salvation was offered, the more he renounced his own people, whom he regarded as replaced by the "new Israel." Let it be clear: it is with Paul's "new Israel" that the church began its career. Indeed, this became the message of its mission to the world: to Gentile and Jew, Greek and barbarian, slave and free man, this new Israel of the spirit was not only open and receiving; even more important, it alone could confer God's rewards and promises. "Paul often speaks about Jews and Greeks," wrote Martin Buber, "but never in connexion with the reality of their nationalities: he is only concerned with the newly-established community [the infant Church]."[4]

It has been claimed that the Christian mission launched by Paul, and followed by the church ever since, represented a more universalist, more global and democratic stance than the narrower, seemingly ethnic and folk-oriented views then held by the leaders of Judaism. The thrust of the Pauline effort to convert the peoples of the region to his new religion was propelled by a double-pronged message: the tribalism of the Old Israel is finished; the universalism of its successor, the Church as the new Israel, has begun. Put another way, it was as if Paul were saying that the Jewish mission was dead, and deserved to die; the mission of Christianity was now born, and it alone deserved to live.

I do not believe that one can fully understand his radical break with his own people without recognizing that "Paul's formula" was his pragmatic way of pitting his "universal" mission against the "national" mission of his people. He was offering "Judaism without Jews" to the world and the gift of life everlasting, while the Pharisee-rabbis in their approach to the pagans seemed earthbound by insisting on preserving the integrity of the Jewish people as the concrete vehicle of their monotheistic teachings. To the rabbis, a convert not only accepted the monotheism of their faith but also its ethics, and this could only be done by becoming a practicing member of the community of Israel. With Paul, pagans could by-pass this arduous route of the here-and-now: their Christian baptism conferred upon them instant membership in an other-worldly community—the "universal," redemptive, church of Jesus Christ.

I do not regard Paul's use of such phrases as the "old" or "new" Israel as the enunciation of new doctrine alone. It was as much his "political" and competitive way of offering "more"—of contesting the successful expansion of the "old" Israel among the pagans, and especially the Romans, which the missionizing activities of the Pharisee-rabbis had already achieved. I am convinced that Pauline Christianity was forced into its anti-Jewish stance as a result of the missionary success of the rabbis. It was always looking to offer "more"—more salvation—in order to compete with and defeat the Jewish promise.

In the three centuries which followed the death of Paul, Jews and Christians kept on vying with each other, competing strenuously for converts, across the Roman empire. Despite the attempts of Paul and those who followed him to make Judaism appear as a tribal religion of a defeated, fossilized culture, if it were not for their political misfortunes at the hands of imperial Rome following the fall of Jerusalem, the thrust of Judaism and of the Jewish people as a missionary force might not have slowed down. It is important to ponder the implications of even a short history of the "Jewish mission" to discover why Paul's Jewish problem still remains a major Christian problem: the "old" Israel and its mission have never died.[5]

The Jewish Mission: A Short History

Even before the rise of Christianity, Jews were not among the most liked peoples of the ancient world. Resentment toward them can be traced principally to their conviction that Judaism, as the one revealed and true religion, was destined to become the universal faith of mankind. As one scholar has noted: "No other religion in their world and time made any such pretensions or cherished such aspirations. It was an exclusiveness the rest of mankind did not understand and therefore doubly resented." He goes on to explain that their unremitting criticism of "the vices of heathen society was not adapted to make them liked in an age that knew nothing of jealous gods, and when all manner of national and personal religions, native and foreign, lived amicably and respectfully side by side."[6] Imagine, then, what would happen when Christianity arose and claimed for itself the self-same universalism of Israel! By conventional definition, a universal and true religion can not be shared by any other universal and true religion. It is, therefore, not surprising that Christians soon came to regard Judaism not as a universal faith, but only as a narrow, surpassed, tribal religion. By the Middle Ages, as we shall soon see, Judaism, unlike Christianity or Islam, would learn how to accept a "shared universalism" which made room for both of her "daughter" religions in the divine economy.

But we are getting ahead of the story, for the Jewish mission to the world had been successfully at work long before Christians came upon the scene. George Foot Moore has tersely described what was involved:

> . . . the [Jewish] belief in the future universality of the true religion, the coming of an age when "the Lord shall be king over all the earth," when "the Lord shall be one and his name One," led to efforts to convert the Gentiles to the worship of the one true God and to faith and obedience according to the revelation he had given, and made Judaism the first great missionary religion of the Mediterranean world. When it is called a missionary religion, the phrase must, however, be understood with a difference. The Jews did not send out missionaries into the *partes infidelium* expressly to proselyte [sic] among the heathen. They were themselves settled by the thousands in all the great centres and in innumerable smaller cities; they had appropriated the language and much of the civilization of their surroundings; they were engaged in the ordinary occupations, and entered into the industrial and commercial life of the community and frequently into its political life. Their religious influence was exerted chiefly through the synagogues, which they set up for themselves, but which were open to all whom interest or curiosity drew to their services. . . .

> . . . in the Hellenistic world, polytheism and idolatry were so decisively the characteristic difference between Gentile and Jew that the rejection of these might almost seem to be the renunciation of heathenism and the adoption of Judaism; and if accompanied by the observance of the sabbath and conformity to the rudimentary rules of clean and unclean [the dietary laws] which were necessary conditions of social intercourse, it might seem to be a respectable degree of conversion. Nor are utterances of this tenor lacking in Palestinian sources; e.g., the rejection of idolatry is the acknowledgment of the whole law.

> Such converts were called religious persons ("those who worship, or revere, God"), and although in a strict sense outside the pale of Judaism, undoubtedly expected to share with Jews by birth the favor of the God they had adopted, and were encouraged in this hope by their Jewish teachers. It was not uncommon for the next generation to seek incorporation into the Jewish people by circumcision.[7]

Many outstanding Roman notables as well as members of royal houses were known to have adopted Judaism as their own faith, as well as membership in the people of Israel. Among the rabbis themselves, there were a goodly number of converts or children of converts to Judaism. Indeed, Jews never forgot that Ruth, the ancestress of King David himself, was born a Moabite, a member of a nation which had perennially fought Israel before voluntarily accepting the God of Israel and the people of Israel as her very own. Ruth's classic proclamation of loyalty still remains a favorite quotation from the Hebrew Bible: "Entreat me not to leave you or to return from following you; for where you go I will go, and where you lodge I will lodge; your people shall be my people, and your God my God; where you die I will die, and there will I be buried" (Ruth 1:16–17).

Instruction in the law and customs of the community was an integral part of the Jewish conversion rite, and for male converts circumcision was also a preliminary religious requirement. (During the period when the Temple still stood, it was expected that the proselyte would also participate in a sacrificial meal, for which a burnt-offering was brought.) After these obligations had been fulfilled, final conversion to Judaism was consummated by means of the ritual of immersion or baptism. At the conclusion of baptism, after all the other requirements had been met, the new convert to Judaism was considered a full-fledged member of the community, as if he had been born a Jew. In the words of the Talmud: "A proselyte who embraces Judaism is like a new-born child."[8] All former sins were done away by conversion. The Christian ritual or sacrament of baptism was first a Jewish rite.

Yet in spite of this "open-door policy," there was never complete unanimity among the Talmudic rabbis with regard to active missionizing. In marked contrast to the attitude of Christians—then or now— there was always the fear that if Judaism officially adopted a policy of vigorous missionizing among non-Jews, the religious ideals of ethical monotheism might be compromised for the sake of gaining new members. Many rabbis were thus extremely cautious and conservative. In their eyes the Jewish "mission" was not geared to conversionary activity, but was instead caught up in the desire that Judaism serve as an influence on the non-Jewish world so that all mankind might become more receptive to its universal monotheistic teachings. They were concerned that they might be required to dilute these truths if they were to engage in energetic overt efforts to "win souls" among the pagans. There is ample evidence from the Talmud to indicate that some rabbis feared that, rather than turning from idolatry, the pagans might retain some of their heathen practices in coming over to Judaism and thus destroy the higher and more subtle meanings which monotheism taught. Then, of course, during periods of political instability, some rabbis were also concerned that recent converts would turn against them as informers to the governing powers.

Earlier we noted that the Talmudic rabbis had made possible the entry into the folk and faith of Israel of many thousands of pagan converts, most notably among the upper classes of Rome itself. We have also seen how, after Christianity was born, with its rival claims as the "true religion," the pace of Jewish missionary efforts seemed to abate. What happened? And in what ways has the Jewish impulse to bring the whole world "under the wing of the one God" changed and altered course since that time?

The Mission Alters Its Course: The Effects of Christian Triumphalism

The persecution of the Jews instituted by the Roman Emperor Hadrian represents a turning point in the history of Jewish proselytizing. In 132 c.e., the Emperor promulgated bans against public Jewish instruction as well as circumcision. These edicts made it most difficult for Jews to carry on their own religious life; they were put on the defensive. It was difficult enough for those who had been born Jews to continue their own religious practice. Now it became even more difficult to seek new converts to Judaism.

On the other hand, Christianity from its earliest beginnings was a community composed of converts; without them there could be no church. Unlike Judaism, it was in the earliest years a zealous faith-group consisting wholly of new adherents; it was not formed on a natural, organic, or national base. Moreover, as we have seen, Paul had charged the infant church with the need to convert the world to its universal saving qualities as the "new Israel." In accordance with his doctrines, the whole world stood in need of redemption, and all peoples, including the Jews, could come to God only through *"the way"*—by staking their lives and their faith on Jesus. At the very core of Christianity stood the cross, the sign of salvation, which was to be carried to all—pagan and Jew alike.

Until the time of Hadrian, throughout the Roman Empire, Judaism and Christianity had been rivals in gaining new adherents. After the decrees of the Emperor were promulgated, Jewish missionizing receded until it was barely a perceptible force in Jewish religion. On the other hand, the Christians pursued converts with unremitting zeal and vigor. Since conversion in Paul's teaching did not require circumcision, Hadrian's anti-Jewish decrees did not hamper the spread of the

Christian mission. On the contrary, it indirectly led the way to the expansion which was to follow, up to the time of Constantine when the entire Empire became officially Christian.

In the Middle Ages, particularly after the Fourth Lateran Council in 1215 and the oppressive papal edict of Innocent III (which required Jews to wear a "badge of shame" on their outer clothing), it became virtually impossible for Jews to "compete" with Christians in gaining new converts. It would also be most difficult for Jews to establish spiritual or intellectual contacts of a serious nature with either the Christian or Muslim worlds. Pre-rigged polemical debates—not democratic dialogues—were set up by a triumphalist Church to prove Judaism's inferiority to Christianity. These usually culminated either in the burning of Jewish books, repressive ordinances, or even the outright expulsion of Jews. In spite of this the royal family of Adiabene, a province of Parthia, converted to Judaism in the first century of the Christian era, and its Queen, Helena, spent many years in Jerusalem. (Her body was later brought there to be buried in a tomb that is still standing.) Later in the fifth century, the kings of Himyar (Yemen) in southern Arabia adopted Judaism, and in the first half of the eighth century the upper classes of the Khazars, a kingdom of Turkic stock in the Volga-Caucasas region, converted as well.

Additionally, although it is infrequently remembered, Jews had actually established a series of independent "kingdoms" in several far-flung diaspora communities. These ranged from Malabar in India, where an autonomous Jewish principality survived for almost a thousand years until its destruction in the fifteenth century, to a group of Jewish kingdoms in Ethiopia, which lasted for at least a millenium until their downfall in the seventeenth century. Some scholars are also of the opinion that "as late as the ninth and tenth centuries there was still an extensive Jewish kingdom that stretched from the hills of Ethiopia through the vast expanses of Sudan, and as far as the Atlantic coast," including the Berber country of North Africa.[9] Inevitably, in the course of those centuries, many local Hindu, Ethiopian, Berber, and other tribespeople adopted Judaism as their faith and became members of the Jewish community.

It is difficult to ascertain the extent of proselytism in the Middle Ages. While historical sources refer only to a few isolated cases, there must have been a steady influx of converts, despite the absence of authoritative Jewish records on the subject. For one thing, one Church Council after another records warnings and punishments to any Christian who consorts with Jews, harbors them in his home, or adopts any Jewish ceremonial or religious practices. The latter were contemptuously called "Judaizers," and they were especially cautioned against emulating or affecting Jewish ideas or styles. Of these we shall have more to say later.

Indeed, it is a matter of record that for over six hundred years until the beginning of the twelfth century, more than forty separate Church Councils kept enacting and re-enacting laws which repeatedly warned professing Christians of dire punishments should they persist in observing the Jewish Sabbath, celebrating Jewish festivals, or attending synagogue services. That the highest Church authorities felt the recurring need to reiterate these prohibitions—every fifteen years on the average—is a sure sign that Judaism must have been a magnetic force for many Christians, and that over many centuries a significant number of them continued to be attracted and even converted to it.

In addition, although we have no written documentation of the facts, visual anthropological evidence points to still another remarkable clue to the ongoing process of conversion to Judaism, even in the face of strong external religious opprobrium. There are marked physical differences between various Jewish communities which point to some merging of the scattered, local Jewish communities with the settled members of their host nations. The resemblance of various Jewish communities throughout the Diaspora to the dominant ethnic types of their own separate environment may very well be the result of the influx of "outsiders" who converted to Judaism, even during the most intolerant centuries of the Middle Ages. Thus, many German Jews still bear the physical appearance of their Germanic descent; and so it is also with Polish, Russian, Ukrainian, Italian, Chinese, Yemenite, Indian, North African and Ethiopian Jews—to mention only a few. The distinguished anthropologist Raphael Patai has put it well:

> "The historical record of proselytism tells us only a very small part of the story, most of which is, and will forever remain, unknown. The striking physical similarity [however] between the Jew and the non-Jew in every country in which Jews settled not later than the end of the Middle Ages can serve to confirm that the non-Jewish genetic influence on the Jews must indeed have been considerable."[10]

In North America in only the last several decades, another unusual phenomenon has appeared, one that can indeed be documented: each year over 10,000 persons are converting to Judaism.[11] To be sure, almost all of these are Christian women (Christian men comprise only about 20 percent of the total) who are marrying Jewish men and establishing Jewish homes. While this number is not one of major proportions, the phenomenon itself is most significant: it was almost never this way in recent years in Europe. The fact is that conversion to Judaism is taking place freely—in the face of generally negative popular Jewish opinion and without benefit of rabbinical persuasion. In an open American society Jews can easily "opt out" of Judaism and convert to Christianity when they marry across religious lines. That there are increasing numbers of Christians who are accepting Judaism, in a situation where the Jewish partner could have gone the other way, does say some things that are significant.[12] It demonstrates that there are Christians today who regard Judaism as a fitting personal choice. It sheds light, too, on the vitality of Judaism, even among those Jews who might otherwise appear by their intermarriage to be only marginally related to Judaism.

Indeed, after many years of pondering this new Jewish "opportunity" in America, the Union of American Hebrew Congregations in 1983 established a permanent "Commission of Reform Jewish Outreach." Its declared purpose was to engage in active programs "to encourage both the non-Jewish parents in mixed marriages and their children, along with the 'unchurched,' to convert to Judaism—to become 'Jews by choice.' " It is a program, as well, for those without a religious preference who may want to consider Judaism as one of the alternatives to make their lives meaningful. While the Orthodox and the Conservative—the two other major Jewish denominations in America—are still reticent about seeking converts, this radical departure by a large and powerful group, the Reform Jewish movement, may yet prove to be the first successful organized attempt at Jewish proselytizing in the history of the Diaspora. Not since the times of the Pharisees had such a view taken serious hold of any part of the Jewish religious community. "Jews by choice" has now become a new category of religious experience in the contemporary American Jewish community.

Maimonides: "Shared Universalism"

We have seen that the fact Jews accepted but did not seek converts was due in large part to the changing vicissitudes of their political fortunes after Christianity took over the Roman Empire. But I believe that at the heart of the matter there was a deeper ethical and theological reason for this unusual situation. After all, it is a strange condition to be in, and difficult for many people to grasp. "How can you be willing to accept converts," the sincere questioner will ask, "and yet not vigorously pursue the 'Jewish mission'?" He quizzes further, and suggests forcefully: "Either you believe in your mission or you do not; either you proselytize or you do not!"

Judaism's most respected medieval theologian, Maimonides, had set a new course for the Jewish mission by redefining the meaning of religious universalism. He insisted that universalism does not demand a monolithic "totalitarian" religious viewpoint, nor does a universal God require or depend upon a universal church in which he is worshipped. His view, already posited in the the Talmudic age, can be summed up in the rabbinic dictum: "The righteous among all the peoples of the earth have a share in the world to come." While the rabbis of the Talmud required Jews to fulfill the 613 commandments enumerated in the Torah-law, non-Jews, in their view, could be adjudged righteous if they observed but *seven* of these commandments. The Seven Commandments required of the sons of Noah, as this special "Torah" for the non-Jew (also called the "Noachide laws") came to be known, were considered to be the basic rules of morality binding on all mankind. All people were commanded to refrain from (1) idolatry; (2) incest and adultery; (3) bloodshed; (4) blasphemy; (5) injustice and lawlessness; (6) robbery; and (7) inhumane conduct, such as the eating of the flesh of a living animal.

Maimonides, living courageously as a physician-philosopher and eminent rabbi in medieval Spain, and looking out upon the contending forces of both Christianity and Islam in his native land, could still say: "All these teachings of Jesus the Nazarene and the Ishmaelite [Muhammed] who arose after him were intended . . . to prepare the whole world to worship God together as one."[13] In his view, universalism was no undivided monolith. Rather, he was calling upon his fellow Jews to recognize that Jewish universalism could prosper from a sharing of the mission with the two monotheistic daughter religions of Israel. He went so far as to equate the repudiation of all forms of idolatry with the ultimate purpose of Judaism. "Whoever denies idolatry," he wrote, "confesses his faith in the whole Torah, in all the prophets, and all that the prophets commanded from Adam to the end of time. And this is the fundamental principle of all the commandments."[14]

In the view of many other medieval Jewish theologians, there was a divine message in the fact that God had scattered the nations across the face of the earth, multiplied their languages, and frustrated the desires of the builders of the Tower of Babel to "make themselves a name," by forcing the world to become "of one language and of one speech." (See Genesis: 11:1 ff.) Like Maimonides, these teachers were not committed to the idea of a single, universal religion; they preferred a multiplicity of nations and languages. Despite the origin of all men in a single man—Adam—they regarded the enormous differences among the peoples of the earth as an added reason for admiring God's creation.[15]

It is this special brand of religious universalism by which Christianity needs to be confronted. In its pristine days, when it was still virtually a "sect" within Judaism, Christianity emerged as a unifying force in a world which was decaying for lack of a centrifugal, transnational force. The early Christians sharply criticized the Pharisees as too separatist, too self-concerned, too parochial in clinging to the doctrine of the divine election of Israel as the chosen people. When Paul taught that in Christ there is neither Jew nor Gentile, Greek nor barbarian, he was addressing himself specifically to what he thought was the ethnocentric provincialism of the Jewish community in the view it held regarding its own chosenness.

But a crucial paradox developed. Whereas Christianity rejected Israel's special relationship to God as producing too narrow a worldview, it substituted itself as the new Israel—the elect of God, and proceeded to deify its church as the mystical body of Christ. While the Pharisees may not have been especially interested in the religious fate of the heathen nations—and this remained a scandal to Christianity which was intent upon universalizing its mission—these Jewish teachers never refused the righteous non-Jew a share in the salvation that was the reward of righteousness.

Christian "universalism," however, has had a difficult time finding a proper place for the non-Christian in its esoteric scheme of things-to-come. The Roman Church has insisted that Christ is God-like and that the Church is Christ. Orthodox Protestants have not gone much beyond this, substituting for this doctrine the affirmation of its faith in "the universal priesthood of believers." Thus, for devout Christians, faith in Jesus as the Christ is still *the* way to eternal salvation.

This is why Christianity, and the world beyond it, needs to be reminded of Judaism's own universal mission. For Judaism still insists—and by its continued corporate existence persistently maintains—that while God is one, his children are many, and the proper universal task of each is to live by His teaching, leaving final judgments only to Him.

No people is essentially wayward, and mere mutual toleration of each other's errors cannot be the final approach to truth. Only when we validate as divine the separate roads which lead to the divine can we develop the true love of each other which is the ultimate concern, the final and consummate goal of a common humanity.

James Parkes, wise student of Judaism and Christianity (and himself an Anglican clergyman) has aptly and pithily summarized this need: "Judaism is a way of life, and it converts by communicating some part of its way of life to the nations among which and within which it lives. Because of this . . . the world, so to say, notices when a Jew becomes a Christian; and the convert must cease to be a Jew. But it does not notice when Jewish influence affects the political and social life of a Christian community, and the community itself does not notice that it has been in some respects converted to Judaism."

This explains why most Christians have little awareness of the question, and only when "famous" people convert to Judaism do they realize that this religion, like their own, is also a conversionary faith.

Yet be it remembered: Judaism does not seek converts. It seeks instead to convert the peoples of the world to the higher implications of their own monotheistic faiths. Religious Jews believe that this may happen not so much by making others into Jews as by making themselves into better people.

Why Jews Rarely Convert

All of this may help to explain why, despite the centuries-long endeavors of Christians and Muslims, Jews have rarely converted to these other religions.[16] I do not know how many millions of dollars or man-hours are still being expended by a variety of churches and sects in what can only be described as vain and futile attempts to convert Jews to their "one true religion." This too must be seen as still another Christian problem—so-called "Christian love" turned into Christian hostility, or even hate for Jews, as happens so often to rejected suitors. I have people like Martin Luther, in mind—and even lesser lights. Luther, the proverbial "founder of Protestanism," was initially very kind to Jews. He had his reasons. His view of the future foresaw that the Jewish people would convert to Christianity en masse and thus hasten the return of Jesus. Frustrated when they refused to convert in the early years of the Reformation, he turned on them, and by the end of his life wrote the vilest statements against Jews.[17] Many of Luther's antisemitic lines have been quoted by Protestants for over 400 years. They were even used by Julius Streicher as part of his defense at the Nuremberg trials.

It never seems to fail: when I ask Christian emissaries or missionaries why they continue to spend time and energy on us "non-convertible Jews," they unfailingly reply that theirs is a special mission of "Christian love"—they are doing what they do, because of a divine and biblical mandate whose call they must follow. Until the Jews convert to Jesus Christ, they fervently maintain, there can be no "second coming" of their Lord, and Jewish obstinancy in not seeing things their way is no less a scandal to them than it was to Christians in earlier days, during the time of his "first coming." "Salvation," they proclaim, often quoting but misunderstanding their own Scriptures, "is *of* the Jews": until Jews become Christians, they sincerely believe their Bible says, there can be no messianic peace in the world.

By now, many mainline churches seem to have learned that they can not depend on Jews to swell their ranks. Yet while they may have officially abandoned their Jewish evangelical departments, or their boards of missions to the Jews, many of these self-same Christian denominations still cherish the hope that somehow, some day, Jews will truly see the "Light" of their Lord, Jesus Christ. To those whose Christianity is deeply tied to the spirit of missionizing evangelism, the Jews are still the largest prize they openly or inwardly covet.

History, however, is not on their side. When there is decisive competition between two rival and contending missionary faiths, one will invariably hold sway over the other. When this takes place, the air is charged with a dramatic feeling of "either-or," as was the case in the first centuries of the Christian Era, when both Judaism and Christianity were vying for converts. Many of the early Christian Church Councils dealt with the problem of "Judaizing" practices within the Church, seeking to root these out because of their desire to make certain that prospective converts made no mistake about the *Christian* character of the Church. Obviously there was fear that in some ways a missionary Judaism might capture the heart, if not the body, of the Church.

A good case in point was the decision taken by the Church Council at Nicaea in 325 to separate the new religion from the old in the celebration of its most holy day, Easter. Until then, this day had been celebrated by Christian congregations throughout Asia at the same time as the Jewish Passover. The Nicaean Council decided, however, that henceforward Easter would be celebrated independently of the

Passover, by setting the day as the first Sunday after the full moon of the spring month. It would be a "movable feast" and no longer linked to the Jewish calendar. The text of that decision makes these tell-tale points:

> It would be unworthy for us to follow for this holy feast the custom of the Jews who soiled their hands with the most monstrous crimes and remained spiritually blind. Henceforth we wish to have nothing more in common with the people of the Jews, who are hostile to us, for our Saviour has shown us another way. . . . It would indeed be contrary to good sense to permit the Jews to boast that we are not able to celebrate Easter without their instructions [from their calendar].

Similarly, the rabbis of this period made every effort possible to steer clear of rituals which might seem overly similar to those current in Christianity. In the first centuries of the Christian Era, as the Jewish and Christian missions dramatically competed with each other, the traffic between the two communities was relatively heavy: Jews were converting to Christianity, Christians to Judaism, and pagans to one or the other.

But once Jews reworked their concept of the mission, and no longer actively engaged in proselytizing, the situation changed radically. If Jews had remained interested in winning Christians over to Judaism—as Christians are still interested in "saving" Jews—it is conceivable that in such a spirited contest many Jews might fall away from Judaism and accept Christianity. It is still difficult for many to understand why Jews do not accept Christianity in greater numbers, because they are unfamiliar with this new Jewish concept of universalism. Since Jews now believe that in all monotheistic faiths the one God is worshipped, if ethical behavior is the end-product, they do not see Christianity as a rival, and thus are not attracted to it by the magnetism which rivalry often creates. Christianity can survive, and at its side Judaism may grow and create . . . and Jews see in this situation not the curse but the blessing of God. For Jews, both in their practice of Judaism and in their world-view, do not equate unity with uniformity. Unity is based upon a recognition of the existence of vital differences among men who can nevertheless cooperate through acts of mutual understanding and helpfulness. Uniformity, on the other hand, stifles and retards the development of creative relationships because it desires to obliterate rather than to recognize differences.

Much of the hate in the world has, sadly, been the result of strong religious rivalries—all in the name of God. Here again is another reason why most Jews—excepting possibly those who are unwilling or unable to withstand the social pressures which are the lot of a member of a minority—have not found it necessary or seemly to accept Christianity.[18] Essentially, to do so would mean that they would be giving up their own brand of ethical universalism in exchange for a "Christian universalism" which requires uniformity as regards faith in its messiah.

Some have said that the Jews, who have given the world the concept of messiah, surely need not hold out stubbornly to the Christian world, claiming that the Messiah has not yet come. Instinctively, however, Jews have distrusted all would-be claimants to messiahship. As far as they are concerned, the "Messianic Age" which Christians claim arrived with the coming of Jesus has not brought peace to the people of Israel. Far from it: Jews have suffered in the past at the hands of devout Christians, men who excused their unethical behavior by blaming the Jews for not accepting Jesus. This kind of "religious" thinking surely could not succeed in drawing Jews closer to Christianity.

But even if Christian history had not been marred by the blind hate of religious zealots—even if Judaism had had as uneventful a relationship with Christianity, as, say, Buddhism—Jews would still find it difficult to accept the idea of Jesus as Messiah. There are at least three reasons for this:

While Jews contributed the idea of messiah to the treasury of world thought, and while Judaism still holds onto its original significance, Jews somehow have sensed that as an ideal it was inspiring, but in actuality, it has been quite unfulfilling. Many men besides Jesus have proclaimed themselves the Jewish messiah. At the moment that they also claimed supernatural powers and boasted of special kinship to divinity, however, they were rejected by their strongly monotheistic people and could no longer be contained within the community and the faith of Israel. Even those Jews who stray far from their religious heritage, and do not faithfully observe Jewish law, are instinctively on their guard against the possibility of personifying a God in the name of Messiah. Some Jews may adhere to the Law in less strict fashion than their forefathers, but as Jews they are monotheists in no less strict a construction.

Orthodox Jews, of course, believe in the coming of a Messiah, but only in the form of a man, not a God. They envision one who will serve as the "anointed one," the king of Israel, to lead his people as the "light of the nations." The Messiah, they believe, will not come until Israel is restored to its place as the messiah-people, a moral example to the world of the teachings of the Lord. *Until the Messiah comes, Jews must remain Jews.* Indeed, they contend that he will not come until all Jews become better Jews, until they scrupulously observe the Law, thus becoming worthy of their special role as the teachers of the nations.

Most Conservative and Reform Jews do not accept the idea of a personal messiah and surely cannot be expected to accept the Christian Messiah. These Jews speak of a "Messianic Age" yet to come. They would say that in essence, the Jewish messiah idea never fully centered upon the personality of the man (he was but a symbol) but rather would be experienced in the "Days of the Messiah." The special role of Jewish messianism, that which sets Judaism apart and makes its viewpoint distinctive, is the driving force of its ethical optimism. Most peoples have spoken of a Golden Age in the past tense; Jews alone believe in a Golden Age yet to be: not outside of history, but within it. Although these Conservative and Reform Jews do not personalize the messiah, perhaps because they fear that such envisioning might lead to idolatry, they are impelled religiously by the hope for the improvement of mankind and the ultimate achievement of the Good Society—the Kingdom of God on earth. This Kingdom of God they have equated with the Messianic Age, and peace on Earth is its chief hallmark.

As Jews see it, Christian messianism has tended to deflect the interest of its followers away from the ethical demands God makes upon the human community, and toward preoccupation with "salvation by faith" alone. "Salvation" is the reward bestowed upon the Christian faithful, but not in our own world; only in some mystical "other world." St. John refers to this Christian messianic world as a "kingship *not* of this world" (John 18:36). But Jews always understood, and understand still, that the messianic world is God's world and that God's world, exalted and idealized, can be found in *this* life. As a result, Judaism never became a world-weary religion, and could never despair of man's ethical possibilities; its messiah-idea is intimately linked to a belief in man's spiritual potential, not his spiritual failure. Even the Orthodox Jew who persists in personalizing the messiah idea still sees him only as "a righteous man ruling in the fear of God," his function being to help bring ethical perfection to the world. The progress of humanity, however, does not depend upon him, but upon humanity itself. In the long run, and in this world, God is going to be the winner, because man, whom He created, will learn to repent of his evil ways and do good works.

Christian preoccupation with sin is still another barrier to Jewish acceptance of Christianity. This insistence that man is a sinner, merely because he was born a man, seems to Jews a moral pessimism which is not in consonance with their way of thinking. Modern Christian teachers have made much of a "crisis theology." Many of those who are "returning to religion" have been attracted by this mysterious leap of faith which helps to overcome anxiety about man's frailty and finitude. But Jews, because of the background of their own world-views, sense that this "new" theology is not new at all; it has a familiar ring to it. It is but a modern restatement of what has been a perennial Christian obsession with man's death and earthly mortality. But how does one hurdle these obstacles, Christian theologians ask, if not through faith in Jesus? Christian faith eliminates the crisis by offering eternal bliss in the hereafter. Believe in Jesus and destroy death; believe in him not, and be consigned to eternal damnation.

This threat of doom and damnation has been hurled at Jews throughout all of the Christian era, ever since their synagogue was labeled by some as the "Synagogue of Satan." Yet in these very periods Jews experienced some of their greatest moments of spiritual creativity. The "Dark Ages" never reached them. Their rabbis, scholars, and philosophers continued to develop and heighten their intellectual, scientific, and religious traditions, while most of Europe remained ignorant and superstitious.

This ceaseless spiritual energy may not be unrelated to still another fundamental barrier to Jewish conversion. Jews do recognize "crisis" in their world-view, but not the crisis created by the forbidding face of death. The crisis which Jews understand is the crisis which results from an unfulfilled life. This is what motivates the Jew to seek ethical solutions rather than to leap away from life in the name of faith. Why, Jews ask, create additional anxieties by constantly confronting man with the burden of Original Sin and the mystery of the unfathomable world to come? In the words of Abba Hillel Silver, Jews prefer to focus their efforts upon men's "needless and profligate waste of their limited years, the unassayed tasks, the locked opportunities, the talents withering in disuse, and all the summoning but untrodden ways of mind and soul which give rise to men's spiritual malaise and the deep-rooted and undefined sorrows of their lives . . . Whatever is inherent, universal and inevitable in the race of man does not constitute a crisis."[19]

* * *

Jewish spiritual energy, as we have seen, did not cease with the advent of Christianity. To believe that it did is another clear example of the problem facing Christians, and helps to explain why they still offer us their faith—as if we Jews did not have a creative religious and cultural life of our own. Christian historians and theologians have contributed enormously to the myth of the pariah, the "deculturated" Jew, by the ways in which they and their precursors have read the past. Their studies and analyses have something in common: they invariably reconstruct the history and culture of the western world from the solitary angle of a "Christian vision." They see that world as essentially their preserve. Both their cast of principal characters and their descriptions of the interaction of peoples and ideas usually focus only on Christian areas of influence. They write of Throne and Altar as the key centers of power—and it is power which concerns these historians most. Because throughout the Middle Ages, up to and including modern times, Jews were not only excluded from the sources of power but were also thought to be a "defeated race," Christian historians have thoughtlessly neglected to take the Jewish factor into account. Often, in fact, they completely avoid and discount it.

It is time to rewrite the story of Western ideas, which blinded historians long-biased in favor of Christianity have been offering students of history. It is surely time, too, to address this Christian problem, in order to correct this myopic vision of Jewish life, its cultural creations, and its religious uniqueness.

NOTES

1. Quoted from John G. Gager, *The Origins of Anti-Semitism* (p. 193). See footnote 5 below for fuller reference.

2. Salo Baron, *A Social and Religious History of the Jews* (New York: Columbia University Press, 1937), Vol. I, pp. 229–30. See also his *History* (1952 edition), Vol. II, pp. 76–88. See also Michael Grant, "Paul the Discontented Jew," *Midstream*, Aug./Sept. 1976, pp. 32–40.

3. Baron, *supra.*, p. 232.

4. Martin Buber, *Two Types of Faith* (London: Routledge & Kegan Paul, 1951), p. 172. Buber regards this view as "rigid Paulinism."

5. Contemporary scholars—both Christian and Jewish—have debated the question: Was Paul a product of Rabbinic, or Pharisaic Judaism? Or was he more influenced by Hellenistic thought, which was more closely akin to paganism? A large and growing literature among Christian scholars in particular places Paul closer to Pharisaism, while it distances him from pagan sources within the Greek world. W. D. Davies, noted Pauline scholar, places Paul squarely inside the Jewish camp. He goes so far as to claim that "for the Apostle the Christian Faith was the flowering of Judaism . . . The Gospel for Paul was not the annulling of Judaism but its completion, and as such it took up into itself the essential genius of Judaism." See his *Paul and Rabbinic Judaism* (New York: Harper and Row, 1967), p. 323. I consider such an argument as groundless, and indeed, as a form of theological sleight-of-hand. Faithful,

self-respecting Jews fully understand that the "completion" of Judaism within Christianity, in itself constitutes its "annulment." See also Davies' *Christian Origins and Judaism* (Philadelphia: The Westminster Press, 1962).

More recently, a debate has also been raging among Christian scholars concerning Paul's role in promoting anti-Judaism. It is, however, based more on "strained exegesis" than on the explicit phenomena of history—the actual consequences of Pauline teaching in the hands of Church leaders. John G. Gager, in an altogether engaging way, has stressed the need to "reinvent Paul," (his own phrase) since he refuses to accept the "traditional interpretation of Paul, long established and almost universally held by historians, theologians, and exegetes of Pauline letters" which held that "Israel, Judaism and the Torah are no longer valid, if indeed they ever were so, for forgiveness of sins, redemption, salvation, or full membership in the people of God." (John G. Gager, *The Origins of Anti-Semitism: Attitudes Toward Judaism in Pagan and Christian Antiquity* [New York: Oxford University Press, 1983], p. 197.)

Despite Gager's valiant and appealing efforts "to save Paul from the charge of anti-Judaism" (relying on earlier efforts in this direction of people like Markus Barth, Krister Stendhal, E. P. Sanders, and Lloyd Gaston) the fact remains that even if Gager is right, he is wrong. It is one thing for a modern ecumenist, seeking rapprochement between Christians and Jews, to "reinvent" the historical Paul, in order to help Christians change their attitudes toward Jews. It is quite another to obliterate from history the manner in which traditional Church leaders used what they believed Paul had (negatively) taught about Jews and Judaism, and then proceeded to translate into official Church policy. We can try to change current prejudicial attitudes—and we, of course, should. But we cannot change the historical and *phenomenological* dynamics of Paul—to "reinvent" him by means of novel *exegetical* twists and turns.

Thus, even Christian theologians like Paul Van Buren, who regard Paul himself as a "Pharisee" and friend of Jews, are sometimes prepared to admit that he had laid the groundwork for future antisemitism. "What can scarcely be denied," Van Buren writes, "is that an anti-Judaic conclusion was the consistent result of the way in which the Gospels, and also Paul, were read and interpreted by Christians from the second to the twentieth centuries. They are still read by many in this manner. This reading is the foundation for the distinctive theological anti-Judaism of the Christian tradition. It is the theological root of antisemitism." See Van Buren's "The Theological Roots of Antisemitism: A Christian View," in Alex Grobman and Daniel Landes, eds. *Genocide: Critical Issues of the Holocaust* (Chappaqua, N.Y.: Rossel Books, 1983), p. 88.

It strikes me, moreover, that some of these scholars miss the more important point—one that is being made here—namely that irrespective of either the sources of his theology or of a new exegesis of his teachings, it is the *politics* of Paul, the pragmatic ways in which he redirected the idea of the Jewish mission, that is crucial. In this process, as I have noted, he virtually behaves as an antisemite: he uses Jewish ideas while denying the Jewish nation any significant right to continue its covenantal group existence. *By insisting that they have lost those rights to the church—the "new Israel"—Paul (or at least those who acted in his name) laid the foundation for Christian antisemitism, as well as its anti-Judaism.*

Discussing Paul from the Jewish side, in 1976, Michael Grant wrote: "Lately, Jews have written brilliant books about Paul; Samuel Sandmel [*The Genius of Paul,* 1970], Richard Rubenstein [*My Brother Paul,* 1973] and many others. Such writers achieve a degree of sympathy with their subject that earlier Jewish students had lacked, since they tended to regard Paul with acute distaste, as the arch-apostate." Grant then goes on to make the point with which I am in full agreement: "And I am not sure that, from a Jewish point of view, the old view is wrong. Paul *was* the arch-apostate." Further, Grant adds an interesting conjecture: "Historical 'might-have-beens' are a somewhat sterile exercise. But I would suggest that, had it not been for Paul, Judaism might eventually have conquered the Roman empire instead of Christianity, replacing it as the faith destined to become numerically predominant in the ancient world, and then in the modern world as well." See Michael Grant, "Paul the Discontented Jew," *Midstream,* Aug./Sept. 1976, pp. 39–40.

6. George F. Moore, *Judaism in the First Centuries of the Christian Era* (Cambridge: Harvard University Press, 1927), p. 323 (Vol. I).

7. *Ibid.,* pp. 323–25.

8. Tos.: *Kiddushin* 5:1.

9. See Itzhak Ben Zvi, *The Exiled and the Redeemed* (Philadelphia: Jewish Publication Society of America, 1957), pp. 285; 298.

Ben Zvi also maintains that before Ethiopia "was Christianized, the Jewish element in the population was influential and, indeed, powerful, under the influence of the kings of the Himyar dynasty who had ruled over that country, too, in the third century C.E. There were ups and downs in the fortunes of Ethiopian Jewry. Three religions contended for exclusive dominance: Judaism, Christianity and Islam" (p. 286). Moreover, "under the reign of the Christian Ethiopian ruler Zera 'a-Jacob (1438–1468), several princes of the provinces of Salamat and Sameean left Christianity and embraced the Jewish faith" (p. 296). In the western part of the Sahara Desert, at Wadi Dera'a, it is believed that Jews "enjoyed an autonomous existence since very ancient times, perhaps as early as the days of the Roman, Byzantine and Vandal invasions, and even resisted the forces of the Fatimid Idrees" (p. 298).

10. Raphael Patai and Jennifer P. Wing, *The Myth of the Jewish Race* (New York: Charles Scribner's Sons, 1975) p. 90.

11. According to one expert, Dr. Egon Mayer, about 100,000 American Jews marry each year, and a third of them marry non-Jews. He estimates the number of conversions to Judaism at more than 10,000 annually, involving mostly middle- and upper-class people. *New York Times,* November 10, 1985, p. 15.

12. This contemporary tendency is in stark contrast to the wave of "pru-

dential baptisms" or "expediential conversions" which had swept across German and other Western emancipated Jewries in nineteenth century Europe. Perhaps as many as 200,000 Jews seemed to agree with Heinrich Heine that the baptismal certificate was not only "the admission ticket to European society," but also a necessity for those Jews who wished to attain coveted social, economic, or political positions. See Raphael Patai, *The Jewish Mind* (New York: Charles Scribner's Sons, 1977), pp. 279–282.

13. Maimonides, *Mishneh Torah*, "Hilkot Melakim," Ch. 11.

14. Maimonides, *Hilkot Avodah Zarah*, 2:4. Earlier, in the Talmud itself, we have similar references. Rabbi Johanan stated that "anyone who repudiates idolatry is called a Jew." See *Megillah*, 13a.

15. A cardinal teaching of the early rabbis was that human diversity was, in fact, divinely ordained, and had been built into God's creation. Thus, as early as the *Mishnah (Sanhedrin* 4:5), we find this dictum: ". . . Only a single man [Adam] was created for the sake of peace among mankind, that none should say to his fellow, 'My father was greater than your father . . .' Moreover, only a single man was created to proclaim the greatness of God, for man stamps many coins with one die, and they are all like to one another; but God has stamped every man with the die of the first man, yet not one of them is like his fellow. Therefore every one must say, 'For my sake was the world created.' "

16. This was uniformly true except for approximately one short century (c. 1830–1930) in western Europe, where thousands of newly-emancipated Jews "voluntarily" converted to Christianity—*pro forma*—in the hope of gaining thereby, social and economic position within Gentile society. See *supra.,* footnote 12.

17. For a concise description of Luther's changing positions on the Jews see Franklin Sherman, "Luther and the Jews," in *Genocide: Critical Issue of the Holocaust* (Chappaqua: Rossel Books, 1983), pp. 91–94.

18. See above footnotes 12 and 16.

19. Abba H. Silver, *Where Judaism Differed* (New York: Macmillan, 1956), p. 284.

PART TWO

Restoring Jews to the Mainstream of History

"For it is the supreme irony of Jewish history that the new ground captured for Judaism by Alexander Janneus (102–76 B.C.) brought to birth, within a hundred years, a Galilean Jewish prophet whose message was the consummation of all previous Jewish experience, and that this inspired Jewish scion of forcibly converted Galilean Gentiles [sic!] was then rejected by the Judean leaders of Jewry of his own age. *Thereby Judaism not only stultified its past but forfeited its future.*"[1] (Italics added.)

Arnold J. Toynbee

". . . The use of federal principles to organize Jewish communal life [is] a system as old as the Jewish people itself, having its origins in the federation of the twelve tribes under Moses. The very term 'federal' is derived from the Latin *foedus*, which means covenant, and is an expression of the biblical idea of *brit* [covenant], which it defines as the basis of political and social relationships among men as well as between man and God.

99

". . . In essence, a covenant creates a partnership based upon a firm legally defined relationship delineating the power and integrity of all the partners but which, at the same time, requires them to go beyond the legal definition to fully realize the relationship. In other words, the covenant relationship is to social and political life what Buber's I-Thou relationship is to personal life"[2]

Daniel J. Elazar

"As a permanent minority for some two thousand years, Jews were forced to seek the kinds of openings that were available to newcomers. As a rule, wherever they settled they found the established positions occupied by members of the majority. Hence they were forced to look for new opportunities. When they found and used such opportunities, they were working for both their own benefit and that of society as a whole. I have long believed that *much of Jewish history ought to be rewritten in terms of the pioneering services which the Jews were forced to render by the particular circumstances of their history.*"[3] (Italics added.)

Salo W. Baron

NOTES

1. Arnold J. Toynbee, *A Study of History,* Abridgement of Volumes I–VI, by D. C. Somervell (New York: Oxford University Press, 1947), p. 485.

2. Daniel J. Elazar, ed., *Kinship and Consent* (Washington, D.C.: University Press of America, 1983), pp. 21ff; see also his *Community and Polity: The Organizational Dynamics of American Jewry* (Philadelphia: Jewish Publication Society, 1976), pp. 86–7.

3. Salo W. Baron, *From a Historian's Notebook* (New York: American Jewish Committee, 1962), p. 34. A reprint of Professor Baron's testimony before the Jerusalem Court in the trial of Adolf Eichmann. (See also *American Jewish Year Book*, Volume 63, 1962.)

CHAPTER VI

Jewish Self-Government in Exile: The Unbroken Covenant

WITHOUT GOD'S COVENANT THERE WOULD BE NO JEWISH NATION: IT shaped their very beginning, and they never abandoned it. The continued existence of the Jewish people as a unique community— from the destruction of the Temple in the first century, to the Crusades of the eleventh century, and the Holocaust of the twentieth—should be ample proof that the covenant still abides. But from the very first, Christians have had a problem with Israel's covenant. With the coming of Jesus, they have stoutly maintained, the "old" covenant was annulled, and a "new" covenant" established with the Church alone.

The profound irony of Arnold Toynbee, and of lesser Christian historians and preachers of the same mold, is that instead of writing history, they re-write it—to conform to this pre-conceived Pauline christology. Small wonder, then, that Toynbee and company miss the most obvious irony of all: that Jews continued to expand and deepen their covenant-community long after Christians had dismissed them from history. It is a puzzlement: that self-same "old covenant" which Christians after Paul regarded as defunct was responsible for saving Jews from the oblivion those others had prepared for them. But the paradox does not end there. By keeping alive their own covenant, Jews also helped to set the pattern for the non-hierarchical church

101

which some Christians sought to establish both in the Old World and the New.

No serious student of history can avoid the living connection between the so-called "old covenant" of the Jews and the shaping of American history. W. E. H. Lecky reminded us that "in the great majority of instances the early Protestant defenders of civil liberty derived their principles chiefly from the Old Testament."[1] With strong support from New England pulpits, the common man in Yankee towns consistently opposed the absolute powers of both kings and bishops, quoting the admonitions of Moses and of Samuel against the corrupting powers of authority. The spirit of the *Mayflower Compact*, and other American documents such as the Salem pact and the Connecticut code of 1655, breathe the language and sentiment of biblical, covenantal thought. That the Pilgrim fathers labeled many of their political and social documents "pacts" or "compacts" is no accident. They did so because they were deeply and fundamentally committed to the biblical concept of a covenanted community— where power is shared only by the mutual consent of the contracting parties. The language of Governor Winthrop's sermon preached aboard the ship *Arabella*, while still in midocean en route to the New World, makes this abundantly clear:

> . . . Thus stands the cause between God and us; we are entered into Covenant with him for this work; we have taken out a Commission; the Lord hath given us leave to draw our own articles; we have professed to enterprise these actions upon these and these ends; we have hereupon besought him of favor and blessing. Now if the Lord shall please to hear us, and bring us in peace to the place we desire then hath he ratified this Covenant and sealed our Commission, and will expect a strict performance of the Articles contained in it . . .[2]

The truth remains, however: most often, even when Christians invoked the covenantal language of the Hebrew Bible, no matter what it was they were saying, they usually were not thinking of the continuing "Jewish covenant," but rather of the older biblical one, which they believed they themselves had inherited. For them, a living, pulsating, and creative Jewish community could only be a thing of the biblical past. They had little idea—or at best only a fuzzy one—that the Jewish people was still thriving and still seeking to fulfill its mandate: to implement God's word in the social institutions it had built as the vehicle for their covenant-community. That old "Christian problem" masked their vision.

The standard Christian view of the exile imposed on the Jews by the

Romans is the product of Pauline theology. It consists of several hinged and complementary parts. Your dispersion throughout the world, Christians have been telling Jews, is a punishment to fit the crime: a sign of your defeat and of our ultimate victory. Had you accepted the true Messiah, you could have kept the covenant, and won the world. Now that you have refused to live up to your agreement with God, He rightly visits upon you eternal wanderings. You broke God's covenant, and for your many sins, He properly punishes you with exile—a visible sign that He will continue to annul his covenant with you until you return to Him—through our Lord Jesus Christ.

Were they right? It is time to test their thesis.

Illiteracy Begets Hostility

The great Christian potentate Charlemagne was unable to write his own name. In 799, at coronation ceremonies marking his ascendancy as Emperor, he could only make the two lines that formed the "u" of his Christian name, Carolus. The rest was filled in by the priestly scribe who attended the cathedral services.

What, then, shall we say of the larger population—those who made up the rank-and-file of Christendom? While Jews were then basking in the light of their "Golden Age" of literature and culture, Christians were in darkness.

It is no surprise that the leaders of the Church in the days of its dark ages could manipulate its unsuspecting believers into accepting any and all myths about the Jews. Illiteracy abounded throughout Christendom, and superstitions of all kinds—especially those which blamed Jews for many of the social evils of the times—could gain ready acceptance. The gulf between the rulers and the ruled was also of no small significance: the abject poverty and the miserable conditions imposed upon most of the population by greedy feudal lords and venal, princely bishops, played their part in grinding down the spirit of a de-classed population.

The myths creating the image of the "demonic Jew," which helped to divert medieval Christians from their poverty and affliction, left no room whatever for any awareness of the real Jewish world. As one writer put it: "The mythical Jew, outlined by early Christian theology and ultimately puffed out to impossible proportions, supplanted the real Jew in the medieval mind, until the real Jew to all intents and purposes ceased to exist. The only Jew whom the medieval Christian recognized was a figment of the imagination."[3]

What myths about Jews had Christian theology, with its emphasis on "Jewish perfidy," and its equation of the synagogue with the "synagogue of Satan," puffed out? And in the mind's eye of the mass of benighted and impoverished medieval Christians—who, indeed, were the Jews? What was their "real" face like—behind the mask of their mysterious and unaccountable presence—to a sea of faithful Christians? By way of résumé, here is a concise, composite picture, which helps make palpably real the abstracted contempt for Jews which Christian theologians had been cultivating for centuries:

> They [the Jews] are creatures of the devil, with whom they conclude secret pacts and whom they worship with obscene rites; they offer sacrifices to demons; they conduct secret meetings where they plot foul deeds against Christian society and practice a blasphemous ceremonial; they mock and despise the Christian faith and profane its sacred objects; they stink; their eyes are permanently fixed earthward; they often wear a goat's beard, and at their conventicles disguise themselves with goats' head masks; their heads are adorned with horns, and their wives trail tails behind them; they suffer from secret ailments and deformities; they are cruel and rapacious; they buy or kidnap children and slaughter them to Satan; they consume human flesh and blood; they believe that the sacrifice of an innocent life will prolong their own lives.[4]

How, indeed, could Christians with such views know or understand that at that very hour the Jewish covenant-community was building an advanced society, far beyond the high walls of a spiritually impoverished Christendom? Little wonder, then, that many of their heirs and successors remain ignorant to this day of the ways in which that Jewish community, even in its dreary exile, had already laid the foundation for the contemporary welfare state. Theirs was not a private covenant contracted for the benefit or personal fulfillment of the individual. The community, and the example it could set for all the nations, was ever paramount.

Responsibility and Commitment

Anyone who reads the Hebrew Bible without bias will recognize that the Jewish people was called upon to fulfil a special vocation as a "model community." What was permitted other nations was prohibited them. (Even the purely ritual laws, Jewish teachers explained, were designed to set Israel apart. To "set apart" is the primary meaning of "holiness"—only a people "set apart" can see itself as having a "holy purpose".) The Canaanites might offer their children as sacrifices to their God, Moloch, but for all their intermittent backsliding, the Israelites under the watchful eyes of their prophets were urged to serve as a "light unto the nations." That surely would not win popularity contests with Canaanites, by any other name called!

In the backlight and hindsight of history it is not difficult to see how a people set apart would run afoul of all sorts of powerful authorities, not excluding, of course, the virtually omnipotent Church. A "holy people" is usually reviled by others—damned for being what they say they are; damned, as well, for falling short of their aspirations. In the real world of passion and violence to be a "light unto the nations" can be a painful ambition. This calling may make you a crucified people, which, ironically, is precisely what Jews did become at the hands of those who should have known better: the very people who were protesting a different and distant crucifixion.

Nor did it help matters that in the first three centuries of their dispersion Jewish teachers were interpreting exile as a spiritual opportunity, and not as the religious disaster which Christians regarded it. In the view of the rabbis the increase in the number of converts to Judaism gave heightened meaning to their own dispersion. "The Lord did not exile Israel among the nations save in order that proselytes might join them," is the way some Talmudic scholars viewed the exile.[5]

When, however, the full might of the Roman Empire was added to the power of the Church—after Constantine's acceptance of Christianity—it became impossible to compete with the force of the Christian mission. Jews began to look to themselves and the powers they themselves possessed as a covenant-community to buttress their own self-esteem and to give new meaning to their dispersion. Without despair, they turned their attention to building their own "just society," within their own communal life. This strengthened their resolve to serve as God's witnesses, without the trappings of state power, or of church establishment, or of a land of their own. In time, their own "welfare-state-within-a-state" would emerge.

It is surely a matter of some importance to uncover the continuing source of Jewish strength which enabled the Jewish community to retain its own spiritual integrity in this reduced situation. How could they survive as a religious minority in the face of the powerful and successful attempts by medieval Christian clergy to stifle them? When these clerics were not busy exploiting Jews they were advising feudal chiefs and monarchs to expel them from their jurisdictions. Historians are largely silent on this subject, principally because they are usually wholly ignorant of the history of Judaism after Christianity. They are generally unskilled in either medieval Hebrew or Aramaic, the languages in which most of the primary sources are written. They would hardly know how to fathom a page of the Talmud, or to read in the original the vast literature relating to the religious, cultural, or legal issues which dominated Jewish community life in those years.

Occasionally, one does find Christian scholars who have specialized in post-biblical Jewish studies. Although only a tiny number, they have understood what virtually all their colleagues either miss or overlook: that Jewish life in the Middle Ages remained a *continuum*—it was an outgrowth of its own unbroken historical covenant, and still rooted in the social idealism of the Hebrew Bible and in the more recent Talmudic expression of its teachings. Far from seeing exile as a final judgment of doom, Jews simply applied their Torah-law wherever they resided, and though the Christian world still regarded them as a "race rejected by God," they themselves were not about to relinquish their own sure hold on their own covenant. George Foot Moore explained the basic reasons for this:

> In no sphere is the influence of the highest conceptions of Judaism more manifestly determinative than in that to which we give the general name of justice, including under it, *first*, fair dealing between man and man, the distributive justice which gives to each his due; *second*, public justice, the function of the community in defining and enforcing the duties and rights of individuals and classes; and, *third*, rectitude, or integrity of personal character. In all parts of the Bible justice in the broad sense is the fundamental virtue on which human society is based. It is no less fundamental to the idea of God, and in the definition of what God requires of men.[6]

Their responsibility for and commitment to public or social justice was rooted in a carefully honed system of personal ethics. There was no way to build their humane society without first ensuring that its private constituents—each and every one of its members—would also be held responsible for his own acts. So it was that the covenant-community first turned its attention to the sphere of interpersonal relations—the ways in which individuals dealt with one another—before setting out to build the community. It is worth noting some of the key elements of this code of personal, ethical practice which characterized the inner life of the Jewish community.

The Sacred Center: The Family

It was the family which served as the Jewish sacred center, where interpersonal relationships of all sorts were learned and practiced. It was the essential carrier of the tradition—the wider community in microcosm. This helps explain why celibacy was extremely uncommon, and in fact, disapproved of by the rabbis. They taught that a man should marry at eighteen, and that if he passed his twentieth birthday without being married, he was in possible transgression of the divine law. Students of the Torah, however, were permitted to delay their marriage for a few years longer, so that they could complete their studies before taking on the obligation of supporting a wife and children.

Husbands were required by marriage contracts to work for their wives, and to provide food, clothing, and shelter, in addition to satisfying their physical and spiritual needs. Fathers were obligated to support their children, and to teach their sons the Law and commandments. Hand in hand with this requirement went the injunction that fathers had also to teach their sons a trade. Rabban Gamaliel taught: "Study combined with a secular occupation is a fine thing, for the double labor makes sin to be forgotten. Study of the Torah which is not also accompanied by work, will in the end come to naught and bring sin in its train."[7] In like vein, Rabbi Judah, son of Ilai, said: "A man who does not teach his son a trade, teaches him robbery."[8]

Among the most important injunctions was the commandment which focussed on filial piety: "Honor your father and your mother, that your days may be long in the land which the Lord your God gives you" (Exodus 20:12). The rabbis taught that "great is the honoring of father and mother, for God makes more of it than of honoring Himself." Indeed, "when a man honors his father and his mother, God says, I impute it to you as if I were dwelling among them and they had honored me."[9] Traditional law also required that a son not sit in the place where his father usually sat, nor talk in a place where he was accustomed to talk, nor contradict him. And it was expected that children would keep sacred their parents' memory—honoring them in death as in life. Moreover, in a community where learning was regarded as the central, pious pursuit, and the study of the Torah-law regarded as an act of worship, it was natural that the honor due one's parents would also be accorded one's teachers. Careful codes of etiquette governing the relations between pupils and their masters were set down and punctiliously followed.

The family "altar" was its home, and virtually all of the prescribed religious ceremonies were performed there—the synagogue never became its surrogate. The family home was the first and foremost "holy place" in a community which comprised many sacred places—the school, the synagogue, and the court of justice, to name but a few. It would not be easy to destroy the will-to-live as Jews in a community where parents and teachers were revered, and the home-life of its members was regulated by sacred laws and observances. It would, indeed, be possible to burn or loot synagogues, as did the Christian Crusaders, in the vain hope that Jewish life would be undone thereby. But the vital center of Judaism in all of the exiled communities was not so much the synagogue as the home. It was the sacred customs and manners of the home—the relationships between the generations of elders and disciples—which neither fire, nor flame, nor deep-seated hatred could fully uproot or totally destroy.

Labor and Commerce

The network of moral obligations and the sense of mutual interdependence provided by the Jewish family were meant to be extended beyond the family, to reach out to the marketplace as well. Thus, various regulations carefully defined relationships with laborers and hired hands. The biblical law had originally laid down the basic obligation: "You shall not defraud your neighbor and you shall not rob. The wages of a hired servant shall not remain with you over night until morning" (Lev. 19:13). The rabbis, however, extended the provisions of this law to include aliens and strangers, as well as the members of the settled community.

They were especially concerned with the human needs of the wage earner and enacted into law additional protective legislation. An employer, for example, may not insist on a longer day's work than is customary in each locality, even though he might be willing to pay higher wages than usual. If a person was hired by the day to do one kind of work and completed the job before night fall, he could not be coerced into doing still another job, unless it was lighter than that for which he was originally hired. Moreover, wherever it was the custom for the local employer to furnish food, this, too, was understood to be covered by his work agreement. At the heart of these new rabbinic laws governing the internal life of the Jewish community, there was a profoundly sensitive regard for the honor and the feelings of others— especially for the weaker and less advantaged members of the society.

Manual labor was so highly regarded that virtually all of the eminent rabbis supported themselves and their families by some trade or craft. This helps explain why fathers were enjoined to teach their sons a trade: not only because it secured for them a livelihood, but because of the moral influence and dignity of labor itself. "Flay a carcass of a dead beast in the market and earn a wage," rabbinical law decreed, "and say not, I am a great man; it is beneath my dignity!"[10]

Laws governing unlawful gain in commercial transactions, or "wronging with words" in business dealings, were also to become part of the expanding covenantal experience of the Jewish community in exile. Business transactions came to be regarded as part of the moral and religious obligations of Jews, and not merely as impersonal, mundane activities without effect upon human character and integrity. Rabbi Judah, son of Ilai, ruled that a shopkeeper should not give children sweets (parched grain and nuts) to attract them to buy items at his shop when they were sent on errands. He also believed that a merchant should not cut prices to draw customers away from other dealers. (He was opposed on this matter, however, by a majority of the court, who held that a merchant who sells under the market price should be admired gratefully, because the whole community benefits from the price reduction which his competitors would also have to make!)[11]

Similarly, the adulteration of food for sale was sharply denounced in community law. If, for example, water had accidentally gotten into a jar of wine, the owner could not sell the wine at retail without first apprising the buyer of the dilution. He could not sell it to a fellow merchant at all, even with such notice, it being assumed that the latter would buy the wine at a reduced price only with a fraudulent purpose in mind. On no account was it permissible to "doctor" articles for sale to make them look better than they were. All of these practices were condemned as methods of achieving unlawful gain. Sharp business practices such as these were not only illegal but were also seen as an affront to God's Covenant.

"Wronging with words," whether in business transactions or other human relationships, was regarded as a form of stealth—"stealing a man's mind." Flattery and blandishment, the customary ways of accomplishing these deceitful ends, were strongly condemned. Neither may one say: "How much will you sell me this for?" when he has no intention of buying, for by arousing false expectations he is morally considered to be engaged in a form of cheating. Similarly, to a person who has already repented, one may not say: "I remember your former deeds." Nor may one tell a new proselyte: "We remember the deeds of your ancestors." Rabbi Jose summed up the general rabbinic attitude as well as the community ideal when he declared: "Let your neighbor's property [and person] be as dear to you as your own; and set yourself diligently to learn the Torah-law [to enhance your ethical awareness]; and let all that you do be for God's sake."

These admonitions were, in fact, made the basis for personal behavior inside the Jewish community. Nowhere, however, do we observe their application as much as in the laws governing the obligation of each Jew to assist and support the poor and the needy. Communal institutions were established to mandate this concern as a public responsibility. Yet as in the case of the relations within one's own family, so it was in connection with the requirement to help one's neighbor in need: the laws were not only incumbent upon the community, but had to be seen as a personal responsibility. The Jewish "welfare state" did not come into being as a result of the default of the individual; it was, rather, an extension of the individual—personal, moral concern "writ large."

NOTES

1. W. E. H. Lecky, *History of the Rise and Influence of the Spirit of Rationalism in Europe* (London: Longmans, Green, 1913), II, p. 172.

2. Quoted in Alan Simpson, *Puritanism in Old and New England* (Chicago: University of Chicago Press, 1955), p. 23.

3. Joshua Trachtenberg, *The Devil and the Jews* (New York: Meridian Books, 1961), p. 216.

4. *Ibid.*, p. 215.

5. See Babylonian Talmud: *Pesahim* 87b.

6. George F. Moore, *Judaism in the First Centuries of the Christian Era*, Vol. II (Cambridge: Harvard University Press, 1927), p. 180.

7. Mishnah: *Abot* 2:2.
8. Tos: *Kiddushin* 1:11.
9. See Babylonian Talmud: *Kiddushin* 30b.
10. Babylonian Talmud: *Baba Batra* 110a.
11. Mishnah: *Baba Metziah* 4:12.

CHAPTER VII

The Just Society: Origins of the Welfare State

As PART OF HIS LARGE LEGAL CODE WHICH BECAME THE BASIC MEDIEVAL compendium of Jewish law, Maimonides included three full chapters dealing with the exact manner in which Jews were to govern themselves in matters dealing with aid to the poor and the succoring of the disadvantaged. It was altogether fitting and proper for him to deal with such matters in a legal code, since in Jewish law the giving of aid to the less fortunate is not regarded as "charity" in the Christian sense, a voluntary act of gracious kindness. It is, rather, an act of social justice required by religious law, and not merely dependent on the "good-heartedness" of the donor. It is because of its basic "this-worldliness"—the accent being placed on the covenantal demand to build the good and just society here and now—that the Jewish community long ago established the framework for what we today call the modern welfare state.

Indeed, what Maimonides was codifying in twelfth century Spain became not only the practice of medieval Jewish communities the world over, but may still be seen as the driving force which animates the contemporary Jewish community. It is a never-ending source of amazement to me to observe, for example, the network of social, philanthropic and educational institutions created by a voluntary North American Jewish community. In addition to assisting in the relocation and resettlement of several million Jewish refugees—principally in Israel, but in other places, as well—the "welfare community" of Jews in the United States, Canada, and elsewhere in the

113

free world not only pays taxes to the national treasuries of the countries of their own citizenship, but freely, voluntarily, and unceasingly, engages in a system of self-taxation to support those pressing Jewish needs. If one were to add up all the funds contributed directly by the six million Jews of North America to all Jewish charities—at home, abroad, and for the Israeli poor—the sum has been reliably estimated as exceeding an amount of over two billion dollars annually. Such gifts could not possibly have been pledged and collected if the donors had only thought in terms of personal philanthropy—of doing "good deeds." They were the prior result of a communal Jewish consciousness that had been sharply honed through time, one based on a profoundly religious idea: the shared Covenant and the interdependence of fate which Jews possess in common.

We can understand how this consciousness was built into the Jewish community process even in medieval times, by noting with care the key portions of Maimonides' "Code of Benevolence," as his regulations came to be known. A selection follows:[1]

7:1: "It is a positive command that one give to the poor as much as is fitting for each recipient, assuming that the giver can afford it."

7:2: "Whoso, beholding a poor person in search of help, hides his eyes and fails to grant alms, violates Scripture" [Deut. 15:7].

7:3: "You are commanded to assist a poor person according to his needs. If he lacks clothing, he should be given clothes. If he is in want of household furnishings, such should be purchased for him. If he be without a wife, provision should be made for his marriage. A woman who is unmarried should be provided with the means of becoming united with a husband."

7:4: "For the orphan who comes asking assistance to marry, a house should be rented and a bed and all needed furnishings provided. Thereupon, and only thereupon, should the marriage be brought to pass."

7:6: "If an unknown person implores: 'I hunger, give me food,' investigation is omitted and food granted immediately. If being unclad, that suppliant says: 'Clothe me,' then investigation takes place to rule out imposture. If, however, the applicant is someone who is known, clothes are granted. They are granted promptly, without investigation, and in keeping with the applicant's social rank."

7:7: "The non-Jewish poor are succored and clothed together with the Jewish poor, in the interests of good will. Toward the door-to-door mendicant, one is obligated not to the extent of any considerable gift but only to the extent of a trivial gift. It is forbidden to turn away a suppliant poor person empty handed, though one grant no more than a single berry."

7:9: "Upon a poor person who declines to accept aid, ruses are employed: aid is extended in the guise of a present or loan. But if a wealthy person starves himself because he is too stingy to spend some of his money on food and drink, he is simply ignored."

7:10: "One who refuses to contribute to charity or who contributes less than is fitting becomes subject to legal compulsion. He is penalized with stripes, such as are inflicted for recalcitrance, until he pays the amount levied. In his presence, distraint is laid upon his possessions and whatever is proper for him to give is taken from him."

7:13: "A poor relative takes precedence over all other poor. The poor of one's household take precedence over the poor of one's city and the poor of one's city over the poor of any other city."

8:10: "The ransoming of captives takes precedence over the succoring and the clothing of the poor. None among the sacred acts is more noble than that of ransoming captives."

8:11: "If townsfolk have collected sums for the rearing of a synagogue and thereupon occasion arises for some momentous act of charity, the funds collected shall be expended for that charity . . . Even though the stones have already been chiseled and the beams already shaped for the edifice, these may be sold for the ransoming of captives. They may not be sold with any other intent."

8:15: "A woman takes precedence over a man in the matter of assistance with food and clothing, and in the matter of ransoming from captivity because a man can go begging, which a woman, with her great sensitiveness, can not do."

10:2: "Never has a person become impoverished by practicing benevolence, and never has there resulted from benevolence any evil or harm . . . All Israel and those attached to them are like brothers."

Perhaps the best-known and most frequently quoted of these injunctions of Maimonides are those which he conveniently placed under the general rubric of "Eight Degrees of Benevolence." In effect, they serve as a summary of his code, reminding his fellow Jews all over the world that to do away with the need for charity is, in fact, the highest form of charity. Helping to rehabilitate and positively restructure the lives of those who have been afflicted is at the heart of the Jewish welfare community. This constitutes justice-in-action.

The Eight Degrees of Benevolence of Maimonides

"There are eight degrees of benevolence, one above the other:

• "The highest degree, exceeded by none, is that of the person who assists a poor Israelite by providing him with a gift or a loan or by accepting him into a business partnership or by helping him find employment. In a word, by putting him where he can dispense with other people's aid.

• "A step below this stands the one who gives alms to the needy in such a manner that the giver knows not to whom he gives and the recipient knows not from whom it is that he takes. This exemplifies performing the meritorious act for its own sake.

• "One step lower is that in which the giver knows to whom he gives but the poor person knows not from whom he receives. [Examples were the great sages who would throw coins covertly into poor people's doorways.]

• "A step lower is that in which the poor person knows from whom he is taking but the giver does not know to whom he is giving. [Examples were the great sages who would tie their coins in their scarves which they would fling to hang behind them, so that the poor might help themselves without suffering shame.]

• "The next degree lower is that of him who, with his own hand, bestows a gift before the poor person.

• "The next degree lower is that of him who gives only after the poor person asks.

• "The next degree lower is that of him who gives less than is fitting but gives with gracious mien.

• "The next degree lower is that of him who gives morosely."

The Ransoming of Captives

How can we explain why Maimonides—and all the other great medieval Jewish teachers—mandated the ransoming of captives as *the* imperious charitable need? How shall one understand why many Jews, far removed from other Jewish communities, could be made to respond with such urgency—even to the extent of giving up the building of their own institutional community life? Why was the "ransoming of captives" put at the top of the list of Jewish moral duties?

True, the Talmud taught Jews that they shared an interdependence of fate and had laid down the rule that "all Israelites are responsible for each other." Yet generalizations such as these are often relegated to the limbo of unpracticed ideals. Christianity also preached doctrines of "brotherly love" and "Christian charity," yet the unbroken history of medieval wars throughout Christendom is a harsh reminder of the refusal of its monarchs and rulers to take seriously either "brotherhood" or "peace." Power feeds upon power: the Church itself had often blessed the implements and symbols of power—the armadas and armies of mighty Christian warriors, some of whom were even canonized as saints years after their demise.

The powerlessness of the Jews throughout history has been, of course, the curse that led to their exploitation, and then their expulsion from many Christian lands. It produced their permanent and fragile minority status throughout the world. Ironically, however, powerlessness and its concomitant persecution also contributed a positive element to Jewish community life. It sensitized group awareness and made painfully clear a continuing need to federate in order to defend and protect one another. Nor was there any escape from this urgent sense of mutuality: somewhere in the world, at any given time, some Jews needed other Jews. There seemed always to be Jews in need of actual physical rescue. It was this condition which would give moral, if not political significance to Jewish self-government. A deeply religious commitment drove Jews to seek the welfare of their beleaguered comrades—even those far away. It was grounded in a simple idea, "There, but for the grace of God, go I."

One can view the vast programs of social and human welfare which Jewish communities around the world have established in our own time only within this historical and moral context. Disadvantaged Jews still have a priority claim upon more advantaged Jews. The contemporary drive to "ransom Jews" is but another way of saying what Jews have learned well inside Christendom: Jewish survival depends upon Jews in the first instance, and not solely on the help of others.

In recent times Jews have been hard at work ransoming their captives in various lands; whether in connection with the survivors of Hitler's Holocaust; or the millions of Jews they redeemed from unstable and untenable existence in Arab lands (e.g. "Operation Magic

Carpet" that rescued the Yemen Jews); or the over one quarter-million Soviet Jews thus far resettled in Israel or countries of the West; or, more recently, the airlift to Israel from Ethiopia, in which the remnants of a once much more populous Jewish community (called "Falashas" or "strangers," by their host country) were saved from the African famine of the mid-1980s. These moral demands upon Jews could no longer be satisfied by the humane responses of individuals alone. Large-scale problems gave birth to the need for large-scale efforts, and only a galvanized community, focussing on these major issues—and not merely well-motivated, or even "charitable" individuals—could address them effectively. Federation became the order of the day. Indeed, it was the result of similar concerns for mutual aid and protection that medieval Jews had uniquely transformed themselves into a welfare-community in the first place.

The causes for Jews falling into captivity were many and varied. When the Romans besieged Jerusalem in 70 c.e., many Jews were taken prisoner and made into slaves. This was the first of a long series of Jewish "captivities" within Christendom, that would plague their history for almost two thousand years. When the first Crusaders reached the Holy Land in 1099, they also managed to take scores of Jews captive, causing the Alexandrian community in Egypt to mount major efforts to "buy" them back, redeeming the Jewish captives with large ransoms. From time to time, a number of leading rabbis were kidnapped by brigands, who demanded payment for their release. They, too, were redeemed by their fellow Jews. Then again there was widespread piracy along the Mediterranean coasts which over the years took many hundreds of Jews captive—as did the Tartars and the Cossacks farther to the east, in Poland and Russia. They also were ransomed by Jews in many countries who banded together for that purpose. Indeed, in seventeenth-century Venice, Jews organized the "Venetian Confraternity for the Redemption of Captives," which even had a branch in Hamburg. The organization required such huge funds that it found it necessary to institute an income tax on its members, in addition to exacting an export duty on all goods shipped by Venetian Jewish merchants to their Jewish correspondents elsewhere.

By far the largest strain placed upon these Jewish welfare communities was the problem of Jews who had been cast out of one exile or another. The expulsion of the Jews from Spain in 1492 unleashed many thousands of them on the rest of Europe. The captains of the vessels on which Jews sailed often enslaved them. From one chronicler of the period we learn: "In the Greek islands of Corfu and Candia, the Jews sold the gold from their synagogue ornaments to raise money for freeing such slaves. In Turkey, the Jews were received by the Sultan, Bajazet II, with extraordinary kindness, and the native Jews of his realm vied with their Italian brethren in the efforts they made to serve the Spanish exiles. Moses Kapsali, the most noted Turkish rabbi of the time, travelled from congregation to congregation and levied a tax on the native Jews to defray the cost of 'liberating the Spanish captives.' "[2]

It would be a mistake to believe that only external, negative pressures were at work in fashioning the Jewish community into a strong moral and social force. Communities as well as individuals usually respond to crises or emergencies more actively than they would to the ordinary and regular necessities of day-to-day community life. An emergency cannot be denied or shunted aside—even if it never seems to end—but a widow or an orphan, for example, who need constant succor, might be put off. Yet in the course of time, especially after the tenth century, each Jewish community made certain that even the so-called "routine" and mundane needs of their own dispossessed and downtrodden would be met. A network of benevolent agencies would be established, each with its own area of human and social concern, to insure that every local Jewish community would be zealously engaged in assisting those who needed a helping hand. To participate in such charitable undertakings came to be regarded as a *mitzvah*—a divine commandment—undertaken without regard to reward. Piety, in such cases, demanded it, not some crisis elsewhere. As a result, such activities, although not performed in response to external pressures or calamities, were seen as a mark of good Jewish "citizenship," and regarded as synonymous with religion itself.

How did this "welfare community" come into being? And what lessons can it teach Christian writers and readers of European history?

The *Kehillah:*
The Autonomous, Covenanted Community

There had been a Jewish community in Babylonia from the days of the first captivity, following the destruction of Solomon's Temple in 586 B.C.E. Most of its members, however, had returned to Jerusalem a generation or so later when the ruling Persian authorities granted them permission to come home to rebuild the sanctuary they would call the Second Temple. But after Rome sacked Jerusalem and destroyed even this temple, thousands of scholars and their disciples began streaming eastward to the area between the Tigris and Euphrates rivers, to what had been the birthplace of their ancient patriarch Abraham, in old Sumer. In the short space of two centuries this old-new Babylonian Diaspora community would boast of a population of about one million Jews, with three important academies of higher learning: in Sura, Nehardea, and Pumbedita. These were destined to become the major centers of rabbinical teaching in the diaspora. Indeed, it was at these very schools that the tractates of the so-called *Babylonian Talmud*, the principal repository of Pharisaic traditions, took shape and were finally edited in the sixth century. While a minority of Jews remained in Zion under Roman rule, for eight centuries following the fall of Jerusalem the seat and source of Jewish religious life and autonomy centered in Babylonia.

There the religious heads of the Talmudic academies legislated the laws by which Jews throughout the diaspora were governed. This situation continued for some time, even after the major academies started to decline and Jews, in the seventh century, began moving out of Babylonia to other centers—especially to countries in and around the Mediterranean littoral and North Africa. Babylonian hegemony in religious and communal matters finally came to an end in the tenth century, and thereafter we see the rise of a series of independent, self-governing Jewish communities to be found in North Africa, Italy, Germany, Spain, France, Palestine, Turkey, the Balkan countries, Poland, and Lithuania. Gone were the days when outstanding religious leaders in Babylonia, whose authority had been recognized throughout the Jewish diaspora, could serve as the lone, central guides for far-flung communities elsewhere.

As a result of this new situation, the local *kehillah,* or community, emerged as an autonomous unit, each with its own elected and appointed leaders, rabbis, and teachers. The *kehillah* had its own courts with authority to deal with civil, administrative, and sometimes even criminal cases; it levied and collected taxes in order both to pay the head tax imposed on the community by the non-Jewish rulers and to finance the educational and social services of its own community. Sometimes a federation was established, consisting of more than one *kehillah,* in areas or countries where conditions warranted it.

It is only with the rise of nationalism in modern times that there began to emerge in Europe what we now know as the monolithic, centralized state: a government which unites all of its constituent parts under its single rule and authority. The so-called medieval European "state" was essentially an admixture of feudal and churchly authority, and it expressed no interest in serving as a central power. In fact, it was a "state" which actually consisted of a variety of separate corporate and autonomous powers—the Church, the aristocracy, the landed burghers, the labor guilds, and the like. Aliens living within its midst—like the Jews—were never recognized as "citizens," yet generally were granted rights to their own autonomous communities and laws, provided, of course, that they paid the required taxes and levies. Governments operated on the assumption that it was their right and duty to impose especially heavy levies on the Jewish community, a kind of "toleration tax" for the privilege of living in their lands. To collect these monies, the authorities found it more convenient to receive them *in toto*, and arrangements were established whereby taxes were paid directly by the community, rather than by individual Jews. As a result, Jewish communities could exist as cohesive, independent, and autonomous units—as long as their leaders accepted responsibility for delivering the required taxes in bulk. This situation suited Jews well, since it allowed them to live under Jewish law, to elect their own *kehillah* councils, and to establish and manage a wide variety of communal institutions—especially those devoted to social welfare. Despite its alien status, the Jewish community could become, in effect, a "state within a state."

But their "Jewish state," or more properly their *kehillah*, was worlds apart and radically different from all those other medieval corporate groups. To read about medieval Jews in most histories written by Christians is to be left virtually in the dark about what, in fact, set them profoundly apart from the rest of society. Occasionally, these standard histories give a token nod to the Jews: they may mention a leading Jewish light here and there, like a Maimonides, who served as court physician in Spain, or some other singular Jewish worthy. Students of these texts, however, are usually left with the distinct impression that Jewish life within medieval Christendom was either vegetating or drying up. Little wonder that Jews play no positive role whatever in the story of Western civilization as told by mostly non-Jewish historians As they have it, Jews were principally money-grubbing usurers who preyed on Christian merchants—greedy, indolent, benighted, and little more! (I will have more to say about this later on, when analyzing the role of Jews in medieval commerce.)

The shoe, however, is really on the other foot. These "scholars" are themselves less than industrious. They have only to consult the communal records of one Jewish *kehillah* after another to note the true sources of our contemporary notions about the necessary and crucial role of government in providing education, social welfare, medical, and other humane benefits to all of its citizens. When this idea of the "welfare state" first arose in the political and philosophical tracts of some late-nineteenth-century English scholars, it was considered revolutionary. Indeed, in some quarters even in the West it is still not wholly acceptable, especially by believers in the "divine right" of capitalism, or by those who trumpet economic theories of *laissez-faire*.

Yet by whatever name we call it, the "welfare state" is here to stay. Governments in retrenchment may try to reduce Social Security benefits, or pensions for the disabled, or aid to needy working mothers or students. They cannot, however, completely abdicate their central role in assisting the disadvantaged: it is their social entitlement! It is interesting to note in this connection that both Catholic and Protestant church groups are now often in the vanguard of movements which call upon their governments to act responsibly toward the poor and needy, the disadvantaged and the disabled. No longer do they see these needs merely as acts of "Christian charity"—they are finally regarded as the essential elements of any responsible society: acts of justice and not merely of charity.

This is precisely the way the Jewish tradition and its leadership centuries ago were interpreting their own Covenant—as the demand which social justice continually makes upon the leaders of a community that is bound together in covenantal love. One Christian problem in past centuries was its inability either to see or to understand that this "Jewish covenant" was profoundly at work in the very communities they were then helping to expel from one Christian land or another. (As we have seen, they were certain that the covenant had died long before.)

It is important, then, that we look at those Jewish communities—some of them living in the very shadow of the Vatican—to see what their "old" covenantal responsibilities may still teach Christians and Jews even now.

Local Autonomy: The Welfare Community at Work

The trade-off by which medieval governments permitted Jews to employ their own legal system within their autonomous communities in exchange for payment of enormous taxes proved to be of tremendous importance. As a result of this arrangement, the Torah-law was able to serve as a kind of political constitution, the basis for all community action. For Jews the study of their law would also be valuable socially and politically in addition to its intrinsic religious significance. Scholars were viewed as the natural leaders of the community, and the higher academies of learning which produced them were accorded the greatest respect by the people. This legal self-rule in effect distinguished the Jewish community from all other religious groups. It transformed Jews from being only a religious community. And in the medieval European Diaspora it made them into a national-political entity.

The cornerstone of Jewish political theory in the Middle Ages was borrowed from the Talmudic dictum: "The majority can not be rogues."[3] This teaching served as the foundation for a democratic process. It made clear that a majority, merely by virtue of the fact that it is a majority, cannot arbitrarily violate the basic rights of the minority. There were other democratic safeguards: the leaders of the *kehillah* were viewed as judges of a court, and "clean hands" became a precondition for holding public office. "The elders of the community," a major medieval law code, the *Shulhan Arukh*, held, "who are appointed to deal with public or private matters, are viewed as judges, and he who is disqualified from judging because of wrong-doing cannot be appointed to sit among them."[4]

It was in this way that the power of the rabbis of Talmudic days now came to be lodged in the hands of the people themselves through their representatives on their community councils. The *takkanot*, the decrees and ordinances of these *kehillah* executives, were considered binding upon all members of the community, as if they had been legislated by the Torah itself. Yet an interesting principle was also at work—the idea of local autonomy. Since each Jewish community was regarded as a micro-image of Israel's larger covenant, all of its constituents—the leaders and the public alike—were regarded as partners who had voluntarily consented to associate.

Precedents and customs established by other Jewish communities elsewhere did not go unnoticed in their own locales, for in theory they were free to legislate their own laws as their own local conditions dictated. Of course, the overall Jewish tradition was not openly disregarded by any of these community councils—the larger Jewish covenant was never forgotten—but neither were the federal, democratic principles of local rights abrogated. In a real sense the medieval

Jewish world was actually a "community of communities," federated locally as well as across the continents. The communities were connected not only by kinship but also by mutual consent, partners in the Covenant, and not merely passive subjects of others.

These principles were a far cry from the manner in which the rest of Europe was then being governed or controlled by the Church. The hierarchical powers of medieval Christendom were everywhere in place, despite the fact that from time to time there were local challenges to authoritarian papal power. Whenever these became too oppressive, Church Councils would be called into being to address not only "church-state" problems of governance, but also local heresies or other deviations from the established central policies of the Vatican. Though governed by traditional Jewish law and concerned for the general safety of Jews everywhere, the local Jewish community and the elders elected to its councils decided and determined their own fate.

These unique characteristics of the welfare community of medieval Jews still play an important role in the decentralzied, non-hierarchic Jewish community of our day. Indeed, as a result of the diversity and wide dispersion of distinctive Jewish communities in the medieval past, one cannot really speak of uniformity or orthodoxy in Judaism. Local and regional variations were valid: the *minhag,* or custom, of each separate Jewry was supreme. The Jews of Italy, for example, did not follow all the practices of the Jews of Germany, France, Poland, or Lithuania. Moreover, Jews who lived principally under Muslim rulers—in Spain, North Africa, and other parts of the Mediterranean and Near Eastern world—were known as *Sephardim* (*Sepharad* means Spain, in Hebrew) and their community life and religious practices differed measurably from their brethren, the *Ashkenazim,* who lived primarily under Christian rulers in Europe. (*Ashkenaz* means Germany, in Hebrew).

Everywhere we turn in Jewish life today we find lingering influences of the democratic inheritance of the medieval Jewish principle: the central importance of each local community as a self-governing, autonomous unit. While uniformity characterized the Church, Jews were more accustomed to what has been called their unity-within-diversity. As will be noted later in greater detail, these very attitudes and practices of medieval Jews also helped to set the stage for the "Judaization" of the Catholic Church when the Protestant reformers of the late Middle Ages set about to challenge central Christian authority by emphasizing the spirit of "congregationalism" over against the distant but crucial and ever-present powers of episcopacy and papacy.

But we are somewhat ahead of our story. It still remains for us to see how these local communities actually "programmed" their ideas of social justice into the specifics of laws and institutions. To do this, one can choose at random any of the hundreds of different Jewish communities across medieval Europe. Here we will focus on a single community as a reflection of many others. To demonstrate the irony of the Christian problem, it is instructive to examine the community of what might be called "the Pope's Jews"—those who lived in the ghetto of Rome, virtually within eyeshot if not earshot of the Vatican.

The ghetto, it should be noted, was a Christian invention. Its name derives from the fact that the first of these, established in Venice in 1516, was located in the neighborhood of an iron foundry, which in Italian was called *geto*. A generation later, in 1555, Pope Paul IV instituted a ghetto for the Jews of his city, Rome. It was located on the left bank of the Tiber, where the Jewish quarter, the *septus hebraicus*, had existed for some time. When the papal edict established the area as a ghetto, however, high walls were placed around the section and curfews instituted. A single church was permitted to remain near the gates of the wall. It was left in place to promote forced conversion of the ghetto inmates, who were required by the Vatican to attend church services on Saturday mornings—the Jewish Sabbath—where fiery conversionist sermons were virtually hurled at them.

The Roman Ghetto, covering an area of less than three hectares, with over 130 houses containing about 4,500 inhabitants, reflected a density greater than anywhere else in Europe in its day and probably even than the worst shantytowns of our times. Small wonder that a seventeenth century French Christian visitor, chancing upon it as a tourist and lacking the eyes to penetrate into its spiritual core, could write: "What they call *il ghetto* is the Jewish quarter, which is surrounded by walls and closed by doors so that this perfidious nation shall have no communication with Christians at night; as they are not able to live elsewhere or enlarge their district, which is bordered on one side by the Tiber and on the other by the street of the Fishmarket, and because there are a very large number of them, this riff-raff multiplied extremely; this is why several families live in the same small room, so that the whole quarter stinks, continually and intolerably."[5] Yet something very profound was stirring beneath these horrible externalities—which were, of course, the result of the coercive harshness of Church authorities who had insisted on herding these Jews together. In spite of its dire physical plight, this was a compassionate, caring, covenantal community.

A Jewish chronicler of the Middle Ages describes the welfare organizations of the Roman ghetto in the seventeenth century:

> The benevolent societies were grouped under four heads: (a) those for the relief of the poor, (b) those which were concerned with the burial of the dead, (c) those which provided for the aged, (d) those which served religious and educational objects. At this period seven societies devoted their energies to the provision of clothes, shoes, linen, beds, and warm winter bed-coverings for young children, school children, the poor, especially women, widows and prisoners. Two societies provided trousseaus and dowries for poor brides—under which category was sometimes included the loan of jewelery to those who possessed none; another society brought help to the houses of those who met with sudden deaths, and yet another was founded for visiting the sick. Other societies performed the last loving services to the dying, conducted the purification before interment, and attended to the burial.
>
> The women of Rome had their own society, too, though even when this was not the case they were associated with the men in administering such charities as were concerned with the relief of their own sex. In addition to these societies, a special association devoted itself to collecting alms for the Holy Land.[6]

All of these special benevolent societies were established with the agreement of the community council, the *kehillah*. The latter also administered the *tamhui*, or community kitchen, as well as the *kuppah*, which arranged for the distribution of food or monies to the poor, especially in honor of the Sabbath, or on the eve of religious festivals. In addition, the *kehillah* was responsible for managing the communal hostelry, or inn, for the reception of poor travelers or vagrants. We also know of the extensive sanitary services provided by the Roman community—as well as other communities. It supplied a hospital (called *hekdesh*, or sanctuary, in Hebrew), communal physicians, nurses and midwives. In keeping with traditional Jewish law, the community ruled that a gift or legacy destined for the building of a synagogue could be diverted to the erection of the hospital, which was usually part of the community hostelry.

* * *

The walls of the ghettos came down with the birth of the modern nation-state, as recently as the nineteenth century. With the rise of

nationalism and the strengthening of the power of central government, the rule of the Church—the Second Estate—began to decline.
Modern revolutionary spirits, both in France and the United States,
sought to sever Church from state. As the political hold of the Church
on government became weaker, and the division between religious
and secular authority more marked, the medieval period may be said
to have come to its end. When this new era came upon the scene,
Jews were tentatively offered "emancipation"—an opportunity to participate for the first time as secular citizens in the new national life.
Inevitably, in such a situation, the covenantal Jewish community of
the older time would experience difficulty. Instead of serving as the
"Jewish government" it had to wither away—if Jews were to be fully
emancipated and join with their fellow citizens in pursuit of the new,
central national interest. Newly emancipated Jews at first seemed to
believe that they were no longer Jews—they were en route to becoming good Germans, good Frenchmen, good Italians, and the like.
Indeed, they were entrapped by the spirit of the "Enlightenment,"
which in retrospect can now be seen to have been a thinly veiled form
of "liberal antisemitism."

A major Jewish historian recently noted the reasons for the failure
of the emancipation process for both Jews and Gentiles. "The predicament of emancipated Jewry" in nineteenth-century Europe, Jacob
Katz wrote, "was rooted not in one or another ideology, but in the fact
that Jewish Emancipation had been tacitly tied to an illusory expectation—the disappearance of the Jewish community of its own voli-
tion." But this, of course, did not happen. As a result, Katz concludes,
"a certain uneasiness, not to say of outright scandal, was experienced
by Gentiles. The internal contradiction at the heart of Jewish Emancipation—the granting of civil rights to a people, in the hope that it
would disappear—began to exact its cost. If gaining civil rights meant
an enormous improvement in Jewish prospects, at the same time it
carried with it a precariously ill-defined status which was bound to
elicit antagonism from the Gentile world."[7] To which I would add still
another reason, one which clearly points up how "liberal" antisemites
often cover over their Jewish antipathies: while they trumpet individual rights to liberty, they often deny the freedoms necessary for group
survival. Two centuries ago, Clermont-Tonnère, a member of the
French Revolutionary Assembly, summed this up neatly: "We must
refuse everything to the Jews as a nation, but must grant the Jews
everything as individuals." All would be well with them, that older

pseudo-liberal emancipation taught, *if they would only stop being Jews.* Similar views still ring out from time to time, especially from the ranks of the radical left.

But the facts of history have taught Jews otherwise. True, the older order of Jewish self-government had passed; the earlier political contexts were gone, and with them, the old structures of Jewish life. But Jews were more than "private persons"—they formed a living community. Accordingly, Jews needed to be able freely to remain Jews, even if definitions of their group status or political nationality had changed dramatically since the Middle Ages. A truly amazing fact emerges, however, even in the free and open Western society of our own times: Jewish "self-government" never died with the Middle Ages; it lives on in the voluntary association of free Jews determined to assist their fellow Jews everywhere. They may give new names to their charity organizations, or embark on new-style fund-raising efforts. The forms change; the substance abides. No matter how others may describe them, they still define themselves in the way their Talmudic rabbis had seen them—as "compassionate children of compassionate parents." They live not only as helpful citizens of the various lands of their current domicile, but also as Jewish citizens, proud of their unique ethnic and religious culture. From those Pharisee-rabbis they have learned the secret of survival, even in their dispersion, by living effectively within two civilizations at once—their own, as well as those of their new communities.

The Christian world may observe. If it wishes, it may also learn. To do so, however, requires an effort to appreciate the Pharisaic legacy: the ways in which the first rabbis helped to ensure not only their religous survival, but their cultural and intellectual development as well.

To do so, it is necessary to recast older attitudes toward the work and the world of the Pharisees, to see how their efforts have contributed to a highly literate, culturally alive Jewish society that would never know the "Dark Ages" of European history.

NOTES

1. For a commentary on this code, as well as its legal sources in Jewish law, see Abraham Cronbach, "The Maimonidean Code of Benevolence," in *Hebrew Union College Annual* (Cincinnatti: 1947), Vol. XX, pp. 471–540. The "Code of

Benevolence" is part of Maimonides' treatise *Matnot Aniyim*, which occupies chapters 7–10 of Section VII of his *Mishneh Torah*—the most definitive legal work of the Middle Ages.

2. Israel Abrahams, *Jewish Life in the Middle Ages*, (New York: Atheneum, 1969), p. 337.

3. Babylonian Talmud: *Baba Batra* 100a.

4. See section on civil law, *Hoshen Mishpat* 37:22, in the *Shulhan Arukh* (Code of Jewish Law). For a wide-ranging discussion of the basis in Jewish law of the medieval corporate community see the authoritative essay by Menachem Elon, "Power and Authority: Halachic Stance of the Traditional Community and its Contemporary Implications," in Daniel Elazer (ed.), *Kinship and Consent* (Washington D.C.: University Press, 1983) pp. 183–208.

5. Quoted in Leon Poliakov, *Jewish Bankers and the Holy See: From the Thirteenth to the Seventeenth Century* (London: Routledge and Kegan Paul, 1977) pp. 188–89.

6. Abrahams, *op. cit.*, pp. 326–7.

7. Jacob Katz, "Misreadings of Anti-Semitism," in *Commentary*, July, 1983, p. 43.

CHAPTER VIII

Appreciating the Pharisees: The Oldest Schools and Universities

Seated across from me at my desk, a serious young man steeped in Christian piety seeks to engage me in religious dialogue. He wants to know the secret of Jewish religious survival: why do Jews remain Jews?

I give him the same answer I have given numerous other friendly and truth-seeking people who are eager to make a fresh, unencumbered start in Christian-Jewish relations. I tell him that Judaism, as we know it today, did not begin with Moses, the Prophets, or other worthies of biblical religion. It began with the Pharisees—the ancient rabbis and their Talmud.

That Pharisaic world, the bedrock of all that has come to be known as "Judaism" since the Temple's fall, I tell these Christian ecumenists, has become still another obstacle in the historical Jewish-Christian divide. "You begin to understand Judaism only by learning to appreciate the Pharisees. And in this process, unlearning will be as important a tool as learning itself. Be prepared to shed almost everything you have ever heard about them from your Christian teachers. They have set up the Pharisees as strawmen, as the key foils of their anti-Jewish polemic. Beware, however: one may never judge the true nature of either men or movements from evidence adduced by their enemies."

My friend is surprised. Not begin with Moses? Not start at Sinai

131

itself? And these Pharisees? He has already learned "all" he thought he needed to know about them from the pages of the New Testament itself. Why need Christians begin their study of Judaism with them?

I remove my copy of the *Oxford English Dictionary* from its case, and turning to the appropriate page, read to him these entries:

"Pharisaical: Resembling the Pharisees in being strict in doctrine and ritual, without the spirit of piety; laying great stress upon the external appearances of religion and outward show of morality, and assuming superiority on that account; hypocritical; formalist; self-righteous." And again, "Pharisee: An ancient Jewish sect distinguished by . . . their pretensions to superior sanctity; a self-righteous person; a formalist; a hypocrite."

He begins to "see," black on white, my reasons. Perhaps for the very first time, it dawns on him that even in the ordinary day-to-day uses of simple discourse, age-old remnants of an ancient Christian prejudice have become part of our speech, our attitudes, and even the way we think. He is confronted directly with what I have been calling the Christian problem. He perceives, perhaps, that the lexicons of our language and our lives are still in need of demythologizing, if the truths about Judaism are to be unveiled, to be viewed in their own light. Perhaps, too, he can understand how to apply the moral implications of what Spinoza is reputed to have said in another connection: What Paul says about Peter tells us more about Paul than about Peter.

It is pleasant to report and refreshing to note that Christian ecumenists are just now also being told by some of their own leaders what rabbis have been telling them all along. In 1982, a study unit of the (Protestant) World Council of Churches, a select group on "Dialogue with People of Living Faiths and Ideologies," met in Bali, Indonesia, and took a giant step forward in this direction with its proposed new "Guidelines for Jewish-Christian Dialogue." It is useful to pay heed to what these Christian teachers are now beginning to perceive:

> It should not be surprising that Jews resent those Christian theologies in which they as a people are assigned to play a negative role. History has demonstrated over and again how short the step is from such patterns of thought in Christianity to overt acts of condescension, persecution and worse. . .
>
> For those reasons there is special urgency for Christians to listen, through study and dialogue, to ways in which Jews understand their

history and traditions, their faith and their obedience "in their own terms." Furthermore, a mutual listening to how each is perceived by the other may be a step toward overcoming fears and correcting misunderstandings that have thrived in isolation. . .

. . . In the understanding of many Christians, Judaism as a living tradition came to an end with the coming of Christ and with the destruction of the second temple as God's people, and the Judaism that survived is a fossilized religion of legalism.

In this view the covenant with God with the people of Israel was only a preparation for the coming of Christ—after which it was abrogated. Judaism of the first centuries before and after the birth of Jesus was therefore called "Late Judaism." *The Pharisees were considered to represent the acme of legalism, Jews and Jewish groups were portrayed as negative models, and the truth and beauty of Christianity were thought to be enhanced by setting up Judaism as false and ugly.*

Through a renewed study of Judaism and in dialogue with Jews, Christians became aware that Judaism in the time of Christ was in an early stage of its long life. *Under the leadership of the Pharisees the Jewish people began a spiritual revival of remarkable power which gave them the vitality capable of surviving the catastrophic loss of the temple.* It gave birth to the Mishnah and Talmud and built the structures for a strong and creative life through the centuries. . .

Christians should remember that some of the controversies reported in the New Testament between Jesus and the "scribes and Pharisees" find parallels within Pharisaism itself and its heir, Rabbinic Judaism. These controversies took place in a Jewish context, *but when the words of Jesus came to be used by Christians who did not identify with the Jewish people as Jesus did, such sayings often became weapons in anti-Jewish polemics and thereby their original intention was tragically distorted. . . .*

Judaism, with its rich history of spiritual life, produced the Talmud as the normative guide for Jewish life in thankful response to the grace of God's covenant with the people of Israel. Over the centuries important commentaries, profound philosophical works and poetry of spiritual depth have been added. *For Jews, the Talmud is as central and authoritative as the New Testament is for Christians. (Italics added.)*

Sensitive religious leaders now realize that they must begin to reappraise many of their long-standing, narrow, and often anti-Jewish definitions. In this process they should be seeking to rediscover the Pharisees. In earlier chapters I have traced some of the contributions the Pharisees made to their own people. But to help restore them to their proper place in world history, it is important to recognize what this small "Jewish sect" was able to accomplish for the wider realm of human culture, in the space of only a few centuries. How, then, should we now regard and appreciate the Pharisees?

From a Sect to a Cultural Force

It is one of the greatest success stories of history that a handful of spiritual laymen, unsupported by the vast, inherited authority held for centuries by Jewish priests under biblical law, could in the short span of less than two hundred years create a revolutionary new religious style, and new institutions, as well, that not only would help their people outlive the shock of their Temple's destruction but would prepare the way for their future survival across their dispersions and in all their exiles.

The Pharisees were essentially plebeian tradesmen and artisans, who in the words of one scholar "thought they were banding together for the protection of their ritual. Actually, they were laying the foundations for a world civilization."[1] In his view, "Pharisaism is the anomaly of religious history. Nationalist and ritualistic in origin, it became universal and philosophic in outlook. Though it admitted but thousands to formal membership, it included millions (of whom many were not Jews) among believers in its doctrine. The Pharisees disappeared as an organized society in the third century of the Christian era, but their influence on western spiritual thought still endures."[2]

Keeping these broader views in mind, we would do well to avoid making the "genetic fallacy" which would equate their seemingly archaic and narrowly ritualistic origins with the cosmic and universalist sweep of their later development. We commit a genetic fallacy every time we wrongly identify the ultimate meaning and significance of ideas or customs with their genesis. Oftentimes ideas came into the world much less developed and mature. (A handy example of a genetic fallacy is to equate a handshake with its earliest origins: the extension of unarmed hands by opposing warriors, to prove that they were weaponless. A "warm," or a "friendly," or even a "firm" handshake have become symbols with altogether different connotations, as the custom of handshaking grew away from its more primitive origins.)

I set out this *caveat* concerning the Pharisees, in particular, because when we seek to discover their origins and place a spotlight on their earliest activities, we discover something unnerving. The essential idea they first propounded seems both arcane and archaic when contrasted to their later and larger visions concerning human freedom, learning, the glories of diversity, the rational uses of knowledge, or their conceptions of international peace and morality. And what was it that first brought them into league with one another, to stand apart from the rest of the House of Israel? Ritual purity, pure and simple. It was their staunch view that if their people were indeed to constitute "a kingdom of priests and a holy nation," as set forth in the Torah, then the primary and fundamental way to achieve this higher destiny was to observe, in great detail, the biblical laws of levitical purity, not only when entering the Temple, but in every-day acts and in all interpersonal relations.

The Pharisee washed his hands frequently, bathed often, and sought to make certain that nothing he owned, touched, purchased, or stored in his house, would be defiled by contamination with "impurity"—a running sore, a corpse, a cemetery, an infectious disease, and such like. It is likely that later offshoots of their order—the Essenes, various apocalyptic sects, and even the first Jewish-Christians, or Nazarenes—adopted this Pharisaic model in their own ways: by ablutions, immersion in brooks and rivers, and, even later, by baptism in the Jordan.

Yet there would be major differences between the Pharisees, and all the other Jewish sects, differences that would ultimately insure a role for Pharisaism as a world-force, even as they rendered the other sects irrelevant to Jewish survival. Unlike the Sadducees, theirs was the unique view that the Torah and its moral teachings would survive the loss of the Temple, and that Jewish fulfillment of these precepts, and not only loyalty to Zion, was paramount. Nor did the Pharisees succumb to the urgent messianic passion of apocalyptic sects like the Essenes. Theirs was a more patient, future-oriented vision, rooted in man's capacity to change and grow; it also regarded world peace and warlessness as the preeminent requirements for the messianic arrival. Man, in other words, had first to perfect society: the moral re-making of mankind would have to precede the messianic time. The human community, the Pharisees believed, would have to work infinitely harder than it had, to become morally worthy, before the messianic age could be anticipated. They renewed the older prophetic tradition by shifting emphasis from a preoccupation with cultic concerns to a studious search of what it was that God demanded of moral men.

From the Temple, to the Home, to the Community

To achieve this kind of moral readiness for the better world to be, the Pharisees staked out their own, new territory. If to others "a man's home is his castle," to these Jewish pietists, a man's home, and not merely the official Temple, was his first and pre-eminent sanctuary, and the table was perceived as its "altar." Food, thus, became clearly more than nourishment; it was a gift from God and the means whereby man, at his family table, sanctified and praised the Creator daily and regularly, and not alone on visits to the Temple.

The table too was transformed in Pharisee homes into a place of learning. Words spoken there were meant to edify, ennoble, and instruct. In a real sense, the table served as the first school, and even after other, more formal educational institutions would be established, the table would continue to serve as a "school" throughout life, every time a meal was eaten. In this way, the Pharisees began to emerge as more than "puritanical pietists." They were also the learned teachers—laymen, to be sure, but teachers who could rank equally with the priests.

Pharisees considered the meal as a "sacrifice" of thanksgiving to the Lord, and the company seated around the table on which it was offered as a "religious fellowship." The "table fellowships" created by the earliest Pharisees, like their ablutions, would later infiltrate other sects, including the first Jewish Christians. Indeed, the early Christian *agape* (love-feast), and later the Eucharist (the offering of thanks) itself, were outgrowths of this Pharisaic ideal of the fellowship of priest-like believers, united in community, seated at the meal—at the "altar-tables," of each Jewish home. So it was that for Pharisees the home, as altar and as school, became as important as the Temple itself; as a moral center, it surely would be as pure. It is important to keep this novel if apparently simple Pharisaic ideal in mind as one very important reason why the fall of the Temple in 70 c.e. did not spell the end of Judaism. In a certain sense, as we shall soon see, the Pharisees turned that curse into a blessing: they made the home into a portable sanctuary which, once *the* Sanctuary was destroyed, could move wherever Jews would live. By elevating the home into a permanent altar, they not only de-clericalized Judaism but accomplished even more. In the process, they sought to transform each individual into a priestly person who would be morally responsible for his own behavior and ethically sensitive to the demand that the entire community behave as a "kingdom of priests." They radically transformed the older monotheistic cultic religion into an international cultural community profoundly committed to a system of monotheistic ethics.

To those who have only met the Pharisees casually in church Sunday School classes, or who have heard about them only from the pulpit, listening to the New Testament read or expounded, these extraordinary, even revolutionary, achievements may not be easily recognized or appreciated. How so?

Why Some Christians Err

To many Christians, the Pharisees seem to be only hypocritical and self-righteous men. This is so because they are brought into the New Testament story only in order to "explain" why it was that most Jews did not accept Jesus as the Messiah. The Pharisees are thus made to serve as the arch symbols of *the* adversary. And they often appear in the New Testament as wooden, stereotypical characters, or as "straw men" to be beaten off by the beleaguered disciples of Jesus and as the villains who stood in the way of his acceptance as the true Messiah by the whole Jewish community.[3]

Accordingly, the word "Pharisee" itself, as we have seen, continues to serve as an epithet of derision. How could it be otherwise, given the fact that descriptions of the Pharisees by New Testament authors are couched in querulous words heaped upon them by their adversaries, the early Christians? No fight, experience teaches, is as fierce as the one among brothers: each knows the weaknesses of the other. When Jewish Christians described their own brothers who were Pharisees as "hypocrites," or as "children of vipers," they were merely re-echoing words which Pharisees themselves had used in describing fellow Pharisees in the heat of their own inner disputes or intellectual arguments. Indeed, the references to this point, as paraphrased by George F. Moore, great Christian student of rabbinic Judaism, are especially instructive, even amusing:

> That many who bore the name Pharisee were a disgrace we have on rabbinical testimony. Both Talmuds have a list of seven varieties of Pharisee, of which only one—or none at all—gets a word of approval. The first four are designated by what were perhaps old nicknames at the enigmatic significance of which those who recorded them in the Talmuds could only guess, and did not guess alike. In the Palestinian Talmud they are the "shoulder Pharisee," who packs his good works on his shoulder (to be seen by men); the "wait-a-bit" Pharisee, who (when someone has business with him) says, Wait a little; I must do a good work; the "reckoning" Pharisee, who when he commits a fault and does a good work crosses off one with the other; the "economizing" Phar-

isee, who asks, What economy can I practice to spare a little to do a good work? the "show me my fault" Pharisee, who says, show me what sin I have committed, and I will do an equivalent good work (implying that he had no fault); the Pharisee of fear, like Job; the Pharisee of love, like Abraham. The last is the only kind that is dear (to God).[4]

Indeed, to close off this "defense" of the Pharisees against Christian stereotypes on a positive note taken from the Pharisaic sources themselves, here is the most accurate self-description available of what Pharisees aspired to:

This is the way that is becoming for the study of the Torah: a morsel of bread with salt you must eat, and water by measure you must drink, you must sleep upon the ground, and live a life of trouble, the while you toil in the Torah. If you do thus, "Happy shall you be and it shall be well with you"; happy shall you be in this world, and it shall be well with you in the world to come. Seek not greatness for yourself, and crave not honor more than is due to your learning; and desire not the table of kings, for your table is greater than theirs, and your crown greater than theirs; and faithful is He, the master of your work, to pay you the reward of your labor.[5]

From the Home to the Academy: A Unique Educational Innovation

I have suggested earlier that the religious genius of the early Pharisees can be comprehended by recognizing but two of their many revolutionary achievements:

(1) That the sanctity and purity of the Temple be extended from its public domain to the private world of human relations, and especially to the home, so that all Israelites recognize that they constitute a "kingdom of priests and a holy nation."

(2) That in this process of transference and extension, religious authority would shift, too, so that the right to teach and expound the Torah-law be moved away from the exclusivity of the Temple priests, and shared by the learned laymen—the Pharisee scholar-teachers themselves.

The second of these propositions, of course, was based on the Pharisaic innovation which held that in addition to the Written Torah of Scripture, there was a "tradition of the elders," or an "Oral Torah," which was as old as the Jewish people itself—indeed, received by Moses at Sinai—and which the Pharisees relied upon in their expanded interpretations of Scripture. The Sadducees, as already indicated, adamantly opposed this notion of a "twin-Torah," insisting that only the written and recorded words of Scripture were authoritative as law, and they alone were entitled to dispense judgment based upon its literal meanings. They refused to recognize the existence of that "second Torah" of the Pharisees—the so-called "Oral Law" or tradition.

I want to dwell for a moment on the first of these two innovations, one that is often overlooked. There are no known historical references that can readily explain how it was that the Pharisees were able to assume their ultimate role as the official recognized spiritual teachers and judges—and thus, the leaders as well—of their people. After all, they faced a formidable vested group—the priests—which did, in fact, stand fast by biblically mandated rights as the judges and expounders of the Torah. A plausible explanation is the one I suggest: the private home became the new Temple, the new school, and the new base of Pharisee support among the common people.

We need only turn to the earliest teachings of the Pharisees compiled in the *Mishnah*—the first codebook of their vast Talmudic literature that would follow—to find verification. One of the very first Pharisees, Jose, son of Joezer, who lived in the middle of the second pre-Christian century, was actually describing the Pharisaic platform when he said, "Let your house become a regular, stated meeting place for learned teachers [the Pharisees]; sit in the dust at their feet, and thirstily drink in their words."[6] A few years later, still another Pharisee-teacher, Joshua, son of Perahiah, was explaining the style of their pedagogic program. Study was not to be left to chance, nor could true learning take place in isolation without an authoritative teacher as guide. "Provide yourself," he advised, "with a teacher, and get for yourself a fellow student."[7] Both of these themes—the house as a place for advanced study, and the need for authentic, traditional guidance—would be frequently re-echoed in later Talmudic writing. But that these had already served as the prototype of their academies of learning of the future, and were in vogue two centuries before Jerusalem's fall, is highly significant. It supports the view that even though the Pharisees had first banded together for what may be called puritanical ritualistic purposes, they soon began laying the foundations for their greatest innovation—a sanctuary that would serve the people long after the loss of the Temple. That sanctuary would become more than a ritual center: it would be the school for higher learning, open to all, without regard to class or caste—the learned laymen's response to what had become, in priestly hands, less a prophetic and more a cultic religion. Learning, the Pharisees were saying, is in itself an act of worship within the prophetic tradition: to know and understand the word of God in order to deepen moral and spiritual sensitivity. When the Pharisees, in their synagogues, recited the well-known words, "Hear, O Israel! The Lord is our God, the Lord alone" (Deut. 6:4),[7a] they thought of it as "*Understand*, O Israel!" To listen—to God or to man—but not to fathom the depths of what one hears, is virtually not to hear at all.

It was probably not until after 70 c.e., when the Romans destroyed the Temple in Jerusalem, that what we now know as the Beth Midrash, an academy of higher learning, began to emerge as an institution, fully independent of private homes or of some of the synagogues to which it was also attached. By that time these schools had become so important to the life of the community that it was ordained that a building occupied by a synagogue may be transformed into a school, but not contrariwise. To do so, the Rabbis taught, would be a "descent in sanctity."[8]

These academies, it must be clearly understood, were not "theological seminaries" or "professional schools" where outstanding virtuosi would train for the rabbinate. They were concerned, rather, with the instruction of the whole adult community, the cobblers and the smiths, as well as tradesmen, in order to elevate the religious and cultural standards of the entire adult population. This enterprise, as George Foot Moore has suggested, "created a unique system of universal [adult] education, whose very elements comprised not only reading and writing, but an ancient language and its classic literature. The high intellectual and religious value thus set on education was indelibly impressed on the mind, and one may say on the character of the Jew, and the institutions created for it have perpetuated themselves to the present day."[9]

All of this was made possible, despite the utter destruction and the attendant despair visited upon the capital and its religious institutions by the Romans, principally as a result of a momentous decision taken by the leading Pharisees as the Roman war against the Jews was reaching its climax. As we have seen, small groups of Pharisees, even years before, had splintered off from the party's mainstream to found their own messianic or apocalyptic communities: the Dead Sea sect at Qumran, as we have noted, was one of these. There were others, too—and some scholars even regard the first Nazarenes, followers of John the Baptist and Jesus, as still other Pharisees who sought to avert the severe decrees of Roman destruction and pillage by preaching and believing in the "end of days" and the imminent recompense to be awarded their long-suffering people with the advent of the Messiah. The mainstream of the Pharisaic party, however, could not accept any of these apocalyptic ways as the solution to the problem of Roman evil. They were too pragmatic, too concerned with society to flee this world. In the end, they opted for the school and the Torah to be taught there as their religious answer to Roman oppression.

Consider the way one scholar has described that fateful hour and that crucial decision, and its continuing echo effects across the continents from that time forward:

> While "the sword without and terror within" ravaged Jerusalem, a venerable old teacher quit the wall that harbored misfortune and fled to the enemy. The Roman general gave the fugitive, no less a personage than Rabban Johanan ben Zakkai [the leader of the Pharisees], a friendly reception, and promised to grant one request that he would prefer. The rabbi modestly asked that he be allowed to open a school at Jabneh [Jamnia], where he might teach his pupils. The imperator had no objection to this harmless desire, for he could not suspect that its consummation would enable Judaism, apparently so weak, to outlive Rome, for all its iron strength, by thousands of years . . . The last eighteen hundred years of Jewish history, however, are the best justification of the wisdom of Rabban Johanan. That the Jewish nation has survived the downfall of its State and the destruction of its national sanctuary is above all due to this great genius, who made of religious study a new form in which the national existence of the Jews found expression, so that by the side of the history of nearly two thousand years of suffering we can point to an equally extensive history of intellectual effort. Studying and wandering, thinking and enduring, learning and suffering fill this long period. Thinking is as characteristic a trait of the Jew as suffering, or, to be more exact, thinking rendered suffering possible. For it was our thinkers who prevented the wandering nation, this true "wandering Jew," from sinking to the level of brutalized vagrants, of vagabond gypsies.
>
> In Jabneh, Rabban Johanan kindled the eternal light of the Torah— the light that was never to be extinguished. Usha took up the work begun at Jabneh, and was in turn replaced by Sepphoris, and after the sun of learning in Palestine had past its meridian and hastened toward its setting [third Christian century], it appeared in the sky of the East [Babylonia]. Nehardea, Sura, and Pumbedita for eight hundred years radiated a brilliant light, and their lustre rivalled that of Jabne and

Sepphoris. When, toward the beginning of the eleventh century, darkness spread its wings over the Babylonia Jews, a bright day dawned in European countries. Cordova, Gerona, and Barcelona in Spain; Mayence, Worms, Speyer in Germany; Lunel, Montpellier, and Narbonne in Provence [France]; and Troyes, Rameru, and Dampierre in Champagne are stars of the first magnitude in the heaven of Jewish learning.[10]

Rabban Johanan ben Zakkai was the quintessential Pharisee—he believed that study was a religious act because it was the means for the molding of moral character. Nor was study merely ritualistic, to be performed only on stated occasions. It was a lifelong preoccupation, which explains why the Pharisees felt that one should always remain a student. Since all education was also moral education for religious Jews, there would be no "former students"; only "current students," in unending pursuit of higher learning and wisdom. To my own teacher, Professor Louis Finkelstein, I am indebted for the manner in which he has linked these ideas to what Johanan ben Zakkai did at Jabneh. Asked by a favorite pupil, Rabbi Joshua ben Hananya, as they walked through the ruins of Jerusalem, how Israel could obtain forgiveness for its sins without a Temple, Rabban Johanan replied: "We have a means of atonement as effective as the Temple itself—acts of loving kindness." The reply may appear astonishing, Dr. Finkelstein suggests, from the man who in the last days of Jerusalem had devoted his time not to remedial action for the suffering about him, but to the establishment of the Academy at Jabneh, where the study of Torah could be perpetuated. But the inconsistency, we are told, is superficial. In the establishment of the Academy he promoted loving kindness. He was enabling the pietist to master the science of life so as to act justly and love mercy. Indeed, so clearly was this understood by later disciples, that the record of Rabban Johanan's achievement in the establishment of the Academy at Jabneh is cited as an illustration of *gemilut hasadim*—acts of loving kindness.[11]

It is thus no exaggeration to claim for Jews that they were in effect the fathers of higher education and the builders of the first "universities" long before the idea of a university would first be tested in Europe, and even longer before adult education came upon the cultural scene in very recent times, and then only in western countries.

The First "Universities"

Of course, the chief purpose of their schools of higher learning was to teach "Jewish knowledge"—the mastery of biblical law. But to say this is also to make the point that by "biblical law" these teachers meant to include an understanding of the laws of nature, the traits of human nature, and the moral manner of comporting oneself in "God's world," an understanding of which these rabbi-scholars ardently believed was susceptible to human analysis and rational probing. Accordingly, it is wrong to describe either the early Pharisees or the later rabbis as narrow legalists or mere pedants. The Mishnah itself defines the Pharisee who aspires to become a wise man, as "one who is capable of learning from all men."[12] Indeed, in his consideration of a controversy between Gentile men of learning and members of his own academy, Rabbi Judah the Patriarch, the chief scholar in Palestine toward the end of the second Christian century, concluded and then ruled that "their view is preferable to ours."[13] Later, in Babylonia, a well-known rabbi-scholar established as axiomatic law: "Whoever says a wise thing, even if he is a non-Jew, is called wise."[14]

A careful study of their writings will also reveal that these Pharisee-rabbis were in close touch with the ruling philosophies of their own day. While they discarded the polytheistic basis of those teachings, they were also quick to adopt Greek philosophical logic and mathematics, and rules of Roman jurisprudence, not to mention the lessons they had learned from the study of philology—which included foreign languages—to help them probe the deepest meaning of language itself. They were, as a result, profoundly related to their surrounding cultures, whether Greek, Roman, or Persian. Indeed, the Talmud is replete with many "loan words"—perhaps as many as three thousand—borrowed from these neighboring societies, as well as many of their parables and popular sayings which had achieved international currency and had filtered into Jewish thought.[15]

Their interests carried over into the realm of science as well. It was not exceptional for them to consult the pagan Greek physicians, for example, in order to learn the laws of anatomy with greater precision than was available to them from their own sources.[16] Indeed, it became an important goal of many Jewish scholars in medieval times to become masters not only of medical science—even the Muslim and Christian population turned to them for advice and treatment—but to achieve prominence as mathematicians, astronomers, and even as cartographers. It is not widely known, for example, that two major early medieval centers of medical education and practice in Salerno and Montpellier, were probably founded by Jews, who also helped to develop and expand both schools. (The fact that medieval medicine for a long time was virtually a monopoly of Jewish and Muslim scientists may have much to do with the long-standing Christian prohibition against the "defilement" of its priests if they came in contact with human blood, diseased persons, or corpses. As we have already seen, these priestly rules themselves hark back to the levitical legislation of the Torah itself.) Indeed, in Andrew White's landmark nineteenth century work, *Warfare of Science with Theology*, the author writes: "To the Jews is largely due the building up of the School of Salerno, which we find flourishing in the tenth century . . . Still more important is the rise of the School of Montpellier; this was due almost entirely to Jewish physicians; and it developed medical studies to a yet higher point, doing much to create a medical profession worthy of the name throughout southern Europe."[17]

It is interesting to note that Jews—most of them rabbinical scholars—were on several occasions even granted the right to open universities of their own. In 1466, they embarked on a venture to establish such an institution in the Kingdom of Sicily. King John formally authorized them to set up a university, also called a *studium generale*, in any city they might choose, to engage and discharge doctors, jurists and others, "and in said university to arrange the introduction in all the approved sciences for those who seem proper thereto and others."[18] There is, however, no clear evidence that this unusual university was actually ever established. In the following century, in Mantua, a similar scheme was initiated by Jews in northern Italy, but again, we have no records to indicate that it ever materialized.

Despite these apparently failed attempts, those Jewish schools of higher learning noted earlier, whether in the East, in North Africa, or across the map of Europe, had, in any case, long functioned as universities where accumulated Jewish wisdom was the fundamental curriculum. Yet as we have seen, such explorations would inevitably include discussions dealing not only with specifically religious themes, but given the humanistic interests of both the scholars and the students, they would reach out to psychological, scientific, and literary themes, as well. Moreover, in certain respects these Jewish academies even went beyond the standard academic practice of most universities—whether medieval or modern—in which the principal educational dynamic was reflected in the magisterial relationship between the instructor and his students: the one who "gave," and the others who "received." Jewish academies brought scholars and disciples into direct contact—scholars who openly exchanged and debated their views with each other; and disciples who were not only expected to ask or debate questions with the scholars, but who were also encouraged to express their own views, some of which came to be accepted by their teachers even in preference to their very own. Rabbi Hanina, a leading Palestinian scholar of the third Christian century, provides us with a clue to the democratic, collegial style of those early Jewish "universities." "From my masters," he said, "I have learned much, and from my colleagues I learned more than from my masters; but I learned most from my students."[19]

As a result of Pharisaic efforts, universal literacy prevailed virtually among the entire Jewish community. Yet it should not be assumed that all who attended schools for higher learning as full-time students went on to become scholars. True, as we shall soon see, it was the Pharisees who were the first in history to organize public instruction for young male children within a "universal" educational system. In a most tell-tale, dramatic way, this points up the contribution these Jewish leaders made to the democratization and universalization of education, especially since most histories of education have led us to believe that it is the Greek and Roman legacy which was principally responsible for this massive cultural and humane achievement. It is a matter of record that the schools in all Hellenistic cities were essentially urban and discriminatory; they were never intended to encompass all of the residents of their communities. The majority of rural persons, whether in Egypt or in any other Hellenized country, never attended schools at all. In contrast, the Jewish elementary school was intended for all male children. Pharisaic legislative reforms made it obligatory for every community to attend to their education at the very time that the prestigious Greco-Roman civilization was still offering instruction to only a select few.

"A father should bear with his son"—keep him in school—"until the age of twelve," and only after that age could he request him to participate in his own work or have him learn a trade. So ruled the scholar-judges at the Usha academy in Palestine in the middle of the second century.[20] In fact, learning a trade was a goal which occupied the attention of most members of the population. Full-time scholars who went on to study at the higher academies were in relative terms much fewer in number. The rabbis themselves give us some idea of these ratios. "Such is the usual way of the world," they report: "A thousand enter the Bible school [elementary school], and a hundred pass from it to the study of the Mishnah; ten of them go on to Talmud study, and only one of them arrives at ordination as a rabbi-scholar."[21]

Nevertheless, these new traditions shaped by the Pharisees insisted that adult education was a life-long duty required of the entire population, and incumbent upon all Jews, even those who were artisans or tradesmen, and not academic scholars. To achieve this important agenda, it was arranged that the academies be required to open their doors wide every Sabbath afternoon—on the weekly day of rest from manual labor—so that the entire population could attend the public lectures given regularly to the assembled crowds by their leading scholars. While attendance at these educational programs was not obligatory, they were considered central to the mores and value-system of the community, and few could resist the prevailing social pressures by not participating.

Indeed, in Babylonia, beginning with the third Christian century, a major educational innovation was introduced by the scholars who presided over that country's Jewish academies—a custom which was to continue for long centuries thereafter. Known as the "Kallah"— most likely a Hebrew equivalent for what we would now call "extension courses"—it was convened by the chief scholars of each academy for two full months in each year: one in the month of *Adar* (at winter's end); the other during the month of *Elul* (at the close of summer). References in the Talmud indicate that on many occasions more than 12,000 persons were in attendance, men who had sought and received permission to leave their work, in order to join in the intensive study periods.[22] The rabbinical courts had even ruled that litigants who wished to attend the *Kallah* were not to be summoned to appear before them during these study months, in order not to cause these people to interrupt their studies.[23]

Some teaching methods adopted by the *Kallah* were remarkably similar to usages at modern universities. At the close of the *Kallah*, texts for the next one were announced by the academic heads, allowing participants to ponder them during the months intervening. At the end of each of the lectures (the daily sessions sometimes lasted far into the night) the floor was opened for questions, answers, and general discussion. Then, in the final week of the *Kallah*, the head of the academy would test and examine those who aspired to join the regular academy as full-time students, who would receive stipends in order to devote themselves wholly to scholarship. That such advanced educational principles and procedures became a permanent part of the Babylonian Jewish landscape for many centuries following the exile from Jerusalem is further evidence of the remarkable cultural revolution engineered by the Pharisees alongside the religious innovations of their liberal and expansive interpretations of the older biblical law. In a profound sense, these were their continuing answers to the older Roman evil: to produce and inspire a literate and cultured community which had knowledge of, and took increasing pride in, a tradition it would not permit even exile to destroy. This fundamental Pharisaic contribution is still very much at work within the contemporary Jewish community as well.

Compulsory Elementary Education

The Pharisees anticipated the modern public school by some seventeen centuries. This did not come about all at once, yet as the Talmud itself describes it, by the middle of the second Christian century, stringent rules were put into place which required that "teachers of young children should be appointed in each district and town and that children enter school at the age of six or seven."

Rabbi Judah said in the name of Rav:

> Verily, the name of that man is to be blessed, to wit, Joshua son of Gamala, for but for him the Torah would have been forgotten from Israel. For at first if a child had a father, his father taught him, and if he had no father he did not learn at all . . . they then made an ordinance that teachers of children should be appointed in Jerusalem . . . Even so, however, if a child had a father, the father would take him up to Jerusalem and have him taught there, and if not, he would not learn there. They therefore ordained that teachers should be appointed in each prefecture, and that boys should enter school at the age of sixteen or seventeen. [They did so] and if the teacher punished them they used to rebel and leave school. Finally, Joshua son of Gamala came and ordained that teachers of young children should be appointed in each district and each town and that children should enter school at the age of six or seven.[24]

It is interesting to note that when Talmudic authorities wished to describe the importance of one city or district over the other, they habitually did so by indicating the number of schools and pupils to be found there—other considerations played no role. Education was not provided completely free, however; parents had to pay the wages of the teacher. But the city or town council was required to participate as well, in order to pay for the tuition of the sons of the poor, as well as of the orphans, since neither of these groups were in any position to pay these expenses. As a result, classes were open to all: the sons of paupers and rich men; the children of notables who sat alongside the offspring of the "ignorant"; and all, together, even the children of "wicked men," joined one another in attending classes. Learning was taken very seriously by parents and teachers—and presumably, by the children—alike. Rabbi Samuel son of Shilath, early in the third century, hammered home this point: "Less than six [years old] do not accept them; at six years of age accept them and stuff them [with Torah knowledge] like oxen!"[25] Indeed, so seriously did the Pharisees view the importance of the education of the young that they went so far as to lay down the rule proclaimed by no less a personage than Judah the Patriarch, chief scholar of Palestine at that time: "One may not suspend the studies of school children even for the rebuilding of the Temple, itself."[26]

These are surely views no other Jewish group or sect—especially not the Sadducees—could have espoused at that time and with such evident fervor. Nor could any other Jewish party in the years immediately preceding or in the centuries which followed the destruction of Jerusalem have been capable of insuring the creative survival of their people in the manner of the Pharisees.

For these achievements, it is important to review and revise old attitudes to the Pharisees—attitudes forged primarily by theological arguments and fighting words enunciated two thousand years ago in the midst of a "religious battle" that can no longer be relevant today. Serious and sincere Christian-Jewish dialogue should recognize that much of what the Pharisees achieved has also become part of our democratic and humane culture.

The Pharisees' principal contribution to the western world may still be seen in our contemporary open and democratic societies which are dominated by a penchant for education and research that knows few boundaries or borders. Their heirs in the darker and almost-closed medieval society of Europe would continue to play an even more crucial role in helping to bridge a variety of lands, peoples, and cultures.

For all of its intolerance and meanness to Jews, the Middle Ages proved to be a rich and seminal time in Jewish history—a time when Jews would serve as the catalytic agents for cultural and economic change and growth.

NOTES

1. Louis Finkelstein, *The Pharisees*, (Philadelphia: Jewish Publication Society, Second Revised Edition, 1940), p. xxx. For a good one volume overview of the Pharisees, see also Jacob Neusner, *From Politics to Piety: The Emergence of Pharisaic Judaism*, (Englewood Cliffs: Prentice-Hall, 1973).

2. *Ibid.*, p. xxix.

3. As recently as April, 1985, on the "Op-Ed" page of the *New York Times*, Harvey Cox, a professor of Christian theology at Harvard Divinity School, writing on "The Trial of Jesus," still implicates the Jewish community and their Pharisee-leaders in the death of Jesus. The Sanhedrin, which was composed of both Sadducees and Pharisees, Cox alleges, "had to get rid of Jesus."

In a sharp rejoinder, a second Christian theologian—one much more versed in the history of that period—A. Roy Eckardt, wrote a "Letter to the Editor" which was headed: "Responsibility for Jesus' Death Is a Nonquestion." Eckardt wrote, *inter alia:*

"Equally specious is Mr. Cox's allegation that Sanhedrin members 'had to get rid of Jesus.' Much more serious is his attempt to make large numbers of Jews collaborators of the Romans in Jesus' crucifixion. That accusation has long since been exposed as untruthful. The National Conference of Catholic Bishops has correctly declared, 'The Jewish people never were, nor are they now, guilty of the death of Christ.'

"Jesus was a messianic revolutionary, who was executed with unnumbered other Jews by the Romans under Pontius Pilate (anything but the flunky of alleged Jewish conspirators that Mr. Cox tries to make him). Jesus the Jew died as the beloved, though failed, deliverer of his people from the hated Roman oppressor. *The New Testament documents culpably shift Roman responsibility for Jesus' crucifixion onto 'the Jews.' That finding is an all-decisive truism of responsible historical scholarship, which Professor Cox fails to make clear.* (Italics added.)

"But the infinitely more fateful question is why the Christian world must keep driving itself to raise the issue of Jewish linkage to Jesus' death. The psychological and moral problem here extends to expressions of Jewish innocence as much as of Jewish 'guilt.' What is there in the collective Christian psyche that demands repeated, unrelenting concentration upon the 'place' of Jews in Jesus' trial and crucifixion? Where is the moral legitimacy in keeping this kind of pot boiling? It is not even a half-century since the Japanese attacked the United States, yet there bygones can wholly be bygones, and Americans can enjoy every available Japanese automobile.

"After 2,000 years the question of responsibility for Jesus' death is a nonquestion, or ought to be. It ought to have been buried long ago, together with all other efforts at hostility to Jews. Rather than concentrating upon reputed Jewish (and Roman) 'malice' in the death of Jesus, Harvey Cox could more responsibly expend his time in fighting the Christian malice toward Jews that the churches inculcate every 'Holy Week.'" See *New York Times*, April 16, 1985.

See also Franz Mussner, *Tractate on the Jews: The Significance of Judaism for Christian Faith* (Philadelphia: Fortress Press, 1984), especially Chapter 5: "Theological 'Reparation,'" pp. 154–214. The description of the author by his translator, Leonard Swidler, a leading American Catholic ecumenist, is significant: "Franz Mussner . . . a Roman Catholic New Testament scholar . . .

was no different from the vast majority of the rest of Christian scholars, namely, filled with undisturbed prejudices against Judaism. Then with Vatican II and its aftermath, he underwent a *metanoia* and ventured forth on the rereading of the Scriptures, which are at the basis of Christian teaching, with new eyes as far as Judaism is concerned. . . . The critique of Christian teaching is at times severe, but the author is clearly still a committed Christian (or perhaps better, *because* the author is a committed Christian . . .) . . . The small but growing number of Christian theologians working in the area of Jewish-Christian dialogue are already doing this." (See Swidler's "Translator's Foreword," p. viii.) A noted Jewish theologian, Michael Wyschogrod, in a review-essay of Mussner's book, regards it as a landmark work, which, along with several others, helps set the stage for a new era in Jewish-Christian dialogue. See his "A New Stage in Jewish–Christian Dialogue," *Judaism*, Summer, 1982, pp. 355–65.

4. Based upon the Jerusalem Talmud: *Berakot* 14b; and *Sotah* 20b; and on Babylonian Talmud: *Sotah* 22b. Quoted by George F. Moore, *Judaism in the First Centuries of the Christian Era* (Cambridge: Harvard University Press, 1927), Vol. II, p. 193.

5. Mishnah: *Abot* 6:4.

6. *Ibid.*, 1:4.

7. *Ibid.*, 1:6.

7a. For this translation of Deut. 6:4 see *The Torah: The Five Books of Moses* (Philadelphia: The Jewish Publication Society of America, 1962), p. 336 (including notes).

8. Mishnah: *Megillah* 3:1.

9. Moore, *op. cit.*, Vol. I, p. 322.

10. Louis Ginzberg, *Students, Scholars and Saints* (Philadelphia: The Jewish Publication Society, 1928), pp. 35–36. All Jewish scholars are of the opinion that Johanan ben Zakkai "guided both the faith and the people of Israel beyond the disaster of the destruction of the second temple and then laid foundations which have endured to this very day" (Jacob Neusner). For an imaginative description of the life and times of ben Zakkai see Jacob Neusner *First Century Judaism in Crisis* (Nashville: Abingdon Press, 1975).

11. Professor Louis Finkelstein, "Hasideanism in Transition: From Jose ben Joezer to Jabneh." (Based upon unpublished, undated lecture notes.)

12. Mishnah: *Abot* 4:1.

13. Babylonian Talmud: *Pesahim* 94b.

14. Babylonian Talmud: *Megillah* 16a.

15. See especially two works by Saul Lieberman: *Greek in Jewish Palestine* (New York: Jewish Theological Seminary of America, 1942), and *Hellenism in Jewish Palestine* (New York: Jewish Theological Seminary of America, 1950). See also Martin Hengel, *Judaism and Hellenism*, (London: SCM Press, 1974). Vol. I, Chapter II: "Hellenism in Palestine as a Cultural Force and its Influence on the Jews," pp. 58–106.

16. See Babylonian Talmud, for example, *Niddah* 60b.

17. Andrew White, *Warfare of Science with Theology* (New York: D. Appleton, 1896), Volume II, p. 33. In Salerno, in 846, Arabs and Jews had joined together to found the first university in Europe specializing in medicine. In Provence, at the University of Montpellier, Jewish teachers offered courses in medicine ranging from surgery to ophthalmology.

18. Cecil Roth, *The History of the Jews of Italy* (Philadelphia: Jewish Publication Society of America, 1946), p. 216.

19. Bablyonian Talmud: *Taanith* 7a.

20. Babylonian Talmud: *Ketubot* 50a.

21. *Midrash Rabba* on Ecclesiastes 7:28.

22. Babylonian Talmud: *Baba Metzia* 86a.

23. Babylonian Talmud: *Baba Kamma* 113a.

24. Babylonian Talmud: *Baba Batra* 21a.

25. Babylonian Talmud: *Baba Batra* 21a; also *Ketubot* 50a.

26. Babylonian Talmud: *Shabbat* 119b.

CHAPTER IX

Jews as Inter-Religious Brokers: Commerce, Culture, and the "Judaizers"

HISTORY TRANSFORMED ONE SMALL NATION TUCKED AWAY IN A TINY corner of the world into a cosmopolitan, international people.

Ironically, this unprecedented but tenuous status imposed upon Jews from without—often the clear result of Church-inspired restrictions and expulsions—caused them to play a distinctive and unique role among the nations. Unwittingly, they became the intermediaries between continents and cultures—the human bridge that connected East with West, Christendom with Islam. They functioned as vital liaisons and conduits in the realms of commerce, culture, and religion. And though their important role as cross-fertilizers of ideas and institutions has traditionally been minimized or overlooked, it is clear that this factor in Western civilization has produced far-ranging benefits. It is a story more historians should have told us about. Their almost complete silence on the subject is still another facet of the Christian problem: an inability to ascribe positive significance to the creative ubiquitousness of the Jewish presence within Christendom.

Their Almost-Universal Presence

The Jews, variously called Semites, Orientals, and non-Aryans, were in fact among the very first Europeans. They reached Germany

153

sometime in the first or second century of the Christian era, almost one hundred and fifty years before the Germans themselves finally crossed the Rhine. By the early fourth century, there was already a flourishing Jewish community in Cologne. Strabo, the Greek historian and geographer who was Julius Caesar's contemporary, had already written of Jews in his *Geography* that "it is hard to find a spot in the inhabited world where this race [*sic*] does not dwell or traffic."[1]

From Arab sources we also learn that Jews constituted the majority in many cities across the Iberian peninsula before its reconquest by the Christians. Granada, for example, known as the "last citadel of Muslim culture in Spain," was once called by Muslims *Igranatat al Yahud*—"Jewish Granada"—not only because of its extremely large local Jewish population, but also because the Muslims themselves recognized that Jews had actually founded the city several centuries before it had become the capital of the Moorish kingdom. Similarly, of neighboring Lucena, it was said by Arabs that "the entire township consists of Jews." Other Arab sources inform us that Barcelona, located in the heartland of Spanish Christendom, had "as many Jews as Christians," before the reconquest of Toledo in 1085.[2]

Farther to the north, in France, Germany, and England, Jewish numbers were not as large, yet in some towns, like London, at least one out of twenty inhabitants was a Jew. Salo W. Baron has noted: "The influences emanating from this single, centrally located community [of London], through its ramified business contacts with nobles, clerics, and burghers; its extension into rural England by virtue of frequent, though legally precarious, land tenures; and its manifold relations with the European continent, may have given many a stimulus to the rise of the medieval English civilization."[3]

He further remarks that

> . . . fuller consideration of personal relationships between Jews and Christians would elucidate many aspects of Jewish influence . . . there were innumerable instances of the daily exchange of ideas as well as goods between the two groups, exchanges which in their totality undoubtedly had even farther-reaching effects. Agobard, the well-known anti-Jewish archbishop of Lyons during the Carolingian age, speaks of his "almost daily" meetings with Jews. Other, less prejudiced Christians had still fewer objections to conversing daily with their Jewish neighbors. Positively or negatively, such relationships must have helped shape the medieval outlook in a direct, though often intangible, fashion . . .
>
> . . . These personal contacts may have diminished in both frequency

and intimacy after the rise of official ghettos toward the end of the Middle Ages; but they were never completely severed, except through the physical removal of Jews through expulsion.[4]

Ironically, tensions that existed between Christians and Muslims sometimes worked in favor of the Jews. Jewish merchants, it seems, were the only persons who could pass freely between the two spheres of influence—one controlled by the Crescent, the other by the Cross. Less than two centuries after the rise of Islam, Jewish merchants already held a virtual monopoly on all trade that moved between the separate hegemonies of Church and Mosque. In 847, the well-known Arab travel writer Ibn Khordadbeh, who also served as Postmaster-General of the Caliph of Baghdad, described the amazing ubiquitousness of Jewish merchants. In his *Book of Roads* he wrote:

> These merchants speak Arabic, Persian, Roman [Greek], the language of the Franks, Andalusians, and Slavs. They journey from west to east, from east to west, partly on land, partly by sea. They take ships in the lands of the Franks, on the Western Sea [Marseilles, on the Mediterranean] . . . and make for Antioch . . . They embark in the Red Sea and sail to El-Jar [the port of Medina] and Jeddah [the port of Mecca] . . . They sail down the Tigris for Oman, Sind, Hind, and China . . . They also make different journeys by land . . . starting from Spain or from France to Morocco, then to Tangiers, whence they march to Kairowan and the capital of Egypt . . . Sometimes they take a route from Constantinople, passing through the country of the Slavs . . . or they embark on the Black Sea and arrive at Balkh [Afghanistan] betaking themselves from there across the Oxus, to continue their journey toward Yourt, Toghozghor, and from there to China.

These Jewish merchants did not serve only as cultural intermediaries between Europe and the East. They undoubtedly introduced the West to many luxuries in exchange for furs and nonprecious metals. Scholars have established that these commercial travellers introduced Europeans to such items as oranges, apricots, sugar, rice, cinnamon, sandal-wood, camphor, sofas, and mattresses! These are only a few of the many "exotic" products that Europe had never before laid eyes on, and which are now regarded as staples. But soon enough the unique contribution of the Jews would not be limited only to the items they were exchanging. It would go to the very heart of the economic system itself.

What factors were responsible for turning the Jews away from their older pursuit of agriculture and leading them to the broader highways of commerce and trade?

Agriculture and Land Tenure

Many in the West, even those exposed to a higher education, have been led to believe that medieval Jews were essentially Shylock-like moneylenders rapaciously intent on grinding out their "pound of flesh."[5] Closer to the truth is the fact that while some were merchants, in early Europe, many had been farmers or craftsmen. Jewish social and economic life was radically altered only when papal edicts—especially Innocent III's "Fourth Lateran Council" in 1215—targeted Jews as "outcasts" by requiring them to wear the "badge of shame" publicly. Until the end of the twelfth century, personal relations between Christians and Jews had been on the whole fairly friendly. By then, however, the prelates of the Church sought to prevent close relations between the two groups. Not only was the badge then instituted, but at the same time Jews were prohibited to own Christian serfs, churchmen fearing that the latter might be converted to Judaism. Since farming was dependent upon slave hands, in one fell swoop this ecclesiastical ban removed many Jews from agriculture. But there were other insidious factors as well that drove Jews away from this occupation, one in which they had in fact excelled over the course of many centuries.

The eminent medieval historian James Parkes has laid bare certain other issues regarding land tenure. The following adversely affected Jews:

> The Jew had absolutely no certainty that he could bequeath property to his son, so that there could not be with him, as with the ordinary Christian possessed of a certain competence, the hope of rooting and securing his family in permanent property. The facts about inheritance, in so far as Jews are concerned, are as uncertain and contradictory as almost every other fact of medieval Jewish lilfe. If the maxim be stated that the Jew could not bequeath property, there is ample evidence to support it; if it be replied that the average Jew obviously did bequeath property to his children, and they as obviously enjoyed it without disturbance, this is also amply proved. The one fact which emerges from this contradiction is insecurity, and this would be much more evident when the inheritance was land, which could not be concealed, than when it was goods, which might be hidden or whose value might be reduced for "probate."[6]

Living in constant uncertainty concerning the rights to land tenure was surely a fact of negative impact for those Jews who might have wished to continue farming. In addition to legal turmoil and confusion, one had also to take into account the growing unrest among Christian peasants who were periodically stirred up by anti-Jewish sermons, especially in the weeks immediately preceding Easter. The last straw, of course, were the expulsions from England, France, and the Iberian peninsula, which struck each of these Jewish communities from the thirteenth through the fifteenth century. In England expulsion took place in 1290. It was followed shortly thereafter in France, where Jews were expelled in 1306 and in some parts of the country a few decades later. In Spain, in 1391, the Jewish population was heavily persecuted, so that only a smaller remnant of that long-standing community would remain until their final and complete banishment in 1492. While Jews may have been "permitted" to own land, in the light of these uncertainties and mortal fears, it would be more objective to say that it was not the Jew who withdrew from the land but the land that withdrew from him.

For many centuries before their expulsion from western Europe, Jews had been welcomed as highly prized farmers in the very lands from which they would later be forced to flee—France, Spain and Portugal. They had been attracted as new settlers to these regions because they brought with them from various parts of North Africa and the Mediterranean basin well-practiced skills and refined techniques of land cultivation which these countries desperately needed. In many cases, too, the new crops they brought to these parts of Europe gave them special status as pioneering and highly productive tillers of the soil.

From the rabbinic legal literature of tenth-century Spain, we learn that there were many innovative Jewish farmers then living in Andalusia, some of whom had even pioneered new irrigation schemes in their cornfields and orchards. In Sicily and elsewhere in Italy, Jews were also among the first to cultivate the mulberry. The flourishing silk industry related thereto was largely controlled by them. Where suitable conditions allowed, Jews also specialized in dairy farming, fruit-growing, and even in viticulture. Indeed, the great medieval Rabbi Solomon Itzhaki—better known by the acronym "Rashi"—grew grapes for a living so that he could freely offer his services as a teacher of biblical and Talmudic subjects at his adult academy in the French district of Champagne. Benjamin of Tudela, that peripatetic Jew who in the middle of the twelfth century travelled thousands of miles in order to observe Jewish life on several continents, found several Jewish communities wholly engaged in farming in Greece as well as in the Balkans.

Economic historians agree that in the twelfth century a money-economy finally replaced barter in most of Europe. One student of that era reports:

> This transition came in Western Europe mainly in the eleventh and twelfth centuries. It spread from the king as the head of the military state downwards; he found it more efficient to keep an army of mercenaries under his continual control than to depend upon the often unwilling service of his vassals. Hence the increasing practice of commuting the duty of military service for a fixed sum (named "scutage" in England), and this later on led to general taxation not alone of vassals but of all persons living in the territory under the control of the king. The same practice was soon followed by abbeys and monasteries who desired to build, and by the superior nobles who wished to have a force at command, or desired to build castles, or to go on crusade. For all these purposes, warfare, taxation, building, or crusading, actual cash was much more efficient than aids in kind or service.[7]

A curious and fortuitous combination of circumstances now came into play. It would affect not only the lives of European Jews but would also serve to provide the "actual cash" that now became essential to fuel the economic expansion about to begin in Europe. In this major transition from late feudalism to early "capitalism," the Jews of Europe, who could no longer effectively remain on the land, would play a major economic role—especially in light of their successful pre-history as innovative travellers and merchants.

Nationalism and Europe's New Money-Economy

To understand properly the new and, at first, indispensable role of Jews as "money merchants," it is important that we stake out the differing attitudes toward interest between the Church and the Jewish community.

In line with the view of Thomas Aquinas, the Church believed that it was unjust "to sell something which does not exist." Accordingly, all interest came to be labelled "usury" and was prohibited as *mercatura illicita*, or illegal commerce. Those who engaged in the practice were subject to excommunication, although on the church principle that one may commit hostile acts against one's enemy—*ubi jus belli, ibi jus usurae*—it was permitted to take usury from Jews. In point of fact, however, the Church was simply not ready for the transition from an agrarian to a commercial economy. Loans in an agrarian economy were extremely dangerous because in the event of default on principal or interest lenders could foreclose and take away the farmer's land—his only source of livelihood. A ready and venturesome group of capital risk-takers was urgently required. Because, by then, many Jews had been virtually driven off the land, this was a new economic function they were prepared to perform. As a result, and perhaps even in spite of itself, Europe would benefit: cash was made available for many cultural, religious and commercial undertakings. (Indeed, when we marvel at some of the great artistic and architectural achievements of many of the grand medieval buildings still standing in Europe, little do we realize that they could not have been built without massive expenditures of money, which not even the kings or lords of the time could privately accumulate).

A penetrating analysis of the Jewish position was offered by my teacher, the eminent historian Salo W. Baron:

> From biblical times there existed the outright prohibition, "Unto thy brother thou shalt not lend upon interest" (Deuteronomy 23:21) . . . The approach of the ancient and medieval interpreters to that passage was based on ethics and psychology rather than economics. We are told in the same verse that "unto a foreigner (or stranger) thou mayest lend upon interest," but it did not occur to any of these interpreters to look for an economic rationale for this distinction. Under the conditions of ancient Palestine, lending money to a fellow Israelite usually meant extending credit to a needy farmer or craftsman for whom the return of the original amount plus the prevailing high interest was an extreme hardship. At the same time the foreigner, that is, the Phoenician-Canaanite merchant, as a rule borrowed money in order to invest it in his business for profit. Such a productive form of credit justified the original lender to participate in some form or other in the profits derived by the borrower . . .
>
> . . . On the other hand, economic realities particularly in countries like medieval England, France, northern Italy, and Germany, where banking became the very economic foundations of many Jewish communities, forced the Jews to make some theoretical concessions . . . (Rabbi) Meir ben Simon of Narbonne argued that "divine law prohibited usury, not interest . . . Not only the peasant must borrow money, but also the lords, and even the great king of France . . . The king would have lost many fortified places [castles], if his faithful agent, a Jew of our city, had not secured for him money at a high price." . . . Addressing his own coreligionists, a German rabbi, Shalom ben Isaac Sekel, insisted that "the reason why the Torah holds a higher place in

Germany than in other countries is that the Jews here charge interest to gentiles and need not engage in a [time-consuming] occupation. On this score they have time to study the Torah. He who does not study uses his profits to support the students of the Torah."[8]

Jews were thus unaffected by any prohibitions of their own laws from lending to Gentiles. Since they were also outside of the sphere of the canon law of the Church, they could not be prevented from engaging in money-lending. In the process, Jews shored up much of the European economy for three centuries beginning with the twelfth. They were regarded as the recognized money merchants by virtually all of the upper classes—including churchmen—who required funds for travel, building, fighting, or even crusading. Indeed, records indicate that Aaron of Lincoln, England's fabled twelfth-century Jewish financier, advanced the funds required for the building of nine Cistercian monasteries, as well as the abbey of St. Albans! All of this would of course be forgotten in England when its Jews were expelled in 1290.

It would, however, be a mistake to think that all Jews in this period were active as money-lenders. It is equally false to imagine that all Europeans had already come into the orbit of the money-economy. In feudal Europe, even down to the eighteenth century, a large number of inhabitants probably never used money throughout their entire lives since they were still mostly vassals serving on the large rural estates of their lords. Jews surely had very little contact with these people. Jews now found it necessary to live in larger towns, and in their dealings with burghers, artistocrats, bishops, and church leaders, those Jews who practiced money-lending came into regular contact with the Christian world. This was especially significant as regards their relations with the royalty of Europe and the members of their courts.

With kings and emperors, Jews enjoyed a most ambivalent relationship. When they were needed as capital providers, all went well; when they could easily be replaced by others, kings vied with one another in expelling all of "their" Jews. By the thirteenth century, a serious challenge to Jewish money-lending began to appear on the European scene. This came from the bankers in northern Italy, who, with the assistance of high church officials in the Roman Curia, set themselves up in direct competition to Jewish lenders. Indeed, these financiers, collectively known as "the Lombards," were often angrily referred to by Jews as "the Pope's usurers." In many ways, this title aptly fitted them: they came into prominence by supplying money to debtors of the Church all over Europe, who were required to pay cash regularly for their papal dues remitted to Rome. The great might of the Roman Curia assured these Lombards almost immediate success—for they could invoke the threat of excommunication for those who did not pay their debts, however usurious.

Nevertheless, the lasting political influence of Jewish money-lending can be seen in the way it had earlier served the purposes of many European kings. Jews who helped these monarchs consolidate their "nations" into central powers—often in direct opposition to the interests of the Church in Rome—assisted in the growth of a new sense of nationality, a force that would ultimately crush medieval feudalism with its strong ties to the papacy. Their success in this direction, however, was not without its sacrifices. Even when in favor with these monarchs, Jews were still regarded as their property—as part of the royal right of "eminent domain." As a result, properties belonging to Jewish money-lenders were always potentially the property of kings. Moreover, "in allowing the Jew to sue for his usurious debt in the king's courts," writes one historian, "the kings naturally claimed their dues, and, in addition, taxed them to an amount which was never under a fifth and often reached as much as a quarter or a third of their income . . . In fact, in this way, the kings of England and Spain, and to a less extent the kings of France and the emperors of the Holy Roman empire, became the arch-usurers of their realms."[9]

In addition to their indirect economic role in buttressing the sense of nationhood descending upon Europe even before the rise of Protestantism, Jews played an even greater religious and cultural role in helping to set the stage for the Reformation itself.

Jewish Religious Influence: "Judaizers" and Others

Balaam, the pagan soothsayer and wizard, had been employed by an enemy of Israel, Balak, king of Moab, "to come . . . and curse this people." The biblical episode, of course, ends on a happy note: Balaam sets out to curse Israel and ends up by blessing them.[10] In similar vein, over the centuries Christians showed their contempt for Jews by labelling with the name "Judaizer" colleagues who engaged in unorthodox practices or heresies. History suggests, however, that what was used as an epithet of reproach and derision turned out to be an affirmation of the importance not only of those dubbed "Judaizers," but, ironically, of the continuing influence of Judaism itself. What was cursed proved a blessing, even if sometimes in disguise.

One writer provides us with a concise history of the term "Judaizer." His description leads to a single, clear conclusion: "Judaizing" became, in effect, a code word for "Jewish influence." He notes:

In the decrees of the Church Councils, the term gained currency from the time of the Council of Laodicea in the fourth century onward. It was used by Christian ecclesiastics like Agobard, who charged Christians at Lyons (in the ninth century) with Jewish inclinations and habits. In the historical literature of the twelfth and thirteenth centuries, the term "Judaizer" won frequent place, and came to designate either individuals or groups, who, as in Lombardy, adopted a Jewish outlook on life, and Jewish forms of ceremony and conduct. It was employed to designate certain heretical groups which had challenged Papal authority. Papal Bulls during these centuries when heresy flourished are filled with references to "Judaizers" and "Re-Judaizers," the latter term being applied to Jewish converts to Christianity who later returned to their original faith.

The age of the Renaissance and Reformation found the phrase "Judaizer" popular in every camp of the Christian Church. The Catholic party used it to designate the reform movements of Wycliffe and Lollard, and employed it against Reuchlin, Luther, Melanchthon, Zwingli, Calvin and their contemporaries. The Reformers in turn accused others of their opponents of "Judaizing" . . . It was an irony of circumstances that the Church itself should be accused of "Judaizing" by the Catharist heretics and later by the Protestant Reformers in their turn.[11]

It seems clear to me that this amounts to a grudging awareness of the vitality of Judaism, despite dire Christian predictions of its early demise. How else can we explain recurring references to religious ideas and structures—closely resembling Judaism itself—which like a ghost that would not go away, kept reappearing inside Christianity itself! If we strip away the rhetoric and the polemic, we are sure to find that the Protestant Reformation cannot be fully explained—not even by political or economic theories—without taking into account the positive influences of Judaism itself, not to mention those "Judaizing" tendencies in general.

The essential connection between Judaism and many of the key ideas of various early Protestant groups was in the need of the reformers to rediscover the "Old Testament." They intended to make the Bible the source of their own authenticity, as against Canon law and Church tradition that served as the fountainhead of Catholic authority. But this "biblical connection" of Protestants did not, of course, spring into being overnight. For many centuries, even in certain older Catholic circles, Christian intellectuals and philosophers had been turning to the study of Hebrew, and even to medieval Jewish philosophy, to come closer to the sources of their own beliefs.

Medieval Christian thinkers were affected by Jewish thought in a variety of ways. Usually, it was through the medium of Latin versions of books of Jewish philosophy that had been translated from the original Hebrew. There are numerous examples, but only two will be cited here. The first is a major philosophical tract, *Mekor Hayyim* ("Fountain of Life") which was translated into Latin around 1160 as *Fons Vitae*, by Dominicus Gundisalvi, the Archdeacon of Segovia, together with Johannes Avendehut (originally Ibn Daud), a well known Spanish physician who had converted from Judaism. There is, in fact, a good deal of amusement connected with this significant work. For many centuries, Christians had actually believed it to be the work of a person they had dubbed Avicebron, and whom they thought to be a Christian scholar. Only little more than a century ago, in the 1850s, was it belatedly "discovered" that Avicebron was actually Rabbi Solomon ibn Gabirol (1020–1058) of Spain! And all through these many centuries it was *his* text—that of a Jew—which Church scholars regarded as a classical work and used as the critical basis for their own philosophical and theological learning. It had a neoplatonic orientation and, accordingly, was welcomed by many Church scholastics already nurtured on the philosophical speculations of St. Augustine concerning the nature of form and spirit.[12]

Ironically, the great Moses Maimonides (1135–1204) became in very many important ways one of the leading philosophical and theological mentors of the Catholic intellectual community of the Middle Ages. His *Guide to the Perplexed* (1190) first appeared in the Arabic language which he wrote using the Hebrew alphabet. Shortly after its initial appearance it was translated into Hebrew for those Jews who did not understand Arabic. A few decades later, an anonymous author translated this book—which sought to harmonize the philosophical thought of Aristotle with the monotheistic teachings of the Hebrew Bible—into Latin, as *Dux Neutrorum*. From this translation it came into vogue all over Europe among many Christian theologians— Alexander of Hales, William of Auvergne, Albertus Magnus, and Thomas Aquinas, to mention only a few.

Thomas Aquinas (1227–1274) was the eminent disciple of Albertus Magnus: both had strong Jewish associations. In his chief work, *Summa Theologiae*, Aquinas refers frequently and approvingly to Rabbi Solomon ibn Gabirol's work, *Fons Vitae*—although, of course, he believed it to be a work of a Christian. But it was Maimonides' *Guide to the Perplexed* that influenced Aquinas most. An interesting, yet infrequently noted paradox came into play: Aquinas was accused by his Christian adversaries of having succumbed to "the ideas of Jews and Pharisees," while many Jews found his philosophical arguments so attractive that his works gained currency in Jewish circles in the form of Hebrew translations. No better example of cross-fertilization can be adduced. Think of it: Jewish ideas that had entered Aquinas' own Christian philosophy returned to Jews, full circle.

Sometimes the influence of Judaism on medieval Christianity was the result of the direct assistance of Jews, or Jewish converts to Christianity, who served either as collaborators or as teachers. Actually, there were many more personal intellectual encounters between Christian and Jewish scholars than we might suspect, especially in countries like Italy from the thirteenth through the sixteenth century. Some of these contacts even involved direct collaboration and joint efforts. Records are available to show that numerous Christians were attending Jewish services. Salo Baron reminds us that "as early as the ninth century, Agobard had bitterly complained of some Christians in the archdiocese of Lyons who claimed 'that the Jews preach better to them than our priests.' In Spain and Renaissance Italy, especially, where the social intercourse was more intimate and the Jewish preachers were in better command of the vernacular, Jewish sermons were often extremely popular among the educated classes."[13] He goes on to state, however, that no one shall ever really be able to gauge the extent of the transmission of Jewish concepts to the Christian public through these oratorical performances. I would demur: these were not merely "oratorical performances" as such. I would hazard an educated guess that despite the obvious impossibility of recourse to any recorded proof of the lasting influence of these Jewish sermons— by their very nature, the effects of even the best of sermons tend to be ephemeral—attendance at medieval Jewish services, was a brave Christian act that made an important statement. In the intolerant Middle Ages, Christians who voluntarily attended a synagogue in order to listen to Jewish sermons were clearly not going there merely as curiosity-seekers or as spiritual tourists looking for exotic experiences. Undoubtedly, they carried over into their own Christian communities some of the "unusual" religious ideas or scriptural interpretations they had first heard from Jewish pulpits. As a practicing rabbi—one might say as a "participant-observer"—I am a frequent witness to a similar process taking place today but, of course, in a radically different, open and free society. Indeed, even the same cautious historian—Salo Baron—might agree, for he also writes that "one may take it for granted that in innumerable instances [in the medieval period] individual Christians, clerics as well as laymen, sought the advice of their Jewish friends in the interpretation of obscure passages in the Old Testament."[14]

But these informal contacts would ultimately lead to a larger role for

Jewish religious thought once the Old Testament began to appear in translation. This was especially true in western Europe. Now entire Christian populations, and not merely a small number of learned clergy, would be able to read and study "Jewish ideas" as inscribed in the Hebrew Bible itself. They were no longer totally dependent upon their clergy as the sole source of Biblical knowledge or inspiration. The influence of the translated Jewish scripture was enormous.

From the point of view of Christian religious history, the Hebrew Bible became a necessary tool in strengthening the new and rising movement of Protestant dissent. Without an accessible and understandable Hebrew Bible translated into the vernacular of English- and German-speaking countries, it is difficult to see how Protestantism could have taken hold at all. Yet few church people today have been schooled to understand how much the Reformation, as well as the politics of the modern nation-state, are indebted to the Jewish ideas of the Hebrew Bible. It is time to recognize those crucial Jewish elements; they are an integral part of Europe's crossing over from its older and outworn medieval culture to the birth of modern society; from the twilight of the Middle Ages to the dawn of our own, newer age.

NOTES

1. See Marvin Lowenthal, *The Jews of Germany: The Story of Sixteen Centuries* (Philadelphia: Jewish Publication Society of America, 1936), p.2. Strabo himself died fifty years before the Jews were exiled from Jerusalem by the Romans in 70 C.E.

2. Salo W. Baron, *Ancient and Medieval Jewish History,* ed. Leon A. Feldman (New Brunswick: Rutgers University Press, 1972), p. 242.

3. *Ibid.,* pp. 243.

4. *Idem.,* pp. 243–44.

5. It is instructive to note that Shakespeare's play, *The Merchant of Venice,* which depicted a repulsive Jew by the name of Shylock as one of its leading protagonists, was written at a time when no Jews were living in England. The negative imagery of a rampant Jewish stereotype was in itself sufficient to allow the playwright to communicate to audiences nurtured only on tales about mythical, demonic Jews.

6. James Parkes, *The Jew in the Medieval Community* (London: Soncino Press, 1938), p. 264.

7. Joseph Jacobs, *Jewish Contributions to Civilization* (Philadelphia: The Jewish Publication Society of America, 1919), pp. 205–6.

8. Salo W. Baron, et al, *Economic History of the Jews* (New York: Schocken Books, 1975), pp. 52–54.

9. Jacobs, *op. cit.*, pp. 209–10.

10. See Deuteronomy, chapters 22–24.

11. Louis I. Newman, *Jewish Influence on Christian Reform Movements* (New York: Columbia University Press, 1925), pp. 1–3.

12. See Solomon ibn Gabirol, *The Fountain of Life*, trans. Harry E. Wedeck (New York: Philosophical Library, 1962), Introduction (unpaged).

13. Baron, *Ancient and Medieval Jewish History*, p. 256.

14. *Ibid.*, p. 254.

CHAPTER X

The Influence of the Translated Hebrew Bible: Language, Religion, and Politics

TRANSLATIONS CAN BE MIGHTY TOOLS IN FORGING LINKS AND BUILDING bridges.

It was only when the Bible was made available in a non-Semitic language, a language that travelled throughout the ancient civilized world, that its message could be brought beyond the household of Israel. This was the result of the first Greek translation, which came to be known as the Septuagint.

The Septuagint (short form of the Latin *septuaginta*, meaning "seventy") made possible the transmission of Scripture from Egyptian Jews, responsible for the translation, to the Christian Church, whose converts were principally Greek-speaking pagans. It seems fairly certain that without this Greek version, and later additions based upon it, the conversion of Europe to Christianity would have been virtually impossible. This epoch-making translation in itself provides an interesting sidelight on history.

The *Letter* or *Epistle of Aristeas* (285–247 B.C.E.) claims to be a reliable contemporary account of how the translation came to be made. According to this narrative, Demetrius of Phalerum, the royal librarian, suggested to the then-reigning Egyptian king, Ptolemy Philadelphus, that a copy of the Torah of the Jews be placed in the royal library. A mission was sent to Jerusalem headed by Aristeas, who was loaded

167

down with many valuable gifts and a letter to the high priest Eleazar. The priest then forwarded a copy of the Pentateuch to the Egyptian king, in the hands of seventy-two elders, six from each of the tribes of Israel, who were able to translate the original into Greek. The seventy-two translators were sent off far from the capital city to a quiet island to undertake their work. Each day they translated—every man for himself—and then they met to compare results and to agree upon a common rendition. After seventy-two sessions of rigorous labor they finished the translation. It was given to Demetrius, who had it read to the Jewish community; they delighted in it and asked to receive a copy. King Ptolemy heard the books read before him, expressed his favor, and directed that the translation be added to his library where it would be carefully watched over.

While this delightful story must not be written off as complete fantasy, the initiative for the translation most likely came from the Jews of Alexandria rather than from the king or his librarian. The Jews were participating in Greek life and needed a text most of them could understand, one which might also be read by Egyptians, whom the Jews were interested in influencing. In any event, an historical landmark had been reached when the Pentateuch arrived in Egypt in a form that could enter into the mainstream of Hellenistic life. In due course, the translation of the Pentateuch prodded the translation of the Prophets and the Writings, and by the middle of the second pre-Christian century, the process of translating the entire Bible into Greek had been completed.

For almost two centuries, the Christian Church had no sacred books other than the Hebrew Scriptures taken from the Jews. It was only toward the close of the second century that what is now called the New Testament was joined to the Hebrew Bible. Both formed the Scripture of the Christian Church. It was about this time, too, that the Christians set about arranging for their own translation of the Hebrew Bible—one that might suit their own religious purposes. Two such versions were made—one in Latin, the other in Syriac, a sister language of Aramaic then spoken in northern Syria. (This language survives in a few isolated parts of the world, as for example in certain localities in India, where the Roman Catholic Church still conducts its Mass in this ancient Semitic language.) The Syriac translation, known as the *Peshitta* (which means "the Simple"), was based in part upon the then-current Hebrew text, and embodied a number of the traditional interpretive meanings. There are, however, some intermixtures of style, which seem to point to the fact that the Septuagint, which was the Bible version used by the Church, was also used as a basis for the translation.

The first official Latin version goes back to this second century, too, although it was based upon a number of obscure and early translations from the Greek. But around the year 380, at the request of the Roman Bishop Damasus, a better translation was called for. This undertaking was assumed by Jerome (346–420), later canonized as St. Jerome, who set out for Palestine toward the end of the fourth century in order to acquire a thorough knowledge of Hebrew at the hands of Jewish teachers. With their assistance he completed a new translation, which attempted to use the Latin then common to the speech of the people. Thus this version received the name "The Vulgate" (from *vulgata*, meaning "common"). This work was not altogether acceptable to the Church in Jerome's own day, but, with the passage of time, it became more and more the Bible of the Roman Catholic Church. Finally, in 1546, at the Council of Trent, it was named the only authentic Latin translation to be used in the educational and religious work of the Church.

For a long time, Greek and Latin versions of the Bible dominated Church circles. Since average Christians could no longer read or write these two classical languages, the Bible text itself was closed to them; they could only hear "about" it from the priests of the Church. Then, beginning with the end of the fourteenth century, and continuing for almost three hundred years, a spate of translations began to appear in the English language. However, the first of these great translations, that of John Wycliffe, which saw the light around 1381, was not based on the Hebrew original, but rather on the Vulgate—which had been full of mistranslations. Wycliffe, who knew no Hebrew, merely noted some of the errors of that Latin translation in the margins, but he offered no new information or corrections of its many errors. It remained for William Tyndale (1484–1536) to produce the first English Bible translation actually based on the Hebrew original. Unfortunately, he had only completed the first Five Books of Moses, the Pentateuch, when he was killed in 1536. His translation appeared in 1530. Thereafter, a number of newer translations followed: Miles Coverdale's, published in 1535; the Genevan Bible, prepared by a group of English exiles in Geneva and published in 1560; the Bishops' Bible of 1568; the Douay Bible of 1610, which became the official English version of the Catholic Church; it was not based on the Hebrew original but on Jerome's fairly faulty Vulgate text.

Despite the growing interest in the Hebrew text of the Bible, most

Christian scholars still retained their inherited attitudes of anti-Judaism. In 1516, even Erasmus made known his concern that Christians ought not rely only on the Hebrew text of the original, and stated he "feared that *the study of Hebrew will promote Judaism.*" (Italics added.) Nevertheless, the need to authenticate the text by getting back to its roots was too strong and irresistible a force by the time the seventeenth century arrived with the winds of Protestant change. Accordingly, the so-called Authorized Version, or the King James Bible which appeared in England in 1611, would in fact lay great store in the Hebrew original. The German translation by Martin Luther, "father" of Protestantism on the continent, was similarly based on the Hebrew.

Indeed, the joint effect of both the King James and the Luther translations, as was clearly intended by the Protestant reformers, was to open up the pages of the Bible to the masses of people, and thus make biblical religion directly accessible to the layman. The growing piety of the century was linked to a new sense of national aspiration. As the modern period was opening, the view that each country had the national right to establish its own form of Christianity—*cuius regio eius religio*—became the dominating Protestant principle. The colloquial Bible translations were no mere symbol of this new religious-national orientation of Protestantism; they were, in fact, at the very core of the issue. If they were not the principal cause for this radical departure, they were surely high up on the list of causes.

Moreover, "with the spread of Hebraic studies," as one historian explained, "and increased zeal for accurate Bible translation in England, the Hebrew text attained its rightful place as the best available source for true knowledge of the Scriptural word. Despite the uncertainty of many passages in the 'Textus Receptus' of the Jewish canon, it has served as the foundation for Christian Biblical scholarship, and has aided in a reconstruction of many doctrines based upon misreadings and misinterpretations of Old Testament sources."[1]

The Bible and the English Language

It has been well said that no education without a knowledge of the Bible may be regarded as truly liberal. The best in English literature, not to speak of the great writings of the world, is hardly comprehensible without an understanding of the biblical background of many of its allusions and depictions. And it is clear why this should be so. Until the beginning of modern times and the growth of humanistic, secular culture, the peoples of the world knew no real history save that recorded in Hebrew Scriptures. Since the religious authorities were responsible for what educational activities were afforded their people, it was the biblical story of man to which they pointed, and which they used as the basis for their knowledge of society and humanity.

The beginning of modern times was also the beginning of national awakening; nationalism as the central instrument of public policy was virtually unknown until not long before the American and French revolutions of the eighteenth century. As the nation-state came into its own, so did a consciousness of its purpose come to the fore-ground—and schools, organized by governments rather than only by religious groups, now began to teach national as well as spiritual ideals. To inculcate these views, it became necessary for the first time in the West to see history as a reflection of national character, and not only as the story of the divine in human affairs. Ever since, with increasing tension, conflicts between the secular purposes of the state and the religious desires of the churches have arisen in the broad arena of democratic education.

It is not my purpose to enter into the great church-state debate in the matter of education. It is important to note, however, the ines-capable fact that Western culture until recent times was thoroughly immersed in the religious teachings of Christianity, and in that situa-tion the Bible had served as the core of the educational curriculum. Ironically, here again Christianity, especially its Protestant brand, found itself teaching Jewish history as if it were the history of the Church and the world. The story of mankind was encompassed in the adventures of ancient Israel, and the purpose of history was dis-covered by studying the unfolding of divine intervention in the drama of that people's survival. Moral philosophy was taught as it emerged from the pages of the Law and Prophets. The geography of the Holy Land, the place names of biblical sites, and references to the cities and lands which found their way into Scripture, were carefully studied and eagerly digested. In short, for centuries the Hebrew Bible supplied Western culture with its principal textbook for the knowl-edge of worldly as well as religious ideas.

That such an intimate connection between the Bible and Western culture could not have been easily severed even after the rise of modern secularism is obvious. For the very fabric of our society—the literary, social, and even the political strands—had already been interwoven with the thread of biblical values. This is true for the English-speaking peoples in particular.

For them, the Hebrew Bible had virtually become a national monument; so much of their own national cultural history had been rooted in it. Biblical eloquence deeply penetrated English literature: Caedmon, the progenitor of English poetry, won distinction and popularity for his paraphrases of Bible stories; the *Chronicle* of King Alfred the Great was based on the Hebrew Book of Chronicles; Shakespeare, dean of English writers, made abundant and fruitful use of biblical characters and quotations; John Milton, student of Hebrew, made the Bible the essential source of most of his great works; Shelley, Keats, Tennyson, and Browning, not to mention scores of lesser-known poets, were directly and fundamentally influenced by the cadences and grandiloquence of biblical rhythms.

It was, of course, the grandeur and the sweep of the King James translation that singularly aided and abetted the growing links between Hebraism and Anglo-Saxon thought and culture. A key to this is the scarcely remembered yet highly significant fact that the English language before 1611 was still in a highly fluid and unfinished state. The King James Version, which was itself to attain the status of virtual inspiration, and which was often the only book possessed by an English-speaking household, helped to shape the language, to standardize it, and to fill it with a rich addition of idiomatic expressions. Through it filtered the mighty and colorful streams of biblical imagery and linguistic suggestion. Those who have made a study of language know that it is infinitely more than a means of communication; it is a key to the thought process and mentality of a people. Wittingly or not, as the King James translation became the principal literary standard by which the English language was measured, family after family came to think in Hebraic terms and to evaluate life in relation to the biblical-Hebraic frame of reference. No Jews, of course, participated in that great translation of 1611—they would have to wait many years to be welcomed back to England after their expulsion in 1290. But clearly the Jewish spirit had hovered over the work-tables of those inspired translators: page after page of the King James Version demonstrates how heavily those who produced it had relied upon the incisive biblical commentary and grammatical studies of the great Spanish-Jewish exegete, Rabbi David Kimhi, who was also known by the acronym *"Radak."*[2]

Hebrew Words Enter Our Language

Because they lacked either the words themselves or the conceptions conveyed by the words, many Western tongues had to borrow from the Hebrew vocabulary of the Bible. Not only has the English language been enriched by loan words from the Hebrew—words like *amen, Armageddon, cherub, hallelujah, jeremiad, jubilee, Paradise, Sabbath (sabbatical), Satan, shibboleth, shekel,* and many, many others—but so have other European languages. And there is a host of religious terms which may be derived from Greek or Latin, but whose semantic significance is essentially Hebraic. Words like *adoration, angel, benediction, Lord, prophet,* and as we have seen, even *Christ,* are but a few examples of the many Hebrew ideas and expressions that have travelled from their native habitat to our own via the circuitous route of Athens and Rome.

Mary Ellen Chase reminds us how much of the Hebrew Bible has actually entered into our daily living in word, phrase, image, and simile:

> Think for a moment how in the course of a single day spent in the homely, necessary details of living we clarify and illuminate our talk with one another by the often unconscious use of its language. An unwelcome neighbor becomes "gall and wormwood" or "a thorn in the flesh"; a hated task "a millstone about our neck"; we escape from one thing or another "by the skin of our teeth"; we earn our bread "by the sweat of our faces"; . . . in moments of anger we remember "a soft answer turneth away wrath"; intrusions upon our sleep are "the pestilence that walketh in darkness"; we warn our children to be "diligent in business" so that they may not "stand before mean men"; or prophesy that if "they sow the wind they shall reap the whirlwind" . . . we heap "coals of fire" on the heads of recalcitrant children or of harassed wives or husbands; having no servants we are ourselves "hewers of wood and drawers of water"; we long for a time when men "shall beat their swords into ploughshares and their spears into pruning hooks"; and after an irritating session with ration books, we are forced to remember that "better a dinner of herbs where love is than a stalled ox and hatred therewith."[3]

This is but a minor sampling of the way in which the vivid and unique expression of the Hebrew language and the moral overtones of biblical insight have become integral to the culture of English-speaking peoples. We may "speak English," but, to a large extent, fed by biblical food for thought, we often "think in Hebrew."

In Early America

It has been correctly stated that "Puritanism was in essence, the rebirth of the Hebrew spirit in the Christian conscience."[4] As a result, not only was Pilgrim America a convenanted community in the style of the Jews, but it also molded its public life in the cast of the Old Testament. Village, town, and city were given Hebrew names to reflect this intimate feeling of interrelatedness: Bethlehem, Canaan, Dothan, Eden, Goshen, Hebron, Jordan, Jericho, Mount Carmel, Nimrod, Pisgah, Rehoboth, Salem, and Zion are but a few examples of hundreds more.[5] Abraham, Isaac, Jacob, Ezekiel, Amos, Isaiah, Israel, Moses, David, Ezra, and other biblical heroes were also the proud names of thousands of children born to Christians in early America. Sometimes the more remote the biblical name, the greater its popularity. Even "Shear-Yashuv" and "Maher-shalal-hash-baz" had been adopted in some instances. Indeed, there was one Puritan dog whose master had named him "Moreover" because a stray verse—not a dog!—mentions: "Moreover the dog came and lapped up the water."

This fixation of many early American settlers on both the Hebrew language and the Hebrew Bible can be traced to the education they had received in England. British Puritanism, after all, had mothered them and cradled them in the Hebraic spirit. Not only was their Protestant theology rooted in a heavy reliance on the literal inspiration of the Bible, but the England of its day also shared in the Hebrew revival that accompanied and followed the Protestant Reformation. The study of Hebrew in England flourished from 1600 to 1660—from the reign of James I to the Restoration—and the knowledge of Hebrew was widely diffused throughout the country. There were even some Christian Talmudists who had taken up the study of rabbinical literature.

When Puritans began arriving in America, the first settlers brought with them a sense of total identity with the ancient Israelites. Many cultural and ideological streams have gone into the making of the Anglo-Saxon mind and mood; these pilgrims to America, however, were such indefatigable readers of the Hebrew Bible that they staunchly believed they were themselves reenacting ancient Israelite history on the shores of the "New World." They had virtually adopted the mind-set of the Hebrews: England was their "land of Egypt," King James I, their "Pharoah," and they even thought of the Atlantic Ocean as their "Red Sea." They were living not alone in America, but in the "New Canaan," or the "Promised Land"! Indeed, when Benjamin Franklin and Thomas Jefferson drafted a seal for the new United States it pictured Pharaoh seated in an open chariot passing through the waters of the Red Sea in hot pursuit of the Israelites. Moses stands at the other shore and causes the sea to inundate Pharoah and his charioteers. Beneath the seal was their motto: "Resistance to tyrants is obedience to God."[6]

Clearly, the founding American fathers, men of Christian conviction, had understood the Hebrew Bible as having special, personal, and national relevance to their bold experiment in government and nation-building. They did not see it as some remote fossilized document that depicted the culture of an ancient people long forgotten. For them, it had the power of immediacy and directness. It was *their* Bible, not merely a collection of curious Hebrew documents.

Their strong abhorrence of the monarchy as an institution cannot be fully explained or understood unless we realize how deeply they identified their political and not only their religious destiny with ancient Israel. They knew that in the history of Israel the institution of a human king was established only as a concession to the weakness of the people. Far from possessing divine rights, human kings in the biblical view, were subject to all of the ills of flesh, and were the objects of repeated moral admonition at the hands of prophet after prophet. Indifference to human misery, callousness of spirit, oppression of the weak and the poor—these and other royal failures, are mercilessly depicted in the scriptural stories. The prophets never fail to reprove, criticize and point their fingers at a king who lifted his heart above his brethren.

Serious researchers of early American history have discovered that this "Jewish connection" not only was part of the mores and culture of the time, but had also profoundly influenced the laws and constitutions of the oldest communities in America. It is part of their ongoing Christian problem that so many American historians have glossed over this phenomenon. The result is that large numbers of university students in the United States, even some on the graduate level, are virtually ignorant of the ties that unite Judaic ideas of justice and morality, to the founding fathers of the country. To cite but one example from many, the foreword to the *Pilgrim Code* of 1636, will surely help put the matter clearly before us:

> It was the great privilege of Israell of old and soe was acknowledged by them, Nehemiah the 9th and 10th that God gave them right judg-

ments and true Lawes. They are for the mayne so exemplary, being grounded on principles of moral equitie as that all Christians especially ought alwaies to have an eye thereunto in the framing of their politique constitutions. We can safely say both for ourselves and for them that we have had an eye principally unto the aforesaid platforme in the framing of this small body of Lawes.[7]

It is especially important today in view of those who would argue that a "Christian America" is the ideal toward which the republic ought to strive, to underscore the country's profound relationship to Jewish ideas. The Jewish factor in the Middle Ages can often be overlooked with impunity, for we are at so far a remove from those times that buried documents alone are insufficient to awaken us to that distant reality and truth. What, however, can be said of American historians who systematically overlook the Jewish factor which was at work in the founding of the nation? True, fewer than six million Jews in the United States constitute less than three per cent of the total population today. True, too, that even up to the time of the American revolution they numbered no more than 2,500 souls; and on the eve of the Civil War there were still hardly more than 150,000 of them in the country. Yet even the perceptive John Wesley, noted British Protestant reformer, on a visit to Georgia in 1737 realized that the Sephardi Jews he had met there—probably only a handful—were spiritually very much alive. "I began learning Spanish," he writes, "in order to converse with my Jewish parishioners, some of whom seem nearer to the mind that was in Christ than many of those who call him Lord." Wesley may have had it in his own mind to convert these would-be "parishioners" to his own faith, but his equation of the "mind that was in Christ" with the mind of Judaism hints at his own surprise at the personal influence the Jews had upon him.

What accounts for the reticence of many teachers even now to teach their students that at the birth of the republic Judaism was not only very much alive but was also very much taken into account? The "forgotten Jews" put into historical limbo by many of these social scientists were few in number; spiritually, however, they were powerfully present. Here again, sadly for these historians and even more sadly for their students, it is their own persistent anti-Jewish bias which blocks their clear vision and prevents them from coming to terms in more positive ways with the Jewish fact of life.

NOTES

1. Louis I. Newman, *Jewish Influence on Christian Reform Movements* (New York: Columbia University Press, 1925), p.96.

2. Rabbi David Kimhi (1160–1235) was the author of a masterly grammar and dictionary, the *Mikhlol*, or compendium. Max L. Margolis has written of him: "When at the revival of learning in the early sixteenth century Christian Churchmen, following in the footsteps of Jerome in the fourth century, sought instruction in Hebrew at the hands of Jewish scholars, all that these teachers could impart to them was a digest of the labors of David Kimhi. In 1506 the humanist Reuchlin wrote the first Hebrew grammar and dictionary produced by a Christian scholar, and his teachers were Jacob Jehiel Loans and Obadiah Sforno. Sebastian Münster and Paul Fagius were the pupils of Elias Levita (1469–1548), a versatile man who became the link between Kimhi and the Christian Hebraists . . . The influence of Kimhi . . . may be traced in every line of the Anglican Translation of 1611 [the King James Version]." See Max L. Margolis, *The Story of Bible Translations* (Philadelphia: The Jewish Publication Society of America, 1917), p.61.

In a masterful and thoroughly engaging study of David Kimhi, the author, Frank Talmage, tells us that "when the Christian scholars of the Reformation began their study of Hebrew, it was largely to Radak [the acronym formed by his name: Rabbi David Kimhi] that they turned. Directly or indirectly, they were all his disciples: Reuchlin, Münster, Pagninus, Luther, the masters of the King James Version." See Frank Talmage, *David Kimhi: The Man and the Commentaries*, (Cambridge: Harvard University Press, 1975), p.58.

3. Mary Ellen Chase, *Life and Language in the Old Testament* (New York: Harper and Row, 1955), pp.56–57.

4. Abraham A. Neuman, *Relation of Hebrew Scriptures to American Institutions* (New York: Jewish Theological Seminary of America, 1943), p.6.

5. See Moshe and Lottie Davis, *Map of Biblical Names in America* (New York: Associated American Artists, Inc., undated).

6. Quoted in Oscar Straus, *The Origin of the Republican Form of Government in the United States of America* (New York: G. P. Putnam's Sons, 1885), pp.119–20.

7. Quoted in Louis I. Newman, *op.cit.*, pp.637–8. For a comprehensive and scintillating discussion of what the author calls the "American-Hebraic idea," which he finds manifested in the rule of law; the rights of conscience; the pursuit of human happiness; the democratic ideal; and the celebration of human dignity, see Milton R. Konvitz, *Judaism and the American Idea* (Ithaca: Cornell University Press, 1978).

PART THREE

The "New Jews" and Their Christian Neighbors: Continuing Problems in the Dialogue

Christianity contains within itself the tension between paganism and true religion . . .

. . . Whenever the pagan within the Christian soul rises in revolt against the yoke of the Cross, he vents his fury on the Jew.[1]

Franz Rosenzweig

Over the centuries Christians have generally lived with the tacit assumption that a "good Jew" is either a dead Jew or a Christian. So, alternately, they have consented to the death of Jews and prayed for their conversion. They have kept alive a notion of the "curse that bears down on this people" (Bonhoeffer), and they have said that God loves Jews "for the sake of the Fathers" (Vatican statement.) But Christians have never really said that God loves the Jew for what he is now. They have never been able to acknowledge the current legitimacy of his vocation and commitment, or the continuing relevance of his covenant and witness. Christians have lived with a vision of "a world without Jews." There is as yet no clear evidence that we have come to the end of that long tradition and its agony. One can only hope.[2]

J. Coert Rylaarsdam

The Holocaust is the final act of a uniquely unique drama. It is the hour that follows logically, inexorably, and faithfully upon a particular history of conviction and behavior. It is the climax that succeeds the drawing up, over many centuries, of the requisite doctrinal formulations. It is the arrival of the "right time" (kairos) following upon all those dress rehearsals, those practice sessions of the Crusades, the Inquisition, and the like. The Holocaust is the consummation of all of them . . . Only the final destruction remained to be carried out . . . Here was the implementation of the dominant theological and moral conclusions of the Christian church . . . All in all, *we were following orders*—the remorseless, gathering of commands of nineteen centuries.[3]

Alice and A. Roy Eckardt

Christians have difficulty understanding that the passage through the Holocaust to a restored Israel is for the Jewish people comparable to crucifixion and resurrection.[4]

Franklin H. Littell

NOTES

1. Quoted by Jacob B. Agus, *Modern Philosophies of Judaism* (New York: Behrman House, 1941), p. 193.

2. J. Coert Rylaarsdam, letter to editor, *Christian Century* LXXXIII, 43 (October 26, 1966), p. 1306. The expression "a world without Jews" is actually borrowed from the title of a book by Karl Marx.

3. Alice and A. Roy Eckardt, *Long Night's Journey Into Day* (Detroit: Wayne State University Press, 1982), p. 57.

4. Franklin H. Littell, *The Crucifixion of the Jews* (New York: Harper and Row, 1975), p. 130.

CHAPTER XI

Christianity and the Holocaust

"THERE ARE SOME THINGS THAT WEARY OF SPEECH; THEY WELCOME silence."[1]

Surely the murder of six million Jews, among them one million children, causes words to die on one's lips. For almost two decades after those numbing, genocidal events, Christians barely spoke of them. Church councils scarcely considered them, only faintly remembering. Jews, too, though hardly forgetful, kept their wounds and memories largely to themselves, as they slowly began the painful work of rebuilding the shattered lives of those who had somehow survived. In those days, too, they rarely spoke of or described the horrors, and when some few did, their voices were muted, almost inaudible to others.

"Death brings to Jewish lips a prayer of glorification that speaks not of death [the doxology called the *Kaddish*], so let these six million dead rest in peace undisturbed by words of reproach that cannot touch them or regenerate the living who killed them. Silence in the aftermath; *words only in the anticipation of new disaster.*"[2] *(Italics added.)* Until the 1960s, even the most sensitive Jews felt this way. Not until the very eve of that decade would the word "Holocaust" be "invented" to refer specifically to the death of six million Jews.[3] No clear language or vocabulary was yet at hand that would in an instant—in a single, unmistakable, and penetrating locution—say what should have been said. Not words, but silence was virtually everywhere.

But the silence of the Jews then was of a far different order from the silence of the Christians. Jews know this, but many Christians still do not and that problem remains as an obstacle even now in our new "age of dialogue," when the word "Holocaust" comes more easily and quickly to the lips of many.

It will be helpful to understand how it was that what was barely mentioned mere decades ago—regarded almost as taboo—has now become part of the common realm in television programs, magazine articles, books—even Christian theological books—and on the inter-faith lecture platforms of churches and synagogues. Even now, how-ever, when *some* Christians and most Jews are "silent" no longer, the "Holocaust" means different things to each group. Before we explore this phenomenon, we need first to examine both of those older, yet vastly different silences, to see what they may still teach. To do so in proper perspective, we must note with reverence that there were indeed *some* Christians who did set a different example for their own co-religionists. They had refused to stand idly by.

"Righteous Gentiles"—Christians Who Saved Jews

It cannot be forgotten that there were Christian martyrs who willingly endangered, or even sacrificed themselves, in the hope that they could save their Jewish neighbors. Jews have especially remem-bered. In Jerusalem at Yad Vashem—the national shrine memorializ-ing the six million Jewish victims of the Holocaust—an honored place is reserved for those "righteous Gentiles," as the Jewish tradition refers to them, who served the cause of justice and mercy in their own godly ways. Overlooking the capital city of the Jewish state, high atop a once barren, rocky hill, is a quiet avenue known as *l'Avenue des Justes.* Here trees have been planted by Jews, each dedicated to the memory of every European Gentile known to have saved the life of even a single Jew during the Holocaust. The street is now verdant with evergreens and carob trees. Further, as a dramatic sign of the love and reverent esteem in which these people are held by Jews, in May, 1985, on the occasion of the fortieth anniversary of VE Day commemorating the close of World War II in Europe, the Israeli government conferred honorary citizenship upon all known "right-eous Gentiles"—living or dead.

These people must have numbered in the thousands. Some worked clandestinely, and as a result have remained unknown. Others con-sidered their efforts a "religious duty" for which they would accept no public acknowledgment or publicity after the war. Still others, fearing reprisals from antisemitic neighbors or groups, cloaked their life-saving work in anonymity. Then, as in Denmark and Greece, there were also whole populations who rallied to the Jewish cause. In October, 1943, when the Danes learned of the German plan to deport their fellow Jewish citizens, rescue committees sprang up overnight and went into action. At great risk to their own lives, they transported the entire Danish Jewish community—some six or seven thousand souls—under cover of darkness, across the Sea of Malmo to safety in Sweden.[4] Many hundreds of Greek Jews were also transported from the Greek islands to Turkey by their Christian neighbors. In Holland, a Nazi attempt in 1941 to effect the mass deportation of Jews was met with a general strike by Amsterdam workers. And in Finland and Bulgaria, the strong and openly expressed antipathies of local populations prevented the deportation of Jews which had already been ordered by the Nazis.

There are others, too, whom Jews remember with feelings of awe and reverence. Among the most notable are Raoul Wallenberg, who served as the plenipotentiary of the king of Sweden, and Charles Lutz, a Swiss Consul, who persistently intervened against the edicts of the Nazis, and whose efforts helped to save tens of thousands of Hungarian Jews from imminent death.[5] Not to be forgotten is Jean-Marie Mussy, once president of the Swiss Confederation, whose careful and skillful negotiations with the Nazis helped virtually at the eleventh hour to snatch several thousand doomed Jews from the Theresienstadt and Bergen-Belsen death camps.

Not many churchmen, however, risked their reputations to defy the authorities in favor of the Jews. When they did, it was usually a personal choice, not an official one. One Jewish scholar notes:

> How important the individual feelings were for the rescue operations of Jews can be proven by the different attitudes of two bishops in Lithuania in 1941. When a delegation of Jews from Kovno approached Bishop Brizgys to ask for help, he answered, "I can only cry and pray myself; the Church can not help you." On the other hand, Bishop Rainis of Vilna preached to the monasteries that help be given to Jews. He also refused to bestow his blessing on a Ukrainian auxiliary battalion attached to the German Army, because the battalion participated in actions against the Jews.[6]

An American Catholic priest, at the conclusion of his careful study of *Vatican Diplomacy and the Jews During the Holocaust, 1939–1943* reminds us that Pope Pius XII did not instruct his diplomats or priests to denounce the racial laws or the deportations. Instead, he "chose reserve, prudence, and a diplomatic presence in all the capitals over any other goal or needs. Vatican diplomacy failed the Jews during the Holocaust by not doing all that it was possible for it to do on their behalf." It pursued "a goal of reserve rather than humanitarian concern . . . it betrayed the ideals it had set for itself. The nuncios, the secretary of state, and most of all, the Pope, share the responsibility for this dual failure."[7]

All of which makes more poignant the quiet but searing testimony of one unforgettable Christian who died a martyr at Nazi hands. He saw things quite differently from Pius XII. This man from Holland, a devout member of the Plymouth Brethren, explained why he had to oppose the Nazis: "Anybody who takes part in the persecution of the Jews, whether voluntarily or against his will, is looking for an excuse for himself. Some cannot give up a business deal, others are doing it for the sake of their families; and the Jewish professors must disappear for the sake of the university. I have to go through these difficult days without breaking, but in the end my fate will be decided and I shall go like a man."[8]

How do we explain these widely differing Christian choices? While diffident about generalizing regarding the varying attitudes of Christians to Jews, a leading Holocaust historian, Yehuda Bauer, does throw some light on the question. He writes:

> In Poland, Lithuania, Latvia, and the Ukraine, in Croatia and Romania, the attitude of the overwhelming majority of the local population, including that of the majority churches, and excepting the left-wing political parties, ranged from hostile indifference to active hostility . . . Minority churches tended to protect Jewish minorities . . . On the whole, the tragic situation of the Jew in a Gentile environment was one in which the Jew could only appeal to mercy, compassion, and loving kindness. In some places he met people who had these qualities; *in most places he did not* . . . The Jew was powerless, and the *European background of antisemitism* did not permit for more than a partial reassertion of humanism in the attitude toward him.[9]

It is against this background of "European antisemitism" that what was largely a "Christian silence" must inevitably be viewed. To do so is not to diminish, but rather to add meaning to the lives of those several thousands of "righteous Gentiles" who lived and died as *faithful Christians.*

The Second Christian Silence

The exceptions—the relatively few and notable "righteous Gentiles"—help prove the rule. During the twelve years of Hitler's "kingdom of night" which culminated in 1945, most Christian churches distanced themselves from the Holocaust, whose destructive force was moving inexorably toward the fulfillment of Hitler's "final solution to the Jewish problem": the wholesale slaughter and destruction of that people, for no other reason than that they were Jews. But even after the war, when the work of reconstruction and reconciliation should have begun—even then, few Christian leaders or their church councils reached out to assist the remnants of European Jewry. Worse still, few, if any, actively sought to address their own crucial religious question: the meaning of the Holocaust for believing and practicing Christians.

The second silence of the churches must surely be related to their first—their almost total acquiescence to, and acceptance of, Hitler's anti-Jewish measures in the 1930s and 1940s. The so-called "European background of antisemitism" was, in fact, little more than its own Christian history. In a monumental work on Hitler's destruction of the Jews, Raul Hilberg has carefully documented this fact. To put things into capsule-form, he constructed a chart to buttress his claim that the Nazis "did not discard the past; they built on it. They did not begin a development; they completed it."[10] Even a cursory glance at Hilberg's table provides us with clues to the questions surrounding the double silence of the churches. In some ways, these questions apply with even more force to Church behavior *after* the War, since, by then, they were no longer constrained by issues of "prudence" or "diplomacy," but should have been liberated sufficiently—and capable of speaking out—in order to proclaim the judgments the Holocaust had for them.

Hilberg's Table:
Church Law and Nazi Anti-Jewish Measures

CHURCH LAW	NAZI MEASURE
Jews and Christians not permitted to eat together, Synod of Elvira, 306	Jews barred from dining cars (Transport Minister to Interior Minister, December 30, 1939.)

Jews not allowed to hold public office, Synod of Clermont, 535	Law for the Re-establishment of the Professional Civil Service, April 7, 1933
Jews not allowed to employ Christian servants or possess Christian slaves, 3d Synod of Orleans, 538	Law for the Protection of German Blood and Honor, September 15, 1935
Burning of the Talmud and other books, 12th Synod of Toledo, 681	Book burnings in Nazi Germany
Christians not permitted to patronize Jewish doctors, Trulanic Synod, 692	Decree of July 25, 1938
Christians not permitted to live in Jewish homes, Synod of Narbonne, 1050	Directive by Göring providing for concentration of Jews in houses, December 28, 1938
Jews not permitted to be plaintiffs, or witnesses against Christians in the Courts, 3d Lateran Council, 1179, Canon 26	Proposal by the Party Chancellery that Jews not be permitted to institute civil suits, September 9, 1942
Jews not permitted to withhold inheritance from descendants who had accepted Christianity, 3d Lateran Council, 1179, Canon 26	Decree empowering the Justice Ministry to void wills offending the "sound judgment of the people," July 31, 1938
The marking of Jewish clothes with a badge, 4th Lateran Council, 1215, Canon 68 (Copied from the legislation by Caliph Omar II (634–44), who had decreed that Christians wear blue belts and Jews, yellow belts.)	Decree of September 1, 1941
Construction of new synagogues prohibited, Council of Oxford, 1222	Destruction of synagogues in entire Reich, November 10, 1938

Christians not permitted to attend Jewish ceremonies, Synod of Vienna, 1267	Friendly relations with Jews prohibited, October 24, 1941
Compulsory ghettos, Synod of Breslau, 1267	Order by Heydrich, September 21, 1939
Christians not permitted to sell or rent real estate to Jews, Synod of Ofen, 1279	Decree providing for compulsory sale of Jewish real estate, December 3, 1938
Jews not permitted to act as agents in the conclusion of contracts between Christians, especially marriage contracts, Council of Basel, 1434, Sessio XIX	Decree of July 6, 1938, providing for liquidation of Jewish real estate agencies, brokerage agencies, and marriage agencies catering to non-Jews
Jews not permitted to obtain academic degrees, Council of Basel, 1434, Sessio XIX	Law against Overcrowding of German Schools and Universities, April 25, 1933

Why, then, in the years immediately following World War II, did so few churches or their leaders fail to see that there was a relationship between the long and continuous history of Christian anti-Judaism and the end product of Nazism—the calculated murder of one third of the Jewish people? Many of their communicants still hid their faces, or, even worse, placidly accepted the doom of the six million in Hitler's Europe as a divine judgment for the "Jewish rejection of Jesus."

Sensitive souls among them are now inquiring: how could we have failed to see that the Holocaust was a judgment upon us as Christians, and not upon the Jews as Jews?[11] How could we not have understood that six million unredeemed crucifixions have left us with blood on our own hands? As a Jew, I draw strength from the growing number of devoted Christians who are now willing to state, without hesitation or equivocation, that *after Auschwitz, the central moral test and religious question for Christianity is the survival of Jews in a Christian world.* Indeed, all of those earlier issues relating to this question—which I have called "the Christian problem"—are now beginning to be re-examined, reviewed, and in some quarters courageously acted upon.

Yet I am convinced that Jews still have a crucial role to play in this process. Without Jews to raise these questions, to remind the churches repeatedly, and tirelessly to confront Christian conscience with the moral and religious implications of these spiritual shortfalls, there are strong signs that new silences will again prevent them from coming to terms with their "Christian problem."

This is what makes a thorough understanding of the Holocaust and its implications for Christianity so crucial for the outcome of any religious dialogue between Jews and Christians. To suppress a serious discussion and analysis of the Holocaust out of "genteel" concerns for personal sensitivities, or out of fear of erecting barriers to ongoing and continuing encounters, is to miss the point, if not the ultimate purpose of these dialogues altogether. In the language of Robert McAfee Brown, a leading Christian ecumenist, "each partner [to the dialogue] must accept responsibility in humility and penitence for what his group has done, and is doing, to foster and perpetuate division; each partner must forthrightly face the issues that cause separation as well as those that create solidarity."[12]

These words originally addressed to the Catholic-Protestant encounter are probably of even more force when applied to the meeting of Christians and Jews. It is especially in light of earlier Christian silences that Jewish partners to the dialogue have a special role to play: to help "sear into memory" what many Christians may have forgotten.

I have borrowed the phrase "sear into memory" from a high prelate of the Catholic Church. When, in May, 1985, President Reagan decided to visit the cemetery at Bitburg, Germany, where many S.S. troops were buried (Reagan proceeded with this trip despite agonized pleas of many Americans and the Jewish community in particular urging him to cancel his plan), Cardinal John J. O'Connor, Archbishop of the Roman Catholic Archdiocese of New York, joined in the protest. He said that he was not prepared ever to forget those who perpetrated the horrors of World War II. He declared: "I cannot forget it as a Christian and I am grateful that it is our Jewish brothers and sisters who keep reminding us. It must be seared into our memories."[13]

The "new Jews" of the 1980s are prepared to serve as untiring prods to Christian conscience. Beginning in the late 1960s, they began to opt for a different posture than the one taken by their parents or friends two decades before. The latter, as already indicated, had been "Jews of silence." They rarely invoked the Holocaust; they hardly ever spoke publicly about those dreaded events. The "new Jews" of our time, however, lose no opportunity to remind the world that "silence" is a mortal sin; it is the mother of future catastrophes.

How was it that the silent Jews of only a generation ago have been replaced by a contemporary community bearing this new Jewish identity? And what does their new "Holocaust awareness" tell us about the future of Christian-Jewish dialogue?[14]

"Jews of Silence" No Longer

The "silent Jews" of the fifties and sixties are now virtually a thing of the past. But why were Jews so reticent then to speak up—to teach the world the meaning of Auschwitz? Why did it have to await the arrival of a new breed following Israel's Six Day War of June, 1967, for most Jews to take strength from selfhood, and to proclaim their "declaration of independence from Christian charity" as Holocaust theologian Emil Fackenheim phrased it?[15] There are no easy answers, but I include the following items as contributing factors:

1. In the decades immediately following the Holocaust, the survivors themselves were too traumatized, too shattered, to speak of the unspeakable. Many chose to shield their children from the wounds, and refused to talk about their experiences even in the privacy of their homes. How then could they begin to deal with these questions publicly?

2. The Jews of North America, while physically unscathed, were, nevertheless, emotionally enfeebled too. They reflected a community shot through with self-doubt: How could this have happened? How could we have allowed this to happen? Remorse was coupled with guilt. And there was shame: the feeling of having been reduced to virtual nothingness in the sight of the world.

3. But there was to be a new pride as well—pride in 1948 in the establishment of the State of Israel; pride in the amazing spectacle of young Israelis fending off the attacks of five invading Arab armies. Holocaust memories were dimmed by new Jewish strength.

4. Jewish hearts and minds thus turned toward Israel as the effective answer to the Holocaust. If North American Jews did not speak about the Holocaust, perhaps it was because they began to focus on Israel and its urgent needs. They were too busy building "the kingdom of light" to concentrate then on "the kingdom of night."

5. A rash of large-scale problems requiring immediate attention also served to turn Jewish attention away from the past. Vast Jewish populations had to be rescued quickly from Arab lands—from Yemen to Iraq to North Africa; and the remnants of Hitler's destruction—from Romania, Italy, Bulgaria, and Yugoslavia, and elsewhere on the continent—had to be brought "home" to Israel.

6. In the new optimism about Israel, Jews came to believe that liberal-minded, humane Christians would share their feelings. Israel was "equality"; it was "democracy"; it was "America" itself—a new nation comprised of oppressed immigrants making a new home. Surely North American Christians could be relied upon to appreciate these qualities, even if they had not "appreciated" or assisted the ghettoized Jews of Poland, Hungary, or Romania.

7. Pope John XXIII and the Second Vatican Council of 1962 also brought Jews additional reassurance. Were not Catholics, and many Protestants, too, opening the way to a new beginning, to an "era of good feeling"? Fraternal dialogues were now called for; they would replace hostility or indifference and bring understanding. If there was still no serious reflection on the part of Christians concerning the religious implications of the Holocaust for them, neither were Jews then looking backward. Zion restored would be a source of blessing to Christians as well as Jews. A new Jewish day was dawning; a new Christian-Jewish history was about to be written.

It was only in 1966 that the phrase "Jews of Silence" entered the vocabulary of our times. It served as the title of a book by the pre-eminent Holocaust author, Elie Wiesel. The title was in many ways enigmatic.[16] The book itself was a proclamation to the English-speaking Jewish world, urging it to spare no effort to help redeem a forsaken diaspora—Soviet Jewry. At first glance, the title appeared to refer only to the beleaguered Russian Jews, some three million strong, who were constrained from being fully themselves—condemned to "Jewish silence." But Wiesel meant much more. He was also thinking of Jews in the free world who had themselves willingly become "Jews of Silence"—who could become activists to help liberate Russian Jews. Here was a Holocaust survivor, whose riveting books on the Holocaust still lacked any appreciable audience, cautioning his people that for all of their other preoccupations, unless they placed the meaning of the Holocaust at the center of their own Jewish experience, they might well be forfeiting their obligation and opportunity to prevent a new one.

That book, in addition to the amazing and indefatigable efforts of a new body of activists comprised largely of Jewish university students, was the start of a new dawning. Not to see the miserable condition of Russian Jewry as somehow related to the older Holocaust events—as a form of spiritual and cultural genocide—was really to be blinded by our very freedom. The phrase "truly to be free as Jews" now began to take on new meanings. Henceforth, free Jews would be on guard to help avert impending catastrophes to their people. Silence would be replaced by acts as well as words, "in anticipation of new disaster." There would be protests and demonstrations, too, to prevent the Christian world from closing its eyes to the spreading poison.

The birth of these "new" and truly free Jews can be traced to approximately that time, some two decades after the end of World War II. This new personality was strengthened after June, 1967, as a result of the events surrounding the Six Day War in Israel. And it was also the "third silence" of the churches, caused by Vatican Council II, that brought about the shift.

The Third Christian Silence

I have said that Vatican Council II was a source of some reassurance to Jews. Yet one cannot overlook some of the disquiet and confusion it also deposited in Jewish hearts. In his search for "church renewal"— *aggiorniomento*— Pope John XXIII convened the Second Vatican Council, in 1962. It could not have been foreseen that he would stretch the "new ecumenism" beyond his fellow Christians, the Protestants, and reach out to Jews as well. By 1965, however, the Vatican had issued a major decree, part of its final "Declaration on the Relationship of the Church to Non-Christian Religions"—known as *Nostra Aetate*. Section 4 of *Nostra Aetate* dealt with the Jews alone, and it has since been known as "The Jewish Declaration."

The "Declaration" did take into account "the bond that spiritually ties the people of the New Covenant to Abraham's stock," and did state that the Church could not "forget that she draws sustenance from the root of that well-cultivated olive tree on to which have been grafted the wild shoots, the Gentiles." But there had been great and often ugly wrangling within the Council—led by the conservative forces within the Curia, and heavily abetted by Catholic bishops from Arab and Middle Eastern countries and their supporters. The final version passed in 1965 after the death of Pope John and during the new reign of Pope Paul—and even then only after several years of sharp controversy—was greatly watered-down from what had originally been proposed by the preparatory secretariat.

What had been intended as a statement to foster friendship and mark a new accord became severely blunted in its effect, and many North American Catholics were themselves deeply disappointed. In the words of one of them, John Cogley, then religion editor of the *New York Times*, the Declaration became "a reason for shame and anguish on the part of many Catholics and of suspicion and rancor on the part of many Jews."[17] The unwillingness of the Council to deal in any fundamental way with the persistence of anti-Judaism and anti-semitism; its amazing silence concerning the events of the Holocaust; and its refusal to recognize the special relationship of the Jewish people to the land of Israel, became all the more prominent, because in one way or another these issues had been thoroughly discussed at the Council sessions and were then overwhelmingly rejected in the showdown of the final vote. The recorded vote which approved the Declaration was 2,221 to 88. In hindsight, this would be later regarded as an ominous foreboding of what soon lay ahead.

Not many months would pass before there appeared on the horizon the spectre and portent of possible new Jewish dooms. In April and May of 1967, prominent leaders in the Arab world openly began to call for the destruction of the Jewish state and vowed that they would soon "drive all Israelis into the Sea." I can never forget the fear that clutched at the hearts of even those Jews who had wandered from the organized community, as Israel's total annihilation seemed imminent. And then again, the world held its tongue. Even many Jews who were assimilated began streaming back to their own people as the days were ticking quickly away and no nation on earth was either willing to stand in the way of Arab threats or to defend Israel. Indeed the United Nations even assisted President Nasser of Egypt in his plans to be rid of Israel by allowing the Straits of Tiran to be blockaded by Egypt. When these straits were no longer protected as an international waterway under U.N. surveillance, the Egyptians and their allies could attack Israel by sea at will. On May 16, 1967, the official voice of the Egyptian Government, Radio Cairo, openly declared: "The existence of Israel has continued too long . . . The great hour has come. The battle has come in which we shall destroy Israel." One historian has written: "Even as Israel mobilized its forces to defend its life against that threat of destruction, Israeli rabbis were consecrating extensive burial grounds for expected Jewish losses."[18] The vision of a new nightmare descended upon the Jewish community, not only in Israel but all over the world. No Jew then living will ever forget. The spectre of two Holocausts within a single generation became too much to bear. No one moved to help Israel; no voices were raised to give it hope.

Incredibly, in six lightning days in early June, 1967, the Israelis won a "miraculous" victory, one which not only made military history, but which also fundamentally changed Jewish self-perceptions thereafter. The Six Day War, I believe, was chiefly responsible for creating a new Jewish identity in North America and elsewhere in the free world. Before that time, many Jews could only think silently and inwardly of the Holocaust and then only with the lamentation and tears that were enshrined in their earlier recollections of the slain six million. Before that time, they seemed to repress these painful memories—as Jews of Silence—but ever since, the Holocaust was itself turned into a challenge to survive. To remember the helpless martyred dead was now also to vow that it would never happen again. A strong Israel, most Jews came to feel, was the only guarantor of that. As will be noted in greater detail in the chapter that follows, since 1967 virtually all Jews—even those who had earlier distanced themselves from their people and its faith—in near-mystical manner came to regard their own future as inextricably tied to a secure and undiminished state of Israel.

In a strange way it was this third Christian silence that contributed to these repossessed feelings of Jewish solidarity, in which Holocaust memories now played a crucial role.

The anguished words of Rev. Dr. A. Roy Eckardt and his wife, Alice, who jointly wrote a two-part series shortly after the Six Day War, appeared in a leading periodical, under the revealing title: "Again, Silence in the Churches."

> The guilt of the Christian community for its dominant silence amid the Nazi slaughters of the Jewish people has in recent years been increasingly confessed within both Catholic and Protestant circles. Yet when within past weeks the extermination of the entire nation of Israel almost occurred, once again there was silence in the churches.
>
> The few voices that were raised merely helped to make the general stillness louder. When at the beginning of the crisis Protestant and

Catholic organizations were asked by the American Jewish community to call upon our government to stand by Israel, there was no institutional response. The U.S. Conference of Catholic Bishops gave no word and the (Protestant) National Council of Churches was content to urge "compassion and concern for all the people of the Middle East" and the formulating of a solution by the United Nations. Some Christians found an element of presumptuousness in the Jewish request; they claimed it did not allow them to reach a moral judgment of their own. But the fact is that church groups either ignored the entire problem or announced a policy of neutralism . . .

. . . The moral tragedy is that the only tangible way open to us to atone for our historic crimes against original Israel is by assuming a special responsibility for the rights and welfare of Jews. The present refusal to bear this obligation may well reflect the Christian community's wish to exonerate itself from culpability for the long years of antisemitism.

Karl Barth once said: "In order to be chosen we must, for good or ill, either be Jews or else be heart and soul on the side of the Jews." It almost seems that the entire history of Christianity, including the churches' current response to the Middle Eastern crisis, has been an attempt to make Barth's words as irrelevant as is humanly possible. Writing as Christians who oppose that attempt, we say to our Jewish brothers: we too have been shocked by the new silence. And we are greatly saddened. But we have not been surprised. The causes of the silence lie deep in the Christian soul. Therefore we can only mourn and pray and hope.[19]

If, as claimed, the causes for these crucial Christian silences "lie deep in the Christian soul," what, indeed, lies even deeper? What is at the roots—at the bottom of it all? I believe that if Christians would willingly and unflinchingly face up to these silences, which, jointly and severally, hark back to their reluctance to see the Holocaust as a problem for Christianity—they may themselves discover what lies at the roots. They should then find the ineluctable culprit: the clinging pagan elements that still adhere to a Gentile Christianity shorn of its Jewish lifelines. Paganism can perhaps finally be expunged from their midst when Christians seek to fathom what the Holocaust should mean for them *as Christians*. The task is arduous and demanding; it requires hard choices. Indeed, as one Christian scholar, Franklin H. Littell, who himself has made these choices, reminds us: "A Jew has to choose to be a pagan, while a Gentile has to choose not to be."[20]

Choosing Not to Be Pagans

If, from the thousands of stories that have reached us out of the depths of the Holocaust experience, only a single tale were permitted to be told, there is one which fully epitomizes the moral questions facing Christianity and its leaders in these post-Auschwitz days:

> As the German *Einsatzgruppen* (mobile killing units) were about to execute the Jewish population in a small Ukrainian town, a Hasidic Jew walked over to the young German officer in charge and told him that it was customary in civilized countries to grant a last request to those condemned to death. The young German assured the Jew that he would observe that civilized tradition and asked the Jew what his last wish was.
>
> "A short prayer," replied the Jew.
>
> "Granted!" snapped the German.
>
> The Jew placed his hand on his bare head to cover it and recited the following blessing, first in its original Hebrew, then in its German translation:
>
> "Blessed art thou, O Lord our God, King of the Universe, who hath not made me heathen!"
>
> Upon completion of the blessing, he looked directly into the eyes of the German and with his head held high, walked to the edge of the pit and said: "I have finished. You may begin." The young German's bullet struck him in the back of the head at the edge of the huge grave filled with bodies.[21]

Every day of the year, as part of their morning prayers before food may be partaken, traditional Jews pronounce that benediction: praise to the God of Israel for not having been born into a pagan community. But things are very different for Christians. Littell again has clarified this issue by reminding us that "the 'Christian' Gentile can take on again the protective coloration of the dominant society, that is the heathen world; the Jew cannot. When the Jews suffer from antisemitic attacks they suffer for that which the Christians would also suffer if they stayed Christians. But the 'Christians' can homogenize and become mere Gentiles again, while the Jews, believing or secularized, remain representatives of another history, another providence."[22] In their dialogue with Jews, the Holocaust issue becomes crucial for Christians: they can see how important it is for them to cut their pagan ties by returning to their Jewish sources.

The Jewish world view, as we have already seen, regards idolatry and paganism as the root of all moral evil. Pagan idolatry, of course, is not merely the worship of things—of sticks, stones, or nature itself—as some simple minds might surmise from the ancient stories narrated in the Hebrew Bible. Idolatry occurs whenever we absolutize the relative: when we worship the part as if it were the whole, and confuse the means with the ends; or when we trivialize morality by not holding human life as God-given and sacred.[23] The Nazi cult worshipped "blood and soil," and in narcissistic fashion deified their own so-called "Aryan race." In the process, they harnessed their false "gods of science," which many German scientists had made into objects of adoration. As a product of their own pagan mythologies and fictions, the Nazi-Germans and their collaborators saw themselves as *übermenschen*, a superhuman people whose scientific knowledge could be used with impunity to engage in "scientific" barbarities, to be applied to all sub-human types—the *untermenschen*—as a matter of "absolute" right. Inevitably, it was the Jews, arch-enemies of these and all other forms of paganism, who were their prime targets. But it was not Nazism alone that served pagan gods.

When some contemporary Christian theologians remind us that Christians must choose *not* to be pagans, they use as their prime model and object lesson the virtual apostasy of many European Christians during the Holocaust. One such historian writes as follows:

> It has become popular among some churchmen and general historians, to deal with Nazism as a "pagan" irruption—essentially atavistic, tribal, anti-Christian. There is much to be said for the argument . . . The trouble with this line of argument [however] is that it relieves the Christians and their leaders of their guilt for what happened . . . If the churches had used the means of spiritual government at their disposal to call the Nazi leaders to repentance, to return to minimal Christian standards, if the Nazi elite had been excommunicated for failure to respond, then today the churches could say truthfully, "They were pagans. They left our fellowship in the covenant. They were not of us." But the churches did not do this. Instead they retained in their membership and accorded signal honors to traitors to human liberty, mass murderers, apostate Christians. Adolf Hitler died a Roman Catholic, and an annual mass is celebrated in his memory in Madrid. Hermann Goering died a Lutheran. We Christians cannot come back today and claim no responsibility for what they did in the name of law and order and anti-Bolshevism, claiming to protect "religion."[24]

Even now, more than four decades after the Holocaust, there is a growing attempt on the part of some to push those barbaric events far from the concerns of Christendom. Unless these current "revisionist" efforts at downplaying and falsifying the Holocaust are met with a firm Christian response that denies them any standing, the "new Jews" of our time will find it impossible to respond affirmatively to invitations to "dialogue" and "meeting."

"Stealing" the Holocaust

Edward Alexander reminds us that one of the earliest and best-remembered attempts "to steal from the Jewish victims of the Holocaust precisely that for which they were victimized" was the dramatization for the American stage of the book, *The Diary of Anne Frank*. He explains that the playwrights had

> expunged from the stage version all of Anne's (diary) references to hopes for survival in a Jewish homeland and changed Anne's particular allusions to her Jewish identity and Jewish hopes to a blurred amorphous universalism. One example should suffice to illustrate the general pattern. In the *Diary* Anne writes:
>
> "Who has made us Jews different from all other people? Who has allowed us to suffer so terribly up until now? . . . If we bear all this suffering and if there are still Jews left, when it is over, then Jews instead of being doomed, will be held up as an example . . We can never become just Netherlanders, or just English, or just representatives of any country for that matter, we will always remain Jews."
>
> In the stage version, this is reduced to the following: "We are not the only people that've had to suffer . . . sometimes one race, sometimes another."[25]

The lessons to be learned from this single example are many. Morally insensitive persons often relate to the awful particularity of Jewish suffering in clearly amoral fashion, for when they insist on universalizing the unique Jewish condition they succeed in trivializing it. Thus today virtually all urban slums are called "ghettos," and even neighborhood fires are referred to as "holocausts" by the print and electronic media. When the unique Jewish deprivations and degradations are made into universal metaphors for disabilities of all kinds—large or small—not only is the currency of language devalued, but other difficulties, even if not immediately obvious, also ensue. From the point of view of improved Jewish-Christian understanding, for example, this word-play has become a "new game" that helps to obliterate the history of Jewish suffering from Christian memory. As a result, some Christians can be prevented from seeing and learning what they *must* see and learn: both Christianity and Nazism singled Jews out as special and perennial targets for their hostilities. Yet, as Cardinal John O'Connor has cautioned: Christians need Jews to help sear into their memories what they might otherwise forget. Religious dialogue can play an important role in helping Christians listen to the testimony of an important "witness"—the Jewish remembrancer.

The most serious menace of all to healthy Christian-Jewish rapport is a "Holocaust stealth" of an entirely different order. It can be traced to what some have called "Nazi gutter historiography"—a species of "history" that is now a new antisemitic genre: the outright denial of the Holocaust.[26] *The Hoax of the Twentieth Century*, written by a professor of electrical engineering at Northwestern University, for example, not only denies that Jews were murdered by the Nazis, but insists that the gassing installations at Auschwitz were actually only designed for the disinfection of clothes due to typhoid epidemics! There are many other pamphlets and books that similarly distort the facts.

Two significant points emerge from a study of these tactics. In the first instance, "the spiritual inheritors of those who perpetrated the destruction of the Jewish people of Europe, also have discovered that this monstrous and unprecedented crime is the central event of the modern world, the one most likely to enthrall the imagination of those who live in its shadow."[27] In other words, these pseudo-historians are fearful that authentic Christians may now feel obligated to discover why Christianity went wrong in allowing such crimes to be visited upon Jews within the very heartland of Christian Europe. By denying the truth of those crimes, those pagan elements within the Christian world can regain their upper hand over those other Christians who appear prepared "to go soft" on Jews.[28]

Still another fact emerges—one, perhaps, that is even more radically important. If, ironically, some have been spuriously employing the Holocaust itself as a weapon against Jews, it is probably because they are so heavily outnumbered by many other faithful Christians who increasingly confront themselves honestly and contritely by moving the problem of "Christian silence" and forgetfulness to a prominent place on their own religious agendas.[29] Consider, for example, what the President of the West German Republic had to say about these basic concerns, in a remarkably candid and courageous speech he gave in May, 1985, to the full Parliament, on the occasion of the fortieth anniversary of the unconditional surrender of Nazi Germany marking the end of World War II:

> The genocide of the Jews is . . . unparalleled in history . . . every German was able to experience what his Jewish compatriots had to

suffer . . . whoever opened his eyes and his ears and sought information could not fail to notice that Jews were being deported. The nature
and scope of the destruction may have exceeded human imagination,
but apart from the crime itself, there was, in reality, the attempt by too
many people, including those of my generation . . . not to take notice of
what was happening . . . When the unspeakable truth of the Holocaust
then became known at the end of the war, all too many of us claimed
that they had not known anything about it or even suspected anything . . .

The Jewish nation remembers and will always remember. We seek
reconciliation. Precisely for this reason we must understand that there
can be no reconciliation without remembrance. The experience of mil-
lionfold death is part of the very being of every Jew in the world, not
only because people cannot forget such atrocities, but also because
remembrance is part of the Jewish faith . . .

. . . Remembrance is experience of the work of God in history. It is
the source of faith in redemption . . . If we for our part sought to forget
what has occurred, instead of remembering it, this would not only be
inhuman. We would also impinge upon the faith of the Jews who
survived and destroy the basis of reconciliation. We must erect a memo-
rial to thoughts and feelings in our own hearts.[30]

These stirring words should serve as a reminder to both Christians
and Jews that the events and the meaning of the Holocaust must not
be forgotten nor may they be blurred or distorted. If true dialogue
and reconciliation are to occur, these "memories" must be openly
faced and fully probed. The Holocaust must continue to remind both
parties of a fundamental and abiding truth: Both need each other;
both must be able to rely on each other.

Together, Christians and Jews should be able to stand. And standing together, both will find it possible to join their voices in unison,
speaking these words from the most ancient and majestic of Hebrew
prayers—words of rousing hope that still serve as the concluding
signature to the prayers traditional Jews recite three times every day,
every day of the year:

We therefore hope in You, O Lord our God, that we may soon behold
the glory of Your power, as You remove the abominations from the
earth and heathendom is abolished. We hope for the day when the
world will be mended as a kingdom of the Almighty, and all flesh will
call out Your name; when you will turn unto Yourself all of the earth's
wicked ones. May all the earth perceive and understand that only unto
You should every knee bend, and only unto You every tongue vow
loyalty. Before You, O Lord our God, may they bow in reverence, giving

honor only unto You. May they all accept the yoke of Your sovereignty. Rule over them speedily and forever more. For dominion is Yours and to all eternity will You reign in glory; as it is written in Your Torah: The Lord shall reign for ever and ever. And it has also been foretold: The Lord shall be King over the whole earth; on that day the Lord shall be known as One, and only One.[31]

NOTES

1. Arthur A. Cohen, *The Myth of the Judeo-Christian Tradition* (New York: Harper and Row, 1970), p. 172.

2. *Idem.* Although these words appear in this book which appeared in 1970, they were first published in an essay he wrote some ten years earlier. In 1981, the same writer, Arthur A. Cohen confessed: "For nearly a generation I could not speak of Auschwitz, for I had no language that tolerated the immensity of the wound." See his *The Tremendum* (New York: Crossroad, 1981), p. 17.

3. The use of the word "Holocaust" in this connection, was coined by the author, Elie Wiesel, probably around 1959. Yet, even by mid-1961, when Adolf Eichmann was tried in a Jerusalem court, the word "Holocaust" was not yet in vogue. Instead the words used more frequently were "genocide," "final solution," "catastrophe," or "destruction" of the Jews. In 1966, Gideon Hausner, Israel's state prosecutor of Eichmann published his account of these events. Even there the word "Holocaust" does not yet appear. See his *Justice in Jerusalem* (New York: Harper and Row, 1966).

4. For the full story see Lenny Yahil, *The Rescue of Danish Jewry* (Philadelphia: Jewish Publication Society, 1969).

5. See John Bierman, *Righteous Gentile: The Story of Raoul Wallenberg* (New York: Viking Press, 1981).

6. Philip Friedman, *Roads to Extinction: Essays on the Holocaust*, edited by Ada June Friedman (Philadelphia: Jewish Publication Society, 1980), p. 416. See also the late Dr. Friedman's splendid account of Christians who saved Jewish lives in his *Their Brother's Keeper* (New York: Crown Publishers, 1957).

7. See this title by John F. Morley (New York: Ktav Publishing Co., 1980), p. 205. Also see relevant references to the information available to the Vatican concerning the Holocaust, and its reticence to act in any substantial way to prevent the slaughter of Jews: in Walter Laqueur, *The Terrible Secret*, (Boston: Little, Brown, 1981); and Monty Penkower, *The Jews Were Expendable* (Urbana: University of Illinois Press, 1983).

8. See Arieh Bauminger, *Roll of Honour* (Tel Aviv: Hamenora Publishing House, 1971), Introduction.

9. Yehuda Bauer, *The Holocaust in Historical Perspective* (Seattle: University of Washington Press, 1978), pp. 77–8.

10. See Raul Hilberg, *The Destruction of the European Jews* (Chicago: Quadrangle Press, 1961), p. 4. For an engaging discussion of some theological issues related to this question see Seymour Cain, "The Holocaust and Christain Responsibility," *Midstream*, April, 1982, pp. 20–27.

11. See David S. Wyman, *The Abandonment of the Jews: America and the Holocaust, 1941–1945* (New York: Pantheon Books, 1984), p. XII.

12. Robert McAfee Brown and Gustav Weigel, *An American Dialogue* (New York: Doubleday, 1960), p. 32.

13. Quoted in *New York Times*, May 2, 1985, p. 10 (National Edition).

14. It should be noted, however, that some Jewish scholars argue that "over-attention" to the Holocaust has become the new "civil religion"—a substitute faith-system—for too many Jews. There are also those who call this preoccupation with the death of the six million, a "Holocaust Industry," or a "Holocaust Religion," and hope instead, that Jews would concentrate on learning "how the Jews of Europe lived and not only on how they were gassed." See my *The New Jewish Identity in America* (New York: Hippocrene Books, 1985), pp. 262–3. Also see Chaim I. Waxman, *America's Jews in Transition* (Philadelphia: Temple University Press, 1983), pp. 122–123. For a discussion of this question as it relates to the Israeli scene, see Charles S. Liebman and Eliezer Don-Yehiya, *Civil Religion in Israel* (Berkeley: University of California Press, 1983), pp. 100–07.

15. Emil L. Fackenheim, *The Jewish Return Into History* (New York: Schocken Books, 1978), p. 79. Fackenheim wrote: "If Auschwitz is a trauma for Christianity, the state of Israel, being the Jewish declaration of independence from Christian charity, is a trauma for Christian antisemitism."

16. Elie Wiesel, *The Jews of Silence* (New York: Holt, Rinehart and Winston, 1966).

17. *New York Times*, October 16, 1965, p. 8.

18. Lucy Dawidowicz, in "Letters from Readers," *Commentary*, May 1985, p. 18.

19. A. Roy and Alice Eckardt, "Again, Silence in the Churches," in *The Christian Century*, July 26 and August 2, 1967. For a much different view of the failure of Christians to react supportively in aid of Israel during the Six-Day War of 1967, see Martin E. Marty, "Interfaith at Fifty—It Has Worked!", *Judaism*, Summer, 1978, pp. 343–344.

20. Franklin H. Littell, *The Crucifixion of the Jews* (New York: Harper and Row, 1975), p. 63.

21. Quoted in Yaffa Eliach, *Hasidic Tales of the Holocaust* (New York: Avon Books, 1983), p. 185.

22. Franklin H. Littell, *The German Phoenix: Men and Movements in the Church in Germany* (Garden City: Doubleday, 1960), p. 217.

23. The medieval Jewish biblical commentator, "Rashi," expounding the reasons for the failure of idolaters at the Tower of Babel (Genesis 11:7) explains: "One man asked for a brick but [misunderstanding], the other gave him mortar, instead; whereupon the first man killed the second." To idolaters, human life is not as sacred as are trivial, material objects.

24. Franklin H. Littell, *The Crucifixion of the Jews*, pp. 47–48.

25. Edward Alexander, "Stealing the Holocaust," *Midstream*, November, 1980, p. 48.

26. See Lucy S. Dawidowicz, "Lies About the Holocaust," *Commentary* 70:6 (December, 1980), pp. 31–37. See also her *The Holocaust and the Historians* (Cambridge: Harvard University Press, 1981), pp. 4–21.

27. Edward Alexander, *op. cit.*, pp. 47–48.

28. As recently as 1985, two jury trials which attracted international attention were conducted in Canada. Two separate defendants were found guilty of violating Canadian law by knowingly and wilfully spreading "false news" against an "identifiable group." The "false news" in question were the claims by these defendants that the Holocaust was a "Jewish hoax." At the Toronto, Ontario, trial of Ernst Zundel, a professed "lover of Hitler," the defense paraded a string of professional Holocaust deniers brought to Toronto from all over the world, and extravagantly sworn in as "expert witnesses." In Red Deer, Alberta, defendant Jim Keegstra, a former school-teacher, pleaded unsuccessfully that as a believing Christian citizen he had both the religious and democratic right to express his "Christian views" as a classroom teacher, views which not only denied the truth of the Holocaust but which also trumpeted the existence of a world-wide "Jewish conspiracy." While many Christians in Canada were offended by Keegstra, others publicly supported his views and vowed that "as Christians" they would stand behind him. See also Harold Troper, "The Queen v. Zundel: Holocaust Trial in Toronto," in *Congress Monthly* (published by American Jewish Congress: New York) July–August, 1985, pp. 7–10. Also see David Bercuson, and Douglas Wertheimer, *A Trust Betrayed: The Keegstra Affair* (Toronto: Doubleday Canada Ltd., 1985).

29. For a brief but succinct overview of some leading contemporary Christian theologians who have made the question of the Holocaust central to the reworking of their own religious thinking, see John T. Pawlikowski, "Implications of the Holocaust for the Christian Churches," in *Genocide: Critical Issues of the Holocaust*, ed. Alex Grobman and Daniel Landes (Chappaqua, New York: Rossel Books, 1983), pp. 410–18.

30. The text of this historic speech by President Richard von Weizsaecker, as translated by the West German Foreign Ministry, appeared in *New York Times*, May 9, 1985, page 10 (National Edition).

31. This translation is by the author and is part of the copyright of this book.

This prayer, known as *Alenu*, is probably pre-Christian in origin. In the third Christian century, in Babylonia, a great rabbi known as "Rav" incorporated this prayer into the New Year (*Rosh Ha-Shanah*) service. Because it expresses so well the Jewish hope for the future, it was later incorporated into every worship service, as the closing prayer. In 1656, Menasseh ben Israel, a leader of Dutch Jewry, related that the Sultan Selim, on reading this prayer in a Turkish translation of the Jewish prayer book, said: "Truly this prayer is sufficient for all purposes; there is no need of any other." See Joseph H. Hertz, *The Authorized Daily Prayer Book* (New York: Bloch Publishing Company, 1961), pp. 208–209.

CHAPTER XII

The Churches and the State of Israel

A JEWISH SCHOLAR ASKS: "WAS THE STATE OF ISRAEL HISTORY'S ANSWER, or to put it in an even more vulgar way, the reward the Jewish people received for the murder of its sons and daughters during the Holocaust?" And he answers: "emphatically *not*."[1]

Clearly the proclamation of the new state in 1948 by the relative handful of Jews then living in Palestine was only the culmination of a long and arduous process begun almost seventy years earlier by small, steady streams of young, idealistic Zionists who had dared to come to a malaria-infested country of arid deserts and swampy marshes. They came "to build the land and to be built by it."

What these *kibbutzniks*—many were formerly rabbinical students in East Europe now turned co-operative farmers in Palestine—lacked in numbers they possessed in ardor. Their fervor reached across the Jewish world, and I remember catching it too while still a young child growing up in New York City in the 1930s. In those days, other American Jews, then in the vast majority, used to say of the small group of us who had already caught this "Zionist contagion," that "one doesn't have to be *meshuga*, or crazy, to be a Zionist, but it surely helps!"

Those were the days before the whole Jewish world was "Zionized." Many Jews still regarded the idea of a Jewish state in a harsh, tiny land area as the unrealistic fantasy of young fools and idealists. Those young fools, however—not unlike very much older ones in the days of biblical Amos—have turned out to be the "sons of prophets," if not prophets themselves. Perhaps, as some of us now believe, there could not have been a Holocaust had there been a

Jewish state, say, only fifty years ago. Alas, though thoughts such as these cannot possibly rewrite recent history, they do serve as the underpinning of what is now the post-Holocaust Jewish mood: Never again!

Indeed, the stability and security of the state of Israel have become religious imperatives. Now Jews understand that if the Jewish people does not survive neither will Judaism. This mood, as we have already seen, began to grip most of us after 1967. Even in the minds of most Jewish theologians, survival is now regarded as a "divine commandment" on a par with the other 613 commandments of the Torah. In the words of Emil Fackenheim, who himself left North America to take up permanent residence in Jerusalem, Israel is at the crux of Jewish survival: "For almost twenty-five years [before 1967] I . . . held to a definition of Jewish faith in which, systematically, all historical events were considered irrelevant. [But in 1967] I formulated the only statement I ever made that became famous: that there now exists a six hundredth and fourteenth commandment—Jews are forbidden to give Hitler a posthumous victory . . . if we live as if nothing happened we imply that we are willing to expose our children or their offspring to a second Holocaust—and that would be another way of giving Hitler a posthumous victory . . . I think that I have been rightly understood by *Amcha*—the [whole] Jewish people."[2]

It is no longer a source of great wonderment, therefore, to the many individual, faithful Christians who have seriously encountered Jews, that these questions of survival and of the security of the state of Israel are bound into a single knot. Yet for those churches that continue to remain hostile—or to use their own oft-repeated language, "neutral"—to the idea of Israel reborn, Rosemary Ruether, a leading Christian theologian has some words of caution. Quite properly, she states that "every criticism of Israel is not to be equated with anti-Semitism." She goes on to say, however, that "there is no doubt that anti-Zionism has become, for some, a way of reviving the myth of the 'perennial evil nature of the Jews,' to refuse to the Jewish people the right to exist as a people with a homeland of its own. The threat to Jewish survival, posed in ultimate terms by Nazism and never absent as long as anti-Semitism remains in the dominant culture of the Diaspora, lends urgency to the need for the Israeli state."[3]

Professor Ruether digs down even deeper to get to the fundamental "Christian problem" in this regard:

> The end of Christendom means Christianity must now think of itself as a Diaspora religion. On the other hand, the Jewish people, shaken by

the ultimate threat to Jewish survival posed by modern anti-Semitism, have taken a giant leap against all odds and against two thousand years of urban Diaspora culture, and founded the state of Israel. The Return to the homeland has shimmered as a messianic horizon of redemption from the exile for the Jewish people for many centuries. But Christianity dogmatically denied the very possibility of such a return, declaring that eternal exile was the historical expression of Jewish reprobation. Now this Christian myth has been made obsolete by history.[4]

I am perplexed. Many educated Christians I know can readily agree with these penetrating observations of this Catholic theologian—not to mention similar expressions by other advanced Christian thinkers.[5] But when they do, they are, most often, not prompted by the teachings of their own churches, but by their own humane and democratic impulses. As for the churches themselves, they are traditional—and sometimes also political—institutions that often reflect those old, unresolved Christian problems. They tend to look upon some of these forward-looking theologians as threatening to their own established traditions, rather than as trend-setters for a new wave of thought.

Christians and Jews are joint survivors of Auschwitz and together we should be seeking to learn its scorching lessons. Why, then, in these post-Holocaust days, are there still churches whose neutral public stance concerning Israel flies in the face of the obvious—the domino effect which Israel's fate must now have upon the fate of all other Jews? What happens to Israel affects them all. Why are so many churches neither willing to recognize the fact of a Jewish national state nor capable of empathizing with the spiritual reassurance it now affords all Jewish communities regarding their own destiny as Jews? A brief examination of the positions on Israel of the liberal Protestant mainline churches; their more conservative, evangelical counterparts; and the Roman Catholic Church, is in order.

Protestant Liberal Mainliners

A word, first, about the cast of characters to follow.

In North America there are now about 110,000,000 Protestant adherents of many varieties, divided generally into two major camps. The mainline churches—sometimes called "liberal," to differentiate them from those that are more conservative—represent thirty-two Protestant (plus the Eastern Orthodox) churches that are in league with the World Council of Churches. (In the United States, their country-wide umbrella group is called The National Council of Churches; in Canada, the counterpart is known as The Canadian Council of Churches with thirteen church groups in affiliation.) The so-called "evangelicals" have been gaining ground steadily at the expense of the liberals, especially since the 1970s. The former group, also referred to as "fundamentalists," tends to be more loosely federated, and usually consists of smaller and less affluent religious fellowships, many of whom are located in the "Bible Belts" of the southern and western United States. Latterly, however, they have been achieving a much larger following from a wide variety of groups, possibly because of their effective use of radio and television, and doubtless, as well, because of the rising fortunes of conservative forces in religious as well as political life. For every forty "liberal Protestants," about sixty today are affiliated with various evangelical church organizations.

Until the emergence of the "new pluralism" in the 1970s, the liberal Protestant groups had been regarded as quintessentially "American." It was they, primarily known as "WASPS," who controlled virtually every important power group in the country. In the first seven decades of this century, it was these Protestants who also took an active interest in the Middle East. Indeed, immediately after the Second World War, many of them assumed leadership in various political activities, affirming their "liberal" view that as a matter of justice, a Jewish state as well as an Arab state should be established in the region. Moreover, the huge investment of money, effort, and personnel by these mainline churches in major missionary activities in the Middle East brought the leaders of these denominations into intimate working contact with Arab interests in Egypt, Iraq, Lebanon, Syria, and what is now Jordan. Part of this missionary network, for example, is the American University in Beirut, founded and supported by American Presbyterians and, more recently, the Bir Zeit College on the West Bank, in the Christian Arab city of Ramallah—a "Presbyterian" college that has close links to the Palestine Liberation Organization. Mainline liberal Protestant churches also tend to be closely aligned with Third World countries, and as a result are predisposed to supporting Arab political claims against those of Israel.

There is, accordingly, a strong tendency on the part of many mainliners to identify with the views held by the Arab Christians of the Middle East. Unfortunately, however, Christian churches in the Arab world—Protestant, Orthodox, or Catholic—have no desire what-

soever for dialogue with Jews, nor do they share in the more democratic religious outlook of many Western churches. One observer
noted:

> In 1977, the patriarch of the Syrian-based Antiochian Orthodox Church,
> Elias IV, visited the United States. At a news conference in Washington,
> he declared that Jews had little "historic connection" with the territory
> of the state of Israel. Speaking through his interpreter, Elias said, "As far
> as we Christians are concerned, we are the new Israel. All the proph-
> ecies of the Old Testament were fulfilled by the coming of the Messiah
> . . . After the destruction of the Temple, the Jews were dispersed.
> Those who remained lived in peace with the Arabs and the Christians"
> until modern times when, he said, "outsiders" came into the land . . .
> The clear intention of such a position is to theologically delegitimize the
> Jewish state and to deny it any authentic linkage with the biblical
> promises of land and peoplehood.[6]

In June, 1967, when "the lights were going out" in Israel and in
Jewish hearts all over the world, most mainline liberal churches affiliated with the National Council of Churches in the United States or the
Canadian Council of Churches, adopted a quiescent, apathetic view.
These country-wide organizations have since continued to side
largely with the Arab states and to disregard Israel's need for security
in the face of the belligerent "no-peace," "no-recognition," "no-nego-
tiation" stand still enforced by all Arab states save Egypt. One astute
Christian academic pithily summarized the "problem" Jews may continue to experience with these liberal Protestant groups for some time
to come: "The thing [that] the nineteenth century Liberal Protestant,
the Christian humanitarian, cannot grasp, is the Jew who is a winner,
a citizen soldier of liberty and dignity, who does not have to beg
protection of a patron or toleration of a so-called Christian nation . . .
This is precisely the reason why Israel is a stone of stumbling, and
why also the generally covert anti-Semitism of liberal Protestantism
can be just as dangerous as the overt anti-Semitism of the radical
right."[7]

Protestant Fundamentalist Evangelicals

What of that "radical right" so closely interconnected with many
"born again" Protestants, and other fundamentalist types like the

"Moral Majority," who speak so longingly of a "Christian America?" Often they also speak out on behalf of the state of Israel as "Concerned Christians" who reject the frequent pro-Arab pronouncements of their avowed adversaries, the liberal Protestant churches.

These evangelical churches pose a quandary for many Jews. We are aware that these fundamentalists are essentially triumphalist Christians whose "Christian Zionism" does not conceal their expectation that Israel will fade away at, or before, the "second coming" of Jesus as the acknowledged Messiah of the Jews. Nor do many of these fundamentalists take the liberated step, as have many other Christians— Catholics and Protestants alike—of renouncing the validity of the Christian mission to the Jews. The conversion of the Jews still remains an integral part of the theological position of many of their churches.

We must ask what in fact constitutes the basic religious platform of these fundamentalists, and what role do they assign to the Jews?

Richard John Neuhaus has recently offered an interesting and succinct answer to these important questions. It is, however, an answer that cannot resolve the problem for all Jews:

> Most fundamentalists boil[ed] their case down to insistence upon five "fundamentals": the inerrancy of Scripture (the Bible contains no errors in any subject on which it speaks); the virgin birth of Jesus (the Spirit of God conceived Jesus in Mary without human intervention); the substitutionary atonement of Jesus Christ (on the cross he bore the just punishment for the sins of the entire world); his bodily resurrection; the authenticity of the biblical miracles; and pre-millennialism . . .

> . . . While all orthodox Christians say Jesus will return most fundamentalists are "dispensationalists" who derive from "Bible prophecy" a quite precise blueprint and timetable for the return. There are, they believe, dispensations or ordered events and time periods predicted in the Bible. Jews are critical to the final act. There is considerable confusion over whether this means that (in any case) the Jews will finally be converted to Christianity . . .

> . . . Christians of all persuasions have had a difficult time finding a secure theological place for living Judaism. There is little problem with the Jews of the Hebrew Scriptures (the Old Testament, as Christians say) and dispensationalists have an important role for Jews in the End Time, but Judaism between the biblical prophets and the eschaton is something of an anomaly . . . Fundamentalists . . . are increasingly insistent that this mystery (of Jewish survival) means that the nation that blesses the Jews will be blessed and the nation that curses them will be cursed. It is less a sense of guilt over the Holocaust—which is viewed

as something perpetuated by other people in a distant land—than of Divine purpose that gives Judaism and the state of Israel such a special place in the fundamentalist world view.

Of course some Jews protest that it is demeaning to be fitted into a theological system to which they do not subscribe . . . Some (other) Jews take a more pragmatic view in welcoming fundamentalist support for Israel in particular. Irving Kristol recently noted, "It is their theology, but it is our Israel."[8]

Events have indeed taken a paradoxical and enigmatic turn. Liberal Protestants, professing their ecumenical outreach, have all but rid themselves of their older desire to convert Jews to Christianity. They also publicly profess their abhorrence to any form of antisemitism—but not including anti-Zionism. Despite these changes, they have not produced a church leadership that is fully sympathetic to or supportive of the state of Israel. Their adherents in the pews are often far more sensitive to the problems of the Jewish state than their ministers in the pulpits, or the church administrators and bureaucrats of their national councils. Their religious thinking does not require a reborn Israel, nor do Jews have any special role to play in their theology. What they now see when they look out upon Jews is a people who may once have been victimized by Christians, but who no longer merit any special Christian concern for their future. For them, Israel is just another small and distant country—an ordinary "piece of real estate" as some of their leaders have put it to me—which represents for them more of a political issue than a religious or cultural solution and fulfillment. Some go so far as to regard the Palestinian Arabs as "the new Jews" who are in greater need of sympathy.[9]

On the other hand, the fundamentalists have taken Israel to their heart, and, for esoteric theological reasons that are surely unacceptable to Jews, appear to have become reliable allies in the struggle of the Jewish people to renew itself and to survive. Can we feel comforted, however, when the right thing is being done for the wrong reason?

We Jews now have something of a uniquely Protestant problem. How can we engage in serious dialogue with those who do not accept Israel as an integral part of our Jewish being? And how can we meet in truly religious encounters with those "fundamentalists" who, still harboring hopes for our conversion to Jesus Christ, cannot see us as fully equal partners?

In ways that could not have been foreseen, the Roman Catholic Church—the largest, most powerful of all Christian groups on earth—has been radically altering its own views of Jews. Ironically, it may yet be able to offer some helpful insights into this Protestant-Jewish dilemma.

The Roman Catholic Church and Israel

In some ways, the most interesting and promising development in the area of Christian-Jewish dialogue can be found in the manner in which the Roman Catholic Church—especially in North America—has recently been responding to questions about Israel. The Vatican Council's "Jewish Declaration" of 1965, as we have noted, was in many ways a flawed document, owing to the large number of compromises and concessions that the Council had made in response to vociferous protests against Israel by Arab Christian bishops and patriarchs. But because of growing pressure on the Vatican, principally by its own North American hierarchy, those previous grand evasions of the meaning of Israel for the Jewish people were slowly being redressed by new guidelines. In 1975, the newly established Vatican Commission for Religious Relations with the Jews issued its own "Guidelines and Suggestions for Implementing the Conciliar Declaration—*Nostra Aetate*, Number 4." They addressed themselves especially to questions concerning the profound relationship of Jews, as well as Judaism itself, to the Land of Israel, and to sensitive matters touching on Christian proselytization of Jews.

That same year the American bishops picked up the thread of these Vatican guidelines and issued their own fundamentally new "Statement on the Jews"; one, it is clear, that must have emerged from a sharpened awareness that Jews would shy away from their earlier invitation to join in "fraternal dialogue," if it were held within the framework of the Vatican's "Jewish Declaration" of 1965. Now the American prelates filled in the gaps by noting *for the first time* that "an overwhelming majority of Jews see themselves bound in one way or another to the land of Israel. Most Jews see this tie to the land as essential to their Jewishness. Whatever difficulties Christians may experience in sharing this view, they should strive to understand this link between land and people." And on proselytizing, they applauded the Vatican guidelines: "Dialogue demands respect for the other as he is; above all, respect for his faith and his religious convictions."[10] The prelates expressly disapproved of all efforts on the part of Catholics to convert Jews.

By exposing itself to serious discussion with thoughtful Jews the Church was beginning to listen to Jewish thought. Without a doubt, these new attitudes, revolutionary by all previous Catholic standards, were also the result of what some of their own pioneering theologians were saying as a result of their own new and more intimate contact with their Jewish counterparts. One of them, Rosemary Ruether, has compressed these new issues in a nutshell: "It is in Israel that the myth of Christian anti-Judaism comes to an end. Here, the dispersion is overcome, and the Jewish people regathered into the ancient home-land, contrary to [all] that Christian theory that denied this possibility. The Zionist messianic vision of the Return confronts the Christian doctrine of eternal misery and dispersion of the Jewish people to the end of history."[11]

On the political level, too, the Vatican of late has been relaxing some of its earlier harsher attitudes toward Israeli policy. Although it does not as yet maintain formal diplomatic relations with Israel, it has virtually all but abandoned its older position which had called for the "internationalization" of Jerusalem. Now it speaks only of "interna-tional guarantees," by which it primarily means free access to the holy places in and around the "holy city." Some Catholics have even described the present state of Vatican-Israel relations as "more than *de facto*, and less than *de jure*," and point with pleasure to growing contacts, some of which have not been widely publicized, between the two.

There are still others, like Dr. Eugene J. Fisher, executive head of the Secretariat for Catholic-Jewish Relations of the [American] Na-tional Conference of Bishops, who point out that historically "Jews could and did turn to the papacy for protection in times of trouble." Indicating his agreement with a Jewish source, he goes on to say: "Pius XII in essence broke with the traditions of the medieval popes. It is precisely because the medieval papacy managed to speak out for the Jews *in extremis* that the silence of the Vatican during World War II is all the more deafening."[12] The underlying point behind comments such as these is clear. These Catholics are telling Jews that they are now mindful of the tragic mistakes of the past. But more importantly, they are also reassuring Jews, that like them, Catholics, too, are ready to proclaim: Never again![13]

It seems fairly obvious to me that as a result of the friendlier Catholic positions on Israel, some of the liberal Protestant churches may also modify their own attitudes regarding the importance of the Jewish state to the future of both Judaism and the Jewish people. Indeed, there are signs that this Roman Catholic review of its own positions has already influenced the World Council of Churches—the international stronghold of liberal Protestantism—to begin to do the same. In 1982, that Council's select study unit proposed new

"Guidelines for Jewish-Christian Dialogue." For the first time, these liberal Protestants were also beginning to see that Israel's fate had to be taken into account and reckoned with, if they were to attempt serious religious dialogue with Jews. It is instructive to pay heed to the words *they* were now using—truly echoes of similar language the Catholics had begun to employ only a few years earlier: "The words from the World Council of Churches Guidelines on Dialogue that one of the functions of dialogue is to allow the participants to describe and witness to their faith 'in their own terms' are of particular significance for the understanding of the bond between the Land of Israel and the Jewish people. This bond has, after many centuries of dispersion, found expression in the State of Israel. The need for the State of Israel to exist in security and peace is fundamental to Jewish consciousness and therefore is of paramount importance in any dialogue with Jews . . ."[14]

* * *

Issues arising out of the Holocaust, and those which surround the future of the state of Israel must be faced squarely, openly, and honestly if Jews are to participate in good conscience in true dialogue with Christians.

Earlier, I suggested that the day may yet come when Christians will join Jews in ridding the world of the abomination of paganism, and stand together to recite that very ancient and stirring prayer I quoted. That serious but joyful day can only come about *when "the Christian problem" arising from the Christian past is resolved.*

But there is still another prayer I believe we Jews and Christians may one day join in reciting too, out of the depths of our collective souls. It is not an old prayer; it is, in fact, the newest of all Jewish prayers, composed by the Chief Rabbinate of Israel shortly after the birth of the state. When both of these—the newest and the oldest of our prayers—can also be soulfully recited by our Christian neighbors, it will be a sure sign that not only has the old Christian problem been addressed, but that these newer Christian problems arising from the Holocaust and relating to the state of Israel have been dealt with too. Perhaps, then, Christians and Jews will also stand together to recite these hopeful words:

> Our Father in Heaven, the Rock of Israel and her Redeemer, bless the State of Israel, the beginning of the dawn of Jewish redemption. Shield her with the wings of Your love, and spread over her the tabernacle of Your Peace.

NOTES

1. Yehuda Bauer, *The Jewish Emergence from Powerlessness* (Toronto: University of Toronto Press, 1979), p. 77.

2. Emil Fackenheim, "To Mend the World," in *Viewpoints: The Canadian Monthly* (Toronto: October–November, 1983), pp. 2–3. See also his "Reflections on Aliya" in *Midstream*, August/September, 1985, pp. 25–28.

3. Rosemary Ruether, *Faith and Fratricide* (New York: The Seabury Press, 1974), p. 227. See also my essay, "Contemporary Renewal and the Jewish Experience" in L. K. Shook, ed., *Renewal of Religious Thought: Proceedings of the Congress on the Theology of the Renewal of the Church, Centenary of Canada, 1867–1967* (Montreal: Palm Publishers, 1968), Vol. I., pp. 265–281.

4. Ruether, *op. cit.*, pp. 226–227.

5. See, for example, Eugene Fisher, "Anti-Semitism: A Contemporary Christian Perspective," *Judaism*, Summer, 1981, pp. 276–282.

Dr. Fisher discusses what he calls "new forms of anti-Semitism" and points out that "Israel exists as the last refuge of Jews, not only from Europe after the Holocaust, but from Arab persecution as well. . . Thus, while it is true that one can criticize particular Israeli politics without in any way being antisemitic (Israelis do it all the time and, frankly, there is a lot to be critical of in any government, including Israel's) the 'slide' into antisemitism, I would say, occurs whenever either of the following factors enters in:

" (1) The criticism amounts to a questioning of the right of Israel to exist. The United States has been justly criticized for its politics toward American blacks and Indians, its treatment of Japanese citizens during World War II, and over Vietnam—but nobody questioned its right *to be* on the basis of these clear crimes against humanity.

" (2) Israel is held to a stricter moral code to justify its existence than are other states. Indeed, given the process involved, Israel has a clearer legal and moral right to exist than do most nations today. Here, often enough, there is a reflection of ancient Christian theological polemics against Jews, excoriating them for not "living up" to their own Law (which the accusers never bother to try to understand, anyway). Israeli policy is often viewed through the prism of classical antisemitism, e.g., the charges of Israeli 'intransigence' which often could be taken out of the pages of the sermons of Chrysostom [an early Church Father] on Jewish 'obduracy' and the traditional polemics against the Pharisees" (p. 280).

6. A. James Rudin, *Israel for Christians* (Philadelphia: Fortress Press, 1983), pp. 125–126.

7. Franklin H. Littell, "Observations," *Congress Bi-Weekly*, February 20, 1970.

8. Richard John Neuhaus, "What the Fundamentalists Want," *Commentary*, May, 1985, pp. 44–45. For an expansion of Kristol's favorable view of the

fundamentalist position on Israel, see David A. Rausch, "The Evangelicals As Zionists," *Midstream*, January, 1985, pp. 13–16.

9. For a careful review of the mainliners' pro-Arab stance see J. A. Emerson Vermaat, "The World Council of Churches, Israel and the PLO," *Midstream*, November, 1984, pp. 3–9. On p. 9 the author makes a telling point: "The official views of umbrella organizations like the WCC or the NCC are not shared by many of those whom they claim to represent. However, the people in the pew are often ill-informed on the policies of the radicalized ecumenical elite which has estranged itself from the very essence of theology in order to commit itself to political causes."

10. See Leonard Swidler, "A New Stage in Jewish-Christian Dialogue," in *Judaism*, Summer, 1982, pp. 363–4. See also his "Catholic Statements on Jews: A Revolution in Progress," in *Judaism*, Summer, 1978, pp. 299–307.

11. Ruether, *op. cit.*, p. 225.

12. Eugene J. Fisher, "The Holocaust and Christian Responsibility," *America*, February 14, 1981. Dr. Fisher relies here on material he quotes from a Jewish historian, Yosef Yerushalmi. Yerushalmi's view is that the anti-Jewish massacres by medieval Christians were "principally the work of the rabble" and were often interrupted or contained by cardinals and popes rather than being the consequence of their instigation. For a different view—which does not completely exonerate medieval popes and cardinals—see Sam Waagenaar, *The Pope's Jews* (La Salle, Illinois: Library Press, 1974). A most succinct evaluation of this matter has been offered by the French Jewish historian Leon Poliakov: "Over the centuries the papacy tried to make the Christian governments respect the teachings of the fathers of the Church on the subject of the Jews. These teachings had two facets, one of which was the necessity for conserving the remnants of Judaism, and the other the equally necessary abasement of the Jews. On numerous occasions the popes protested strongly against the massacres and persecutions of the Jews; on equally numerous occasions they warned the Christians against the Jews and their influence, and these warnings led innumerable Christian hearts to draw bloody conclusions." See Leon Poliakov, *The History of Anti-Semitism: From Mohammed to the Marranos*, (New York: The Vanguard Press, 1973), Vol. II, p. 303.

13. It should be pointed out, however, that within the organized North American Jewish community there are still divisions of opinion concerning the real progress that has been achieved by the Catholic Church on matters pertaining to the Jews, especially under the leadership of John Paul II. In June 1985 the Vatican's Commission for Religious Relations with the Jews issued its "Notes on the Correct Way to Present Jews and Judaism in Preaching and Catechesis in the Roman Catholic Church." There were many expressions of disappointment with this document by leading rabbis and Jewish theologians who maintained that the "Notes" represented a retreat from earlier Catholic statements, particularly as regards attitudes toward the state of Israel and the Holocaust. In turn, Catholic leaders replied that the "Notes" should be under-

stood as they were intended: "as another step along the way to the goal" of making "ourselves understood to one another as well as in understanding the other . . . a beginning and not by any means a finished product." See especially Eugene J. Fisher, "Interpreting *Nostra Aetate* Through Post-Conciliar Teaching," in *Conservative Judaism*, Vol. 38 (1) Fall, 1985, pp. 7–20. See also Judith Banki and Alan L. Mittleman "Jews and Catholics: Taking Stock," in *Commonweal*, September 6, 1985, pp. 6–8.

Additionally, beginning in October 1985 as twentieth anniversary ceremonies commemorating the promulgation of "The Jewish Declaration" of Vatican II lauded the "new rapprochement," differences in Jewish leadership opinion concerning the future of that relationship began to surface in the public press. Front page articles in the *New York Times* quoted the views of the American Jewish Committee: "There have been more positive Catholic and Jewish encounters in this country in the last 20 years than there were in the first 1,900 years of Christianity." (Rabbi A. James Rudin, director of inter-religious affairs of the American Jewish Committee, in *New York Times*, October 20, 1985, p. 1). But soon, thereafter, less reassuring views were aired publicly by leaders of the American Jewish Congress and the American Section of the World Jewish Congress. One of their leading spokesmen, Rabbi Arthur Hertzberg, in an Op-Ed column in the *New York Times* (December 4, 1985), explained his group's position: "There is something very wrong with the dialogue between Catholics and Jews . . . the Roman Catholic Church has used every tactic to avoid the issue that matters most to world Jewry—recognition of Israel. . . . The joint concern of Jews and Catholics for all the human decencies cannot be praised again and again as sufficient for the dialogue. . . . The relationship between world Jewry and the Catholic Church requires a new beginning. . . . That, for Jews, means that Israel has to be a central issue on the agenda. . . ."

14. Quoted from "Guidelines for Jewish-Christian Dialogue," issued by the Study Unit of the World Council of Churches, its select group on "Dialogue with People of Living Faiths and Ideologies." Issued in Bali, Indonesia, in January, 1982.

Epilogue:

If I Were a Christian

SOON AFTER I COMPLETED A DRAFT OF THIS BOOK I DISTRIBUTED A number of working manuscript copies to several learned Christian friends, each a high profile lay leader of his or her Protestant or Catholic church. Their comments and feedback were most valuable; they helped me avoid several errors.

Some time later I invited all of them to what I had envisioned to be merely a social evening at my home. Before the night was over, however, I was fairly overwhelmed by their ardent passions. They were expressing powerful emotions—feelings that ranged from profound shock to outright anger. None remained passive or neutral, and all shared a common reaction. What they were saying can be summarized in a single, painful question: "Why were we not taught to face these issues—our Christian problem—*by our own teachers*, in our schools, churches, and colleges?" And then there was this serious, sincere question which they addressed to the "author-instigator" of their dilemma: "What would *you* do about these issues you have raised for us *if you were a Christian?*"

Because as a rabbi I am essentially a teacher, I reminded them of what one of my saintly predecessors, the gentle Rabbi Hillel, had taught two thousand years ago. An enquiring pagan, a would-be convert to Judaism, had asked Hillel if he could teach him the whole of the Torah-law all at once—as if it could be explained as a short answer to a simple question. Accordingly, in quaint and unforgettable language, he asked: "Can you teach me the whole Torah while standing on one foot?"

The rabbi's answer was a diplomatic gem. Of course, he could do

221

that, he suggested, as he proceeded to summarize the whole of the Law in a single sentence: "What is distasteful to you, do not do unto your neighbor. This is the whole of the Torah. All the rest is commentary." After the questioner, however, had been offered his capsule summary, the rabbi continued: "Now, of course, you must go back to the sources themselves and undertake a never-ending, life-long effort to study and understand them all!"

It is erroneously assumed—even by some accomplished and cultured people—that there are shortcuts to learning and understanding. Unhappily, all such shortcuts lead only to dead-ends: capsule-summaries tend to become slogans; slogans are made into doctrines; and doctrines often become unyielding dogmas that block our way to clear, creative, and independent thought.

Thus, I told my Christian friends, if I were a Christian I would go back to *the Jewish sources* to relearn my Christian history from the roots up. I would be wary of all the short answers and quick fixes—of all the familiar, well-worn Christian slogans concerning Jews and Judaism. I would repeatedly challenge and expunge those Christian teachings that clearly pander to prejudice and ignorance and I would insist that my priest or pastor do the same.

If I were a Christian I would want to know the whole truth about my Christian self. In the pursuit of this quest to rediscover my spiritual identity, I would always remember my indebtedness to Jews and to Judaism. And to help my own Christian community, I would urge my priest or minister to do the same.

If I were a Christian I would engrave on the tablets of my heart the teaching of the late Pope Pius XI, who declared: "Spiritually, we are all Semites." From this I would learn what I must never forget: *Before I can be fully Christian I must also know what it means to be a Jew.*

More than two decades ago I heard a Jesuit priest, Thurston Davis, then editor of the Catholic weekly, *America,* say some of the things that I would also say if I, too, were a Christian. "Catholics, Protestants, or Jews, we *can't* vanish. We have to be ourselves, true to our traditions, until the day when in God's good time he brings us together at last. Unvanishing, unwilling to vanish, in combined strength we must labor. We have so much to do together for the common good. Side by side, before we vanish, let's get some of this work done." What is more: for Christians to avoid reverting to near-paganism, the core of their spirituality must always remain tied to Jewish teachings. This is, after all, a neo-pagan, secular age, and more than ever those who reject both the older and the newer idolatries should be standing together. *The stronger a man's Christian faith, the more Jewish will he regard himself.*

Above all I suggested to these Christian friends that if I were a Christian I would seek to establish a *newer Christian mission*—an inner mission inside every single church, across all the denominations. That newer mission would lead Christians back to their Jewish source, and by means of a life-long, dedicated search for the truth, would seek to eradicate from the thought of the church every last vestige of its Christian problem.

Selected Bibliography

ABBOTT, WILLIAM M., ed. *The Documents of Vatican II*. New York: Guild Press, 1966.

ABRAHAMS, ISRAEL. *Jewish Life in the Middle Ages*. New York: Atheneum Press, 1969.

AGUS, JACOB B. *Dialogue and Tradition: The Challenge of Contemporary Judaeo-Christian Thought*. New York: Abelard-Schuman, 1971.

ALEXANDER, EDWARD. *The Resonance of Dust: Essays on Holocaust Literature and Jewish Fate*. Columbus: Ohio State University Press, 1979.

———. "Stealing the Holocaust." *Midstream*, November, 1980.

ALLEGRO, JOHN M. *The Dead Sea Scrolls and the Christian Myth*. London: Westbridge Books, 1979.

ARENDT, HANNAH. *The Jew as Pariah*. Edited by Ron H. Feldman. New York: Grove Press, 1978.

ARON, ROBERT. *The Jewish Jesus*. New York: Orbis Books, 1971.

BARON, SALO W. *The Jewish Community*. 3 vols. Philadelphia: Jewish Publication Society, 1942.

———. *A Social and Religious History of the Jews*, New York: Columbia University Press, 1952–.

———. *From a Historian's Notebook: European Jewry Before and After Hitler*. New York: American Jewish Committee, 1970.

———. "Population." *Encyclopedia Judaica*, 1970.

———. *Ancient and Medieval Jewish History*. Edited by Leon A. Feldman. New Brunswick: Rutgers University Press, 1972.

———, et al. *Economic History of the Jews*. New York: Schocken Books, 1975.

BAUER, YEHUDA. *The Holocaust in Historical Perspective*. Seattle: University of Washington Press, 1978.

———. *The Jewish Emergence from Powerlessness*. Toronto: University of Toronto Press, 1979.

————. "Whose Holocaust?" *Midstream*, November, 1980.

BAUM, GREGORY. *Is the New Testament Anti-Semitic?* New York: Paulist Press, 1965.

BAUMINGER, ARIEH. *Roll of Honour.* Tel Aviv: Hamenora Publishing House, 1971.

BEN-ZVI, ITZHAK. *The Exiled and the Redeemed.* Philadelphia: Jewish Publication Society of America, 1957.

BERKOVITS, ELIEZER. *Faith After the Holocaust.* New York: Ktav Publishing Co., 1973.

————. "Facing the Truth." *Judaism,* Summer, 1978.

BIERMAN, JOHN. *Righteous Gentile: The Story of Raoul Wallenberg.* New York: Viking Press, 1981.

BOKSER, BEN ZION. *Judaism and the Christian Predicament.* New York: Knopf, 1967.

BOROWITZ, EUGENE. *Contemporary Christologies: A Jewish Response.* New York: Paulist Press, 1980.

BROWN, ROBERT McAFEE, AND WEIGEL, GUSTAV. *An American Dialogue.* New York: Doubleday, 1960.

BUBER, MARTIN. *Two Types of Faith.* London: Routledge & Kegan Paul, 1951.

BURROWS, MILLAR. *The Dead Sea Scrolls.* New York: Viking Press, 1955.

CAIN, SEYMOUR. "The Holocaust and Christian Responsibility." *Midstream,* April, 1982.

CARGAS, HARRY JAMES. *A Christian Response to the Holocaust.* Denver: Stonehenge Books, 1981.

COHEN, ARTHUR A. *The Tremendum.* New York: The Crossroad Publishing Company, 1981.

COHEN, JEREMY. *The Friars and the Jews: The Evolution of Medieval Anti-Judaism.* Ithaca: Cornell University Press, 1982.

COHEN, STEVEN M. *The 1984 National Survey of American Jews: Political and Social Outlooks.* New York: American Jewish Committee, 1984.

CRONBACH, ABRAHAM. "The Maimonidean Code of Benevolence," in *Hebrew Union College Annual* 20 (1947): pp. 471–540.

CURTIS, JOHN SHELTON. *An Appraisal of the Protocols of Zion.* New York: Columbia University Press, 1942.

DANIEL-ROPS HENRY. *Daily Life in Palestine in the Time of Christ.* London: Weidenfeld, 1962.

DAVIES, A. POWELL. *The Meaning of the Dead Sea Scrolls.* New York: New American Library, 1961.

DAVIES, ALAN T. *Anti-Semitism and the Christian Mind.* New York: Herder and Herder, 1969.

————. *Antisemitism and the Foundations of Christianity.* New York: Paulist Press, 1979.

DAVIES, W. D. *Paul and Rabbinic Judaism.* Rev. ed. New York: Harper and Row, 1967.

DAVIS, MOSHE and LOTTIE. *Map of Biblical Names in America.* New York: Associated American Artists, Inc., undated.

DAWIDOWICZ, LUCY. *The Holocaust and the Historians.* Cambridge: Harvard University Press, 1981.

———. "Lies About the Holocaust." *Commentary,* December, 1980, pp. 31–37.

DOBKOWSKI, MICHAEL N. *The Tarnished Dream.* Westport, Conn.: Greenwood Press, 1979.

ECKARDT, A. ROY. "Anti-Semitism." In *Jews and Christians,* edited by George A. F. Knight. Philadelphia: The Westminster Press, 1965.

———. *Elder and Younger Brothers.* New York: Scribners, 1967.

———. *Your People, My People.* New York: Quadrangle, 1974.

ECKARDT, ALICE AND A. ROY. *Long Night's Journey Into Day.* Detroit: Wayne State University Press, 1982 (Revised edition. New York: Holocaust Publications, 1986).

EICHHORN, DAVID M. *Evangelizing the American Jew.* Middle Village, N. Y.: Jonathan David, 1978.

ELAZAR, DANIEL J. *Community and Polity: The Organizational Dynamics of American Jewry.* Philadelphia: Jewish Publication Society, 1976.

———, ed. *Kinship and Consent.* Washington, D.C.: University Press of America, 1983.

ELIACH, YAFFA. *Hasidic Tales of the Holocaust.* New York: Avon Books, 1983.

FACKENHEIM, EMIL L. *The Jewish Return Into History.* New York: Schocken Books, 1978.

———. *To Mend the World.* New York: Schocken Books, 1982.

FERRUOLO, STEPHEN C. *The Origins of the University: The Schools of Paris and their Critics, 1100–1215.* Palo Alto: Stanford University Press, 1985.

FINKELSTEIN, LOUIS. *The Pharisees.* 2d ed., rev. Philadelphia: Jewish Publication Society, 1940.

FISHER, EUGENE J. *Faith Without Prejudice.* New York: Paulist Press, 1977.

———. "The Holocaust and Christian Responsibility." *America,* February 14, 1981.

———. "Interpreting *Nostra Aetate* Through Post-Conciliar Teaching." In *Conservative Judaism,* Vol. 38 (1) Fall, 1985, pp. 7–20.

FLEISCHNER, EVA, ed. *Auschwitz: Beginning of a New Era?* New York: Ktav Publishing Co., 1977.

FLUSSER, DAVID. *Jesus.* New York: Herder and Herder, 1969.

FRIEDLANDER, HENRY, and MORTON, SYBIL, eds. *The Holocaust: Ideology, Bureaucracy, and Genocide.* Millwood, N.Y.: Kraus International Publications, 1980.

FRIEDMAN, PHILIP. *Their Brother's Keeper.* New York: Crown Publishers, 1957.

———. *Roads to Extinction: Essays on the Holocaust.* Philadelphia: Jewish Publication Society, 1980.

FROMM, ERICH. *Psychoanalysis and Religion*. New Haven: Yale University Press, 1950.

GILBERT, ARTHUR. *The Vatican Council and the Jews*. New York: World Publishing Co., 1968.

GINZBERG, LOUIS. *Students, Scholars and Saints*. Philadelphia: The Jewish Publication Society, 1928.

GLOCK, CHARLES, and QUINLEY, HAROLD. *Anti-Semitism in America*. New York: Harper and Row, 1979.

GOLB, NORMAN, and PRITSAK, OMELJAN. *Khazarian Hebrew Documents of the Tenth Century*. Ithaca: Cornell University Press, 1982.

GORDIS, ROBERT. *Judaism in a Christian World*. New York: McGraw-Hill, 1966.

GRANT, MICHAEL. *"Paul the Discontented Jew." Midstream*, Aug./Sept. 1976.

———. *Saint Paul*. New York: Charles Scribner's Sons, 1976.

———. *From Alexandra to Cleopatra: The Hellenistic World*. New York: Charles Scribner's Sons, 1982.

GROBMAN, ALEX, and LANDES, DANIEL, eds. *Genocide: Critical Issues of the Holocaust*. Chappaqua, New York: Rossel Books, 1983.

HAILPERIN, HERMAN. *Rashi and the Christian Scholars*. Pittsburgh: University of Pittsburgh Press, 1963.

HASAN–ROKEM, GALIT, and DUNDES, ALAN, eds. *The Wandering Jew: Essays in the Interpretation of a Christian Legend*. Bloomington: Indiana University Press, 1985.

HELLMAN, PETER. *Avenue of the Righteous*. New York: Atheneum, 1980.

HENGEL, MARTIN. *Judaism and Hellenism*. 2 vols. London: SCM Press, 1974.

HEYER, ROBERT., ed. *Jewish-Christian Relations*. New York: Paulist Press, 1975.

HILBERG, RAUL. *The Destruction of the European Jews*. Chicago: Quadrangle Press, 1961 (Revised and Definitive Edition: New York: Holmes and Meier, 1985. 3 vols.)

ISAAC, JULES. *The Christian Roots of Antisemitism*. Barley, England: The Parkes Library, 1960.

———. *The Teaching of Contempt*. New York: McGraw Hill, 1961.

———. *Jesus and Israel*. New York: Holt, Rinehart and Winston, 1971.

JACOBS, JOSEPH. *Jewish Contributions to Civilization*. Philadelphia: The Jewish Publication Society of America, 1919.

KATZ, JACOB. *Tradition and Crisis*. New York: Schocken Books, 1971.

———. *Emancipation and Assimilation*. London: Gregg International Publishers, 1972.

———. *"Was the Holocaust Inevitable?" Commentary*, May, 1975.

———. *"Misreadings of Anti-Semitism." Commentary*, July, 1983.

KLEIN, CHARLOTTE. *Anti-Judaism in Christian Theology*. Philadelphia: Fortress Press, 1978.

KONVITZ, MILTON R. *Judaism and the American Idea*. Ithaca: Cornell University Press, 1978.

LAQUEUR, WALTER. *The Terrible Secret*. Boston: Little, Brown, 1981.

LAURENTIN, RENE, and NEUNER, JOSEPH, S.J. *Commentary on the Relationship of the Church to Non-Christian Religions*. New York: Paulist Press, 1966.

LECKY, W. E. H. *History of the Rise and Influence of the Spirit of Rationalism in Europe*. Vol. 2. London: Longmans, Green, 1913.

LEWY, GUENTER. *The Catholic Church and Nazi Germany*. New York: McGraw Hill, 1965.

LIEBERMAN, SAUL. *Greek in Jewish Palestine*. New York: Jewish Theological Seminary of America, 1942.

———. *Hellenism in Jewish Palestine*. New York: Jewish Theological Seminary of America, 1950.

LIEBMAN, CHARLES S., and DON-YEHIYA, ELIEZER. *Civil Religion in Israel*. Berkeley: University of California Press, 1983.

LITTELL, FRANKLIN H. *The German Phoenix: Men and Movements in the Church in Germany*. Garden City, N.Y.: Doubleday, 1960.

———. *The Crucifixion of the Jews*. New York: Harper and Row, 1975.

MACCOBY, HYAM. *Revolution in Judaea: Jesus and the Jewish Resistance*. New York: Taplinger Publishing Company, 1981.

———. ed. and trans. *Judaism on Trial: Jewish Christian Disputations in the Middle Ages*. Rutherford, N.J.: Fairleigh Dickinson University Press, 1983.

———. "Christianity's Break with Judaism." *Commentary*, August, 1984.

MARTIRE, GREGORY, and CLARK, RUTH. *Anti-Semitism in the United States*. New York: Praeger, 1982.

MCGARRY, MICHAEL B. *Christology After Auschwitz*. New York: Paulist Press, 1977.

MOORE, GEORGE F. *Judaism in the First Centuries of the Christian Era*. Cambridge: Harvard University Press, 1927.

MORLEY, JOHN F. *Vatican Diplomacy and the Jews During the Holocaust, 1939–1943*. New York: Ktav Publishing Co., 1980.

MUSSNER, FRANZ. *Tractate on the Jews: The Significance of Judaism for the Christian Faith*. Philadelphia: Fortress Press, 1984.

NEILL, STEPHEN. *Christian Faith and Other Faiths*. London: Oxford University Press, 1962.

NEUHAUS, RICHARD JOHN. "What the Fundamentalists Want." *Commentary*, May 1985.

NEUMAN, ABRAHAM A. *Relation of Hebrew Scriptures to American Institutions*. New York: Jewish Theological Seminary of America, 1943.

NEUSNER, JACOB. *From Politics to Piety: The Emergence of Pharisaic Judaism*. Englewood Cliffs, N.J.: Prentice-Hall, Inc., 1973.

———. *First Century Judaism in Crisis*. Nashville: Abingdon Press, 1975.

NEWMAN, LOUIS I. *Jewish Influence on Christian Reform Movements*. New York: Columbia University Press, 1925.

OESTERREICHER, JOHN M., ed. *Brothers In Hope*. New York: Herder and Herder, 1970.

OPSAHL, PHILIP, and TANENBAUM, MARC., eds. *Speaking of God Today: Jews and Lutherans in Dialogue*. Philadelphia: Fortress Press, 1974.

ORLINSKY, HARRY. *Ancient Israel*. Ithaca: Cornell University Press, 1954.

PARKES, JAMES. *The Jew in the Medieval Community*. London: Soncino Press, 1938.

———. *Foundations of Judaism and Christianity*. Chicago: Quadrangle Books, 1960.

———. *The Conflict of Church and Synagogue*. New York: Meridian Books, 1961.

———. *A Reappraisal of the Christian Attitude to Judaism*. Barley, England: The Parkes Library, 1962.

PATAI, RAPHAEL. *The Jewish Mind*. New York: Charles Scribner's Sons, 1977.

PATAI, RAPHAEL, and WING, JENNIFER. *The Myth of the Jewish Race*. New York: Charles Scribner's Sons, 1975.

PAWLIKOWSKI, JOHN T. *Catechetics and Prejudice*. New York: Paulist Press, 1972.

———. "Implications of the Holocaust for the Christian Churches." In *Genocide: Critical Issues of the Holocaust*, edited by Alex Grobman and David Landes. Chappaqua, N.Y.: Rossell Books, 1983.

PENKOWER, MONTY. *The Jews Were Expendable: Free World Diplomacy and the Holocaust*. Urbana: University of Illinois Press, 1983.

PERLMUTTER, NATHAN and RUTH ANN. *The Real Anti-Semitism in America*. New York: Arbor House, 1982.

POLIAKOV, LEON. *The History of Anti-Semitism: From Mohammed to the Marranos*. New York: The Vanguard Press, 1973. Vol. 2.

———. *Jewish Bankers and the Holy See: From the Thirteenth to the Seventeenth Century*. London: Routledge and Kegan Paul, 1977.

RAUSCH, DAVID. "The Evangelicals as Zionists." *Midstream*, January, 1985.

ROSENBERG, STUART E. "Some Attitudes of Nineteenth-Century Reform Laymen." In *Essays in Jewish Life and Thought*, edited by Blau, Friedman, Hertzberg, Mendelsohn. New York: Columbia University Press, 1959.

———. *A Time to Speak*. New York: Bloch Publishing Co., 1960.

———. *The Bible Is for You*. New York: David McKay Co., Inc., 1961.

———. "Contemporary Renewal and the Jewish Experience." In *Renewal of Religious Thought: Proceedings of the Congress on the Theology of the Renewal of the Church, Centenary of Canada, 1867–1967*, edited by L. K. Shook. Montreal: Palm Publishers, 1968. Vol. I.

———. *The Real Jewish World: A Rabbi's Second Thoughts*. New York: Philosophical Library and Toronto: Clarke Irwin, 1984.

———. *The New Jewish Identity in America*, New York: Hippocrene Books, 1985.

———. *Christians and Jews: The Eternal Bond*. New York: Frederick Ungar, 1985.

ROSENZWEIG, FRANZ. *The Star of Redemption*. Trans. by William W. Hallo. Notre Dame: Notre Dame Press, 1985.

ROTH, CECIL. *The History of the Jews of Italy.* Philadelphia: Jewish Publication Society of America, 1946.

ROWLEY, H. H. *The Unity of the Bible.* New York: Meridian Books, 1957.

RUDIN, A. JAMES. *Israel for Christians.* Philadelphia: Fortress Press, 1983.

RUETHER, ROSEMARY. *Faith and Fratricide.* New York: The Seabury Press, 1974.

SANDERS, E. P. *Paul and Palestinian Judaism.* London: SCM Press, 1977.

SANDMEL, SAMUEL. *We Jews and Jesus.* New York: Oxford University Press, 1965.

———. *The Genius of Paul.* New York: Schocken Books, 1970.

———. *Anti-Semitism in the New Testament.* Philadelphia: Fortress Press, 1978.

———. *Judaism and Christian Beginnings.* New York: Oxford University Press, 1978.

SARTRE, JEAN-PAUL. *Anti-Semite and Jew.* New York: Schocken Books, 1948.

SCHECHTER, SOLOMON. *Seminary Addresses.* New York: Burning Bush Press, 1959.

———. *Aspects of Rabbinic Theology.* New York: Schocken Books, Inc., 1961.

SCHOEPS, HANS JOACHIM. *Paul: The Theology of the Apostle in the Light of History.* Philadelphia, The Westminster Press, 1961.

———. *The Jewish-Christian Argument.* New York: Holt, Rinehart and Winston, 1963.

SHEERIN, JOHN B. "Evaluating the Past in Catholic-Jewish Relations: Lessons for Today from the Pain of the Past." In *Torah and Gospel*, edited by Philip Scharper. New York: Sheed and Ward, 1966.

SHERMAN, FRANKLIN. "Luther and the Jews." In *Genocide: Critical Issues of the Holocaust.* Chappaqua: Rossel Books, 1983.

SIMPSON, ALAN. *Puritanism in Old and New England.* Chicago: University of Chicago Press. 1955.

SNOEK, JOHAN M. *The Grey Book: A Collection of Protests Against Anti-Semitism and the Persecution of Jews Issued by Non-Roman Catholic Churches and Church Leaders During Hitler's Rule.* Assen, Holland: Van Gorcum and Co., 1969.

STOW, KENNETH R. *Catholic Thought and Papal Jewry Policy, 1555–1593*, New York: Jewish Theological Seminary of America, 1977.

STRAUS, OSCAR. *The Origin of the Republican Form of Government in the United States of America.* New York: G. P. Putnam's Sons, 1885.

SYNAN, EDWARD A. *The Popes and the Jews in the Middle Ages.* New York: The Macmillan Company, 1965.

TALMAGE, FRANK E., ed. *Disputation and Dialogue: Readings in the Jewish-Christian Encounter.* New York: Ktav Publishing Co., 1975.

———. *David Kimhi: The Man and his Commentaries.* Cambridge: Harvard University Press, 1975.

THOMA, CLEMENS. *Christian Theology of Judaism.* New York: Paulist Press, 1980.

TOY, CRAWFORD H. *Judaism and Christianity.* New York: D. Appleton, 1892.

TOYNBEE, ARNOLD J. *A Study of History.* Abridgement of Volumes I–VI, by D. C. Somervell. New York: Oxford University Press, 1947.

TRACHTENBERG, JOSHUA. *The Devil and the Jews.* New York: Meridian Books, 1961.

TURNER, HAROLD. *From Temple to Meeting House: The Phenomenology and Theology of Places of Worship.* The Hague: Mouton Press, 1979.

URBACH, EPHRAIM E. *The Sages: Their Concepts and Beliefs.* 2 vols. Jerusalem: Magnes Press, 1975.

VAN BUREN, PAUL M. *Discerning the Way: A Theology of the Jewish Christian Reality.* New York: The Seabury Press, 1980.

VERMES, GEZA. *Jesus The Jew.* London: Collins, 1973.

———. *The Dead Sea Scrolls: Qumran in Perspective.* London: Collins, 1977.

WAAGENAAR, SAM. *The Pope's Jews.* La Salle, Ill.: Library Press, 1974.

WALLIS, LOUIS D. *The Bible Is Human.* New York: Columbia University Press, 1943.

WAXMAN, CHAIM I. *America's Jews in Transition.* Philadelphia: Temple University Press, 1983.

WHITE, ANDREW. *Warfare of Science with Theology.* New York: D. Appleton, 1896.

WIESEL, ELIE. *The Jews of Silence.* New York: Holt, Rinehart and Winston, 1966.

———. *A Jew Today.* New York: Vintage Books, 1979.

WYMAN, DAVID S. *The Abandonment of the Jews: America and the Holocaust, 1941–1945.* New York: Pantheon Books, 1984.

WYSCHOGROD, MICHAEL. "A New Stage in Jewish-Christian Dialogue." *Judaism,* Summer, 1982, pp. 355–365.

YADIN, YIGAEL. *The Message of the Scrolls.* New York: Simon and Schuster, 1969.

YAHIL, LENNY. *The Rescue of Danish Jewry.* Philadelphia: Jewish Publication Society, 1969.

Index